THE MACCONWOOD WOLF PACK

Volume I

C.D. GORRI

The Macconwood Wolf Pack
Volume 1
by C.D. Gorri

Copyright 2022 C.D. Gorri, NJ

CHARLEY'S CHRISTMAS WOLF

A MACCONWOOD PACK NOVEL

C.D. GORRI

CHARLEY'S CHRISTMAS
Wolf

BLURB

Rafe Maccon is the Alpha of the Macconwood Pack, *for now*. His rule is being questioned by a rogue Wolf who wants him ousted for breaking an ancient law that states the Alpha must be mated!

He must find a mate in order to keep his position. Seeing their Alpha in trouble, Rafe's Wolf Guard take it upon themselves to find one for him.

Charley Palmieri works a dead-end job and lives alone with her cat until one night when her world is changed forever.

Instant attraction sparks between them. Can Rafe convince Charley to be his before the meeting of Pack elders on Christmas Eve? Will she be his one true mate, for life?

PROLOGUE

St. Lucia's Day – December 12th

He circled the woods once more. His black coat gleamed in the silver moonlight as powerful legs carried him quickly through the frozen terrain. The battle was finished. Another few months of peace and prosperity won together with his allies. All it cost was the blood and sweat of his Pack.

He thought of the young Wolf who had asked for his help. She was tenacious and brave. This was the first time in a hundred years such alliances had been made. He knew he had made the right decision for his Pack. The only way to go into the future was to move forward.

Wasn't that what his father had always said? He tasted blood on the air and tensed. Some of it he recognized. It belonged to his Wolves. But they were whole. That was all that mattered.

The black Wolf reached out with his mind and felt his Packmates' injuries. *No casualties.* The blood-stained ice that covered the forest floor and the sulfuric stink of dark magic invaded his nostrils.

He snarled and quickened his pace. For a moment or two the Dark Witches had almost had them. But they had triumphed. The others were gone. Only his Pack remained. They waited for him. Their *Alpha*.

He slowed down as he entered the wooded enclosure. Pride vibrated in his very being. These Wolves were brave, fierce, and loyal.

As his Guard moved to flank him, Rafe Maccon threw back his head and loosed an ear-piercing howl. It spoke of loss, of triumph, of the end of an era and the start of a new one. This had been his last battle as a warrior.

The time had come for him to fully assume his rightful position as Pack Alpha. His father's death years ago should have triggered that leap in his status, but he had denied his birthright for as long as he could. He had chosen to fight with his Wolves instead. But the time had come for him to lead them.

According to the local White Witches of the Coven Realta, the prophecy had already begun. He and his Wolves needed to ready themselves for whatever came next. He signaled to his Beta and like always, he immediately understood what was needed of him.

Rafe watched him leave with a few select Wolves then he surveyed his Packmates. They stood in front of him, each one muscular and strong with varying shades of fur ranging from palest white, tawnies, reds, and browns to his own midnight black coat. One by one, they lowered themselves on their haunches, lupine heads bowed. He had earned their respect before, but tonight he had gained their undying trust. Now, he had to keep it.

Thunder clapped overhead. A mix of hail and rain began to pour from the quickly darkening skies. The streetlights flickered and the tiny overhead shelter at the bus stop gave no protection whatsoever from Mother Nature's latest onslaught.

"Not now! Come on!" Charley cried.

She huddled into the thick pink cardigan she wore over her one good dress. It was a wool blend which was bound to get ruined in this weather. She had instantly fallen in love with the way it alternately hugged and flowed around her curvaceous body. She especially loved the scalloped hemline.

It reminded her of classic movie stars like Hepburn and Taylor. She used to watch them all the time with her grandfather. She smiled as she looked down at the outfit. The pale ivory suited her dark eyes and hair. The weather was definitely going to ruin it. And on her meager salary it would be months before she could replace it.

She looked down at her matching heels and stomped her foot as puddles began to form on the uneven concrete sidewalk. *Great! That's just perfect!* It just wasn't her day, or her year for that matter.

It was almost Christmas and the nutty weather still hadn't made up its mind what season it was. One day it was in the 90s and the next the thermometer had dropped to the low 30s. The past few months had been very unusual for the typically predictable New Jersey climate. Charley didn't know what to make of it.

She was sure it was because of the holes in the Ozone or global warming, melting snowcaps, and the cattle crisis. Every newsfeed had someone to blame, but not much was being done about finding a solution. She shook her head, thoughts like that were better off left to scientists and people who could actually make a difference.

Charley was just trying to make it through a date. Well, a *blind date* that she didn't even want to go on. And she was already late for it because her boss at Junior's Famous Italian Deli, the third "Junior" as it were, just had to make her clean all the slicing machines and the display cases twice that day!

Not to mention he had her mop the entire floor, flip the chairs, hose down all the rubber mats, secure the freezers and refrigerators, and lastly, Windex the tall storefront windows inside and out! *Ugh.* Only then did he let her leave. And the rat hadn't even paid her.

The deli would be closed for the next six weeks. Junior and his family would be in Italy to oversee maintenance work on his family's villa. *Wasn't that nice for him?* Charley had to bite her tongue all day from telling her boss what she really thought of her forced, not to mention unpaid, vacation.

She barely had enough time to get to her apartment, shower, and change before the bus was scheduled to arrive. Dinner had better be worth it!

A black van pulled over across the street and idled. *Lucky bastard!* Charley sighed as she gave it a brief look. The van had tinted windows and chrome finishes. From where she stood, the engine purred.

Not the usual racket from the delivery vans she dealt with at the deli. *Too nice for this neighborhood,* she thought. *Heat probably works too.*

She tried not to stare at the driver. From what she could see, he was huge and rough looking. And boy, was he looking at her. *Pervert! Yeah, have a good look, buddy!* She thought as she tugged her sweater closer to her body.

She tried in vain to cover her ample assets. No doubt they were clearly revealed through her soaked dress. The bus stop provided very little protection indeed. She turned her head towards the street, as if just looking could somehow make her bus appear. No such luck.

The van remained across the street unmoving, creepy driver and all. Charley shuddered. There was no traffic, foot or car, on the usually crowded Jersey City intersection. It was cold, wet, and dark and she was all alone.

She dug in her purse for her cell phone just as lightning lit up the sky. It was followed by the booming sound of thunder and Charley practically jumped out of her shoes.

The distraction was enough that she didn't see the van pop a u-ey and pull to a stop right alongside her. She didn't hear the door open or see the man with the blonde spiked hair exit the vehicle.

He moved faster than any man should be able to and grabbed her from behind. Charley's heart pounded as a huge hand clamped down tightly over her mouth. She struggled and tried to scream. Cold fear ran down her spine as he dragged her to the now open side door.

"Sorry about this," a deep voice said, and he scooped her up and sat down with her on his lap. She tried squirming, but arms like iron held her still.

"Why this one? I thought the blonde was better?" said a rough voice to her right. She struggled to turn her head but got nowhere.

"No way, dude, he doesn't even like blondes. Not since Stephie. You remember her, that blonde viper was a backstabbing little bit-," said another male voice coming from the front seat.

"Shut up guys! Okay hon, I'm going to take my hand off your mouth and we're going to ask some questions, alright? Nod if you understand."

Charley nodded. She was scared out of her mind, but she wouldn't go down quietly. She waited for him to release her. As soon as he lifted his hand, she opened her mouth and screamed as loud as she could. She threw her head back directly into the nose of her captor.

"Shit! I'm bleeding! Hold her, dammit! No, don't hurt her, get the rag! The rag! Shit!"

Charley dove for the door handle, but the stupid thing was locked. She fumbled for a second, but it was too late. Large hands grabbed her and before she knew it, she was in a grip even stronger than before. Angry tears streamed down her face.

"Let go of me, you perverts! Let me go!!"

She continued to try and twist out of her captor's grasp, just then one of them held a rag over her nose and mouth. Then it was *goodbye, Charley*. Literally.

Sometime later.

"Dude, look!"

"Get ready."

"Hey, she's coming around."

The sound of deep voices pounded inside of her aching head. Charley struggled to open her eyes. *What happened? Where am I?* Her thoughts were all jumbled and confused. She felt awful, like she did after taking a nap when she had a really bad headache.

Charley sprang up from her prone position. That was a mistake. She grabbed her head. It felt like it was going to explode.

She looked down at her lap and saw she was wrapped up in a way too big, green flannel robe. And, yup, except for her panties, she was naked underneath.

"Oh, shit. Here she goes," a resigned voice said.

Charley opened her eyes and took in the mountain sized men surrounding her. A split second passed before she opened her mouth and screamed.

"Aghhh! Who the hell are you people? Oh my God, I've been kidnapped!"

"Now, now, take it easy," one of them stepped

closer and Charley screamed again and flung a pillow at him.

"Back up, buddy! Okay, six huge men, well that one looks like a baby," Charley spoke to herself, but the one she called a baby stiffened.

"Hey, I'm twenty!"

"Wait! Seven! There's seven of you? *1, 2, 3, 4 ,5, 6 and 7!* Okay, don't move," Charley closed her eyes, her mind trying frantically to figure out what the heck was going on.

Seven men had abducted her and brought her to a house. A nice house actually. She opened her eyes again and from her place on a rather huge bed she looked at her surroundings.

A soft down-comforter and pillows in various shades of blue covered the bed, navy and beige curtains hung from large windows, the floors were natural stone, and a huge fireplace crackled cheerfully in the corner. Not so bad, considering she was a prisoner!

"What are you going to do with me? Why am I here? Where are my clothes? Why did you-"

"Wait, let me explain-"

"Oh my God, you're going to kill me, aren't you?!," Charley looked around, but the only thing she could get her hands on were more pillows. Not really helpful when trying to fight off giant kidnappers.

"We're not going to hurt you, okay. None of us are even gonna touch you," said blonde-spike guy.

He had two wads of cotton stuffed up his bloody nose. *Aha, the grabber!* Charley focused on him. Oddly, there was no bruising on his face or around his cotton stuffed nose. And she was sure she had broken it.

"You think I'm going to trust you? You sick pervert! If you're not gonna kill me what are you going to do, huh, rape me? Keep me chained up? Cut me up? Cook me?"

"Jesus, lady, what do you think we are? Animals?" laughter followed.

Charley turned her head. She squinted her eyes as she recognized the six-foot plus man with long, brown hair and his equally long beard.

"Wait a second, I know you! You come in every Thursday for the roast beef and fresh mozzarella!"

"Heck yeah! Best sandwich in a hundred miles," he nodded and grabbed a turkey leg off a plate. He shoved the entire leg in his mouth and pull out the bone clean. *At least he chewed with his mouth closed.*

"Alright, if you're not going to hurt me, then just let me go. I swear I won't tell anybody about this stupid little prank. I promise," Charley knew it wasn't likely, but hey, worth a try.

"Look, we're sorry about all this, but we need you," the youngest of the bunch spoke.

"For what?" her voice came out low and squeaky, but she didn't flinch.

"For our Alpha."

"What are you guys, like, dogs or something?"

"No. We're Wolves," Spikey smiled at her, bloody cotton and all. She wondered if his gleaming teeth didn't grow a bit.

"Uh huh. Okay, I need to be going now."

"You can't go," beard boy spoke up. He seemed sad, but serious all the same.

"Why not? Look, you guys are crazy. I need to leave. I really need to leave, please."

"Just imagine for a second that you believe us, okay? We really *are* Werewolves, and our *Alpha* is about to be usurped by this real assho- not nice guy. You see, according to our laws an Alpha can only rule absolutely when he is mated. Understand? He *needs* a mate in order to take his legitimate place as Alpha and *you're* it. Surprise!"

Charley stood up. Seven pairs of eyes watched her. There was beard guy; spikey bloody nose boy; the teenager; a glowering male who was thinner than the rest and meaner looking; the one talking now who had short sandy blonde hair; and two giants who sported identical killer grins and shocking red hair. And they all believed they were Werewolves. *Oh crap.*

"You're all crazy!"

A growl sounded to the right and she noticed the twins' lips pulled back in identical snarls. Charley clasped her robe tighter and backed up a step.

The slam of a door startled the entire group. All the men stood up a little straighter except for sandy. He stood and rubbed his face.

"Damn, he's back early," he said quietly.

The knob turned and a man entered the room. The breath rushed right out of Charley as she took him in with her eyes. There stood the biggest, most gorgeous man she had ever seen.

He had dark hair that skimmed his jawline. Chiseled features enhanced by five o'clock shadow, and eyes that made her knees wobble. They were deep set and icy blue. She swallowed and looked down. Afraid she'd get lost in those eyes.

Next came his shoulders. They were bigger than any professional football player's, hell, maybe even *two* football players'. Charley had to bite her lip to stop herself from sighing out loud. He was a perfect male specimen. Like something out of a Greek mythological hero story. *Hercules or Odysseus.*

Even then. Charley was sure they had nothing on the man who just walked into the room. He stopped dead in his tracks when he saw her. He shook his head and rolled his eyes. *Okay, not very flattering.*

"Oh shit, you didn't," he grabbed sandy by the

collar, lifting him an inch off the floor and he growled. Yes, *growled*. 'Sandy' dropped his eyes to the floor and bared his throat, hands held up high as if in surrender.

"Damn it, Seff! You kidnapped another one?" his voice seemed to shake the entire room. That was all Charley heard before she hit the stone floor.

Charley rubbed her eyes. The back of her head ached as if she'd hit it. *What a crazy dream!* That's what she gets for agreeing to a blind date. She must have been stood up or something.

How *did* she get home? She stretched. *Mmm, so warm.* She always wanted a real down comforter. Especially this winter when temperatures dropped to single digits almost every night. *Wait a minute, when did she buy this anyway?* It was always one of those things on her wish list, but she could never really justify the expense.

She opened her eyes and looked around. Panic gripped her as ferocious blue eyes as light as a glacier reflecting the sky stared at her. Those glorious eyes were set in the perfectly sculpted face of a man bigger than anyone she had ever seen. Charley inhaled.

"Aghh-," a hand the size of a baby watermelon clamped gently over her mouth.

"I'm sorry, but please, no more screaming. I have a terrible headache," his voice was deep and sincere, and he seemed exhausted. She almost sympathized with him. Till she remembered she'd been kidnapped.

She nodded as much as she could. His hand smelled good. A woodsy, clean scent filled her nostrils. Like cut grass, and Christmas trees, and fresh split wood rolled into one. *Whatever. Focus girl!*

He removed his mammoth hand and Charley looked him over. He sat perched on a wooden chest next to the bed. The seven not dwarves were nowhere to be seen. She was alone. With *him*. She pulled the sides of the flannel robe tighter.

"Oh, well gee, I'm sorry. Seriously, excuse me, *you* have a headache! Allow me to be a little more cooperative with you. After all I *asked* to be kidnapped, dragged into a van, rendered unconscious, stripped of my clothes and held against my will!" by the time she was finished Charley was yelling, out of breath, and ready to hit someone.

A small smile played at the corner of her captor's lips after her tirade, but it quickly turned into a frown. She liked seeing that small smile and the knowledge she had been responsible for it warmed her insides. His glower, on the other hand, did not.

"*Who* stripped off your clothes?" he growled in a deep baritone.

She was embarrassed to admit it was not all that unpleasant a timbre. Especially if under the right circumstances. *Stop it, Charley.*

"I don't know! What part of *rendered unconscious* did you not understand? And-"

"I'll be right back," he was up and walking out the door before she could finish.

Charley was alone. She should have been scared, but what she felt was something more like annoyance. And she was thirsty. Small wonder after all that screaming.

There was a large glass of water on the side table. She downed it in three gulps, reveling in the way the icy smooth liquid soothed her raw throat. She wouldn't have minded something a bit stronger considering her circumstances.

She took a good look around. The bedroom was large, more like a suite. The décor was masculine, expensive and sturdy too. *Not bad, but no liquor cabinet.* Not that she was much into the stuff anyway.

The fire was lower now than when she first came to. She looked down at the green robe she wore. Her dress and things were nowhere in sight. Then it hit her.

She was *alone*! She needed to find a phone! She looked on both end tables, inside the drawers and closets, but there was nothing. No landline, cell, tablet, or computer of any kind.

She did find an antique clock on the fireplace mantle. It was beautifully carved with a scene that was like something out of a fairytale. She was getting quite a lot of that! Anyway, it showed huge Wolves in mid-run through a dense forest. One massive wolf was in the lead, his head thrown back in a fierce howl. She ran her fingers delicately over the wood. *Beautiful.*

Charley's hands trembled as she traced the carving. *Werewolves.* She shook her head. *Look at the clock's face, look anywhere else, Charley. Do not get caught up in this mass delusion*!

Ten-thirty. She had made it to the bus stop by six. Over four hours had passed since then. That mattered very little in the greater scheme of things. No one would be looking for her with Junior's closed.

She lived alone except for Buttercup. That old cat wouldn't notice until his food bowl ran empty. She grimaced. The door opened and tall, dark and crazy came back in.

"I thought you'd like to know that Cat, my little

sister, was the one who undressed you. Your clothes were wet. They worried you'd catch cold," he had the decency to look abashed.

"You do realize that the police won't care that my kidnappers were considerate, right? It's only a matter of time before they come looking for me," Charley bit her lip, but her eyes never wavered.

Hey, some people would consider a deli counter girl an important person, right? After all, she did cut the thinnest, most perfect slice of prosciutto in the whole state of New Jersey!

"You know, it's funny you should say that Carlotta. And, whereas, I am greatly pleased by a well-made sandwich, I somehow don't think you'll be missed, at least not for a while. Junior's will be closed for what, six weeks?"

Charley gulped and closed her eyes. *Dammit. Now what?*

"So, what, Mr. Kidnapper? People will miss me."

"Rafe. My name is Rafe and let's face it, Carlotta, no one is waiting for you," she heard the sympathy in his voice and Charley stiffened.

"How the hell would you know? And where am I?"

How dare he talk to her like that! He didn't know her! He didn't know anything about her! He was nuts, gorgeous, but nuts!

"We're at Maccon Manor, my home. It's in South Jersey. The town is called Maccon, named after my ancestors. We're on the outskirts."

"How original."

"It's my main headquarters, but all the Were-wolves under my care, are welcome. The Macconwood Pack consists of all the Wolves on the east coast of North America. There are about 500 of us in town. The total population is about a quarter of a million. I govern them all. I am their Alpha," his eyes glowed and Charley gasped.

"Great, the *Jersey Shore*, not just a reality TV hell hole, but a haven for Werewolves and their boss who happens to kidnap strangers for shits and giggles!"

His laugh resounded in the room. A deep and pleasant rumble. He walked closer to her. His huge shoulders took up so much space, Charley backed up without meaning to.

"Oh, Carlotta, we are going to get along just fine. But I am sorry you were brought here against your will. You deserve much better."

"Great. You seem decent, you know for a kidnapper, so how about you let me go and I'll send you a Christmas card or something?"

He shook his head and crossed his arms, looking her over from head to toe. Pride held her still despite the need to squirm. She brushed her hair back behind her ears and wished she had looked in a mirror before he returned. *Seriously? Get a grip, girl!*

She was desperate enough to accept a blind date just before Christmas, but Charley was not delusional. Well, not enough to believe she had been kidnapped and brought to the Jersey Shore by a Pack of Werewolves. *Not yet anyway.*

"I promise I will do everything in my power to see that you are protected and treated with care. My Wolves were only doing what they thought was best. I'm sorry. I'm out of time."

"Oh, okay, they were only doing what was best. Excuse me, where are my manners? How dare I express outrage at being kidnapped! So, what now? You bite me and I'm a Werewolf too? We go howl at the moon and chase rabbits?" she tried and failed to not sound hysterical.

"Actually, I love chasing rabbits, but you can't be *made* into a Werewolf. You have to be born one."

"Awe, gee, well, this was fun, but since I'm not a Werewolf, and neither are you really by the way, then we just can't be *mated*. So sorry, but I'll just go now. I was kidding about the police. Really, nobody needs to know."

"Actually, human females are very desirous to Werewolves. Humans are better at producing live young. Female Werewolves have a difficult time with pregnancy. A sad, but accurate fact for my kind. As Alpha, I must have a mate who can give me an heir."

"I'm sorry, what? Do you really think I am going to stay here? So, I can give you *live young?*"

"I'm afraid you have no choice. The simple fact is, I need you."

"R*iiight.* So, if you're a Werewolf prove it."

"Excuse me?"

Hands on her hips she glared at him. She could forgive the whole chauvinistic rant about a female's purpose being to produce live young. After all her own grandfather had told her time and time again that she needed to get married and have babies. But there was no way she was giving in to the whole Werewolf thing. *So, yeah, let's see you get down on all fours buddy!* Damn if that didn't turn her knees to jelly too.

"Prove it. Now."

"I can only change during the full moon."

"Really, isn't that a little cliché?"

"Rumors sometimes hide truth, Carlotta, and the moon will be full very soon. Believe me I *know*. Her phases are ingrained on my very soul, *mmm*," his head hovered over Charley's bare throat and he inhaled deeply.

"You smell like heaven."

Heat kindled in her belly and worked its way up through her entire body. He inhaled again and moaned like she was a fresh batch of cookies. Charley backed up another step. It was not a good move.

The back of her legs hit the bed and she sat down abruptly. The folds of her borrowed robe flew open and revealed long, shapely legs. He reached forward and took her hands, effectively stopping her from rearranging the fickle fabric. He was so warm! She glanced up. His eyes. They were *glowing*!

Charley sucked in a breath. Was it too early for Stockholm syndrome? Because right now all she wanted was for him to close the distance between them and *well-* she didn't know what exactly, but yes, she wanted it alright. He inhaled again.

"I know you find me desirable, Carlotta."

"Conceited much?" she tried to shake it off, pretend it wasn't there. But it was no good. He seemed to know what she was thinking.

"It's not conceit. I can smell it. *Mmm.* No, don't move," his voice was a low dark bass that throbbed up her spinal column.

"Why not?" she crossed and uncrossed her ankles, her nervousness growing with each step he took.

"Your scent. Every time you move, I get more of it. Oh God, um listen. Carlotta-"

"No one calls me Carlotta," she spoke softly, completely enthralled by his face.

He squeezed his eyes shut and kept his head back as if he were trying to create space between them. A losing battle as his body leaned towards her. *Another deep breath.*

"Everyone calls me Charley," she hated the way her voice shook, but she couldn't deny the tiny tremors of excitement that vibrated all over her body.

"Really? That's a shame. Carlotta is a beautiful name. It suits you," he moved closer. It was as if he was being pulled by some invisible force. He opened his eyes. They seemed to glow a shade darker than their usual icy blue. Maybe it was a trick of the light?

Charley licked her parted lips. She leaned back further onto the massive bed. It was as if she had no control, her body was reacting to his in a way that was new to her. And she liked it. Her elbows dug deep into the plush mattress as Rafe's massive body loomed over hers.

"I am sorry, Carlotta, that I can't give you more time. I *must* be mated before the meeting on Christmas Eve. I'll give you anything, everything you've ever wanted. I have money and power. After we invalidate this charge that my rule is illegitimate, I can try and give you your own life. But right now, I need you, Carlotta. Will you help me?" his voice was mesmerizing.

Charley wanted to give him, well, everything. It was absurd! But still, she felt herself nod as he lowered himself so that his body hovered ever so slightly over hers. Like a big dark dream.

"I don't want your money or power," she spoke in a voice she hardly recognized.

It was happening so fast, like a force of nature. Charley wondered if she could still be dreaming. How could her body react so strongly to a stranger?

"Anything you want, I'll give you anything." *Mine. She's mine.*

"I don't care about that stuff, Rafe, I have no family-"

"*Shhh*, it doesn't matter. I'll give you family, Carlotta. I'll give you anything. Just say yes, please, God, say yes."

Charley was captivated by his sudden vulnerability. *He needed her.* Nobody ever needed her before. She worked forty hours a week cutting cold cuts and scrubbing counters. It was a dead-end job, and she knew it.

After her grandfather passed away, Charley was

left alone in the world except for Buttercup. But this man, this gorgeous giant who believed he was a Wolf, *needed* her. She felt it.

"I'm sorry it has to be like this. So sorry, but I have to, they'll know if we don't, if I don't-," he whispered his words so close his breath mingled with hers.

Charley wanted to taste him. She wanted, she didn't know what, but oh yeah, she *wanted*. His lips brushed hers once, then twice. His tongue flicked out across her lips and she gasped.

"*Mmmm*, you taste like cherries," he groaned, and he kissed her again. This time his tongue dipped into her warm mouth and she opened for him with a soft moan.

"It's my Chapstick," she whispered.

"No, Carlotta, it's you," he licked her lips and kissed her again. He pulled back and she groaned her disappointment.

"I can't help this, I'm sorry. Your pheromones are so strong and with the moon this close, it's hard for me to stay in control. I *need* you. I'm sorry. Say yes," his voice rumbled, and Charley nodded.

"Yes, oh yes," she whispered.

Charley barely understood him, but she knew she was saying yes, and God help her she meant it too. The things he was doing to her were incredible. His hands had an easy strength as he lifted her and peeled back the covers. Charley wanted more. She wanted him.

He pushed her gently onto the mattress and grazed her neck and chin lightly with his teeth. Charley clung to him, awash in a new kind of passionate haze she had never experienced before. His long hardness pressed against her thighs and he continued to lick and nip her mouth and neck while he undressed her.

She knew she should fight him. She should struggle to hold onto that virginity she had saved for the one man she would marry. But not even her twelve years of Catholic school could have prepared her for this onslaught of feeling.

How could she fight against something that felt *soooo* good? Why should she? It didn't matter. She still had to try, right?

"Oh God. Don't-," Charley's whisper was agonized. She moved her head from side to side against the soft pillow.

"Don't?" Rafe lifted his head, his blue eyes blazed as he fought to control himself.

"Don't-," Charley whispered again.

"Carlotta, do you want me to stop? Carlotta? -,"

"Don't, don't, oh, don't stop, please, oh please,

don't stop," she felt his relieved smile against her full breast.

"Thank God, oh, thank you," he breathed his reply and took her plump nipple into his mouth. A delighted gasp escaped her lips.

What was he doing? Tugging, sucking, licking, nipping. His tongue seemed to paint a picture across her body. She writhed under his expertise, wanting more. His hands left hot trails of desire along her taut body.

Charley's skin burned and Rafe seemed to know what she needed. He switched his attentions almost before she knew she wanted him to. Caressing, stroking, and squeezing her in ways she had never dreamed could happen to her.

Growing up with only an elderly grandfather hadn't left her much time for boys as a teenager. She attended Catholic high school, took some community college classes, and worked at Junior's part time. Then her grandfather discovered he had cancer.

She quit school, worked more hours at Junior's, and took care of him until he passed away two years ago. That brought her life up to date. She lived alone, with her cat. Worked, read books, and very rarely dated.

But here she was. A twenty-five-year-old virgin about to have sex for the first time ever with her kidnapper, who by the way thought he was a Were-wolf. *Whoa.*

Okay, she knew she'd have to deal with a whole lot of reality the minute she woke up from this nightmare/dream. She'd worry about it then. She'd even check herself into a mental health clinic just as soon as she got home. She'd do anything as long as he didn't stop what he was doing right then.

"I can smell your need, Carlotta, can you feel mine?" he pressed against her, his body hard and throbbing. She strained towards it like he was some goal she wanted desperately to achieve.

"Do you like this?" he growled and licked her with his tongue in long strokes from the tip of her rosy hard nipples down to her navel, and then lower to her inner thighs. She couldn't speak, she just moaned and gripped his hair in her hands. She left them there since he didn't seem to mind.

His hot breath hovered over her core and she flexed her hips instinctively. Charley couldn't think. She wanted something, *craved* something she couldn't describe. His big hands cupped her breasts as his teeth gripped the elastic of her white lace panties.

She felt a tug and knew they were gone. Ripped off with his teeth. *Oh my.* She felt his chest vibrate, a deep rumble as he slowly, reverently lowered his head.

His hands moved to part her. He *looked* at her, all

the while slowly stroking her thighs. Charley's mouth hung open. She couldn't believe what he was going to do. What she was going to *let* him do.

His eyes locked on hers as he lowered his mammoth head and kissed her there. Once, twice with his full lips. He looked up, gave her a carnal smile. His lips glistened with what she knew was her own moisture.

Then his long, thick tongue snaked out of his mouth and he *licked* her. The groan that escaped his throat rivaled her own. He lowered his head and lapped her. Sucking, licking, and nipping gently with his teeth.

Charley gasped and ground herself against his mouth shamelessly searching for something, some pinnacle she knew she had to reach. And then she did. White hot flames seemed to burst beneath her closed eyelids as he worshipped her body with his hands, his lips, and his tongue. She yelled her first ever release.

Rafe purred his contentment as he continued to suckle. *Slowly, soothingly*. She was lost in sensation as he changed position and removed his clothing.

Rafe needed her. *Now*. He cupped her buttocks, lifting her, and positioned his swollen head at her moist opening. He tensed and entered her slowly.

Charley felt him push inside of her. The sting was

brief, but the sense of connection, of communion, was strong. *Him, I've been waiting for him.*

"Carlotta," he murmured. He had to go slowly with her. He rubbed his finger in tiny, feather light circles, oh so gently, so tenderly over her throbbing sex.

Charley moved and Rafe sucked in a deep breath as he pushed even further inside of her. His eyes bore into hers. He needed to watch her as they joined. Her scent filled his nostrils, the Wolf in him demanded he claim her. *Now.*

"Rafe! Please," Charley thrusted upwards, but his large hands captured and stilled her.

"Easy, baby," he whispered and shifted. He cradled her gently in his arms and watched her every reaction as he fully pushed into her.

She felt him stretch her. Her soft body accommodated his pulsating strength. The tremendous rightness of it brought tears to Charley's eyes. She reached up and held his face as he filled her.

She pulled down his head. He allowed her to, his expression tense, until she kissed him. He groaned and opened for her. Her soft tongue tangled with his.

Rafe thought he would explode. For the first time, she initiated contact. He was completely at her mercy. He stilled and waited for her to command him. A Wolf always listened to his mate's desires.

Something inside of her must have known it too because she nipped his lip and pulled on his waist. He groaned aloud and thrust into her. *Mine.*

He pumped until her cries filled his ears. He growled and his hot seed filled her. Making her gasp. He had never felt so satisfied, so complete, as he did in that moment.

"Are you okay?" he trailed soft kisses down her throat and up to her mouth.

Charley could hardly believe what had just happened. It was better than anything she had ever read about. And she had read some mighty descriptive romance novels in her day. She kissed him back, loving the weight of him.

"*Mmm*, better than okay."

"Good, cause I'm not finished yet."

Rafe moved inside of her and she felt him swell instantly. Charley's eyes flew open.

"Is that supposed to happen so soon?"

"I'm a Werewolf, we heal quickly."

"Oh, -"

"But I don't think I could ever get my fill of you, sweet Carlotta," he breathed her name into her mouth as he joined with her.

Charley held on tight as Rafe drove her to the edge of sanity. He seemed to know exactly what she needed in ways she didn't know herself. *My destiny.*

Their bodies were slick with sweat. Rafe cradled her face in his big hands, kissing her as he sank into her welcoming warmth. She bit down just above his collar bone, gasping his name, and damn, if he didn't pump harder. Her spasms milked him, and he threw his head back, roaring his completion.

After what seemed like an eternity Charley opened her eyes. She was utterly spent, but not even exhaustion could stop the smile that spread across her face like sunshine.

Rafe moved down her body. His lips trailed soft kisses as he went. She missed his warmth. She wanted to pull him back on top of her. She should be ashamed, but shame was *not* how she felt. Not at all.

She watched as he tended her. Rafe's tongue snaked out and licked her thighs soothing her sensitized flesh. She couldn't move as she watched him. His dark head moved up and down as he ministered to her hot skin.

She wanted to hold her knees closed, suddenly embarrassed, but she had neither the strength nor the will to deny him. He parted her legs and looked at her with such reverence in his gaze that her heart skipped a beat.

She lay before him completely exposed. Charley sucked in a breath as he bent and licked away the remnants of her first time. He kissed her thighs then moved up ever so slowly to her most sensitive flesh. First, he tended her, then he moved with intent.

Charley gasped and arched off the bed. She undulated against his clever tongue. Her breathing grew heavy. Rafe knelt between her thighs and cocked his head to the side. She could feel the pressure build up in his powerful body as he waited for her response.

She reached up and grabbed his long hard length with both hands. His skin was like velvet. She cupped him and pumped him once, then twice. He threw his head back and groaned. A very satisfying sound. Charley bit her lip then placed his swollen head at her center.

"Are you sure I won't hurt you?"

"I'm sure, Rafe. I want this, I want you."

"*Mine*," he growled.

Charley moaned at the pleasure of him filling her. He was so strong. Hard, large, and sinewy. Like some sort of ancient warrior god.

Charley on the other hand, was soft and curvy. Her body full of dips and valleys. Her skin ivory to his bronze. Rafe kissed her full breasts, and she threw her head back, her hair cascading around her in wild disarray.

She never thought much about her looks. Never thought there was a reason to. She knew she was considered much larger than the norm. Advertisements and the media of the day continued to plaster pictures of ultra-skinny waif like models all over the place as the thing to aspire to.

Super-thin girls and women who were concerned with the size of their "thigh gap", a thing Charley could not possibly measure on herself as it was non-existent. She was always fond of food and when she was younger, she often felt bad about her weight. Dieting hadn't worked. She certainly wouldn't take pills or have surgery to fulfill society's standards of beauty.

In the 50s, she would have been perfect. But Charley couldn't complain. She was healthy, her yearly physicals stated as much. She had the odd date here and there. Guys in high school had told her she would be pretty if she lost some weight, but she shrugged them off and stuck to herself.

And she was glad. Now more than ever. She was in bed with a man who looked and moved like a god. And Rafe, well, he made her feel beautiful.

His expression was both fierce and humble as he traced lines along her collarbone, neck, and face with his long-fingered hands. He leaned down and kissed everywhere he had touched. Worshipping her with his mouth.

She met his lips and touched them tentatively with her tongue. Rafe had to work to control himself.

He could hardly believe her response to him. Could she really be his true mate? *Mine.* His Wolf growled inside of him and he gripped the pillow behind her head so hard it popped.

Down feathers flew around her head and she laughed. Rafe smiled too. *Beautiful.* Her scent, her taste, her passion, the waves of emotion that rolled off her, he'd take it all. She was his.

"You are beautiful," he nuzzled her neck just as she ran her nails down to his buttocks. And *squeezed.* His ability to think froze. He was insatiable, but only for her.

"*Grrr*, Carlotta, I don't think I can be gentle if you do things like that, you should stop-" he growled in her ear. But his mate shook her head and squeezed harder.

"I don't need gentle, I need you," she wrapped her legs around his waist.

This was crazy. Charley knew it. *Later, I'll think later.* Right then she only wanted to feel. She waited her entire life to feel something half as real.

Rafe knelt in front of her, still joined he lifted her legs and put them on his shoulders, going even deeper inside of her. Charley gasped.

He ran his long fingers over her sensitive skin and moved. *More.* He seemed to sense her needs. When he moved inside of her it was like poetry.

Charley did the only thing she could think of. She held on and when she reached the height of their passion she cried out.

"Carlotta," he exhaled her name and Charley watched him as he exploded inside of her.

It was the most intimate moment of her life. Staring into the clear blue eyes of her very first lover. *Her only lover.*

They had made love. She may be a novice, but she knew this was more than sex. The way he looked at her in his moment of release melted away whatever protection she had built around her heart.

"Rafe, *mmm,*" her voice sounded dreamlike and far away.

"Hey, baby, you hungry?" he cuddled her and kissed her shoulder.

"Actually, I think I'd like a shower," Charley felt around for her robe. Her cheeks burned. She couldn't quite meet his eyes.

Rafe wasn't having any of that. The last thing he wanted was for his new mate to feel shame after what they experienced together. He turned her head to face him, she had such beautiful brown eyes.

"Of course, but first I need you to hear something. I, I apologize."

Her heart stopped. *He was sorry they made love.* She

was shameless! Having sex with her captor. And loving it! And he was sorry.

"No, never for making love with you. I'd never apologize for that."

As her heart resumed its beat, she wondered if he was reading her mind.

"What you gave me was a gift and I'll treasure it. Always. But that's why I need to apologize, for *not* being sorry."

Sorry for not being sorry? Well, that's new.

"Carlotta, my men took you without your permission and I just jumped you! I need to apologize for that. It's just that I can't because I am not the least bit sorry that you're here with me right now."

"Oh, thank God," she said and jumped into his arms.

❦ 5 ❧

Rafe dressed then left to get food. He told her to wait for him inside the bedroom, but she was never one to take orders. After a quick shower, she searched his drawers for something to wear.

She found a pair of navy-blue boxer briefs and shrugged. They were the smallest thing in there, so on they went. She laughed as she caught sight of herself in the mirror.

Rafe was at least six feet two inches tall and over two hundred pounds. A good eight inches taller than her. Most of his clothes were going to be way too big. She kinda liked that.

She had to fold the boxers twice to get them to stay up. She topped off her ensemble with a flannel button down shirt. Of course, she had to roll up the sleeves half a dozen times to keep them from falling.

She knotted the shirt tails at her belly button since loose they reached down to her knees. Charley grinned as she braided her hair. *Guess I'm petite compared to someone after all. Take that Mrs. Gunfry!* She thought of her old gym teacher and smirked.

She tried the doorknob and was slightly surprised when it opened. The hallway before her was long and empty. It was certainly larger than any she had ever seen.

She knew she was in a house with eight men, one of whom she spent the last few hours making the most exquisite love with. There was also one other woman who lived there, *the sister*. But that was as far as she knew.

She counted ten doors from Rafe's room till she got to a huge staircase that looked like something out of Twelve Oaks from Gone with the Wind.

She looked around and was surprised at the quiet. *Hmm. Kitchen? Where is the kitchen?* She heard a noise. Like a blender. She followed it and opened the first door she found. *Eccola!*

Charley stood in a giant state of the art kitchen. The walls were painted a pale yellow. There were miles of marble countertops, polished wood cabinets, and stainless-steel appliances.

"Goddamn it, Seff! Did you use all the basil making those damned watermelon juice things again?" tall, beard boy shouted through a door opposite Charley.

She got a look at what he was doing. *Garlic, onions, peppers, tomatoes, basil*. He was trying to make sauce! She tuned out the argument and went to work.

Charley opened the large Subzero Wolfe refrigerator. She put back the peppers and onions and found some fresh basil in a plastic baggie in the veggie drawer. She pulled it out and handed it to beard boy who was standing behind her with his mouth hanging open.

"You know your herbs would last longer of you wrapped the stems in a damp paper towel. These baggies will make them mold and wilt."

She waited while he opened and closed his mouth like a fish out of water. Then he bent his head towards her and sniffed. Charley backed up instinctively. A ridiculously pleased smile broke out on his hairy face and he howled. *Like a Wolf*. Charley's mouth dropped open.

A stampede of men came into the kitchen and Charley felt like a fool. She stood there, half-naked, in front of her kidnappers and they were all smiles and pats on the back. *What the heck? Where was Rafe when she needed him?*

"Well, well, looks like we did good after all," said beard boy.

"Easy boys, you'll scare her. Hi, my name is Seff, uh, Seff McAllister. This here is Randall Graves," the soft-spoken blonde held out a hand. She shook it briefly. *These guys are not normal.*

They won't harm me. That she knew. They seemed to respect Rafe too much for that. Besides, they thought he was their leader. If only she could figure out the cause of this mass delusion.

"Okay, you still with me? The twins here are Kurt and Dib Lowell."

He pointed to the two red headed giants, then onto a tall thin male with a grim expression.

"This is Tate Nighthawk. Conall Truman, you'll remember. You, uh, gave him one hell of a bloody nose, and this is Liam. He's my baby brother."

They all nodded and smiled. Occasionally, they sniffed the air and grinned wickedly.

"Okay. I'm Charley, but I think you know that. Now I'm not saying I forgive you, but I am kind of hungry. So, Randall, what kind of sauce are you making?"

"The inedible kind," said Conall. He tried to duck out of the way, but he was too slow. Randall elbowed him hard in the gut. Tate winced, the twins snickered, and Liam bent over laughing.

"Hey man, you want to cook tonight? Be my guest! I'm a game developer, not a bloody chef!"

He threw his dish towel at Conall and stalked over to the mound of ingredients he had gathered.

"How about I help?" Charley grinned and followed him over to the counter where ingredients were strewn all over. The others followed, their expressions hopeful.

"She can cook?" someone asked.

"Put these away," Charley began sorting through the ingredients she wanted. She asked for a sauce pot and another for the pasta. She laughed as they rushed to do her bidding.

"Okay, for a simple meat sauce I am going to need a small piece of pork shoulder and maybe a beef rib bone or two?" They got her what she needed and watched as she taught not one, but seven males how to make a classic Neapolitan tomato sauce.

"What about staples, like sausage and meatballs?" Liam asked.

"Alright, we can make that too, but you guys are my sous chefs," Charley was no fool, after all she worked in a deli that catered. No way was she going to be chained to the stove in that massive house!

Twenty minutes later her enormous pot of sauce was simmering, an even bigger pot full of water laced with sea salt was just about to boil, and four dozen meatballs the size of softballs were in the oven. Randall was frying eggplant. Liam was chopping ingredients for a salad and Charley was rolling out dough for fresh garlic and herbed breadsticks.

Rafe entered the kitchen at a run, in his hand was a sack of fast food. "Has anyone seen Carl-," his stunned expression said it all. He dropped the fast food where he stood and grabbed her in a rough embrace which she happily returned.

"Hey, I'm okay," she stroked his hair back from his forehead and dropped a soft kiss on his lips. His eyes told her all she needed to know.

"Hey, boss, your mate can cook! Isn't that great!" said Liam from his position at the vegetable chopping block.

"You did all this?" he said as he sniffed the air and almost groaned from the delicious smells.

"Yeah, I was getting hungry, and I didn't know where you went."

"No, it's okay. I- Thank you."

She lifted the pan of breadsticks and placed it in the oven. Rafe smiled appreciatively as she bent over. He growled when he noticed Liam's interest and the young Wolf immediately turned his head elsewhere.

Charley lifted her head and looked at Rafe. *Was that a growl?* She must be imagining things.

"Okay, boys, I need you to set the table, get some

drinks, and grated cheese and we'll start bringing the dishes out in a few minutes."

Rafe was stunned at the way his mate took charge. *And just look at how his Wolf Guard fell into line!* He grinned like a madman. They were taking orders from this tiny woman, who just hours ago, was a prisoner. *Their* prisoner. Now, she was in control of everyone, and she completely took over his kitchen!

Rafe pulled out a chair for Charley next to his. He squeezed her hand and sat down to one of the best home cooked meals he had ever eaten. The rest of the Wolves waited for him to take the first bite. His eyes closed as he savored it.

His Guard smiled and dug in. They were a rowdy bunch, elbowing each other playfully and joshing around. Charley had never had any brothers, but if she could choose a family, she'd love one like this. Their jovial manner and goofing around put her at ease.

Rafe was just as casual in his mannerisms. It was obvious he was in charge, but the entire meal held a touch of informality that made Charley feel relaxed. She watched Rafe as he served himself another helping of pasta and four more meatballs.

He could really pack it away! And she thought they were crazy when they pulled out box after box of rigatoni.

Rafe was so ridiculously proud that his mate had made their meal that he couldn't stop grinning. That's when it hit him. She wasn't *really* his mate. He had promised to let her have her own life.

He stared at her as she laughed at one of Liam's jokes. *How could he let her go?* She looked gorgeous at his table with one leg tucked under the other, dipping a breadstick into her salad dressing. It was as if she were born to be his. And she got along with his Guard.

What if she wanted to leave? What if she demanded he keep his promise? His eyes narrowed. He knew there was no way he could live without her. His Wolf snarled in the back of his mind at the very thought of her out of his life. *Mine.*

After everyone ate their fill Charley stood up to clear the dishes, but Rafe stopped her with a hand on her shoulder. "No need for that, the guys will do it. We have a housekeeper who comes in the mornings. He takes care of things like the dishes, laundry, vacuuming..."

"He?"

"Oh, yeah. We are all for equal opportunity here."

"Really?" she looked at him with those big brown eyes of hers. He found it difficult to concentrate.

He could get lost in her eyes. He sensed her pulse

speed up and he watched as her lips parted. Rafe struggled to keep steady.

54

6

She was beautiful with her long hair in a loose braid down her back, her straight nose, and full lips. Not to mention her figure. His body reacted just looking at her.

His mate had curves to fill his hands, a soft, flat belly, and rounded hips. Her legs were just long enough to wrap around his waist. *Sweet as honey.*

She had been innocent. A precious gift in this age. Now he wanted to growl at every male who looked at her. *Mine!*

Rafe shook his head. *Easy buddy. You'll scare her.* That was the last thing he wanted. His instinct was to protect and see she was cared for.

He knew in his heart she was his true mate, but he had to make her realize it too. That meant restraint. He'd give her some space. Let her see how good they were together.

"I have some work to do, but I picked up a few things for you when I went out. Some clothes and toiletries. Not that I mind seeing you in my clothes."

"That was thoughtful," her eyes rested on his mouth and Rafe swallowed. He hadn't felt like this since he was a pup.

"Um, would you like a tour of the house on your way back to our room?" Rafe wanted to punch himself in the face.

He sounded like an idiot. He saw the looks his Guard gave him. *Great. An audience.* He growled at a decibel Charley couldn't hear. The command unmistakable. *Back off.*

"I'd love it, thanks," Charley smiled. *Good.* He liked her smile.

They stood up and left the dining room. They made a quick detour to the laundry room off the kitchen where he swiped a pair of clean socks from his basket. He bent down and lifted her feet one at a time.

"So, your feet don't get cold."

"Thank you," her breathy answer told him more than her words. She had found the act of him dressing her as erotic as he had. He blinked to calm the beast inside of him that demanded he drag her into a dark room and have her again and again until she couldn't walk away from him. *Really enlightened thinking there, man!*

He stood up to put a little distance between them and started the tour. He showed her around several living/sitting rooms. The main kitchen she already saw, but there were smaller snack areas with fridges and microwaves. Werewolves tended to eat a lot.

There was also a game room, indoor and outdoor swimming pools, a hot tub, a gym, a weight room, a sauna, a ten-car garage with a working lift, fifteen bedrooms, each with its own bathroom and walk-in closet, a first aid room, a security room, a laundry room, two dining rooms, a ballroom, and a handful of offices.

Not to mention outdoor guest houses, poolside cabanas, and a huge fenced in garden with dense woods directly behind them. He also informed her it was a half hour ride to his private beach.

Fresh flowers graced the hallway. There were exotic potted plants everywhere. Lush and green, their fragrance was light and pleasant. The furniture was oversized and comfortable. Most of the rooms had their own working fireplaces and lots of natural light.

Rafe was conscientious and polite throughout the entire tour. A little too formal for Charley's tastes. At times, she felt self-conscious, but then he'd brush her hair back from her shoulder or take her hand, and everything was okay again.

"I think we should discuss our arrangement, Carlotta. On Christmas Eve, I will present you to my Pack representatives, including the elders, and you will be declared officially as my mate," he waited for her to react. This was so unfair. He felt like a jerk. Once he did that, she would be officially his.

"And then I'll go back to my life. That's what you said, I understand. One thing though," Charley bit her lower lip and looked up at the man in front of her. The man who in just a few hours changed her entire life.

"Yes?" Rafe tensed.

Please, don't let her ask me not to touch her again. He knew that wasn't going to happen. Werewolves were renowned for their virility. And his libido would go into automatic overdrive the minute she was officially matebonded to him.

"Can you bring me some of my clothes and Buttercup? My cat?"

Rafe couldn't help it, he lifted her up in a fierce hug. He laughed and squeezed her before placing her gently back on her feet.

"Of course! If you just make a list of what you need, I'll send Seff for you."

"Alright, thanks."

"I'll walk you back then I, uh, have work to do."

"It's ok, you go ahead, I'll find my way," she gave his hand a squeeze and turned to go.

Damn. He felt like a total piece of shit. His boys kidnapped her, literally. He practically forced himself on her, though seduce was the word he chose to employ. And yet she still agreed to help him out, even though he would totally get it if she wanted to drive a dagger through his back. And now, like a big dumb jerk, he had hurt her feelings. He could smell her sadness, it was kind of like moss and lemons, and it pained him.

He walked to his office feeling like crap. As he passed the huge Christmas tree on display in the main foyer he stopped. He would make it up to her, and he thought he knew how. He'd give her a Christmas she would never forget!

7

The first thing Charley did was head back to Rafe's bedroom. *Would it ever be ours?* Her thoughts wandered as she picked up the shopping bag he brought her and pulled out a pair of black lace panties, a matching bra, soft gray leggings and a jade green tunic style sweater. There were also fuzzy socks and a pair of black ankle boots.

After another quick shower, she dressed and reveled in how perfectly everything fit her. It was like he had memorized her exact proportions. Her cheeks burned when she recalled how he had gotten that information.

Charley strolled back towards the kitchen. She dug around and found a pad and blue ball point pen. Her favorite writing tool. She wrote down a list of what she wanted and went to look for Seff.

Instead, she found Randall. He was sitting on a big brown leather couch with an old acoustic guitar balanced in his arms. She watched as he strummed the instrument. He played with the ease of a professional. His eyebrows furrowed as he plucked the strings.

Charley smiled when she recognized the tune. *Bon Jovi*. A favorite of any born and bred Jersey girl. She was no exception.

She opened her mouth and hummed along with him. Randall perked up and nodded at her. She began to sing, and he slowed the tune down to match her style. He ended the song and went right into some Christmas music.

Charley sang along and loved every minute of it. After a few minutes, the room filled with the men of the house. Rafe was notably absent.

Charley didn't let that get her down. After all, he said he had work to do. They ended the set with a soft rock version of *Silent Night*. Applause and whistles filled the room. Seven pairs of curious eyes watched her as she grabbed a bottle of water and took a long pull.

"Damn girl, you got a nice set of pipes," Kurt, or maybe Dib, said and high fived her.

"Thanks, I was in choir back in school. My grandpa loved to sing carols around the tree. Randall is the one with the talent though!" She curtsied to her guitarist and he bowed back. A gentle smile on his face barely discernible through all the thick dark hair.

"Cool! So, you cook and sing, and the boss was smiling when he left. I think we picked the right one, huh, Seff?" Conall joined in, oblivious to all the groans and eye-rolls.

"Shut up, Con! Icsnay on the idnapkay!"

"Dude, for real?"

"It's okay guys. Despite being forcefully taken without my consent by you brutes, I, uh, I've worked out a deal with Rafe. I'll stay and help, then I get my life back. In the meantime, Seff, can you pick these up from my place?" she held out the piece of paper to him with hands that trembled ever so slightly.

Charley was once again dressed in Rafe's big flannel robe. She snuggled into it and ran a hand through her long damp hair. It was past midnight and Rafe still hadn't returned. It was ridiculous for her to feel abandoned, but she couldn't help it.

He didn't exactly choose her. His friends did. A gorgeous, important guy like him wouldn't choose someone like her. No family, no friends, no career. She was cute in her own way, but she knew she wasn't in his league.

Guys like him chose girls who wore a size 2 with

platinum blonde hair and frosty pink lipstick. Not short, chubby brunettes. Then there was the whole royalty thing. *Pack Alpha*. Whatever the hell that meant!

Werewolves, really? Maybe it was like an MC or gang thing? God, she hoped so. True, they were all big and good looking, and yes, they did tend to growl at each other. And, well, *during sex*, Rafe growled quite a bit. But was that normal for men? She didn't know. She had nothing to compare it to.

The doorknob clicked and Charley turned. She held a breath as he walked in. He looked startled to see her. His blue eyes wide as they looked her up and down.

"I thought you'd be asleep," his voice was gruff, like it was the first time he spoke in hours.

"Is that why you stayed away?"

"Yes. I, uh, didn't want you to feel like I was going to expect, you know, anything," he walked in and closed the door behind him.

"Look, for whatever reason earlier, we had sex. I'm not expecting you to force yourself to *be* with me. I'm your 'mate' for show, for this other guy to see, I get it. I can move to another room, -"

Quicker than she could blink he was across the room and kneeling in front of her. Charley backed up, surprised by his incredible speed. She almost slipped off the edge of the bed. He reached out and steadied her.

"Carlotta, believe me when I say that getting you into this mess was the last thing I would've wanted, but not because I had to force myself to be with you. That's the most ridiculous thing I've ever heard! Don't you know how beautiful you are?" he reached up and cupped her face. The look in his eyes made her want to believe him. No one had ever looked at her quite like that.

"I'm not beautiful, I'm cute," she replied softly, mesmerized by the depths of his blue eyes.

"Are you kidding me? With that long curly hair and those amazing brown eyes? And your skin? Soft and smooth and warm."

"I'm fat. And short," she moved out of his grasp and spoke matter-of-factly. Rafe's eyes bugged out of his head. And he pulled her back, so she had to look at him.

"What? Are you insane? Who told you that load of crap? Carlotta, you are beautiful. You look exactly as a woman should. You fill my hands perfectly, as *my* woman should."

"Rafe, I don't want to talk about my looks."

"Fine. Then let's discuss your courage, your brains, your talents as a chef and a singer, your passion, your strength, your heart, there are any number of things we can discuss that would clearly point out why anyone would be damn lucky to have you even look at them."

"How did you know I sing?" Charley looked at Rafe, uncertainty on her face.

h oh. How was he going to explain this without sounding like a stalker? One thing for sure. He'd have to be honest.

Werewolves simply didn't lie. Living in a Pack made it impossible. When people lied, they gave off clues in their body language and their scent. As pups, they were taught to identify emotions and behaviors, so lying was not really an option.

"I heard you. I, uh, watched you. From my office. Common rooms have security cameras. I was just checking you were safe. Werewolves can be dangerous. Randall in particular. He plays music to soothe himself. When I saw you go in there I was concerned, but when I saw you open your mouth to sing, I just had to listen. It was beautiful, Carlotta. Just like everything else about you."

Technically, that was the truth, the rest he would keep to himself. For instance, he couldn't tell her that he followed her with his eyes as she walked from room to room. That he was becoming obsessed with her. That he had to stop himself at least a dozen times from getting up from his desk and taking her back to bed.

When he saw her approach Randall, one of his most dangerous wolves, he had jumped up ready to intervene. Then she sat down and began to sing. Rafe turned the audio on and had gotten the shock of his life.

Her voice was strong and soft, sexy as hell. When Dib high-fived her, Rafe had growled low and deep. Jealousy had almost overcome his reason. He had to use all his strength to deny the temptation to rip off Dib's offending hand.

It was no good being jealous and possessive. Besides, she wanted her old life when this was done. *No!*

Rafe wanted to change her mind. Hell, he needed to. In his heart, he knew his Wolf had claimed Carlotta. Letting her go was going to be damn impossible.

"Charley, call me Charley."

"No, I don't think so. Your name is Carlotta, *my* Carlotta," he dropped a whisper of a kiss on her mouth.

Oh yeah, this is what I've been missing. Charley thought as she tugged him closer. Her first experience with sex and she was a wanton! Insatiable and curious and gloriously wanton. *For him. Only for him.*

Rafe kissed her lips, lingering on her bottom one. He stood abruptly with her wrapped in his arms. That damn robe covered much too much! He placed her on the bed and tugged. It fell open and revealed her sublime nudity. He groaned as he looked his fill.

She was gorgeous, sensuous, and waiting, for *him*. With a low growl, he took off his clothes. He enjoyed watching her response. The catch in her throat, the way her eyes widened. He knew he was large and muscular. At first, he was afraid he'd frighten her, but the way her eyes ate him up let him know she liked what she saw.

He sniffed the air, and it was like a rush straight to his groin. She was ready. Rafe lowered himself slowly and carefully on top of her. Her body opened for him without prompting. His erection found its rightful place between her thighs.

"Slowly, I don't want to hurt you, baby," he had every intention of going slow, but Charley ran her hands down his backside and pulled.

She licked him from neck to jaw. Her lips found his as she wrapped her legs around him. He entered her slowly, closing his eyes tight as he tried to still himself.

She was like a drug to him. The more he got, the more he wanted. Yeah, but it was so much more than that too. She was like the air. He needed her that much.

Charley explored his back, chest and hips with nimble fingers. She squeezed with her legs and his control began to slip.

He nipped lightly at her neck and inside his mind's eye his Wolf came forward. Deep blue eyes glowing, Rafe raised his head and bit down, not to hurt her. To *mark* her. He sucked, *hard*.

She bucked underneath him, driving him closer to the edge. Rafe's chest rumbled with pride as Charley moaned his name. He was the first one to fill her, to taste her, to make her moan. And he was going to do it again.

"Rafe, I didn't ask before and it was foolish of me, but what about safe sex? Condoms?"

Rafe went still for a minute. He had just had the most mind-blowing sex of his life. *No, not sex. Love. They had made love.* He couldn't think straight. His heart was pounding, and his brain wasn't working yet. *The moon. She is calling.*

"Uh, Werewolves don't get sick like humans. Also, you're not ovulating. I'd smell it if you were."

She was beautiful in the afterglow of their love-making. He had explored every inch of her body. Her smell and taste would be forever ingrained on his heart and mind. How could it be that his Guard knew him so well? Whatever the reason, he was grateful.

"Sounds, *mm*, reasonable," she arched her back as he rubbed her stomach in gentle circles. It was the first time she didn't seem to doubt he was telling the truth. That was good.

Charley woke the next morning alone yet, deliciously sated. She blushed when she recalled all the things they had done during the night. She couldn't believe this was happening to her.

This may have all started out as a kidnapping, but it wasn't now. Hadn't been since she laid eyes on him. After all he never forbade her to leave. He simply asked her if she would stay.

And she said yes. For a while anyway. Charley wondered when it would happen. When would he ask her to leave? Wouldn't it be wonderful if it were true? If he really was a Werewolf and he wanted her to be his mate?

She yawned and stretched. Charley felt glorious. Like a new battery, completely charged. Rafe had mentioned something about his strength pouring into her, something called a *matebond*, but she had been too exhausted to listen.

The sound of something breaking and someone cursing made her lose her train of thought. She pulled on the green flannel robe and opened the bedroom door. Charley stifled her laugh at the sight before her.

"Goddamn cat! Get her!"

"Ouch! Oh fu-,"

A series of painful groans and furniture being knocked down followed. Charley knew the problem immediately. Seff held his neck. Red blood ran through his fingers as he tried to get his breath back. Randall was holding an equally bloody scratch on his forearm and Conall was on the floor.

She watched as he tried to wrangle the one and only Buttercup out from under an accent table. Pieces of the broken porcelain vase, fresh cut flowers, and accent marbles were everywhere. Water soaked the carpet and dripped over the side of the table. *Uh oh.*

"Meow!" Buttercup ran and leapt straight into Charley's arms.

"Hey, baby, my little Buttercup, my sweetie," she cooed and stroked the cat's fur. She raised an eyebrow at the three grown men sprawled all over the place.

"Sorry, guys, I should have mentioned he doesn't like strangers. Oh, can you bring up my bags please. Thanks."

"Oh, he doesn't like strangers! Thanks for telling

us that! Could have used a little warning," Conall mumbled as he, Randall, and Seff hefted her suitcases, kitty toys, and one freshly cleaned, bright blue litter box up the stairs.

Charley hid a smile at all their grumbling. Served them right! She had them leave the litterbox in the hall. She set Buttercup down and watched him get acclimated to his surroundings.

"Wait, you're going to let that beast roam the place?"

"That's right. You got a problem with that?"

Seff stopped Conall with one hand up, "No, ma'am, we do not. We apologize if we were out of line. Not used to cats, you know. Werewolf thing and all," he bowed. Randall and Conall followed suit.

"If it's okay with you, ma'am, I'd like to go over some things for the meeting when you are ready? You will need to know how to conduct yourself around the rest of the Wolf Pack and our *guests*, ma'am, if that is okay?" Seff's formality made Charley smile.

So, they were really going to treat her like the whole Alpha female thing, huh. Okay then. Maybe she should take a moment to clear her head. She went inside and began to unpack. Humming thoughtfully to herself.

The walk-in closet was huge, but a space had been made for her belongings. When she opened her bags, she realized they had packed much more than just some of her things.

She hung up a few items and left everything else in her suitcases. After all, her time there would be short. Unless, well, she'd think about that later.

9

Charley rifled through the kitchen. Rafe was in his office and she needed to think. Cooking had always been therapeutic for her, especially when she had a problem. And boy did she ever! *Hmmm, chef salad sounds good.* She got out some fresh produce, a dozen eggs, fresh cheese, and cold cuts.

A couple dozen cheddar drop biscuits and home-made honey mustard vinaigrette would complete the meal. Charley set up her ingredients, sighed, and got started.

Everything she could ever want was right in front of her. And not just inside the kitchen of her dreams, but Rafe, and the others too. She walked over to the extra-large double sink and rinsed her hands. Oh, the

Christmas breakfast she could prepare here! Charley smiled.

She and her grandfather always made a large breakfast to celebrate Christmas Day. It was the one tradition she kept since his passing. Though nowadays it mostly consisted of a single pancake, citrus fruit salad, and a strip of uncured bacon. It was no fun cooking just for yourself.

Maybe she could make some quick cookies for after lunch too? She quickly prepared a batch of butter-cookie dough and was not surprised to find a cookie press and sprinkles in the cabinets. She smiled as she quickly prepared a sheet of her favorite Christmas cookie. Tree shaped with red and green sugar crystals. Just how she liked them.

Her hands moved automatically as Charley thought about what was important to her. She had always wanted to get married and raise a family. In her daydreams, she was the mom who stayed home to raise her children. She'd make them cookies and treats and help them with homework. She'd be there for them.

Maybe it was because her grandpa was her only parent and he had worked long days to keep her in private school. He did his best and she loved him, but she had spent a lot of time with strangers or in after school programs.

She disliked the ideas of daycares and nannies. If she were married to a man like Rafe, he could easily provide her with the security and stability to stay with the kids. *Wait, where the heck did that thought come from?*

She shook her head and winced. No one mentioned marriage. True, she didn't ask to come here, but she never felt so at home before. This place, these men, felt like they were *hers* in a way.

They were polite, funny, incredibly courteous, and sweet. Like the brothers she never had. Then there was Rafe. He was truly one of a kind. A gentle and generous lover. Gracious, intelligent, and he had an air about him that commanded attention.

An innate power that was subtle, yet undeniably strong. Her heart beat faster just thinking of the big guy. Heavy footfalls fell behind her and she straightened her back. *Rafe.*

"Hey," he walked up to her, placed big hands on her hips and kissed her neck. Charley almost dropped her knife. She leaned back into him, eyes closed.

"I'm sorry I had to leave you this morning. There was something I needed to attend to. *Mmm*, smells good."

"Thanks. I guess I missed breakfast. I made enough for everyone."

"I meant you, but the food smells great too. You know, you don't have to do that."

"*Mmm*, I know, but I like to cook."

More footfalls, some sniffing, then groans of pleasure.

"Oh my God, are you making us lunch?" Dib or Kurt said. They both sniffed the air, identical looks of ecstasy on their faces.

"Oh, thou fairest maiden, Charley! Wilt thou honor me as my personal chef forever unto eternity," Liam dropped to his knees at her feet.

"Beat it, pup," growled Rafe, only half kidding.

"Alright, alright, come on, boys, go wash your hands and set the table. Lunch is in ten minutes."

They howled and ran for the lower floor bathrooms. Shoving each other like twelve-year old kids.

"My God, you'd think they never saw food! Animals!" Rafe shook his head and went back to nuzzling her neck.

"Pardon my frankness, but none of you look like you never saw food. And, *mmm*, Rafe unless you want one of my fingers in the salad you better stop that now or I'm afraid I'll cut myself," he stepped back immediately. Charley missed his warmth.

"I'd never let a single hair on your head be hurt," he vowed.

"Good to know. Please carry this inside," she nodded at the pitcher of vinaigrette and the two-giant bowls of salad. He dropped a kiss on her temple and picked up the food easily in his big hands.

She took the cookies and biscuits out of the oven. She scooped the warm, golden biscuits into bread baskets and placed the cookies aside. Charley put the baskets on the dining table and was surprised to see no one eating.

"Isn't it alright?" she had used plenty of cold cuts, cheeses and hard-boiled eggs.

"It's perfect, darling, we were just waiting for you," Rafe pulled out the chair to his right.

"Thanks," Charley sat awkwardly and waited, but no one moved. She reached for the salad and was surprised when Rafe took the tongs from her and filled her plate. He filled his next and passed the dish to Seff. He did the same with the dressing and biscuits.

He surprised her even further by taking her hand and saying a brief grace over the meal. Charley had to blink back tears. They were all being so respectful, so kind. *For her*.

Conversation started and soon they were joking and talking about the upcoming holidays. Charley laughed with real joy as the guys ribbed each other. The front door opened, and she heard a female voice.

"Hello? Anyone home? Hey, is that food?" in walked the tallest, most beautiful woman Charley had ever seen. She was thin, toned, and had long wavy blonde hair.

She had a gym bag slung over one shoulder. A badge on her hip and a gun. Fresh snow dusted clothes and hair, giving her a sort of fresh glow. Charley's eyebrows rose.

"Oh, hey! How you doin'? You were passed out last time I saw you and you had less on," at Charley's blush the woman winked. She dropped her bag, grabbed a plate and helped herself. The men seemed at ease with her except for Tate who ignored her completely.

"Jeez, Cat, slow down. Let me introduce you. Carlotta, this is Catriona, my baby sister," Rafe said with an indulgent grin on his face.

"I'm sorry, are you a police officer?" asked Charley.

"Macconwood Sheriff's department, actually, I'm a deputy. Nice to meet you, officially."

"Well, that's just great! *You*, you're sworn to uphold the law? Congratulations, *officer*, you're an accomplice to a kidnapping!" the room got very quiet.

Everyone averted their eyes except for Rafe and

Cat, who met Charley's glare. She averted her eyes and shrugged her shoulders.

"You know, Charley, you don't look like you're being held against your will. Besides Pack comes first," she dug into her salad.

"Oh, so you're delusional too then. Great, just great!" Charley stood up hands on her hips and walked over to Cat.

"Carlotta, we can talk about this later. Besides, you agreed to stay, -"

"Yeah, but not when your sister undressed me. Hey, I'm talking to you, at least look at me! You had no right! As a woman and a deputy, you should have done *something*. Well, what do you have to say for yourself, young lady?"

Catriona stopped eating and stood up to her full height. Not backing down a step, Charley stood toe to toe with her and stared her directly in the eye. Cat dropped her gaze first. Even before she heard Rafe's warning growl.

"I apologize, ma'am," she grinned and bowed to Charley before reseating herself and taking another bite.

"Hey brother, I like her. Try not to fuck it up," Cat said in a not so whisper to Rafe. In fact, all the Guard seemed to watch Charley with admiration in their eyes.

Charley looked at each of the stunned faces at the table and sat back down next to Rafe. Her posture was stiff, displaying her annoyance, but her heartbeat was normal. Rafe let out a relieved breath. *Yes*, he thought, *I have clearly chosen well.*

"Well, eat!" she commanded, and they did.

10

After lunch Rafe took Charley on a tour of the grounds. It was the first time she saw the house from outside. It took her breath away.

Maccon Manor was a veritable fortress. Big and foreboding, like a castle in a fairytale, made of stone and iron. There were state of the art security fences, cameras, and even a manned gate. Rafe pointed each one out to her. Her safety his foremost priority.

He needed her to see that he could provide protection. For her *and* any future young. *Easy.* He needed to curb all thoughts of any children.

The very idea of her bearing his child made him want to take her, right there on the ground. He looked over the fine form of his mate as she bent down to pick up a pebble. *Damn.* She was beautiful.

Charley appreciated the natural stone walkways and the meticulous landscaping. There were luscious evergreens adorned with twinkle lights and shrubberies surrounded by smooth pebbles that reflected the light like glass. They were sure to be spectacular come spring.

Someone must lovingly tend all this, she thought absently. Rafe held her hand but didn't pull or drag her. He was patient with her questions. And she listened with interest as he explained about the history of Maccon, NJ and its ties to his family.

"There has been a Maccon running Pack business in this area since the first settlers. About five generations back. You see, Werewolves live longer than humans and as a result so do their human mates. We can be killed, but it's difficult. I must tell you that we do have enemies, Carlotta, dangerous enemies. But I swear, I'd die defending you."

Charley didn't know how to react. She cared for Rafe, heck, she might even love him. But how could she help him with this delusion of his when everyone seemed to feed it?

She reached up and caressed his jaw. She knew he meant that part about risking his life for her. She didn't doubt that.

"Carlotta, this rogue Wolf, Skoll, wants me out of the picture. As Alpha, I will always be a target for my enemies. It's important you know I can protect you."

"Rafe, this delusion, isn't real, -"

"But it *is*. You must understand as a Werewolf I *can't* lie."

"What does that even mean? You gonna burst into flame or something if you fib?" Charley tried to joke, but it sounded lame even to her ears.

"No. Different emotions, different states of being have scents. Basically, I can smell a lie and so can other Werewolves. I must be *matebonded* by Christmas Eve. I know I promised to give you your own life, but first you must mate me. Will you?"

"I thought we did already," Charley blushed and Rafe reacted predictably. He wanted her, so very badly.

"I'll cherish our intimacy always, Carlotta, and I'll never be able to thank you enough for the gift of you, but I need more. I need you to formally marry me."

Charley's heart pounded in her chest. She placed a hand over her belly. Could this be her one chance for her dreams to come true? *A husband, a home, family.*

"Of course, you wouldn't have to stay, -" Rafe's voice was low, and Charley felt her stomach tighten. She disliked the idea of their *having* to marry. She wanted to be wanted, to be loved. But maybe she was being greedy.

"Look, I said I would help you, Rafe, and I will. I don't know about all this supernatural stuff, but I believe you believe it. And whatever *this* is between us, I gave you my word."

"So, you will?"

She nodded. Whatever fantasy he believed, it seemed like maybe this would help him resolve some problem. And honestly, she just wanted to be as close to him as she could for as long as possible.

Her insides melted as his face lit up. He grabbed her in a tight hug and swung her around. Kissing her desperately on the lips. Charley clung to him. She felt her legs go weak just as he lifted his head.

"I have the paperwork in my office. Will you come with me now and sign? Then Seff can perform the ceremony. He's licensed to perform marriages."

"You want to do this now?" she looked down at herself. She knew if she left his side even for a minute, her brain would take over and reason would never allow her to go through with it. Charley looked into Rafe's blue eyes. Was she really willing to marry a virtual stranger? She inhaled and nodded her head. There was no backing down now.

Half an hour later she was legally married, in a pair of old worn jeans and a yellow sweater. Rafe held her left hand up and slipped a perfect blue sapphire the size of a nickel onto her ring finger. It was set in a thick platinum band carved with what Charley thought looked like runes.

"It's a star sapphire, the ring of the Alpha female of the Macconwood Pack. It belonged to my ancestors, Eoghan and Ailis," Rafe's voice was deep, and Charley held his gaze. One by one, his Guard entered the room and knelt before them.

"I place this ring on your finger and proclaim to all under my domain that you, Carlotta Marie Palmieri Maccon, are the Macconwood Female Alpha and my mate *semper et in saecula*," he kissed her hand and knelt at her feet. The moment seemed to last as Charley felt a sort of warm vibe spread throughout her body.

She didn't know what was happening. One minute it was all legalities, *one, two, three* and they were married. Then, as if by magic, all the guys in the house and Cat appeared and Rafe said things she couldn't possibly fully understand.

"Holy shit," someone murmured.

"Ooof -"

"*Shhh,* -"

Charley ignored everyone except Rafe. Her new husband's eyes were glowing. His expression intense, he was focused solely on her.

"Come, let's leave them."

"You mean, like, now?"

"*Shhhh*, go!"

Charley ignored the footfalls in the background. Great vibrations were coming from Rafe's throat and hitting her right between her thighs. The door shut and before she knew it, they were alone, and he was on her. Right where she wanted him to be.

His dark brown hair was carelessly brushed back from his face. His blue eyes glowed a shade darker than usual and in them Charley saw heat, desire, and power. In two moves he was completely naked before her. A perfect male specimen.

He was bronzed and muscled with dark curling hair that began on his chest and trailed downwards. Charley's eyes widened. He had thick legs corded with muscles. They stood apart and she was drawn to where he was most masculine. His chest heaved with the force of his breathing. He was beautiful.

Charley felt her own breath quicken as he moved in closer. His nimble hands made quick work of her clothing, then he reached for her hair. He gently pulled her tresses free from the ponytail she had worn all day. He leaned in and Charley gasped as he licked her from neck to nipple.

He had to bend to get close enough, his height so much greater than hers, but he didn't seem to mind.

He lifted her onto his desk and laid her back, licking and sucking as he went. He lavished attention on her breasts and belly. Rafe couldn't get enough of the sweet taste of her skin. He knelt before her and parted her supple thighs.

Rafe's growl started deep in his chest sending vibrations straight through to her core. Charley squirmed in his hands as he leaned forward. His fingers smoothed up her legs and he parted her skin to reveal her most secret place. His breath heated her, she pulled him by his thick hair, but he was immovable. Desire burned through her body. *She needed him*.

His growl grew louder and soon he was kissing her swollen flesh. His tongue delved inside, darting and probing. He rubbed his cheeks against her sensitized thighs. Every touch, every sound, and sensation seemed amplified in the closed quarters of his office, but Charley could no more stop her moans than she could his soul shattering touch. *Why would she want to?*

Rafe held her gently in place with his large hands while he suckled her. She was all honey and cherries and Rafe was greedy for her. He kept at her, licking and kissing, using his fingers and even his teeth, until Charley almost bucked off the desk. Her groans echoed all around him and he felt his own sex grow long and hard. Rafe's body quivered in anticipation. He wasn't prepared for his baser reaction to her complete submission.

The Wolf inside of him was howling and he knew without a doubt this woman was his mate. His destiny. His world. He would do anything for her. He would kill for her. Even die for her. *How would he ever let her go?*

Lightning surges of pleasure shot through Charley's body. She was close. Rafe scented her arousal and pleasure, heck, he *felt* them. It was like her body was calling out in a frequency that only his could answer and it was glorious. It almost brought him to his knees.

Rafe stood, his clothing a careless heap on the floor. They moaned in unison as his engorged sex came into her with a single perfect thrust. He fought for control, but nothing he had ever learned or experienced could have prepared him for the sensation of bonding with his mate on this level. It was beyond all previous notions and expectations.

Charley loved having his weight on top of her. Thick and hard, yet smooth and soft as velvet, he filled her on so many levels. Every kiss, every touch, the slightest movement of his body, the tiniest growl that emanated from his chest, sent her closer to the edge of ecstasy. She had never felt as complete as when he swept her away in his most intimate embrace.

He thrusted into her welcoming heat and Charley knew that nothing could ever be that perfect. Nothing would ever compare to these moments. She cried out, an agonizing moan, as they reached the height of their pleasure, together.

Charley snuggled into Rafe's warm chest as he carried her through the empty hallway as if she weighed nothing. Wrapped in his soft sweater with her clothes piled on top of her he managed to make her feel like a princess. Albeit a princess who had just engaged in some deliciously naughty desk sex.

She smiled and sighed, a satisfied sound. He nuzzled her head as he walked. His steps strong and steady, his voice deep and husky.

"I'm sorry I couldn't wait until we were upstairs. I should have had more control," he seemed shaken, maybe embarrassed.

Charley reached up and stroked his cheek. There was more hair than there was just an hour ago. He looked scruffy and handsome. His lips were slightly swollen, and she felt her cheeks heat as she recalled how they had gotten that way.

"S'okay, I couldn't wait either," she bit her bottom lip as he opened the door to his room and placed her on the duvet. He smoothed a stray curl away from her flushed face and kissed her lips.

⚜ 11 ⚜

"How do you feel, *my Carlotta?*" Rafe's hand grazed her neck, his fingers stroked her softly. He couldn't stop touching her. He had no desire to.

"Mmm, good. What time is it?" Charley felt a little sleepy, but good. So very good. *How could this be real?* She wondered if it was possible for a person, *for her*, to truly be this happy.

"Eight-thirty, baby, no, no don't move," he held her down gently when she tried to sit up.

"It's later than I thought, I should make dinner."

"Don't worry about it. The guys ordered a bunch of pizzas. Are you hungry?" Rafe asked. She shook her head as he bent and kissed her softly.

"Carlotta, tonight is the full moon."

Charley stiffened. Time for the truth. He had to come clean about this whole Werewolf nonsense.

"Rafe, I-"

"Please, just listen. You are my female, my mate, you're protected. Do not be afraid. Our matebond will be complete after tonight," he spoke matter-of-factly. His ice blue eyes held a faraway look and for the first time, Charley felt uncomfortable. She didn't know how to respond. *Poor delusional man.* Tears sprang to her eyes.

"Oh Rafe, you are *not* a Werewolf. Maybe we can get you some help?"

"Trust in me. I beg you. I am a Werewolf. Even if you want to leave after, I need you to understand this is not a delusion. I'm so sorry I didn't have the strength to send you away in the beginning, I just couldn't, one look and I knew you were my destiny," he ran his hand through his hair. Charley thought she saw him tremble.

"My Guard is sworn to protect you now. Just remember, I would die before I let anything hurt you. Don't be afraid."

He drew open the floor length curtains revealing the French doors that led to the terrace. He opened them too, letting the frigid night air creep into the bedroom. He didn't seem bothered by it even in his nudity. *A few more minutes and the moon would be completely full.*

"Whatever you're thinking, please, please know this, I love you, Carlotta."

Big, soggy tears ran down her face as she tried to hold in her sobs. She had waited her whole life to hear those words. What was she going to do when nothing happened? How would she console him?

"Don't worry, sweet, you'll be safe. I swear it. After the Change, I'll stay with you awhile, then I'll have to go," he bent and touched her forehead with his own.

"Don't worry, my love. The Pack has to see their Alpha, but Cat will stay behind to keep an eye out," his head still touching hers he leaned down and licked the tears off her face and neck. She wanted to hold him, to keep him there. But he backed away from her embrace.

He turned his head toward the terrace, a look of anticipation and bliss on his face. That's when Charley noticed the moon. Beautiful, bright and completely full. Its rays seemed to land right on Rafe, encompassing his entire body in an unearthly glow.

Suddenly the air around him shimmered. His breathing increased. He started to sweat, and his entire body vibrated. He was just so large and powerfully built. More muscular than any man she had ever seen. *Beautiful.*

He mouthed something to her. She thought it was, *I love you.* Three words. That's all they were. She thought she had imagined them moments ago, but here he was confirming what she thought was delusion.

Charley sat up on the bed, wrapped in a sheet and watched as the man she had married mere hours ago seemed to shimmer in and out of the moonlight. *I love you*, fitting words for this moment of magic and myth. She wished she could return them, but she was struck dumb by the sight before her.

Rafe's brown hair darkened to a deep blue black. Then suddenly, it wasn't hair, but more like fur and it ran down his arms, his hard belly, and legs. His large human body doubled over. Rafe grunted and groaned. He seemed to be in pain.

Oh my God, Charley ran to help, but Rafe seemed to melt right before her eyes. Where he had been crouched down on the ground only moments before stood a black Wolf the size of a small pony. Charley stopped so suddenly she fell flat on her butt.

The Wolf looked at her. His chest was heavily muscled. His paws massive with long, sharp claws. His eyes were a darker blue, but they were full of knowledge and recognition. Charley crouched down in front of him and stretched out her hand as tears rolled down her face. *A Werewolf! It was all true!*

The Wolf held still as she approached. Unsure of herself, she wiped her face and bent her head down, beneath his. It seemed right somehow.

He walked to her and wrapped his great Wolf body around hers. Heat emanated from him, as well as, strength and power. Charley reached out with shaky hands and stroked his fur. It was smooth and silky, but underneath his body was hard and muscular.

His huge Wolf tongue hung out to the side as she scratched behind his ear. Charley's laughter rang throughout the room when Rafe went belly up like a great big puppy. She couldn't believe her eyes. Fear took a backseat, replaced by wonder and amazement. *A real, live Werewolf! And he was her husband. For however long he wanted her.*

He stood up suddenly, jarring her from her thoughts. He walked over to the terrace and barked. Then he looked over at her then back down to the yard. Charley stood up and went to him wrapped in nothing but a sheet from the bed. It trailed behind her like the train of a wedding dress, and she felt like something out of a dream.

She peered over the railing at the eight magnificent Wolves that were gathered below them. They were all huge, bigger than the average Wolf, but none quite as large as her Rafe. They sat on their haunches and howled into the night air when they saw them both together.

Charley made out a dark brown one with long shaggy fur, *Randall*; a light buff one with short smooth fur, *Seff*; a golden one with shorter fur that spiked into a ridge on his back, *Conall*; a smaller, paler blonde one that could only be Cat; a black one with a scar that zigzagged across his shoulders, *Tate*; two large bright red wolves, the twins *Dib* and *Kurt*; and a snow-white wolf, *Liam*. They were a stunning group. As Wolves or humans.

Charley felt a force, a power almost like the hum of a generator, soar through her body. Suddenly she felt as if she were connected to them all. She could feel their presence touching her heart and mind. Rafe stood out among all of them. His heart the clearest. His love for her strong and pure.

Her chest heaved as the force of that power filled her. All her life she had felt alone, especially after her grandfather passed, but not now. All she felt now was love for this man, this Wolf, who had filled her empty life as no one else ever could.

More Werewolves approached from the dense woods behind the manor. They seemed to be acknowledging her, their new Alpha female. Charley felt her heart swell with pride and wonder.

She turned as Rafe's claws made a clicking sound on the beautiful wrought iron fence that surrounded the terrace. He watched the display with a regal air about him. He acknowledged his Pack with a short howl then turned to her.

"Thank you," Charley said to him, her left hand over her heart, "thank you so much."

His great Wolf head was cocked to the side as he dropped down to his paws and approached her. He licked her hand gently, a soft whine escaping his jaws.

"No, I'm happy. I really am. You're beautiful. All of you," surprised and delighted she wrapped her arms around his furry neck, and he nuzzled hers back.

Rafe gently stepped back from her and she released him. Then he leapt in front of her, blocking her view. She heard the clacking of claws on the stone tiles. A Wolf had apparently jumped up, though they were at least two stories high.

Rafe growled once and Charley noticed it was Cat. The female Wolf lowered herself into a submissive position. She approached Charley and sat down at her feet. Charley steeled her nerves and reached out to rub the female between her pointed ears.

She could not afford to be afraid. In truth, she was more curious anyway. Her musings stopped when Cat's sandpaper-like tongue snaked out and licked

Charley's hand. She grinned at the She-Wolf. They would be just fine.

Cat will stay with you, Rafe's voice whispered in her mind. Charley nodded and wiped her eye as her husband barked once then vaulted over the terrace. He landed soundlessly on the frozen grass below.

She walked over to the French doors and closed them, though she wanted nothing more than to watch. She tried listening for them, but only managed to hear a few distant howls. Cat, on the other hand, seemed to hear things Charley's human ears couldn't pick up.

"So, what do I do now?" Charley mused.

Cat walked to the closet and nudged the door. Charley opened it and watched the Wolf pull a nightgown from a hangar gently with her mouth.

"Maybe you're right, a shower first, then bed."

Charley indulged in a long hot shower. She brushed her damp hair and donned the nightgown Cat had chosen for her. It was soft and practical. She shrugged and went to snuggle in bed. Cat was lying down on the rug. She couldn't tell if the Wolf was asleep or not, but she suspected she was trying to make it easier for Charley by not moving around so much.

Sometime later Rafe came back. She knew him instantly. It was as if her soul recognized his. She opened the terrace doors in her soft cotton nightgown and Cat flew out of them just as Rafe stepped inside.

It was ridiculous to wish she were in silk and lace instead of worn cotton, but she couldn't help it. It was her wedding night, after all. She wanted to be beautiful for him.

As if sensing her mood, he licked her hands gently and nuzzled her belly. Then he leapt up on the huge bed. Charley joined him. She wondered at the idea that she was in bed with a Werewolf. Silk or not, she was with him now and that was all that mattered. It was everything.

She must have dozed off while staring at Rafe. *Her husband. Her Wolf.* She was awake now and the male wrapped around her was all warm skin and hard muscle. And he was happy to see her, judging from the hardness she felt rubbing up against her bottom. She pushed back into him and smiled at his groan.

Next thing she knew, her nightgown was off, and she was up on her knees with him behind her. He gently eased her head down and spread her thighs. She sucked in a breath, more than ready.

Rafe parted her slick flesh with his hands. She expected him to take her hard and heavy. Moisture flooded between her legs as she anticipated how he would fill her. She gasped aloud when his rough tongue found her instead. Charley moaned and rocked back against him as two fingers joined his tongue and entered her from behind.

His thumb circled her most sensitive flesh then his mouth was back, lapping at her. She felt deliciously exposed. Like she had never been before anyone. *For him, only him.*

His chest rumbled against her and she could almost see his smile. A now familiar heat coiled low in her belly. It was a delicious secret the way her body opened for him and only him. She wanted more than his mouth. She tossed her head from side to side gripping the pillow in front of her as she almost lost control.

"Rafe, I want to feel you inside me when it happens."

Then his mouth and hands were gone, and he pushed his long erection into her with a deep groan escaping his lips. He kissed her neck as he went in and out, in a rhythm as familiar as breathing. They spiraled together, he plunging, she pushing back into him. Charley groaned his name as pleasure skyrocketed throughout her body.

Rafe could hardly breathe as her contractions milked him for everything he was worth. *My God*, she was something else. *His mate*. He should never have told her he was going to let her go. There was just no way.

She was part of him now. Part of his heart. He had to make her see that. Being with her like this eased a fear inside of him he didn't even realize he had. Happiness was not something an Alpha Wolf counted on. Duty and tradition were more the norm. But now, *with her*, it was a definite possibility.

His world was different from hers. Packs had rules. His parents were no love match. Mated by contract at birth, destined to control the Macconwood Pack. Theirs was a cold union.

His mother bore him out of duty. His father was slightly better. He took the time to teach Rafe how to be pack Alpha, but little else. After his mother's infidelity yielded his little sister, she fled the manor and left both pups to his father's bitterness.

Rafe had never dared dream his life could be different. He rejected the idea of a betrothal contract, but he knew he'd have to mate one day for his heir. He never thought he'd find a soulmate. Certainly not in a spunky human woman. One whom his Guard happened to kidnap.

He wished he'd seen her first. Met her in a normal setting, courted her, made her fall in love with him. Well, he'd just have to make her see she was his. His mate, in every sense of the word.

He knew it in her scent, he felt it in the vibrations that came from her luscious body when they were together, and he tasted it on the salty sweetness of her skin. Rafe kissed her shoulder as he withdrew from her. He tucked her against him as they regained their breath together. She was his everything. *Mine.*

"M*mm*, morning," Charley said as she opened her chocolate brown eyes to meet the icy blue ones of her husband. He laughed and kissed her curly head.

"Good morning, my sweet mate."

"Rafe?"

"Yes," he stopped breathing. Would she ask to leave now that she had seen the truth? Charley sat up, her eyes grew dark and contemplative.

"Rafe, I want to apologize," he exhaled as she spoke. Relief coursed through his veins. *She wasn't leaving. Not yet.*

"You were telling the truth. I didn't believe you and you were telling the truth. I am sorry for that and

I have so many questions for you, I don't know where to start."

"Anything. You can ask me anything," he clasped her hands in his. He brought them to his mouth and kissed her palms. *God*, he loved her scent. Like honey and something else that was all her.

"Is it painful? When you change?"

"Not anymore. The first few times are rough, Werewolves can only change after puberty and are weak in the beginning, but with time our strength grows, and the pain goes away."

"When you're a Wolf how can you understand me?"

"It doesn't happen with everyone. Abilities differ from Wolf to Wolf. As we are mated, I expected to be able to understand your feelings, I admit I was surprised to understand your words perfectly."

"*Mm*. I heard you too, when you said Cat would stay with me, but it was only after that hum that I felt. The one that like, connected me to all of you. How did you do that, anyway?"

"What do you mean?"

"Well, when I saw you, all of you, it was like when you turn on a generator or go past power lines and electricity is in the air. Well, I felt that, but it went through me and then you were all here. In my mind and my heart. I could feel you."

"Carlotta, I've heard whispers of this, legends really, but never in my wildest dreams-" Rafe's heart stopped for a minute then swelled. She was amazing.

He reached for her beautiful face with his hands, then he kissed her. Tugging on her bottom lip as she wrapped her arms around him. He shuddered with pleasure as she embraced him.

"You're a wonder, my Carlotta. If my recollection of our legends is accurate, you're what we call a *whisperer*. Randall would know more. He is sort of our keeper of legends. That's why he invented that game of his, *WolfMoon*."

"*WolfMoon*, really? I had friends from school who played that!"

"Lots of humans do. He's made the Pack a fortune with it. Most of the money is his of course, but I did front him the funds to start so I own a percentage of his company."

"Wow!"

"I know, right?"

"So, from every movie or book I've ever heard about Werewolves are cursed men. Is that true?"

"Yes and no. Our curse is not that we turn into Wolves. Our curse is that we are kept from our Wolves. We can only merge with them at the Full moon, but that may change now."

"How?"

"There is a group within the European Packs, the *Hounds of God*. Within their circles is an American Werewolf, a teenage girl, she lives here, in New Jersey. Her name is Grazi Kelly. It's possible she can break this curse. It's vital to our survival as a species."

"That's a lot of responsibility for a teenager, but if she lives here, isn't she part of your Pack?"

"Well, that's tricky. She's the Greyback Pack heir, but I have afforded her the protection of Macconwood."

"Okay, sounds reasonable. What about this other Werewolf, this Skoll who wants to hurt you?"

"Don't worry about Skoll, I'll handle him."

He felt her stiffen and rubbed her back. The idea of her even saying the name Skoll sent rage coursing through his veins. He would shred that bastard Wolf if he even looked at his mate.

"When is the meeting with the council?"

"Christmas Eve."

"Well then, we better get started."

Charley spent the next few days going over Werewolf etiquette with Seff, getting to know the rest of the Wolves, and spending endless hours alone with Rafe. He was tender, kind, and always willing to explain things she didn't understand about Pack life.

She always did her best thinking when she cooked, so when she was trying to get through her what-to-do what-not-to-do lessons with Seff, they worked in the kitchen. That afternoon she was preparing a huge roast beef. Seff practically drooled the entire time they spoke.

"What are you doing now?" he asked while going over his list of notes.

"Well, I'm rubbing olive oil onto the meat before I put on my *secret* seasoning. Just kidding, don't look so sad! It's really just Kosher salt and fresh ground black pepper. The olive oil will help the meat seal in its juices when it gets into the hot oven. You want to flash it with intense heat then lower it for about two hours. That way it will be tender, juicy and rare."

Seff growled with anticipation. He cleared his throat, obviously ashamed of himself. Charley just laughed. These guys were always eating. It amazed her how fit they were.

She looked down as Buttercup walked by, fluffing his tail at her as he went. Her cat was certainly more at home amongst a Wolf Pack than she could have ever expected. She hid a smile as Seff backed away from the creature a snarl on his face.

"Don't you worry Seff, I already guessed you guys are big meat eaters that's why I'm making three roasts," Charley laughed again as he refocused on the meat and ignored the cat.

"Now, what does it mean to be Alpha female?"

"Well, you are second only to Rafe. You must never put yourself in a position of submission to anyone except him. No bowing or lowering your eyes. You see Werewolves are very aware of body language. You can and should make eye contact with everyone. You're the Alpha female, it is proper for all of us to shift our eyes after three seconds. No more, no less."

"Okay."

"This is important. Never look away first. Try to think of everyone as a potential threat. Werewolves are notoriously territorial. Rafe wouldn't hesitate to tear someone's throat out if they dared disrespect you. As his female and a human, he will be very protective. It is proper."

"Well, I've been taking care of myself for quite some time now, -"

"Yes, but not under these circumstances. Remember everything you do will reflect on Rafe. The last thing we need is for him to look weak or foolish. Please Charley, you must listen to what I'm telling you. Our stability, heck, our *survival* depends on it."

Charley nodded at him. This was serious business. At her signal Seff lifted the heavy tray into the oven. He slid it onto the rack, and she closed the door.

"I would never do anything to hurt Rafe. Ever."

"I believe you," Seff nodded his head.

"I'm sorry we brought all this down on you. You know the kidnapping and everything. If you still want to leave after the meeting, I'll do everything I can to help."

"Thank you, Seff. For the apology, but I think I may end up thanking you for everything else too," she blushed and began peeling carrots, potatoes, and onions. Her skilled hands moved quickly as she put the veggies in a dish with salt, pepper, and olive oil. After everything was in the oven, she set the timer and grabbed her notes.

Charley found herself alone at the table going over what she had learned. After an hour of instructions, Seff bowed and left her to review. The meeting as it turned out was more of a formal party.

Complete with gowns and tuxes. A seamstress had come earlier in the day with a selection of gowns for her. As a sneakers and jeans kinda gal, it was something of a revelation.

She chose a strapless silk gown in a pale blue that fell to the floor. It hugged her curves in all the right places and ended with a small flair at her feet. The dress was lovely, reminiscent of the 1940s. The color was the perfect backdrop for her ring and would remind everyone of her status. She had chosen it with great care.

13

That was the easy part. The hard part was the list of rules Seff had given her. *Never lower your head to anyone in the room. Never look away first. Never allow yourself to be touched first. Keep pace with Rafe. Follow his lead.*

It was the way they recognized her higher position in the Pack. Rafe was the only one higher than her. She would be seated on his right side. Seff would be on his left. She learned he was the pack's Beta or second in command. Randall was third.

All the Wolves who shared the house were actually an elite group of warriors, handpicked by the Alpha. They were charged with keeping Pack business running smoothly and alerting the Alpha to any problems or new occurrences. Like this business with that teenage Wolf and the foreign Pack. It had huge implications, Seff told her.

Rafe spoke a little about this, but she had no idea the vastness of his reach. There was so much going on in the world that she never could have guessed. *How could she?* She worked at a deli. Her grandfather had been in the army and told her a little about the evil that existed in the world, but to think there was a constant supernatural battle going on was incredible.

"Did you find something you liked?"

Charley's heart thundered in her chest as Rafe spoke from just behind her. She turned and met his gaze. Heat, desire and genuine concern shown in his eyes. His emotions as clear as her own. How could she *not* have fallen for this man? This Werewolf? And she had fallen, so deeply in love with him that she was willing to leave everything she knew to be a part of his world.

"Yes."

"That's good. Did Seff go over things? Is there anything you want to review?"

"Is it true that no one is allowed to touch me? That is unless you permit it. No shaking hands? No kisses on the cheek?"

He answered her question with a nod.

"I don't understand. That sounds very-"

"Strange? Not really. I'm the Alpha. My mate is

mine to protect. Anyone who dared touch you without my permission in a formal setting would be indirectly challenging me."

"What if it happens? What if someone does want to challenge you and uses me to do it?" fear gripped her heart. She knew Rafe needed a mate to hold his position. It was the reason for her abduction after all. But she could not bear to think her presence could possibly cause him harm.

"Don't worry, love," he embraced her.

Charley breathed in the woodsy scent of him and clung. She would have never guessed in a million years that she could feel this way about another person. The thought of harm coming to him was enough to stop her heart cold. Her one hope now was that she would be able to fulfill her role as perfectly as Rafe had filled her heart.

The night of the party came quickly. Too quickly for Charley's peace of mind. She walked down the grand staircase in the most luxurious dress she had ever worn in her entire life. She felt as though she was suspended in a kind of dream. *Magical.*

They were all there at the bottom, waiting for her. Dressed in their custom-tailored tuxes, the men of the house looked gorgeous. But no one lit a candle to Rafe.

He was taller and bigger than all of them. At his

throat was a star sapphire pin that matched her ring. Charley's heart pounded and her breath caught. *I love him.*

The moment he saw her, their gazes locked. Electricity sizzled between them. Rafe's eyes traced her from the top of her gently swept up curls to the tip of her high heeled toes. He inhaled and extended his arm.

"You look beautiful," he murmured as she placed her hand just above his elbow. She didn't notice seven heads bowed in deference to her, nor the broad smiles that came from a few of them. She couldn't tear her gaze away from him.

Rafe kissed her free hand. Approval and something more in his gaze. Charley felt power radiating off him. He looked regal, but there was more to it. He seemed to ooze dominance.

"Thank you, Rafe, you look beautiful too," her breath caught as he smiled at her. She felt her pulse speed up and her heart pounded like mad as love for this man warmed her from the inside out.

The ballroom was decorated for the season and filled to the brim with people. *Wolves,* Charley guessed. Everyone was dressed to the nines. There were tables laden with fine food and champagne. Real holly boughs and pine garland with large blue velvet bows graced the posts and walls. White poinsettias and roses sat elegantly on every table.

Charley blinked back happy tears. A twelve-foot Christmas tree sat in one corner and was completely decorated in blue and silver ornaments. The star on top was a brilliantly lit. It was beautiful. Music played softly in the background, but no one danced.

Charley's gaze was drawn to a tall man by the far wall. He was surrounded by four men. He had dark hair pulled back into a ponytail and he wore a black on black suit. His eyes looked furious when he saw them. Charley moved a step closer to Rafe.

That man looked cruel and dangerous. *Skoll*, she thought. She looked at her husband and her unease was immediately laid to rest. Charley and Rafe stepped into the room together, as one. The music stopped and a man stepped to the microphone.

"Members of the Macconwood Pack and honored guests, it is our pleasure to introduce our Alpha, Rafe Maccon and his bride, Carlotta Maccon."

The room erupted in applause as they entered surrounded by the seven Wolves whom Charley now thought of as brothers. She walked beside Rafe to the center of the dance floor.

Seff had explained this part to her. Like a traditional wedding reception, Rafe and Charley were to open the dance floor together for the first time as husband and wife. She was more than ready. She had dreamed about this moment her entire life.

"Okay?" his blue eyes bore into hers and Charley forgot everyone else in the room. They moved in perfect time with the band.

A violinist stepped forward and Charley couldn't stop smiling. Rafe swirled her and danced her around the room. When the song ended, he leaned in and pressed a kiss to her lips to another outburst of applause.

He led her to the head table where he stood by her side. Together they greeted their guests. Charley had never seen anything like it. No one moved to touch her hand or kiss her cheek. They simply smiled and offered their congratulations.

A group of older men came to them first. They were all handsome in a Sean Connery sort of way and Charley smiled at the approval in their eyes. She held herself erect and followed Rafe's lead.

"This is my mate, Carlotta. Darling, these are the Pack elders, Stephen Dark, Carl Warren, and Devon Blake," Rafe introduced them, and Charley kept her eyes level.

"Congratulations, dear boy. We'll see the documents later," Stephen spoke, and they bowed in turn.

They left, but the procession was just beginning. Rafe clapped his male Packmates on the back, offered the women a smile and a word. Conall and Liam accepted gifts for them, Seff and Randall flanked the couple, and the rest of the Guard stood behind.

The greetings and well wishes went on forever, but Charley smiled through it all. It was as if she was born to fill this role. She had just accepted a glass of water from Seff when she felt her husband tense.

14

Skoll and his men walked towards them. He moved with the slimy gait of a snake rather than a Wolf. His slick backed hair reminded Charley of those 1980s drug cartel movies. Who the heck did this guy think he was? Rafe straightened to his full height. Charley held herself perfectly still.

"Ah, well, it seems you have found a *wife* after all. Well, isn't that just grand. Tell me, you didn't happen to kidnap her by any chance did you, Rafe?" his lightly accented voice reached Charley's ears.

Skoll was huge, but Rafe was bigger still. He met Skoll's stare and after too long a moment the other Wolf looked away. He seemed to grind his teeth as he bared his throat slightly. Rafe growled, a threatening sound, nothing like Charley had heard before.

Coming from anyone else she would have been terri-fied, but she only felt pride that it was her husband.

"I've brought a gift, for the bride," Skoll snapped his fingers, and a pair of hands held a wrapped box out to Charley.

His sinister gaze met hers, but when she didn't back down, he lowered his eyes and thrust the box forward again. Randall stepped forward, took the box from Skoll, and snapped his jaws. His teeth gleamed white from behind his long hair and beard.

"My mate and I thank you for attending our wedding party, Skoll, perhaps now your *concerns* are put to rest, but just in case they aren't, I am happy to take this up in an official arena with you," Rafe's voice had taken on a timbre Charley had never heard before.

"Oh, I doubt your human bride would appreciate a quarrel on her wedding night."

"On the contrary, I believe my *mate* would suit just fine."

Charley wanted to hold Rafe back, but she remained still, a bored expression on her face. Seff had warned her of this. The best thing she could do was appear unaffected.

A contest of wills seemed to be taking place right in front of her and Charley had nothing to do but wait it out. Seff had explained about posturing and respect. What he hadn't told her was seconds would feel like hours as the two Wolves faced down. Rafe was clearly better at intimidation for the simple reason that he was the more dominant Wolf.

"That won't be necessary, *Alpha*, after all, it is a party, gentlemen, madam," Skoll bowed his head again and walked away, his men trailing behind him.

Rafe remained on alert until he was far away from where Charley and the rest of his Guard stood. He made a mental note to have that gift brought to his office for inspection. He didn't want anything that had touched Skoll to come near his mate.

The rest of the night passed in relative ease. Charley laughed and talked. She danced to the amazing band with Rafe, and then with others after she approved of them.

She ate the wonderful delicacies before her and reveled in the holiday spirit that seemed to be with everyone. It had been so long since she had really celebrated Christmas. She felt like Cinderella at the ball, only better. Several of the Pack females were introduced to her by Cat, who wore a gorgeous silver sequined dress.

Charley noticed some tension between her and Tate, but she ignored it. Hopefully, after she got to know her better Rafe's sister would confide in her. After all, she was her sister now too. That made Charley smile even brighter. *If only things were permanent.* Doubts crept into her mind and she pushed them away. *Not tonight.*

The moment came when Rafe and the elders left the room to have their meeting to disprove Skoll's claims that his rule was illegitimate. Seff followed his Alpha armed with the paperwork that would prove their marriage, but still Charley worried. *What if it wasn't enough? Would he have to fight?*

Later that night, still dressed in her gown Charley stepped out onto the bedroom terrace. It was Christmas Eve. Snow fell softly from the night sky, drenching the yard in pure virgin white. Like a dream.

The party was over, the guests had left, and Rafe was still in his meeting. Buttercup circled her feet a few times before retreating to the fireplace. He seemed to like this home full of Werewolves. So, did she. *If only he had asked her to stay.*

She turned and went to the closet. Tears rolled down her face as she got out her suitcases and began throwing her clothes inside of them. She was sure by now that Rafe would have suggested their temporary situation be made more permanent.

Maybe he didn't mean it when he said he loved her?

Charley sobbed softly and tried to zipper the suitcase through tear filled eyes. She didn't hear the door open. Nor did she notice the sight of her husband, horrified at what he saw.

"Carlotta?" Rafe's heart pounded in his chest. It sounded loud as thunder to his sensitive ears. *He was too late. She was leaving.*

"No, no, I'm sorry, you, you told me it wasn't permanent. I guess, I just thought, -" Charley stopped and hid her face in her hands. She was so ashamed of herself. She wasn't one to beg, but for this man she just might.

Rafe dropped the large, wrapped box he held and fell to his knees in front of her. He reached for her hands and gently pulled them from her face.

"Please, Carlotta, I know my world is crazy and scary and different from anything you ever knew, and I would change it all for you if I could. Please don't cry, and please, don't leave. Don't leave me."

Charley gasped. More tears fell. Rafe didn't know what to do. *Did he offend her?* He held his breath, then she threw her arms around his neck and kissed his face. He exhaled and tightened his grip.

"You don't want me to go?" Charley asked.

"Of course, I don't want you to go! Look, look here," he picked her up and brought her to where he dropped the large, wrapped box. He nudged her gently until she tore at the paper.

Inside was a large basket with the name *Buttercup* inscribed on a gold plate that hung from a blue velvet ribbon. There was even a huge fluffy white bed to go inside.

"You see, I even got the little demon his own bed," Rafe nudged Charley with his head and Charley laughed and then cried some more. She hugged Rafe and kissed him again as his arms encircled her and brought her fully against him.

"Stay. Please. Always."

"Wild horses couldn't drag me away, Rafe."

"I love you, Carlotta. I love you so much," his voice grew husky as he held onto her.

"I love you too."

They kissed and undressed each other right there on the floor. Rafe grabbed the comforter and placed her on top of it. Then he touched his hot skin to hers, careful not to hurt her. He kissed her from the top of her head down to her toes.

Their joining was a slow and deliberate union unlike any they had shared. They kissed, and tasted, squeezed and caressed each other, careful not to miss a single inch. He loved her and she him until the soft rays of sunlight crept into the room and touched them both. It was the best Christmas she ever had. Well, so far.

Charley's Wolf. Her mate. For life.

124

The end.

CAT'S HOWL
A MACCONWOOD PACK NOVEL

USA TODAY BESTSELLING AUTHOR
C.D. GORRI
CAT'S
Howl
The Macconwood Pack

BLURB

Cat Maccon, was always a handful, even as a pup. It wasn't easy growing up in an all male household, but this South Jersey Werewolf is tough as nails. She's on a mission to prove herself, causing no end of grief for her older brother, Rafe Maccon, Alpha of the Macconwood Pack.

Cat joins the Maccon County Sheriff's Department determined to be taken seriously among her big brother's Wolf Guard. Okay, maybe one Wolf Guard in particular, *Tate Nighthawk*. Tall, rugged, and handsome. He's the stuff of Cat's dreams, but she's been burned before.

When she is targeted by their enemies, led by the dangerous rogue Werewolf Skoll, Rafe assigns Cat her own personal bodyguard. Knowing how his sister hates to be told what to do, Rafe gives her the one Wolf Guard he knows won't be taken in by her wily ways. Tate Nighthawk himself.

Tate takes his job very seriously and no amount of pouting or lamp throwing will bend him to Cat's will. Even if she is the best damn thing he ever saw. Old memories haunt him when he is forced to spend time with the one woman who he turned his back on. But he won't let that interfere with his assignment.

Stuck alone in the woods together, without any way to contact the Pack, their tumultuous past catches up with them. Will this spunky she-Wolf finally find true love or is she too much for Tate to handle?

PROLOGUE

Maccon High Senior Prom Summer 2009

Cat Maccon stepped out of the rented luxury town car carefully so as not to damage the hem of her long dress. The pale blue chiffon reached the floor in soft layers that danced around her low heels in the cool evening breeze. Spring in South Jersey was unpredictable, but she didn't mind the chill.

In fact, she hardly felt it. She couldn't stop smiling. For the first time in her young life, she was happy. *Really happy.* She looked down at the ground to mask her feelings. She so wanted to be cool and mature. But inside her chest her heart was pounding.

She glimpsed the low-heeled strappy shoes she wore with sparkling accents and bit her lower lip. Were they classy enough? She had no need for the super high heels that were all the rage among her classmates for this year's prom. She found these months ago, at the outlet mall before she was even thinking about prom. They were pretty and suited her. But not high and sexy like most of her class-mates. But then again, she wasn't like most of her classmates.

The girls from school were small compared to Cat. They were short and petite in stature. At almost six feet tall, Cat's height was very unusual. So was her lithe athletic build. Tall, slender, and sculpted. Definitely not the norm for teenage girls who attended Maccon City High School. But her kind were usually built that way.

She inhaled and tried to slow the beating of her heart. He'd hear it if she didn't calm down. And the last thing she wanted was to appear juvenile in front of *him*. She let go of the breath she was holding slowly.

Then she discreetly adjusted the rhinestone studded corset top of her gown. Cat panicked for a moment as she waited for her date to walk around to her side of the car. Did she look okay? She wished she filled out the dress a little more. She counted to three, and that helped calm her down a little. Her gown was very flattering. The saleslady had told her so. And besides, she felt good in it.

The driver of the rented car winked and closed the door behind her. He stood too close for just a little too long, giving her posterior a very thorough perusal. Cat simply ignored him.

He obviously didn't know who she was. Or what. If he did, he would've kept his eyes to himself. Usually, she'd love to teach him a lesson, but not tonight.

No. *Tonight* she only had eyes for the slightly older Wolf who had asked to be her prom date. She still couldn't believe it! It felt like a dream. But he did. He really asked her!

It was kind of last minute, but after resigning herself to going solo, she didn't care. She jumped at the chance and said yes before he even finished his question. It was like fate had suddenly decided to be kind. After years of trailing behind him and her older brother he had finally noticed her!

Cat was determined to make sure he never forgot her too. She'd been kept under lock and key for far too long. It was her night to shine. No rules tonight. No stern glances or angry words. She was going to enjoy herself. For once.

Her father held her firmly under his thumb since she was a pup. The only time she had any freedom at all was when she snuck away to watch her brother and his friends hang out. And they were magnificent.

Forever tackling each other, lifting fallen trees and boulders, racing against the wind, testing their strengths and abilities in fierce, yet friendly competition. How she loved watching them! They'd play their own version of extreme sports, mountain biking, snowboarding, even surfing.

How could she forget those long, lonely Friday nights? When they'd howl at the moon and pick up girls to take to the woods. Mainly, so they could make out. Oh, the things she'd learned in the darkness on those nights. They still made her blush.

Those boys were wild and free in ways Cat had never dared to dream were possible for her. Sure, sometimes she would join them in a pickup game of football or baseball. They'd always find her hiding spots and being a good brother, Rafe would let her play. It wasn't as if they didn't know she was there. Werewolves had really sensitive ears and noses.

They would find her. Sometimes they'd let her stay, other times, mostly the ones involving girls or beer, they would drag her back home, kicking and screaming. She was a stubborn child. And she hated to be home.

Her father was a cruel taskmaster. Always judging, always criticizing, and both his fiscal business and Pack business had come before the care of either of his children.

Their home had been neglected almost as much as their home life. It was always up to her and Rafe to see the household chores were finished. Her father was a firm believer in manual labor.

She was the daughter of one of the most powerful Werewolves in the world. Her father was the Alpha of the Macconwood Pack. His territory included most of North America and yet he had a minimal household staff.

He used them mostly for grounds work. He outright refused to modernize their estate and would scold her if she suggested they upgrade the laundry room or kitchen.

Zev Maccon felt modern appliances were not a right. They were a privilege. And she did not merit them. He could often be heard stating that his children were soft and spoiled. Chores, criticism, physical punishment, and tough love were his means to correct them of those faults.

He did very little entertaining, choosing instead to conduct Pack matters in the woods and pine barrens. Away from the house. Most of the Pack, including the elders, were unaware of Cat's home life.

They did not know that at eleven she handled the household laundry, cleaning, and most of the cooking and her schoolwork. Cat tried telling one of the Pack elders once at a rare meeting that took place in their home, but he simply replied that chores built character. Her father had not been pleased.

Cat always defended the elder in her mind. After all, he couldn't have known that Zev had left it to his children to do all the household chores for him and themselves. He probably wouldn't have believed that most nights she went to bed well past midnight only to wake hours before dawn.

Since she was the only girl, Zev expected her to take on most of the housework, like the laundry, ironing, cleaning the bathrooms, windows, and floors, and the cooking. When she was very small, it was fun at first, like playing house. But that got old. Fast.

Rafe helped as much as he could, but as the only male heir he had *other* duties. She did not envy him one bit. There were nights he came home bloody and beaten.

She was too afraid to ask what happened. She had a rough idea though. On those nights, she could smell Zev all over him. She shuddered at the memory.

The work wasn't the most terrible thing about Cat's home life. No, the worst of it, was that she had no mother to teach her how to do things. When she performed a task incorrectly, her father would spare no insult reminding her of that fact.

He was a brutal critic. It had only gotten worse once she had her first Change. Instead of experiencing the freedom she had watched Rafe and his friends enjoy, she found herself living in a prison.

Her father watched her like a hawk. She was restricted from hanging out with local kids, especially normals. He never allowed her to join any school clubs or take part in any extracurricular activities. She could only go to prom because Rafe had insisted. She was grateful to him. For so many things.

She remembered asking to join the Track team after a new coach had seen her run during Phys.Ed. She had been flattered and proud of herself. Until she told her father. He just smiled at her. That cruel smile of his. The one she knew far too well.

She cringed when he ordered her outside. She realized she had made a mistake. Too late though. The force of his command made her obey though she tried to fight it. He took her out to the edge of the forest that marked their property and forced her to run. She ran the entire night.

It was early spring of her sophomore year and it was a cold and bitter like March usually was. He had her strip down to her tank top and gym shorts. Then he told her to remove her socks and shoes.

She could still hear him snarl the word, "Run!" in her ear. Fifteen miles west then back again, over and over until the sun came up.

Her feet were caked with blood, sharp splinters,

and mud by the time she was finished. She had stepped on countless tree roots, rocks, and bits of sharp debris hidden just under the frozen soil. Afterwards he asked her if she still wanted to run track. Cat said no.

It had been a very long four years of high school. She was ecstatic to see it end. *Just two weeks left till graduation.* That was her mantra.

She was a woman now. Her Wolf was strong inside of her heart and mind. She knew exactly what she wanted. *Tate. It would always be Tate.*

Eighteen years old and more than ready to take charge of her life. With the full moon just a few nights away, she could already feel its power stirring inside of her. She was restless. Hungry.

This was a magical night. A rite of passage. *Senior prom night.* Nothing would ruin it for her. Especially not her father.

Tate Nighthawk was the epitome of the adage tall, dark and handsome. He had corded muscles that rippled around his six-foot three-inch frame. He was quieter than the other Wolves Rafe hung around with.

His hair was dark as a moonless night. His eyes too. His Wolf had that same blue-black coloring. She kept a list of all his features locked inside her heart.

Cat had memorized every inch of him. Right

down to the difference between his Wolf black eyes and his dark brown ones when he was a man. They had a shimmer of gold just around the rims. She tried not to stare.

He and Rafe had spent most of middle school and high school hanging out together. She had practically grown up watching him. Her breath left her body as he circled the car and ran a hand through his shoulder length hair.

She loved how it spilled across his back. He was proud of his Native American heritage. She knew that from the way he carried himself and the way he was always reading books about the Lenape Tribe, the Cherokees, and the Original Keetowah Society.

Cat followed him with her eyes as Tate looked around the crowded parking lot outside of the high school gymnasium. Werewolves did not like crowds.

But *man, oh man*, he looked good in his black tuxedo. And he smelled even better. She took a deep breath through her nose and the Wolf inside of her seemed to purr. His scent was a mixture of pine trees and the ocean air. It reminded her of the first snowfall of winter, but without the chill.

He moved his head from left to right and again, making sure he didn't miss an inch of the property. A breeze lifted his long dark locks and his scent hit her again.

This time it reminded her of a salty, warm breeze blowing off the Atlantic Ocean on a hot summer day. The kind when the sun felt as if it could melt the skin right off you. *Prrrr*.

Her senses were going into hyper-drive. Cat could hardly keep steady. *Tate*. It was all because of Tate. How could one Wolf do this to her? She didn't know, and she wasn't sure she liked it either. He made her feel out of control, reckless, but also alive. And that was good.

He was hot and cold all at the same time and more than a little exciting. She wanted to reach out and touch the hair that he had just pushed back. But she knew better. He wouldn't welcome her touch.

Not yet anyway. *But maybe, with a little luck.* After all, he had asked her to prom. She was determined to make it memorable.

Cat's Pack. She's Pack.

Over and over Tate reminded himself of that fact. More than that, she was the Alpha's daughter and his best friend's sister.

Tate grimaced and looked over the jam-packed parking lot again. It was difficult to scent danger in a crowd. Werewolves tended to avoid them, but this was inevitable. He breathed out quickly and turned back to the one thing he was trying not to look at. *Cat.*

The cool evening breeze lifted the tendrils that surrounded her face in a dance that made her look like something from out of a fairytale. She was a vision in the soft light that came from the setting sun. Innocent and pure. *Beautiful.*

The rest of her honey streaked blonde hair was in some complicated twist on top of her head. She wore a sparkly clip just off to the side. It caught the light every time she moved. Tate's mouth went dry just looking at her.

The way her soft silvery blonde curls fell just around her face made it hard for him to breathe. The entire hairstyle looked like a crown or a halo. Angelic. Magical. Something otherworldly. Something *he* could never touch.

He was nothing. Had came from nothing. A dirt poor nobody and he damn well knew it. Tate had to fight hard to make it to where he was now. And still he was nothing more than a foot soldier.

It had taken him years to get that far. Left on Zev Maccon's doorstep when he was ten years old. No money. No connections. For all intents and purposes, his natural father had essentially abandoned and rejected Tate.

He was alone in the world. Seeing the potential of a strong young Wolf, Zev Maccon had adopted him into his Pack. He sent him to live with a widowed fisherman whose only child had committed suicide just after his first Change.

Young Tate couldn't understand why it was that way with Werewolves. His own mother had proved just as fragile. His father couldn't bare the reminder of his wife and he abandoned Tate at the first opportunity.

He was left to wonder how people who were so strong could be so weak. How could any Werewolf decide to take his or her own life? Leaving behind their children or spouses? Was it really so bad? The separation that is. It terrfied Tate. For many years he was afraid of what would happen the first time he heard the full moon call to him.

After his first Change, he more than understood. The exhilaration of being one with your Wolf was quickly replaced by depression and anxiety on those days after the full moon. The waiting was sheer torture. Weeks felt like years and it was only alleviated when he was whole again. When he was complete again. When he was Wolf again.

He almost didn't make it once or twice, but Rafe had helped him through it. He owed Rafe. Not just for that. But also, for being his friend.

Where Zev saw another strong back and set of teeth for the Pack, Rafe made him feel like a person and more. He made him feel like he mattered. He was valuable. His friendship important.

That was why he said yes when Rafe had asked him to take his baby sister to her senior prom. And that was why he wouldn't lay a hand on her. No matter how damn good she smelled. Or how she looked at him with those crystal blue eyes of hers.

"You ready to go inside?" His voice sounded rough even to his ears, and he grimaced.

"Yeah, sure," Cat's answer was low.

Tate ignored the pounding of Cat's heart in her chest as he extended his arm and led her across the pavement. He refused to note the sparkle in her eyes, the breathy laughter that escaped her parted lips, and her overall excitement that smelled to him like orange zest and rose petals.

The flash of a camera surprised him as they walked through the decorated gym doors and he nearly growled out loud. Cat's hand on his arm was the only thing that stopped him.

Her hand was warm through the sleeve of his tux. It felt good there. Too good. He looked down at Cat and she smiled at him. A dazzling bright smile. *Oh damn!* This was not going to be easy.

Later that night.

The bonfire roared around them and Cat felt as if

her feet hadn't touched the ground all night long. This was the best night of her young life.

For the first time, she felt feminine, beautiful, and free, truly free. Tate had whirled her and twirled her all around the dance floor until she gasped for air. Just like a dream! A wonderful, fantastic dream. And she didn't want it to end.

They got invited to go down to the beach with some of her classmates for an after-prom party. And Cat had jumped at the chance. Anything to make the night last.

She didn't notice the chilly night air or the clouds that had gathered. All she noticed was the man next to her and how he made her feel. As if her heart was singing inside of her chest.

Tate danced with her and only her all night. He held her in his arms, smiled and laughed at her jokes. He made her feel special in every way possible.

To her mild annoyance, he was very, very respectful. His hands never wandered. Not an inch. No matter how desperately she wanted them to. Still, she had a wonderful time.

He was gorgeous to look at, intelligent to talk to, and oh, that smile. Her heart skipped a beat every time she saw that dimple winking at her on his right cheek. And the way everyone had stared at him when they walked in!

Cat had to work overtime to keep in control. She almost snapped at one or two of the girls who had brazenly strutted up to him and asked him to dance. But there was no need.

One look from his black eyes had sent them running. He could be cruel she realized, but that was okay, as long as it wasn't directed at her.

To her, Tate had been kind, funny, and courteous all night. A little too courteous, but she had a plan to change that. Finding her courage, she decided there was no time like the present.

She pulled him by the hand until he stood up and wiped the sand from his very nice backside. He took a swig of the warm beer someone had handed them and put it back down before raising an eyebrow at her.

"What's up, Cat?"

"You'll see," she laughed and pulled up the hem of her dress, kicking off her shoes as she did so. She raised an eyebrow at him, mimicking his own questioning expression.

"Race ya!" She yelled and then she was off.

Cat sped alongside the dunes kicking up sand as she ran and jumping over the tall grass that grew there. She could hardly catch her breath. She was so nervous. Anxious maybe.

"What the heck? Cat!" Tate followed her across

the sand and wondered if the half a beer she had went to her head.

He doubted it since most Werewolves had such a fast metabolism that alcohol had little to no affect unless taken in mass quantities.

He didn't know what she was up to. He just wished he had taken the time to remove his dress shoes before he ran after her. It didn't matter for long. She had stopped running.

Underneath an old rotting dock, down by the edge of the water. That was where he found her. The waves were loud as they crashed into the nearby rocks and sand and Tate realized they were out of sight of everyone else. He ran a hand through his hair. His chest was heaving and not from the exertion of following her.

"Cat, what are you doing? Watch out! Your dress. It'll get all wet."

Cat stopped when they were far enough away from the crowd and the music that they were nothing more than a hum in her sensitive ears. She turned towards Tate, her chest very near to bursting. *This was it.* This was the where and when. She reached behind her, biting her lower lip as her hands moved.

"Cat? What are you-"

Tate couldn't finish his thought. He heard her

zipper being lowered and he froze like a deer in headlights.

She wouldn't, would she? He didn't talk or even to think. A second later, it was too late.

The beautiful blue confection that was Cat's prom dress fell to the compacted sand in a soft *whoosh* that sounded much louder to his supernaturally heightened ears.

She stood there before him, barefoot in the sand, in nothing but a pair of white silk panties. The soft moonlight hit her body through the gaps in the wooden slats of the dock revealing all her perfection in a sensuous play of shadow and light.

Tate gulped loudly. Twice. His eyes drank her in like a man dying of thirst. When he finally spoke, his voice cracked like he was still a pup. Green and wet behind the ears. But damn, she was the most beautiful thing he had ever seen.

"Um, Cat,"

"Tate?"

"You, um, dropped your dress."

Cat's heart pounded in her chest like thunder. Louder than the waves even. She knew he could hear it, but she wondered if it sounded like it was going to bust his eardrums the way it did to her?

She had never done anything so forward before. But this was it. She was leaving for college soon and she knew that she wanted this more than anything in the world.

She wanted *him* more than anything in the world. Since she was just a pup following him and Rafe around. It had always been *him*.

Time seemed to slow down to a crawl. She stood there against the rough support beam, frozen in place. She was just about to lose her nerve. Then he stepped forward. His scent filled her nostrils, sea air and pine trees. Tate stood close enough to touch her, but his hands remained stubbornly at his sides.

His eyes though, his beautiful dark eyes seemed to caress every inch of her from the tip of her golden head to her sand covered toes. He leaned forward, and Cat exhaled the breath she was holding. She swayed on her feet. The wanting was nearly her undoing.

Their heads were close then. So, close that she tasted his breath on the air. It was heady and sweet, and Cat had never felt quite like that.

Any memory of stolen kisses with other boys fell far from her mind. This was the one she had waited for her entire life. This was the culmination of every silent wish, every sweet daydream, every yearning ache of her young heart.

Cat's skin buzzed in response to his strength and energy. It seemed to vibrate in the air. It touched her skin, filled her nostrils, and made her blood sing.

Tate leaned in. His full lips brushed hers in a whisper of a kiss that was so fragile she felt like glass. One wrong move and she would shatter completely.

His lips were so soft, Cat sighed into them. He pressed his body against hers and she clung. Following him wherever he led. Never had anything felt so good.

Her heart thundered inside her chest. Nothing else mattered in that moment. *Just them*. The entire world seemed to spin out of focus and fall away from her. Tate became her only reality.

He moved his lips to her neck, then her shoulder. She opened her eyes and saw his closed in concentration. *God*, he was beautiful to watch.

His dark head was bent in such a way that she saw the slight movement of his tongue under his sweet lips against her skin. She was so pale against him.

Tate was bronzed and hard, like some ancient Greek warrior statue. But he was alive and warm. *So very warm*, she shivered, and goose bumps broke out along her skin.

But Cat wasn't cold. This was pure reaction. A sigh escaped her open mouth and her head fell back as she moved into him. *Closer, mmm, need to get closer.*

Delicious. Tate's brain was in overdrive. He

couldn't quite wrap his head around what was taking place. This was Cat. Little Cat. But damn, she tasted every bit as delicious as he always thought she would.

Fresh, clean, sultry, sweet, with the barest hint of salt. Her skin was all smooth pink and gold. The becoming pink blush visible to him in the pale moonlight. Ready and willing and too sweet to resist. *This is Cat.*

Tate trembled as he reached out with his work callused hands. He couldn't help himself; it was as if he needed to touch her. To possess her. *Mine*, his Wolf growled in his mind's eye.

He brushed his fingertips over the tender slopes of her breasts. *God*, she was so damned soft. Cat purred as he stroked his hand back and forth across her hardened peak. He bit back his own moan as he leaned down and kissed her.

Honey, she was honey in his mouth. His tongue snaked around her soft skin, licking, nipping, kissing her soft flesh. He knew he was getting in over his head when she grabbed at his long hair and pulled him closer.

It took all his strength to draw back from her sweet body. The hazy look in her ice blue eyes made him want her so damn bad. He knew he could never stop if he did what she wanted him to. Her body language, heck, even her scent was begging him to finish what they had started. And if he was honest with himself, he should acknowledge that he wanted her like mad.

Cat dropped her hands to her sides. She didn't know what to do, or rather, what she could do. She had never been kissed like that before and she knew right then that the boys she had tried a kiss or two with had absolutely nothing on the man in front of her.

The world spun around and around when his mouth was on hers. She felt dizzy, alive, insane and so very good that she never wanted him to stop. She smiled and lifted her hands to his face. *Serious.* He was so serious.

Cat pulled him down to her mouth, and they kissed again. This time he lifted his lips and ran them down her neck and shoulder, then down again to her aching breasts. Her nipples tightened, and she purred again, wanting more, wanting him. She hardly noticed the sound of her dress being pulled back up over her body.

Tate raised his head just as Cat's eyes flew open. *He was dressing her?!* Her cheeks burned with humiliation. She felt a tear pour down her cheeks, and she bit back a sob. *She would not cry!*

She felt as though he had ripped her heart open, but she would not cry. That, she promised herself.

She grabbed the dress from him and tried to pull away, but his arms were like iron.

"Cat, we need to talk. Don't run."

"Talk? About what? I just offered myself to you and you rejected me. What's to talk about?"

"It's not that easy, Cat, come on, look at me."

Despite her best efforts, another tear spilled down her face. She shook her head as a nervous laugh escaped her lips. *Would the shame ever go away? Why wouldn't he just let her leave?*

She struggled against him, but Tate refused to let her go. She wiped her cheeks and shake her head as she yanked the zipper closed. Heat burning her cheeks so hot she must look like a beacon in the night! No matter which way she moved, his iron grip held her squarely in front of him.

She threw herself at him. Like a slut. Like her father had said she would. Zev often called her an "easy mark", he said she would be just like her mother. Those words cut her, but never so much as now. *Because maybe he was right.*

"Look, Cat, I know you have a crush on me, but I didn't know-"

"Crush? You think this is some little crush? Tate, is that true?" Hope sparked in her chest. If she could only make him see, it would all be okay.

"Don't be embarrassed, Cat, it's okay."

"No, you see, it's not. I don't have a crush on you. I love you! I always have, Tate. And you must feel something for me too! I mean, *you* asked *me* to prom, you never even looked at me before, but you asked me, so I know you feel something too-"

Tate just couldn't listen to this. Confessions of love from his best friend's baby sister? No way. No how. He knew what he had to do. She would hate him for it, but it was for the best. For both of them.

"Cat! Come on! Stop lying to yourself! I'm only here because Rafe asked me to take you! I didn't want to go to your prom, I mean, do you think I'd need some high school girl to go out with? Come on, Cat, think! Years of watching us in those woods and you really believe I want this? I mean look at you, hardly more than a kid in dress up for God's sake!"

"Go to hell!"

The slap surprised her as much as it did him. Her hand stung with the force of it as she ran back to the bonfire. She was careful to slow down before anyone noticed her supernatural speed.

She caught up with a group of girls she had English class with. They were heading out and offered her a ride. Cat readily accepted. There was no way she wanted to drive back with her *date*! Heck, she never wanted to see Tate Nighthawk ever again!

Tate stood there helplessly as she stormed off

towards the bonfire. He figured he'd just take her home, but she was gone before he made it back. He could feel his cheek swell and imagined the angry red mark that still stung. She packed one heck of a punch for a female. His face was on fire and it was minutes later. He figured he deserved it.

He had never felt so low, but it was better to be cruel now than to let her carry on. At least that was what he thought. He'd talk to her again when she calmed down. He'd explain about why he could never have anything to do with someone as pure and good as Cat. Tate was bad news. She'd see it was for the best.

"Damn it!"

Only he never got the chance to explain. Cat skipped out on her graduation ceremony. She left home days later to begin her classes at her college. She was enrolled in the all-female St. Elizabeth's College at Convent Station, New Jersey.

Zev thought his daughter was being industrious and Rafe, well, he had asked Tate only once if anything had happened between him and his sister.

Lying was futile for Werewolves and since Rafe would one day be Tate's Alpha, he figured keeping secrets would be unwise. Tate sighed heavily and sat down one day the following week.

He told Rafe what had transpired between him

and Cat the night of her prom. He managed to leave out some more personal details. That was one discussion that he wished he could have avoided.

Afterwards Tate felt vindicated, angry, and saddened because Rafe agreed with him. He was not good enough for the younger sister of the heir to the Macconwood Pack.

Not good enough. Never good enough. It didn't matter, anyway.

Cat was gone.

resent day.

Cat panted as she chased the perp down the slippery sidewalk of downtown Main Street in Maccon City. He zigzagged between parked cars and even managed to upend a trash can, but Cat was fast. Really fast.

Stupid friggin' kid! Did he think she would just give up?

She blew back the strands of hair that came undone from her French braid as she ran. She hated complicated hairstyles. But it was the only way to hold back the blonde waves that she kept at shoulder length. She guessed she was sentimental about it, but hey, it was her hair. She'd cut it when she wanted to, and not a minute before!

"Oh, come on!"

The kid decided to take off down a dark alley. *Just great!* Cat's partner was lagging further and further behind. Heck, she had no choice. She couldn't wait for him! Cat gritted her teeth. She had been told by her boss she was not supposed to engage with a perp unless she had the proper back-up.

One glance at her partner and she knew the kid would get away if she waited one more minute to chase him. Cat had no choice. She took off after him, her lips curled into a predatory grin. The chase was the best part of her job and she wouldn't even break a sweat.

"Hey girlie, where ya goin'? Wait up, will ya!"

She shook her head as Carl wheezed behind her. He should probably consider hitting the gym a little more and the donuts a little less. She should try to find a gentle way to bring that up next time they had a moment.

Not to mention the fact that he needed to be corrected about using outdated and inappropriate nicknames for her. *Girlie. Doll. Sweet cheeks.* Was he serious?

She was jogged from her musings when the scent of gun metal reached her sensitive nostrils. Cat exhaled sharply. She listened as Carl clumsily withdrew his gun from his hip holster and then started after them again.

Damn it! She shook her head. There was no need for guns. The kid wasn't armed. He was angry, scared, and judging from his crime, hungry.

The alley curved into a dead end behind an old empty warehouse, and Cat slowed her pace. She held up her right hand, so her partner would see she had spotted him. Though "spotted him" was a loose term.

Her acute hearing had actually picked up on the erratic beating of the kid's heart. He was petrified. And he was muttering something under his breath. She focused on what he was saying. *Hmm.* It sounded like he was praying.

"Hey look, just come on out, nice and easy. There's nowhere for you to go. Listen up, you got caught, it's not the end of the world, just come out slowly, with your hands where I can see them," Cat tried reasoning with the boy.

He couldn't be more than seventeen years old. A street kid, from the looks and smell of him. He probably hopped the bus to the shore looking for easy pickings. But he was out of luck.

It was way too early for vacationers. Still the dead of winter and a cold one at that. Most of the retail stores and restaurants were closed until spring.

She couldn't imagine how desperate he'd have to be to try and rob the local Qwik-E-Mart. The owner, Mr. Taggert, had the place wired with top of the line security cameras linked directly to his cellular phone. He even posted a sign warning would be criminals.

He saw the whole thing play out while he was in the men's room. He dialed 911 before the kid even made it out of the front door.

Mr. Taggert estimated about twenty dollars in goods were taken along with the cash. The kid had filled every pocket he had with beef jerky, soda cans, a couple of bags of peanuts, and candy bars.

Cat waved Carl further back; his heavy breathing was interfering with her ability to hear the perp's heartbeat. And she could tell a lot from a person's heartbeat.

A good Werewolf could tell a person's emotions and state of mind from sight, sound, and scent. Cat was a good Werewolf. And a good cop.

She had a high success rate at the Maccon County Sheriff's Department. She mostly enjoyed her work over the past few years.

Earning her M.A. in Justice Administration and Public Service from St. Elizabeth's College allowed her the possibility to move up quickly in the department. It had been her goal throughout college to make her way to the top of law enforcement. But lately she felt restless.

After her father passed away Cat decided to try and make a life for herself in her hometown. Her brother, Rafe, was the Alpha now. It was a difficult position and he needed all the support he could get. She was miffed when he passed her up for a position in his private Wolf Guard.

But in his defense, Rafe made a lot of progressive changes. She just needed to show him she was as tough and dedicated to him as any of the boys in his Wolf Guard were.

As it was, she didn't begrudge him his decision. She was genuinely proud of him and all his accomplishments thus far.

First and foremost, he had built their old home into a veritable estate. The place had been neglected by their father to almost devastating consequences. Much of the land was near to ruin, but Rafe managed to fix it all and then some.

The house was practically a palace and absolutely perfect for all the politicking necessary to run a successful Pack. He called it Macconwood Manor, same as their father had, only now it rang true.

There were dozens of bedrooms, guest houses, and amenities. Not to mention top notch security, their own private beach, and access to over five hundred acres of private woods owned by the Macconwood Pack and located just behind the Manor.

It was perfect. As soon as the paint had dried, he

had his Wolf Guard move in permanently. It was then that he called Cat to come home.

She had been reluctant at first, but eventually agreed. Cat could never say no to Rafe. She was pleasantly surprised at the change in not only the house, but in the Pack as well.

Rafe managed to fill their bank accounts and create programs for Pack members that involved education, support, and protection. Cat wanted so badly to help implement the changes her brother was making, she just had to prove to him that she could be beneficial.

Rafe had come a long way from not wanting any of the responsibility of being Alpha, to being the best Alpha the Pack had had in a century. She loved her brother and would help him in any way she could.

Their bond was strong, after all few children could say they had been raised under Zev Maccon's roof and survived. The nightmare that was living with their father was something that the two of them would always share.

Still, Cat had moved on from all that. It was the past. She had learned to let go of the past. Coming home was part of the process.

Of course, it was awkward with Tate Nighthawk living in the Manor as well. But he was one of her brother's Wolf Guard and that required he live in the

Alpha's primary residence. Cat just had to pretend it didn't affect her.

She stayed in town as often as she could. Working for the Sheriff's department made it all the easier. She pulled double shifts, worked nights, and stayed out of Tate's way.

All the while she told herself she had a job to do. Inside the Pack and inside the Sheriff's Department. Old wounds scarred over, and life moved on.

She had friends, went out on dates, and she did her job well. She never got serious, but then again, she didn't want to. Relationships were tricky things for Werewolves.

When she first got to college, she was a little gun shy about guys. Nowadays she more than made up for it. No one had any power over her. *Not anymore.* Her life was what she made of it.

But right then, the only life she was concerned with was the one belonging to the kid who had made the poor decision to come into her town and commit a robbery.

It wasn't the food or the thirty-seven dollars and sixty-five cents that he had stolen from the register that upset her. It was the fact he knocked over Mr. Taggert's old dog, Betsy.

As he ran away from the store, he had shoved past the poor girl when she came around the counter to see what was going on. The St. Bernard was about ten years old, and that was pretty old for giant breed dogs.

She was the sweetest old girl Cat knew, and the fact that she had been hurt was downright tragic. The least of Betsey's problems was a dislocated hip from the fall, and she would probably require surgery.

That made Cat angry. That and whatever it was that drove the perp to this point in his life. She decided to try reasoning with him one more time.

"Look, it's not too late. You're young and you made a mistake. You got caught, kid, it's okay, but it's time to give yourself up now. No one needs to get hurt here, understand? You can still make the right decision."

Shit. Cat knew the second he decided to fight his way out. His breathing changed, and his scent altered from the bitter smell of fear, to the more acrid stink of desperation. She waited a beat and there it was, a heavy dose of stupidity to round out his bad decisions. Cat scrunched her nose up from the unpleasant odor. *Here goes nothing.*

She focused in on where she knew he was crouched down. She heard the slight scrape as he picked a broken glass bottle up off the ice and mud caked alley floor. Before he could even decide where to throw it, Cat was on him.

She hefted him up by his sweatshirt collar and banged him against the solid brick wall. His wet sneakers squeaked against it as he tried to find his footing.

His panic was ripe when he realized she had him completely off the ground. He whimpered, his scent turning bitter once again. This time it was much more potent. She wrinkled her nose and prayed that he wouldn't urinate right there.

"Damn lady! Lemme go! Lemme go! What are you, some kind of steroid freak? Put me down! Come on, man, put me down, man! Lemme go!"

Cat growled at the insult but dropped him when she heard Carl approach from behind them. His weapon was still drawn. He only pulled it up when he saw them. Cat sighed and tried not to roll her eyes.

She took out her cuffs and began reading the kid his rights. She had to be careful not to hurt him as she pulled his arms behind him, but it wasn't easy when she was that amped up.

It was already difficult downplaying her superior skills at hunting down and locating perpetrators to her peers on the job. She couldn't very well explain bruising a teenage boy who outweighed her by a good fifty pounds by simply putting on a pair of handcuffs.

"Good job, uh, I would've had him, you know," Carl nodded her way as he wiped his sweaty hands on his pants and put his gun back in its holster. She gave him a thumbs up in return. She didn't trust herself to speak just yet.

Instead, she sucked in the cold air and wiped her nose. She had to remember to look winded as she led the boy back to their squad car while Carl called in the arrest. She forced herself to breathe much more rapidly than necessary.

The air was icy when it hit her lungs, but she kept up the facade of looking tired after the chase. It was necessary to keep the whole Werewolf thing under wraps. Especially with Carl puffing out air and holding his side.

Cat was used to the routine. She kept breathing hard and wiped make believe sweat from her forehead. Though she hated the deception, she understood the necessity. The normal world wasn't ready yet to know about them.

They could never understand the supernatural world that lived among them. After all, they never have. Not since the dawn of time.

The kid didn't put up any struggle as she frog marched him out of the alley. He was much too scared to fight. Cat knew the exact moment when the realization that he was likely headed to jail caught up with him.

Tears rolled down his dirt-streaked face and

desperation seemed to hang like a dark cloud over his head. She had seen it before, a hundred times.

That didn't stop her from feeling sorry for him. *Foolish kid.* Left alone with an older, slower cop like Carl or someone as unpredictable as the recruit, Jonny Dominguez, and this kid might have come out of that alley in a body bag instead of in handcuffs. She shook her head at the madness of it all and kept going.

It was the only way Cat knew how to help. She got the bad guys off the street. But sometimes she wondered if that was enough.

She took in the boy's miserable appearance and wondered what chance he ever really had. He wore old, scuffed sneakers and his jeans had probably seen better days.

He had no coat in the bitter cold weather. He wore a black hoodie instead. It reeked of cigarette smoke, stale peanuts, and spilled cola. She wondered when the last time the kid had had a decent meal and a proper bath.

What was his home life like? Did he have parents who cared? And what about school? He had the looks of a kid who'd been in the system before.

Without knowing anything about his situation, she could guess just how much that had helped him.

She shook her head again. It wasn't perfect, the system, but it was all she had to work with.

If only someone could have gotten to him before he came to Maccon City. It was too late now, Cat thought as she looked at her handcuffs snug tightly around his wrists. It was going to be a very long night.

Cat was too caught up in her analysis of the teen to notice the pair of muddy brown eyes that watched her from a nearby rooftop.

She couldn't feel the malintent of the owner of those eyes. He kept himself well hidden and stood downwind.

His dirty hands gripped the edge of his cell phone tightly as he snapped a few photos before she was out of sight. A few clicks here and there and he sent them to his boss.

Modern technology sure was a marvel. He'd been around a long time, ninety years or so, but like most Werewolves, he looked half his age.

Ninety years and he was doing the same crap he had done when he was just a kid. Tailing and snooping. Getting info for someone else. This job was a sweet one, too.

He'd been hired to tail the new Alpha's sister for the past few weeks. And damn, she was fine as all heck too. Of course, he never got too close and he never ever followed her to the big house. He wasn't stupid. Skoll wouldn't have hired him if he was.

She had no idea he was on her tail. It was weeks now, ever since that poser, Rafe Maccon, had wiggled out of the question to his claim of leadership.

The Alpha had tricked the elders with his marriage of convenience and to a *normal* of all people! But his boss knew the whole thing was a façade. He'd force Rafe to give up his position one way or another. Yeah, with Skoll in charge, everything would be the way it was supposed to be!

Wolves like him could run free and wild like in the good old days. Normals would learn to be afraid of their betters.

Heck yeah! They were playthings, nothing more than toys for Wolves. Skoll would see to it. They'd take over this land. *Damn straight!*

Kidnapping the little sister should get things started nicely for his boss. When the Macconwood Pack failed to rescue her, Skoll could again question Rafe's leadership skills and take over as Alpha.

From the looks of things, getting to her would be easy. The She-Wolf partnered with a normal. A fat, slow one at that. Heck, it must be rubbing off on her cause she looked as if she needed a break after running after some punk kid.

Skoll was gonna be pleased with the information.

Maybe he'd even reward him with a few hours with that blonde she-Wolf before he killed her!

The Werewolf smiled and licked his lips. He'd love to show her what it meant to be with a real Wolf. He knew every sham Wolf had had the little slut in the fake Alpha's Guard.

Who knew? Maybe the brother had her too. He snickered at the thought. He didn't mind. He liked his bitches experienced. He licked his lips.

Soon. This would happen soon.

2

"**O**h, my God! Is that pasta? Charley cooked dinner. Yes! Sweet!" Cat stepped out of her muddy boots and dropped her gym bag on the floor, making a beeline for the dining room.

The tantalizing aroma of freshly cooked food made Cat salivate. She hadn't eaten a hot meal in thirty hours. Her stomach was growling big time as she pulled out a chair and sat down.

"Oh yeah. Charley has outdone herself again," answered Seff, her brother's second in command. She smiled and nodded at the Beta Wolf.

Her new sister-in-law pushed through the kitchen door with a basket of freshly baked garlic bread sticks. Cat almost swooned when the heavenly scent reached her.

"Hey Cat! You hungry?" Charley smiled and set the garlic bread down on the long table. Her husband was hot on her heels with a huge bowl of ziti in meat sauce in his hands.

Cat was in heaven. No one made tomato sauce like their Charley!

"Hey sis, have I told you I love you today?"

"Why, yes, Cat, I believe you did when I put your wet clothes in the dryer this morning."

"Oops, yeah, sorry about that. I was late for work this morning."

"No big deal. I'm just glad you made it home last night."

"Yeah, it was good to sleep in my bed," Cat placed a huge scoop of pasta on her dish and inhaled. She couldn't wait to dig in.

"How was work today, Cat? Everything good?"

"Sure Rafe, it was fine," she wouldn't spoil their dinner with talk of work. Her mind was already replaying her interview with the teenage perp she arrested earlier in the evening.

All her suspicions were confirmed. The kid had been in the system for years. He had run away from countless foster homes, was a high school dropout, and already had five stints in juvenile detention.

His name was Ricky Jones. His parents were deceased, his grandmother was in a nursing home, and he had no other living relatives or nobody who had an interest in him at any rate.

Then there was the latest news that Betsy, the victim's dog, had to be put down after all. Cat was brokenhearted about it.

But she wouldn't share that info here. Nope, family meals were for funny anecdotes and cheerful news. Not the messes she dealt with on a daily basis.

Charley smiled and waited for her to continue, but Cat snagged a piece of garlic bread and bit into it instead. Her sister-in-law's eyes were kind as Cat picked up the basket and passed it down the table.

Dib and dailyKurt entered the dining area with a large bowl of romaine lettuce tossed with homemade Caesar dressing and a bowl of extra sauce for the pasta.

Liam was the last one who made his way into the dining room with a tray of meatballs in hand. One corner was noticeably empty. Cat laughed at his guilty expression when Rafe eyeballed him.

She looked around at her Pack, *her family*, and she was glad she was home. Though she noticed not everyone was at the table. Small conversations broke out amongst everyone, but mostly they were complimenting Charley's cooking and passing around bowls of food.

Cat didn't mind. In fact, she loved it. Dinner had

always been a tense affair when she was a child. Zev liked meat and potatoes and nothing else. Every night the same thing. No spices, no flare, nothing but plain meat and potatoes. And zero conversation. This was much better.

Randall walked in and waved hello. He had a tablet in hand and immediately sat next to Seff. He was showing him something on the screen about Randall's newest upgrade to the online roleplaying game that he created, *WolfMoon*.

The "techie talk" they used went right over Cat's head. Something about back-end tables not being named correctly and causing an error when the game refreshed. Whatever the heck that meant. Cat stared a moment too long at the empty chair to the left of them. *Tate*.

Tate wasn't there.

Oh well. Cat chided herself mentally for missing him. After all, she hadn't said more than two words to him at a time in years. Still, she knew his scent, the sound of his voice, and every inch of his face as if no time had passed at all. *Fool*.

Sometimes she felt as if she were still that gangly girl in pigtails who followed behind her big brother and his buddies just to get a glimpse of what fun was like. Well, at least she wouldn't be distracted during dinner.

She could eat and relax. It was a full-time job, keeping her feelings hidden in front of a bunch of Werewolves. She should feel relieved that she was getting a little break. Except she didn't.

"What's on your mind, Cat? You haven't said a word," Rafe's familiar ice-blue eyes met hers and she knew he was trying to read her.

She held herself perfectly at ease and used all the skill she had to hide her emotions. Years of her father's ridiculing had trained her early on to hide her feelings and hide them well. Of course, being a smart alec helped as well.

"Nah, I'm good. Just a long day at the office. How about you? Everything go smooth here? You tired of the old ball and chain yet?"

"Hey! I resent that! I am not old," Charley giggled as she tossed a napkin in mock anger at her sister-in-law.

"Damn it, Cat!" Rafe almost choked on a meatball at the almost insult and Charley patted his back in soothing circular motions.

"Oh shush, Rafe, she's just teasing."

"Yeah, bro, I'm only teasing. Seriously though, everything okay around here? I haven't heard from any of you in the last twelve hours."

"Well, um, you see-"

"Uh, now that you mention it, um, Rafe?" Charley

spoke at the same time as Rafe. Cat couldn't help but get the feeling that they were keeping something from her.

She watched as Rafe's large hand covered Charley's smaller one. His eyes glowed deep blue as he caressed her hand. Cat tried not to stare at them as they looked into each other's eyes, but it was hard not to.

She envied them. Their obvious love and affection. The way they shared secret messages in that intimate, unspoken language only lovers knew.

Cat bit back a sigh. She was so happy for Rafe. Newly married to his true mate. A normal too.

Charley had agreed to stay and help him out even after the boys had basically kidnapped her from a Jersey City bus stop! *The idiots.*

Just proof that love could turn up in the most unexpected places. Cat couldn't have asked for a more perfect match for her brother.

Charley was domestic. She loved to cook and had a knack for interior decorating. She was in the process of reordering linens and bathroom décor for most of the house.

Cat was just grateful she didn't have to do it anymore. For a few years now, she had been given that job, though she often told her brother it was sexist of him.

She had chosen simple white towels and plain curtains and rugs. High quality, but plain, nondescript. Charley said it had a certain hotel like charm, but Cat knew she was just being nice.

She reassured her she was not insulted in the least if Charley went ahead and redecorated. As a thank you, Charley had tackled Cat's bathroom first. She loved the new tangerine and cream motif.

Especially the cute octopus shaped towel rack. Yup, she was glad in more ways than one that Rafe had found and managed to keep Charley.

She was bright and spunky too, and her temper could rival that of any Wolf! *Hot damn!* Cat walked in on the two newlyweds having an argument last week and just as Rafe got a little too sarcastic, his lovely wife upended an entire pitcher of iced tea on top of his shaggy black head. Cat couldn't breathe, she laughed so hard.

And that feline of hers! Oh man, Buttercup was quite the prince of the Manor. Imagine a Pack of Werewolves brought to their knees by a fluff ball!

Cat even noticed some of the guys buying him toys and treats, even Randall. She could take the beast or leave him, especially since he loved snoozing on Cat's uniform whenever she left it in the laundry room for more than a day. Feline fur was hell on a Werewolf's nose.

"Okay, listen Cat, come to my office later tonight and we'll talk," Rafe's voice brought her back to the present.

"You sure? We can talk now; the boys don't mind. I'm pretty sure Liam is in a meatball coma?"

"What? Me? Meatballs? More? Where?"

Cat laughed at Seff's younger brother and threw a meatball his way. The incorrigible pup caught it in his mouth.

"You pig!"

"Who, me? No way, Kit-Cat, I eat pigs! Whole! I can show you sometime," he waggled his eyebrows, and she threw a spoon at him, hitting him right in the forehead.

"Ouch! Dang it, you silly feline named Werewolf, I was still chewing!"

"You deserved it, Liam," Seff chided him for his disrespectful remarks. Cat just laughed. She didn't mind, it was all in fun.

"Cat, Rafe and I are just a tiny bit worried, there's some stuff we need to run by you, okay?"

"Like what?"

"Uh, just stop by his office tonight after dinner. Oh, and it's *your* turn to load the dishwasher," Charley winked, and Cat sighed.

Ugh! It was her turn and she would do it. Just as soon as she finished her salad. And maybe one more scoop of pasta. *Yum!* That was probably her second favorite thing about being a Werewolf. The food.

Like other Werewolves, Cat's metabolism was supernaturally fast. That was because they tended to run hotter and faster than normals.

Especially during the full moon. The Change from human to Wolf was not an easy thing. In fact, her first Change took almost forty minutes and hurt like hell.

Afterwards she was starving. She took down three rabbits that night. Rafe was the one who stayed with her. Well, Rafe *and* Tate.

She had almost forgotten about that. The two black Wolves had kept guard over the smaller buff colored female that was Cat.

They showed her how to keep control, where to hunt, and when it was safe to rest. Nowadays she managed to Change in under ten minutes. That was something of a feat for Werewolves, though Rafe managed his Change in under three.

It was a job sometimes, keeping up with her appetite. But she managed just fine. After all, it was a necessary part of being a Werewolf.

Of course, eating healthy was important. It wasn't all potato chips and cupcakes, but still Cat was able to eat way more than any of the normals she knew.

In fact, she often snuck protein bars and shakes

on the job. She could get snappy when she was hungry. And she was always careful to keep out of sight.

People could get pretty annoying with the same old "where do you put it" questions. Especially civilians. Officers tended to think she just liked to workout.

Cat wasn't the only Werewolf on the force. There was one other. He was much older than she was. A New jersey native, like her.

She sort of remembered him from way back when. He came around the house sometimes when she was just a kid. Pack business, she guessed, but at the time she wasn't privy to any of that.

Zev Maccon was a cold man and an equally cold Alpha. He didn't treat his Wolves with the same kind of respect Rafe did. Besides Lieutenant Matt Larentia tended to ignore Cat on a daily basis.

She didn't take it personally. She figured he preferred to work alone. Besides, she was only an officer and had no reason to interact with him.

He spoke to her only once that she could recall. She remembered that day. He had surprised her when he cornered her in the breakroom. He looked just the same as she remembered. His blonde hair showed little signs of graying, and his muscular body was the envy of men on the force half his age.

It was when she first went on the job at the Maccon City Sheriff's Department. Lt. Larentia had stopped her and asked about her schedule. His voice was gruff and impersonal.

"Keep the night of the full moon free each month," he had advised, "Otherwise things could get a little hairy."

Those were his exact words.

She had to refrain from rolling her eyes and saying something sarcastic. Still, she took his advice.

Other than Lt. Larentia, the entire department was full of normals. Cat didn't mind. It was the same as college. She did her best to fit in, to be useful, and to serve and protect.

It was difficult maintaining friendships and personal relationships when you had to keep such a tremendous secret. She rarely bothered.

She was just happy to be doing what she always wanted. Making a life of her own, on her own terms, and not stuck in a job or house because her father said so. She cringed as memories of old Zev crept into her mind.

"Earth to Cat!" Liam's voice was close. Without even looking, Cat reached out quickly with her hand and slapped him lightly on the nose. *Boys!*

"Ow! I just want the garlic bread!"

"Here, you bottomless pit!" She shook off her melancholy and tossed him a piece.

The jovial sounds of everyone eating around her put a stop to those pesky memories. *Pack. Family. This is all I need.*

Besides, Charley's food was much too good to bother thinking about her childhood. She sighed and dug in.

"Want me to stay and help you clear the table?" Charley asked from her place next to Rafe. But the look in her brother's eye told Cat that he had other plans for his wife.

"No way, you cooked, I clean. Them's the rules," she winked and smiled as Rafe stood up and pulled his new bride to her feet.

They exited hand in hand as Cat stood and began piling dishes. It was quick work getting everything to the kitchen. That was where the actual work happened, but in all seriousness, she couldn't complain.

Loading the dishwasher was a piece of cake compared to scrubbing pots and pans by hand with nothing but steel wool and baking soda. She grimaced as the smell of metal on metal came back to her.

Cat shook her head. *Nope, don't think about it.* She pushed her memories to the back of her mind for what seemed like the millionth time that night.

What was up with her? She needed a nice, long, quiet vacation. Somewhere she could just sit in peace and waste away the minutes doing nothing except maybe reading or sipping tea. *Mmmm.*

But for now, she was home and stuck with kitchen duty. Cat wasnice,n't going to make a fuss about cleaning up. That would be ridiculous, and she hated silly crap like that.

It was her turn, and fair was fair. Besides, the upgraded kitchen rocked. Just another of Rafe's exceptional improvements to the house.

The entire room was state-of-the art. New appliances, stone tiles, accent lighting, gleaming countertops. And besides, he hired help for the really tough jobs since everyone else had other things to do. It was a dream, truly.

She still hated the smell of wet metal, but the lemon scented detergent filled her nostrils as she flipped opened the cap and she went to work.

Ten minutes into it Cat stopped stacking the dishes and pans and pulled out her cell phone. If she was going to be stuck in there for who knew how long, she might as well listen to some music.

She plugged her phone into the wall dock, complete with charging station and speakers that Rafe also had installed in almost every room. She so loved her brother!

She smiled as she looked at her new smart phone. Her brother had insisted everyone in his Wolf Guard had one. Of course, they were full of top-secret apps made for Pack business by Randall Graves. He was the resident tech genius.

Randall was in charge of pretty much all their security, and anything having to do with a computer. The new smart phones were a way for Rafe to have real time access to his elite detail. It was also a way for them to stay in contact with the Pack as a whole.

Cat was pleasantly surprised when he handed her the brand new, hooked up cell in its pink armored case. She smiled at the memory. She may not be a Wolf Guard yet, but this was definitely a start.

She clicked the button that started her playlist. A little rock-and-roll and Cat was ready to tackle the mess. Cooking for Werewolves left more than one dirty pot.

Boy, was that the truth! She huffed out a breath, then shook her head and danced around on bare feet across the chilly stone floor. After packing away the leftovers, she scraped the dishes into the trash can and began loading them into one of the high efficiency dish washers. They had two.

The monotony of the work was soothing after the day she had. Cat bobbed her head as she wiped and stacked. She joined Gene Simmons for a few verses, belting out lyrics and dancing around in her bare feet across the tiled floor.

Cat wasn't afraid to let her hair down, especially when she was alone. Besides, a little bump and grind was just what she needed. She was having a ball too. Well, she was, until she heard the scrape of one of the high stools that surrounded the kitchen island. And then she smelled him.

Oh crap! Cat turned around to discover the one person in the world she wouldn't be caught dead letting her hair down around. Tate Nighthawk.

He stood watching her with a half grin on his usually stern face. To see that smile on his lips was enough to make her almost drop a plate. *Almost.*

"Do you mind? I was watching that," his deep voice cut through the rock and roll, making Cat's pulse speed up.

"Yeah right," she walked to the phone and quickly stopped her playlist, throwing them into a tense silence.

No way was she going to act like a fool in front of him. Not again, anyway. *Been there, done that.*

"I just packed up dinner. It's in the fridge if you're hungry."

"No, I'm good."

"Okay, so why are you in the kitchen then?"

"I love Kiss."

"Oh."

"So," he pulled out the stool and sat down. His muscles strained against the black t-shirt he wore as he rolled his neck and arms to get comfortable.

"How was work? Sheriff's Department treating you okay?"

"Yup. Fine," she cringed at her one-word answers. When would she stop acting like an imbecile around this man?

"I think we can do better than that, Catriona, don't you?"

"Don't call me that."

"Sorry, I forgot."

"Like hell you did."

"What? It's a pretty name."

"Yeah, right."

"I remember when you were eight, and I mispronounced your name after reading it off your homework, I called you Ca-tree-oh-na instead of Ca-treena, and you called me stupid."

"I did not!" Cat's cheeks burned. She was a difficult child, always on the defensive, but she couldn't believe she had said that!

"Yes, yes, you did! You called me a stupid jerk-faced boy and said I couldn't even read."

"Oh geez, look I'm sorry-"

"Nah, you don't have to say sorry. It's funny, you

know, because I couldn't. Read, that is. Not well anyway. My mother was sort of absentee. Hardly noticed when she swallowed those bottles of pills. And my dad, well, he was hardly, a father. I don't blame them, understand, they did the best they could with what they had. It wasn't until I lived here that I learned anything about anything."

"Tate, I-" Cat's heart hurt for him. She felt a sort of controlled emotion emanate from him. Sadness, solitude, heartache. But mostly loneliness. She wanted to do something, comfort him, hold him, but she remained where she stood.

She knew his mother had committed suicide. Another Werewolf driven to madness and grief for missing her Wolf. She even remembered the day her father brought him into their house.

He was older than her, of course, closer to Rafe's age. He was thin and scarred, with chin length black hair and the darkest pair of eyes she had ever seen. His shoulders were hunched, his clothes old, but clean, his expression grim, and the chip on his shoulder as big as a mountain.

"No apologies necessary, Cat. We were just kids."

"Yeah. It was a long time ago," she watched him as she resumed scraping dishes and placing them into the washer.

"Well, you're certainly not a kid now. You weren't

one the last time we were alone together either. You remember that night, don't you?"

"Look I don't–"

"Not one day has gone by in the last seven years that I haven't thought about it," his whispered confession hit her as if he had shouted it. She wasn't ready to hear whatever this was from him. Before she had a chance to speak, he continued.

"*God*, I have pictured you, standing there with the surf crashing just a few feet away. I can still taste the salt that clung to your skin. You looked for all the world like a sea nymph. Soft and glowing in the moonlight, designed by the gods to make a man crazy from wanting you."

Cat froze. This time the dish slipped right out of her trembling hands. Luckily, it landed on the countertop where it wobbled noisily until coming to a standstill. It was the only noise in the room after Tate's astounding revelation.

Had he really pictured her? Did he think about that night?

Cat had denied herself permission to dwell on the night of her senior prom long ago. She had been determined to get on with her life.

Getting away from the strict rules and brutal chores of her father had been step one. Getting herself a college degree had been step two. And putting Tate Nighthawk as far from her mind as she could get had been step three.

Of course, that last part was tough when she came home to live, but she worked long shifts. He seemed to do the same. They hardly interacted.

And on the rare occasion when they were home at the same time, Tate usually ignored her. She hid her grief and embarrassment with humor and sarcasm.

Cat swore she wouldn't moon over him. She promised herself a long time ago that she was done with men. She would never again put herself in a position where she needed to try to please someone with either her looks or actions.

After her father died and Rafe put off his rise to Alpha, she had thrown herself into her studies. She knew her brother would eventually fulfill his destiny, but it gave her time to make her own. She didn't believe in luck. She believed in hard work.

She would never be a homemaker or happy house-wife. It just wasn't in her. Cat had missed the opportunity to impress upon her father just how useful and strong a female Wolf could be outside of the home, but she wouldn't fail with Rafe.

The first time she had approached her brother with the idea of becoming one of his Wolf Guard, he refused. The second time he seemed to have paused before stating that it was not a woman's place. After that, she worked even harder. The third time, she told herself, the third time he would not be able to say no.

Cat had very little else filling her time. She was forever training. She had a rigorous workout routine, went regularly to target practice, and used weapons such as assault rifles, handguns, crossbows, and knife training, and she recently got certified as an EMT. Cat had all the makings of a Wolf Guard and more. She just had to make Rafe see it.

The one thing she didn't have was a personal life. She hardly dated anymore. She just didn't have the time. Besides, she was a fast study. If she was rejected once for baring her soul, there was no way she was going to do that again.

Anger, pain, and confusion took turns bubbling up inside of her. It was all she could do to not scream at him after all the things he had just claimed.

"What is all this, Tate?"

3

Tate stood up and turned around, his shoulders tense and his jaw clenched. Suddenly the room felt small to him.

What the hell was he doing? That night was best left buried where it was, in the past. Why was he bringing it up now? In the kitchen, for God's sake!

He exhaled. His own scent advertised his frustration. He ran his fingers over the top of his head.

He cut his hair short nowadays, but there were times he missed the old length of it.

He should leave as quickly as possible. *Just walk away, man.* But she looked so damn good. And after what he had just seen, he needed to be near something good, and warm, and alive. Cat was all those things. And more.

He took a deep breath and under the regular

kitchen smells he got a whiff of her. She was feeling something in that moment, concern, sympathy maybe.

He lowered his head. He didn't deserve it. Not after the day he had had.

Sometimes he just plain hated his job. As Wolf Guard, it was his duty to not simply protect his Alpha, but to go where Rafe needed him.

Today that had meant a ride to one of the wealthier suburbs of South Jersey. The home in Little Silver was gorgeous. From the outside, Tate took in the newly renovated colonial and saw what everyone must see.

A happy home. Upper middle class. The family clearly had money, what with the sparkling BMW that sat in the driveway. A Christmas gift for the wife, maybe?

Next to it was a smaller sports car. Not a classic, but close. A late 1980s Corvette. It was painted cherry red. *The father's no doubt.* And in front of that sat a brand-new ATV. Something for the kid, perhaps?

Holiday lights and accents tastefully decorated the outside of the house. There was a little sign that said, "Designed by Two Brothers Lawn Care."

Tate frowned, he always assumed when he was married and had his own home that he would be the one to put up the twinkle lights. Not that he knew much about domestic stuff like that, but heck, he wanted to be the one to do things for his family. If he ever had one.

He shook his head and went back to his perusal of the house. His job was to gather as much information as possible to assess whether this tragedy could have been prevented.

To this family the point was moot, but maybe others could learn from their mistakes. Then again, maybe some things were unavoidable no matter what you did.

A customized mailbox sat nestled in a brick post at the edge of the paved driveway. It was in the shape of a sailboat. The family surname was painted across it in bright red letters. It read *Mallory*.

Tate sat silently in the driver's seat of his large SUV and imagined what kind of mail was inside. The weekly grocery circular, maybe a letter from the kid's school for the annual winter fundraiser, a few late Christmas cards, a magazine subscription. The usual stuff you'd see inside a family mailbox.

From the outside, it was all so normal. Perfect, even. But inside was where he would find the horror of an unchangeable reality.

Mrs. Mallory was resting now. At least that was what he had been told. He took a moment to quiet the Wolf inside his mind's eye before knocking on the door. He knew all too well that is the last moment of inner peace that he'd experience for the next few days or weeks or months.

From the bottles on the side table and the smell in the air after he was admitted to the home, Tate could tell Mrs. Mallory was in a self-medicated sleep as opposed to simply resting.

A couple of valium, a glass of red wine. Not enough to harm her, but enough to numb the pain, he thought as he took in his surroundings.

He took note of everything withholding judgement for the time being. After all, she was a normal. Married to a man for the past seventeen years, who happened to be born a normal to a Werewolf family, as does happen on occasion.

Her husband, Rick, was not a Werewolf. However, he was loyal to the Pack. He had grown up inside of it and was under its protection.

His situation was not unique. Some Werewolves simply did not pass the gene onto their young. *You had to be born a Werewolf.* But even if you were normal born to Wolves you were still Pack.

And no, you could not be made into a Werewolf. All those myths about being bitten were just that, myths, stories, make-believe.

Pack was Pack and with Rafe as Alpha that meant

something it hadn't meant in years. Tate was in the Mallory living room for that reason alone.

Rick Mallory was a small man. Slight of stature with neatly trimmed graying hair, and a freshly shaved face. He appeared to be in shock and opted to remain outside the home when Tate went into his son's room to inspect.

He made the right decision. Calling his Pack contact before the police and coroner must have been an instinctual choice. His wife had wanted to call an ambulance. But Rick had known it was too late.

Tate turned the doorknob, careful not to leave any trace of him in the crime scene. The stink of death permeated the air, but unfortunately for Tate it was a familiar scent. And besides, this was no ordinary death.

Suicide. Another one, he should say. The pup was only sixteen years old. His first Change was three short months ago. Mr. Mallory had said there were no warning signs. At least none he or his wife could see.

Mason came home from school as usual. His father said he was texting his friends, making plans for the weekend. Then he and his wife went out to dinner alone, as they did on Friday nights. Date night, they called it.

When they tried to wake him up the next day, they found him. He had hung himself. Mason had used a fifteen-foot length of strong plasma rope. The kind that was meant for sailing. The boy had looped it over a bare ceiling rafter in his bedroom. One of those industrial, open concept motifs.

The walls of his bedroom were painted a mossy green, and the floors were a dark hardwood. A lime green throw rug sat on the floor. One corner was kicked up as if someone had tripped recently.

Rick Mallory had left the body where he found it. The boy still hung from the rafter. He was still and silent as Tate walked over to examine him.

He touched nothing, only inhaled. Once he got past the scent of excrement and decomposition, he breathed again. There was something else in the air, something a little off.

Tate walked over to the two long windows. The curtains were drawn and there was no natural light inside the room. He pushed them back carefully, using a pen that he took from the right pocket of his jacket.

Both windows were closed and locked tightly. Tate's eyes zoomed in on the layer of dust that emphasized one harsh reality. This boy had not opened a window for weeks.

Stale. The air was stale.

Tate inhaled deeply. His Wolf senses came forth and as always, he felt a rush at being so close to his Wolf. *Soon.* The moon would be full again soon. That was what he told himself.

But back to business. He closed his eyes and made a mental list of everything he could identify. *Dust. Mold. Faint remnants of cleaning fluids. Body soap. Deodorant. Pizza. Chips. Gym socks.* But everything was old. As if the boy had stopped living weeks ago instead of hours.

Strange behavior for a teen. Highly suspect for a Wolf. Tate frowned.

Werewolves had extremely reactive senses. Hearing, taste, touch, and especially smell would be very acute for one who had just had his first Change.

Werewolves needed fresh air, they craved it. The boy's father should have seen this, noted it. He should have called his Pack contact. Weren't his parents concerned at all after his Change? He bit back the angry thoughts that crowded his mind. They wouldn't help the boy now. Nothing would.

Tate turned back to the room for more signs. He noted them sadly. The boy's desk was messy, full of crumpled papers and covered in dust.

Tate noticed his laptop was unplugged. He tried to power it up. It was dead. The boy's smart phone too. They hadn't been plugged in for a while, he guessed.

Whatever the boy had told his father aside, this kid had not been in recent contact with his friends. Of course, Tate could try to verify that, but there was really no need. He'd seen this before.

The green plaid bedspread was carelessly tossed towards the foot of the bed. Dirty clothes spilled from the hamper. There were a few half full bottles of water lying around, but no food.

No evidence of potato chip bags or candy wrappers. No empty plates or fast food cartons. This kid should have been eating his parents out of house and home.

Damn it! There were signs everywhere! Didn't anyone pay attention?

Maybe his family didn't know what to expect, Tate reminded himself. But then again, it was their job to get familiar, to learn, to read the signs! Damn, damn, damn!

What was Mason thinking as he climbed up the stepladder and then kicked it away? *Poor kid.* Tate wanted to scream.

It was a slow and painful way for a Werewolf to die. Sad and alone.

As Rafe's liaison, Tate's job was to investigate the death and console the parents. To Tate, suicide was horrific, tragic, and pointless. It was also far too prevalent amongst his kind.

It took him a full five minutes to get control of himself. Another two for him to be able to walk down the staircase to the Mallory's living room.

He had gotten the information he came for. Before he left the bedroom, Tate looked at Mason Mallory's face as he hung from the rafter.

His skin was a deathly shade of blue gray, but Tate saw beyond that for a moment. He pictured the boy smiling, the wind blowing back his dark hair. He saw who the boy could have been. Inside his mind's eye, from a great distance he thought he heard Mason's Wolf howl.

Tate wiped the single tear that fell from his near black eyes. He desperately hoped the young she-Wolf from Northern, the one he had heard so much about, could break the Curse of St. Natalis as Rafe believed she could.

He had yet to meet the teenager, Grazi Kelly, but he knew the effects of the curse intimately. It was unnatural for Werewolves to change only on the night of the full moon.

It drove most to madness, this forced separation. The curse was the single biggest threat to Werewolves.

Tate only wished the girl could work a little faster.

His understanding of the curse was that it was a punishment for some crime committed long ago.

He couldn't fathom a debt big enough that so many would need to die to fill it. What grievous error could have been made against the Saint? It was hundreds of years ago, maybe a thousand.

The Packs of the world no longer remembered the reason behind their suffering. And yet they continued to suffer.

The Macconwood Pack was the only Werewolf Pack that he knew of trying to rectify the situation. Rafe's idea to be proactive and prevent the deaths was unique.

Tate wholeheartedly supported his Alpha. It was just that sometimes Tate had difficulty being strong and lending support to grieving families when all he wanted to do was scream and break something.

In this most recent situation, the something was the boy's father's nose.

He hated feeling powerless, and that was how he felt about the whole Little Silver tragedy.

He had to remember he wasn't there anymore. He was at the Manor, in the kitchen, with Catriona. Tall, blonde, and lovely Catriona.

He felt like a child with his nose pressed against a store window. Looking at some shiny new marvel that he could never afford. He could almost hear his father's words, "that's not for you." How many times had the old man told him that as a child? How many nights had he lain awake wanting what he couldn't have?

Tate watched her capable hands as she scraped plates and piled them into the dishwasher. Her eyes were focused on her task, but he could tell by the way she held herself that she was giving him her utmost attention. He sat a little bit straighter on the stool.

She had long fingers and clean, short nails. Tate wondered if they felt as soft as they looked. She worked competently, exerting little effort. *Strong, quick, smart.* All words he would use to describe her. Also, *beautiful.* Cat was strikingly beautiful.

He had one heck of a hard time looking away. He wondered how those hands would feel on him. Would she be soft and responsive, or would she lead him by the collar? He didn't think he'd mind either way.

He closed his eyes and swore he could hear her sigh the way she did that night so long ago. The taste of her still lingered in the back of his mind. *Damn, get a grip, dude. It was years ago.*

Tate cleared his throat and looked down at his hands. They were rough and hard. Nothing like hers. He loved working outdoors, though his job nowadays didn't call for it much.

Still, he kept a garden on the Manor grounds,

owned his own hunting cabin that he had built himself, and he worked on his old Camaro when he had the time.

The simple things. His father had told him to "remember the simple things" before he had left him there. Whatever the hell that meant.

When he looked up again, Cat was just pushing the button on the dishwasher. She turned with her hands on her narrow hips and a bored expression on her perfectly symmetrical face.

But he knew better. She wasn't bored. He could smell her interest. *Grrrr.* It both soothed and excited the beast inside of him.

He wished he could trust himself to speak, but he was still hurting for the Mallory pup. Besides, their relationship was tentative at best. He would only ruin it with any clumsy attempt to put what he was thinking into words.

And yet, he couldn't bring himself to leave the room. Just being in her presence improved his mood. He wished he knew what to say to her to break the silence.

He didn't have to wait long. Cat interrupted his inner musings with a long blown out breath. She never was a patient one.

"Sooooooo. Hello there. Uh, hi. Earth to Tate. What the heck are you doing?"

"Sorry?" Tate was so busy watching her expressions change with one emotion to the next that he forgot to answer.

"Okay, let me start slowly. How about some food?"

"What?" *Brilliant, dude. You are a wiz at convo.*

"Food. F-O-O-D. You know, you eat it when your stomach is growling like yours is now? Geez, and here you are, Mr. Wolf Guard, and I gotta explain what food is!"

Cat nodded towards the fridge with exaggerated movements and mimed putting food in her mouth and rubbing her stomach. Tate couldn't help himself, he laughed aloud.

She could be so damned sarcastic! Not to mention adorable. At any rate, she jolted him from his morbid musings, and he was grateful.

That was one of the things he liked about her. She didn't mess around like other women did. No games or acts. She was real.

"Um, yeah, thanks. Sounds good. No worries though, I'll get it."

"Damn straight, you'll get it. I wasn't offering to make your dish or anything. What the heck do I look like anyway?"

"Oh, easy there. Besides, there was a time when you would have."

"Yeah, well, that was a long time ago. My father's not here to make me act the maid."

"You were never the maid type to me, Cat."

His answer was punctuated with a long stare. From the tip of her golden head to the bottom of her size nine's. He smiled as he watched her try not to squirm.

"Stop looking at my big feet."

"They're not big. Look at mine. Size thirteen," Tate held out his booted foot and smirked as Cat raised her eyebrows in exaggerated horror. *Wise-ass.*

She blushed as his perusal lingered on her legs and something stirred inside of him. Could she still be so green? So unused to a man's stare? He couldn't believe that. She was a damned knockout.

He knew beautiful women. He had dated them. *Plenty of them,* truth be told, but he was amazed by his reaction to her.

This was Cat. Rafe's baby sister. He had no business sniffing around her, and he knew it. But he couldn't help himself. His Wolf was growling in his mind and Tate felt his hunger. Heck, he reveled in it.

These days he had a hard time even looking at women, but she, well, she was different. She moved to leave the kitchen and his stomach lurched at the thought of being stuck in there with his own company.

"Wait," the word escaped Tate's mouth before he could stop it.

"Huh? What is it?"

"Please. If you could just sit here, with me. We don't have to talk. I just don't want to be by myself. *Please*," Tate's shoulders were tense. His pain was clear in his voice.

He never would have revealed so much about his feelings to anyone else. It was a new experience for him. Unexpected and scary as hell.

He bit his tongue, waiting for her to respond. It seemed to take forever. His heart pounded in his chest and he gripped his fork so tightly he bent it.

Cat turned to the sink and poured two glasses of water before adding ice. She took a seat across from him and handed him one of the glasses. His dish of pasta was cold, but he preferred it that way.

He released the breath he was holding when she grabbed a pink lady apple from the fruit bowl and bit. They sat together and ate in mutually agreed upon silence.

It was the best dinner Tate had had in a very long while.

❧ 4 ☙

"Oh geez, this sucks," Charley grunted with the effort it took to try and keep up with Cat in the gym room or as the gang nicknamed it, the "Torture Chamber."

Maccon Manor truly did have everything, and the Torture Chamber was proof. Cat's father would have never allowed them to build this while he was alive. *Gyms were for normals.*

This was like having a private YMCA. It was a good thing, too. Werewolves were hard on equipment. Besides, it wasn't easy trying to expel all that supernatural energy in a public gym. What with the pesky business of having to keep what they were secret and all.

The Torture Chamber eliminated the need for that. It was equipped with an indoor track, Olympic sized swimming pool with all-natural salt filtration system, free weights, three separate power racks, special made cast iron eights and kettle bells from twenty to four hundred pounds, a rock wall, monster truck sized tires to pull or lift, a row of punching bags, and top of the line fitness machines.

The floor was poured concrete, polished to a shine and covered in five-inch-thick rubber mats, also custom made.

The Manor was connected to the gym through a covered hallway much like you would see in a college annex. There were security coded keys and thumbprint recognition screens for the Manor residents, but they welcomed Pack members to use it provided they had clearance.

Cat simply loved it.

"Hey! *You* asked *me* to help you lose a few pounds, come on, just a few more minutes," Cat didn't have the heart to tell her new sister that she was only jogging at about a quarter of her normal speed.

"Yeah, but you're brutal! We've been at this for like an hour, Cat! Ooh, I think I need a break. I feel queasy."

"Alright, alright, let's just walk to cool down. Don't forget to sip some water."

"Deal."

"Soooo-"

"So, what, Charley?"

"Soooo, what happened between you and Tate last night?"

"What do you mean?"

"Well, you guys were in the kitchen until midnight."

"Yeah, I was cleaning, and he was eating."

"Come on Cat, tell me!"

"Tell you what? Oh my God, did Rafe tell you about prom?"

"Um, sort of?" Charley slowed down the treadmill and stared at Cat concerned.

"It's okay, Charley, I'm not mad. I just wish he would forget it."

"I'm sorry, I didn't mean to bring up the past. But-"

"But what?" Cat tried to keep her voice even. It's not that she was angry, far from it. It was just that last night had left her more than a little confused.

"But seriously, it took you that long to load the dishwasher?"

"Not exactly. Okay, look, it would have been rude for me to leave him in there all by himself, so I stayed."

"*And?*"

"*And* I ate an apple."

"After you ate three bowls of pasta and a huge

salad? You had room for an apple? *Freaking Were-wolves, ughhh,*" Charley let out an exaggerated sigh and shook her head as she patted her neck dry with a small white towel.

Irony welled up inside of her, but she just laughed. If only Charley knew!Cat often wished she could be soft and curvy, full of dips and fleshy valleys.

Wishing never seemed to work and no matter how much she ate Cat remained thin and toned. She shook her head and quickened her pace.

"Do you know what I would look like if I ate half as much as you? I'd weigh like a million freakin' pounds!" Charley exclaimed with mock outrage.

"Oh please, you look perfect! Besides, my brother can't seem to get enough of you judging from that huge hickey on your neck," Cat laughed aloud when Charley grabbed at her neck with a sweaty hand, her brown eyes huge in her face. Cat smelled her embarrassment but laughed it off as Charley blushed furiously.

She managed to keep a lid on the sudden jolt of envy that she felt. Just barely. Would she ever be happy like that?

"What? Wait till I get Rafe! I told him no love bites where people can see! As if the other one isn't bad enough," she mumbled as she took her curly brown hair out of its ponytail and attempted to cover her neck.

"You mean you have more hickeys bigger than that one? Where?"

"Oh, please, Cat! Like you don't know!"

Cat just wiggled her eyebrows up and down and continued to jog. If only Charley knew how inexperienced she really was. It was almost humiliating to think she was twenty-five years old, and the most she had done with a guy was nothing to write home about.

What could Cat say about it, anyway? Her Wolf had decided long ago who her mate was, but he rejected her. She had heard stories growing up about Wolves whose lives ended tragically because of unrequited love. Cat would never consider that.

She was a modern woman and Wolf. She didn't need a mate. At least that's what she told herself.

She listened to her sister-in-law's chatter about her insecurities. Apparently, body size was a big deal to normals, but Cat could tell she was truly happy.

She could hear it in Charley's voice. She saw it in the way the shorter woman held herself, and the way she smiled all the time. That was good. Cat was glad for her. And for Rafe.

Of course, the way they got together wasn't ideal,

but there was that old saying about desperate times. It all seemed to work out in the end.

Charley was adjusting very well to life in the Pack. And Rafe, well, he seemed to be owning his position as Alpha. He was a great leader, but ever since he married he became something more.

He had heart. He truly cared about the wellbeing of the Wolves he was responsible for. As he did for his mate. Cat knew instinctively that Rafe would not only kill for her, but he would die for her as well.

It was that kind of willingness to sacrifice himself for his true love that left Cat in awe. She had never seen a love like that. But if anyone deserved to be happy, it was her brother. And if the Pack could benefit from it too, then that was just the icing on the cake.

Zev Maccon was not the best role model as a father or as an Alpha. To him, they were both about strength and dominance. He governed the Pack and his family with strict rules and an overbearing presence.

Some of his practices were downright archaic. Especially anything involving women and children. Rafe had gotten rid of just about all of them.

There were some Wolves who didn't like it. They didn't approve of all the changes, but Cat thought that was just too bad for them.

The future of the Macconwood Pack depended on Rafe's ability to bring them into the twenty-first century. Cat was fully onboard.

She smiled as Charley narrowed her eyes and sped up her pace. She chugged from her bottle of chilled spring water, eyeing Cat's monitor the whole time.

Her sister-in-law had spunk. That was good! Cat was equally proud of her perseverance and impressed with the way she tried to keep up with her. Especially with those tiny legs of hers.

Cat always felt like some kind of giant compared to girls like Charley. She was just under six foot tall. If she was being brutally honest with herself, she'd admit she used to think she looked like a boy.

Especially when she was a kid. It took forever for her to develop breasts and even when she did they weren't exactly the most eye-catching thing about her.

Most male Werewolves were taller than she was, so that wasn't really the issue. It was just that they tended to be attracted to normals.

She guessed it was because of their animalistic nature. A normal was someone to protect, to pamper, to defend. Cat wasn't exactly the type to be coddled.

In turn, she didn't really have a type. Okay, well maybe she did, but aside from him there was nothing specific that she looked for in a man.

She dated a few guys here and there. Mostly when she was in college. Only two of them were Werewolves, but neither was anything serious. She had offered her heart once, just once, and he had turned her down.

There would be no second time for her. Nope. Besides, she was totally focused on her career and on getting her brother to see her as more than just his kid sister.

She wanted to be a Wolf Guard. It was just the sort of thing Rafe was always trying to promote within the Pack. Some said he had a feminist agenda. In reality, his agenda was equality. Yes, Wolf Pack's had a pecking order, but under Zev's rules women were beneath even the least dominant of males.

Cat was a dominant Wolf. She knew that her father had been unjust in his assessment of female Wolves. Just like she knew he used brutal tactics to keep her in line.

But if Rafe really wanted to make changes in the Pack, he should begin inside his own home. Cat took out her annoyance on the treadmill, and it wasn't until she heard her name being called that she realized where she was again.

"Cat? Cat? CAT!"

"Huh?"

"Geez, you're really focused when you work out,

aren't you? Anyway, sooooo, you never came by Rafe's office last night," Charley looked at her with probing eyes. Cat knew she'd never leave it alone, so she answered honestly.

"Yeah, sorry, it slipped my mind. Okay, let's go over to the mats and stretch a little. You can use the yoga ball."

"I love the yoga ball! Yay!" They both giggled as Charley clumsily sat on the giant inflatable ball and bounced before sliding off in a fit of giggles. Cat gently pinned her to the mat and the two of them mock wrestled until they ended up in a fit of laughter that left them both unable to speak.

Just then Cat's giant of a brother walked into the gym. His face lost its wide grin when he saw his bride in a heap on the floor, gasping for breath next to his sister. He shoved Cat out of the way and reached for his mate. The Wolf peering out of his eyes was just as enraged as the man.

"What the heck did you do to her?! Carlotta? Oh my God, baby, sit up!"

"Chill dude, she's laughing," Cat slapped her brother on the arm and rolled her eyes when he growled. Freaking Alpha males always showing their dominance.

"Yeah, yeah, I know, you the man!" Still, she bared

her throat to him and averted her gaze. Rafe was not playing.

"Rafe, baby, I'm okay, really! We were just being silly," she reached up and stroked his face. The tenderness in that small movement was too much for Cat, so she turned around.

She felt like a voyeur watching them. However innocent the touch, it was full of something intimate. It was sacred and private. She had no right to that moment. It was theirs, made just for the two of them.

Cat sighed. If only that sort of thing was in the cards for her.

"But since you're here, don't you think you should tell her?" Charley had her arms around her husband and was perched in his lap, stroking his face when she asked the question.

Cat could tell from his body language alone that conversing with his sister was the last thing on his mind right then.

"Um, yeah, okay. Uh, Cat? You got a minute?"

"What? Hell no! I'm a goddamn police officer Rafe, I don't need a friggin' bodyguard!"

Cat's emotions were all over the place. Anger, annoyance, outrage, insecurity, disbelief, fear, then back to anger. Still, she never looked her Alpha in the eyes and never made a move to challenge him. She had too much respect for her brother to act that way. Besides, it was a contest she would never win.

"Language please," Charley's sing song voice interrupted Cat's tirade.

Cat tried to control her temper, but even her Wolf was miffed. Her feelings were always clearer to Cat when the full moon was close.

She counted to ten in her head. She needed to be calm to get anywhere with her brother. Otherwise he would just dig his heels in. And she had no wish to fight, but come on!

"Look, we've picked up some good intel here, and it's possible you're being targeted as a means to get to me."

"So friggin' what? I can handle it, Rafe!"

"You're my sister Cat," he sighed heavily and wiped his face with his enormous hands. Geez, he was big, at least three of her width wise. Almost twice the size of the rest of the men in the Pack.

"Yeah, I'm your sister. You taught me well. I can take care of *myself*!"

"BUT you are also my Wolf. I am the Alpha, you will obey me, Catriona!" The command in his voice made her waver where she stood. It didn't hurt exactly, but it was strong, and it held her still when she wanted to turn away. She whined in her throat and averted her gaze. *Damn Alpha!*

"Yes, sir!" she said with clenched teeth.

"You will have a shadow everywhere you go. Now, I worked it out with Matt Larentia, you will take the next month off."

"Lt. Larentia? But-"

"No buts, Cat. You'll do this my way."

"Fine."

Cat stormed out of the office and slammed the

door. She didn't have to use her supernatural senses to guess the expression on Rafe's face.

No doubt Charley was holding him down with nothing more than a sweet word or smile. Bless her!

Cat knew she overstepped, but she couldn't help herself. She stalked across the house to her room and made her way to the shower.

The hot spray hit her body, and Cat sighed. She was tense. Even after her workout. She scrubbed her body with the vanilla-tangerine scented body wash Charley had purchased for her.

It reminded Cat of flavored frozen custard on the Boardwalk. She closed her eyes and exhaled. Memories played through her mind. Games, rides, frozen custard, and cotton candy. She used to sneak off and follow Rafe and his buddies when she was just a kid.

Man, that was fun! She wished it were summer now. She could use a funnel cake after the bomb Rafe just dropped on her. *A bodyguard! Really?*

She didn't flinch when the bathroom door swung open. Nudity was sort of acceptable for Wolves. Not that she paraded around naked, but there were times during the full moon when she or other Wolves were nude before and after the Change. *Hey, it happened.*

"Liam, is that you?" She knew it wasn't the youngest Wolf of the house the second she inhaled. *Oh crap!* She fought the urge to duck and cover.

She was grateful steam from the shower fogged the glass enough to hide her blush from probing eyes. Black eyes, to be exact.

"Does Liam often come into your bathroom when you're showering?"

"What? No! *Ew*, no way! Why the heck are *you* in here?"

"Rafe ordered me to act as your guard for the foreseeable future."

"Oh bullshit! I don't need a bodyguard!"

"Well, you got one."

"That's just great, sunshine! But I'm pretty sure I can handle things in here!"

"That's a shame, I'm an excellent backwasher. But if you're really sure, I'll wait outside. And, uh, tell Liam to stay the hell out of your bathroom."

Cat flinched when he left the room, slamming the door. Was Rafe out of his mind, assigning Tate Nighthawk to her? Her brother could be a real butt-hole sometimes. *Ugh.*

She took her time in the bathroom. There was no need to rush. Besides, she was in no hurry to confront her new bodyguard.

Cat thought about it. She didn't have any work for the next few weeks. Well, since that was the case, she was going to make the most of her time off. Even if she had Tate hanging around.

"Seriously? 45 minutes in the shower? What were you doing in there?"

"Hey, you don't need to stick around for me!"

"Um, yeah, I do actually. It's my job."

Cat rolled her icy blue eyes and tossed her wet blonde hair out of her face. She had pulled on a pair of black leggings and a long fluffy sweater.

On anyone else it would have fallen to the knee, but on her it stopped mid thigh. The sleeves were oversized, and the neck was large enough to reveal one lean shoulder. She didn't bother with a bra. Her breasts were smallish and high enough on their own.

She wasn't into fashion, but she was a clotheshorse. Whatever body issues she had, she always could put just about anything on and it sort of fell into place.

She knew she looked okay, but she stopped being concerned with how she looked in front of Tate a long time ago. This outfit was just plain comfy. She was still tugging on a pair of knee-high weatherproof boots when she started walking down the hall.

"Where to?" Tate's voice was deep and clear. She had to work hard to mask the effect it had on her.

"I was told you were going to shadow me, not badger me to death with inane questions."

"Suit yourself," Tate's face betrayed no emotion. Still Cat knew she was being rude. Too bad for him.

She didn't ask for his company, and she wanted that to be as clear as crystal.

She headed towards her little convertible and stopped when Tate turned her around with a hand on her shoulder.

"What?"

"If we're going out, it's best we take the box."

Cat rolled her eyes and followed him to the huge suped up SUV parked alongside the driveway. The windows were tinted bulletproof glass. There was a custom satellite hands-free phone system, GPS, and a trunk chock full of state-of-the-art weapons for killing enemies of both the supernatural and normal kind.

He had dubbed it "the box" because of the bulky square shape of the vehicle. Rafe ordered a dozen more of them based on Tate's review. But Tate kept the original. His opinion was important to Rafe.

Cat had never driven one of these babies before, and she wasn't about to pass up the opportunity. She hopped into the driver's seat before Tate had a chance to blink.

He set his jaw, and she knew what was coming, but she wasn't going to budge. The corner of her mouth tilted up, and she raised a blonde eyebrow as she met his dark eyes. She felt for the keys around the ignition but came up empty.

"It's keyless. You need to be added to the database first. Here, let me scan my thumb, then you just push the button," Tate leaned over Cat, his wintergreen scent filled her nostrils. She felt warm in places she shouldn't, and she held her breath to stop breathing him in.

If only she could stop the furious pounding of her heart. His face was close to hers for one fraction of a second too long. She wondered if he was doing it on purpose.

Their breath mingled, and she could have sworn she saw desire in his eyes. She swallowed. Her eyes felt heavy as she stared at his full lower lip. It looked so tempting.

She wanted desperately to taste it, but just like that he was gone. He walked around the car and sat in his seat, eyes forward as if nothing had happened. The roar of the engine snapped her back to attention and Cat put the SUV in gear.

"Where are we headed?"

"I need some things from town since I'm not allowed to work."

"What things?"

"I don't know, *things*, you know, like shampoo, conditioner, deodorant, tampons, batteries for my feminine massager."

"Really?"

"Hey, you asked, buddy!"

"Can't you get a real man to do that for you?"

"Yes, I'm sure I could, but no thank you! Real men smell."

"Wolves don't."

"Oh, yes, they do! Especially when it rains! Then there's all those pesky emotions. Werewolves cannot handle emotions at all!"

"What?!" Tate was stunned. He couldn't believe his ears.

"Listen, Tate, I do not need to deal with anymore cry baby men who want a commitment! Werewolves are the worst, It's all like, you're my territory, yadda yadda, boo hoo. *Ugh.* Let me tell you, I'm fine with Mr. Vroom Vroom!"

Tate laughed aloud at her outrageous commentary, surprising them both. Cat couldn't help but smile. He did not laugh often.

She continued with her quips the entire twenty-minute drive to town. It didn't matter if half of what she said was an outright lie or not.

Tate was feeling refreshed and jovial in a way he hadn't for a very long time by the time Cat put the SUV into park in the almost full lot of the local grocery store.

"Geez, it looks like they're having a sale. What is everyone in Maccon City here?"

"It's worse than a sale."

"Huh?"

"Blizzard warning."

"Oooh. Yeah, everyone's buying their bread, milk, and eggs. Like that ever stopped the snow. But anyway, come on! Those forecasts are never even accurate."

"Alright, let's just hurry up. I smell ice."

"No duh, Tate, it's winter. Who are you, Queen Elsa or something?"

Tate didn't reply. He stood behind her stone faced and unmoving as she grabbed a shopping cart and muttered to herself about ice and Werewolves who thought they were the next Storm Jackson! She didn't see his amused smirk.

True to her nature, Cat was in and out of the store in record time. Tate paused, raising a perfect black eyebrow when she did in fact purchase a twelve pack of double AA batteries. She rolled her eyes and kept shopping.

"Guess you were serious about Mr. Vroom Vroom?"

"You know, men always have their minds in the gutter! Not surprising, you'd remember that bit of our conversation!"

"You know you were the one to bring that up, not me."

"Oh please, you can talk to a woman without bringing up sex or hitting on her?"

"Um, actually, I can. I talk to you all the time."

Ouch that stung. Cat had no intention of letting him see her squirm. She grabbed some snacks and headed to the checkout line.

"Everywhere I go, men are always coming on to the women around them."

"Men and women can be just friends."

"No way. It's almost impossible for them to work together, let alone be friends."

"That's simply not true."

"Oh yeah, I went for a coffee run with the new rookie, Johnny Dominguez, and in five minutes he was all over me."

"What do you mean? What did he do?" Tate narrowed his eyes, but Cat was already in front of him and didn't catch the sudden shift in his posture.

"I mean, what a creep! He's good looking and all. That wasn't the problem. Tall, built, wavy brown hair, tan skin, dark eyes. But he's a cocky jerk. Two seconds we're waiting for coffee and he's like grabbing my ass and trying to stick his tongue down my throat and I'm like oh heck no! I don't even know you."

"What?" Tate growled low and menacingly. Cat was so surprised she stopped short and turned around. He almost walked right into her, amped up as he was.

"What's eating you? Like I can't take care of myself? *Please*! Look, I had his arm behind his back and his face down on the counter in less than five seconds."

Tate shook his head. He needed to keep his attention on what was around them. Not in Cat's office romances. He placed a hand on the small of Cat's back just as she swiped her card and punched in the four-digit security code.

"They should rename this the $100 store, no matter what I come in here for, it costs me $100."

"Let's go."

Uh oh, playtime's over, she thought to herself. She hurried out the door with her bags in one hand. She was already reaching for the gun she kept in the small of her back when Tate pulled out his own nine-millimeter.

"I smell it too," Cat threw her bags in the back and jumped into the passenger seat when the first shot rang out.

Tate was fast. Unlike anything she had ever seen. He returned fire within a second of the first bullet and took down one of the perps.

He fired up the engine, and they peeled out of the parking lot. Another few seconds and they were gone.

"Are you okay? You hit?"

"No, no, I'm fine. But what the hell was that?"

"I'm not sure, but we better call Rafe," Tate pushed the button for the sat phone and within seconds they were connected.

"Wassup?" Liam was always clowning around.

"This is Tate. An attempt was made. I got one of them."

"For real? Damn! Alright, you know what to do! I'll alert the others."

"Copy that."

"What was that? Tate?"

"Listen, you know how Rafe operates. He's had his ear to the ground ever since that business Christmas Eve with Skoll. From what we've uncovered, you are central to a plot to force Rafe's hand."

"What the heck? Why didn't you guys tell me this?"

"It doesn't matter now, does it? We have to go somewhere safe for a few days."

"Why not back to the Manor? The place is a fortress."

"No, the place *is* a fortress and as of two minutes ago it has been completely locked down. No one in or out, including us."

Cat paused for a moment and let that sink in. Her home was off limits and she was being hunted. Her

Wolf snarled in her mind's eye, unused to being prey. Cat refocused.

"Where will we go?" She had no doubt that if anyone could help her get through this, it was Tate. Personal issues aside, he was a steady and capable Wolf. Rafe trusted him. If she was being honest, she'd admit that she trusted him too. His deep voice broke through her reverie and she turned ice-blue eyes to meet his.

"Some place safe."

6

They drove for what seemed like hours. Across back roads and little used truck routes. In reality, they had travelled for a little bit more than an hour when Tate parked the SUV in what looked like a stand of trees.

It was actually a covered garage hidden in the woods off one of the many forgotten roads that cut across that part of the state. Tall trees and a clever paint job hid the building from view. Cat was glad that they had stopped.

A knot was forming in her stomach, and she was getting antsy. Werewolves didn't usually like to be cooped up, and the SUV was beginning to feel cramped. Maybe it was Tate's dominance silently warring with her own. Maybe it was pent up sexual frustration from years earlier. Nope, she was not going to touch that thought. She waited for Tate to speak.

"On the wall, you'll find a couple of backpacks. Inside of them should be some provisions, ammo, first aid, that type of thing."

"You mean we're leaving? Why can't we just stay here?"

"You know better than that. We could've been followed. This place is close to the main road. If the men working for Skoll are halfway decent, they will find us by nightfall. So, grab anything else you need from the car and let's go."

"Fine. Geez," Cat didn't much like the way he reprimanded her. She knew better, but momentary panic made her speak without thinking.

"Damn, you didn't wear a coat, huh? There are a few extras hanging up next to the bags. Put one on."

"I'm fine."

"Humor me, okay?"

Cat's blue eyes narrowed as she watched Tate stuff more ammo into his backpack. He added a choice selection of knives, guns, and other weapons, stuffing them in pockets and belts around his person. The black backpack he held was bulging to the limit by the time he had finished.

"Better safe than sorry, I guess," Tate grunted his reply. Was that a smile? She couldn't be sure. He rarely smiled, and his head was facing the wrong way for her to make that determination.

Cat took a deep breath. She knew the Pack had safe houses all over the state, but she had never actually seen one. The prospect piqued her interest, and she switched into work mode.

Okay, Cat, game on. Her police training kicked in as she opened the back door of the SUV. She put the box of vanilla crisp protein bars that she had just bought into the backpack Tate had told her to grab.

It was already heavy with supplies that he or someone must have pre-packed and left there hanging on a large metal hook that was screwed into the scarred wall. She smelled Werewolf and recognized that this place was used by Pack members.

She smelled a few different Wolves, but the scent that hit her as the freshest belonged to Tate. Her trust in him, in his ability to get them to safety, allowed her to set aside her natural instincts to quarrel and obey his orders.

She rummaged through her shopping bag and added a box of her favorite cinnamon toothpaste and a travel sized bottle of hand cream. She waited until she knew he was looking at her, and then she grabbed the pack of AA batteries and put them inside the bag.

Cat managed to remain straight faced even when Tate raised both eyebrows. He was rarely surprised, and she silently congratulated herself on her ability to shock. She closed the zipper with added oomph and turned her head, flipping her blonde hair to the side.

The camouflage hunting jacket she donned was a little too big for her, despite her above average height. Cat didn't care. It was warm, and the lining was soft. The outer shell was black, which was good for camouflage and it was waterproof too.

That would come in handy if the weather turned ugly, as it had all winter. And Tate had already predicted an ice storm earlier. He had a knack for telling the weather. Maybe it was an old Lenape trick. She wasn't sure, and he rarely spoke of his native heritage.

She closed her eyes and inhaled in an effort to focus her thoughts. *Well, crap, that isn't gonna work.*

Tate's scent was imbued in the fabric of her borrowed coat. *Pine trees and snow. Sand and sun.* Only Tate's scent could be so contrary and so near perfect, she thought.

Cat's Wolf purred in her mind's eye. She had never heard of a Wolf that purred before. No one had until the night of her first Change. She had just caught her very first rabbit, a small gray one, and her medium-sized buff colored Wolf purred her contentment.

Rafe told her it must be her name that caused her

Wolf to make such an un-wolf like sound. Whatever the reason, Cat couldn't seem to help it.

"Well, if you can't help it, own it," those were her brother's words to her after that night.

And she did. As far as she knew, no other Wolf purred. Just her. Right then she was glad that only she heard her Wolf inside her head.

Scent was important to Werewolves and Tate's scent just about drove her wild. She resisted the urge to bury her nose in the collar, but not without some serious effort on her part.

"So, you come here a lot then?"

"Sometimes."

"Well, then you know where we're going."

"Of course, I do."

"Well?"

"My cabin," he answered without looking at her, though Cat had the distinct impression he knew the exact expression she wore. The slightly raised corner of his lips told her that much. Great. She amused him.

"Your cabin?"

"Yes."

"Perfect, just perfect. Don't you think they can find a vacation spot?"

"It's completely off the grid."

"Meaning what exactly?"

"There are times when my duties as Wolf Guard get to be a lot. Whenever I feel like that, I try to get in touch with nature and the elements without all the traps of modern technology."

"I've never heard you mention it," Cat's curiosity was piqued. She thought she knew everything about the man in front of her.

"That's because I don't talk about it."

"Why not?"

"Cause then people ask questions. They don't understand why anyone would want to live without Wi-Fi, I guess."

"Oh."

"What? Don't tell me you're panicking?"

"Of course not, I-"

"I suppose to a modern girl like you it seems impossible to survive a few days without social media."

"I can last more than you can! Besides, you're the one with the twitter account!"

"How do you know that?"

Cat gave him a scathing look and headed for the door. She knew he was goading her, but she always rose to the bait. Maybe it was a throwback to when she was a kid. Always in competition with the boys.

Anyway, she didn't care. She was every bit as

tough and as strong as Tate or any of them! She'd show him.

By the fourth hour of their hike through the semi-frozen pine forests of South Jersey, Cat was beginning to lose her patience. Tate was quiet as ever and focused on wherever the heck they were going.

Most Werewolves had a great sense of direction. There was some innate knowledge of one's whereabouts that only grew more amplified after the Change. After covering miles and miles of ground in rapidly decreasing temperatures, Cat was beginning to question hers.

She was absolutely positive they were going around in circles. The sounds and smells surrounding her told her so. Didn't they pass that same sun-bleached red cedar at least three times? Maybe Tate was losing it, she thought. But even in her mind, that didn't ring true. He was, to put it simply, the most talented Werewolf tracker she had ever seen.

Cat was ready to burst from wanting to scream at him when suddenly, he lifted a hand. With two long fingers he signaled her forward, toward a stand of short pines.

The air felt thicker as she neared them. Her Wolf recognized magic. It was similar to the type of magic that bound each Werewolf together within a Pack. The Alpha's connection to the Pack was always the strongest and so on and so forth according to rank and dominance.

This felt slightly different. It seemed to come from the earth itself as opposed to any one being. Cat tensed. The human half of her didn't exactly trust magic. Except for her beautician. Sherry was simply a marvel when it came to Werewolf skin and hair care. Not to mention nails.

Tate turned his head, a question in his dark eyes. He was at least ten feet ahead of her. She had stopped the second she sensed the magic. Before she could speak, he held his right hand to his lips and motioned for her to follow him.

Whatever her objections, Cat swallowed them. She was used to being independent, but in this situation, she was the less dominant Wolf. Plus, she trusted Tate to lead her to safety. It was as simple as that.

The rocky path was covered in snow and ice. She frowned as she circumnavigated her way over tree roots and slick rocks. This winter was by far the coldest she had ever seen.

The weather had turned nasty early that fall. And that was after a summer with daily temperatures in the high nineties. It had gone from one constant heat wave to unseasonably bitter weather almost overnight.

The reason for that wasn't global warming, cow flatulence, or holes in the ozone layer. It was dark magic and the evil that came with it. After a nasty battle just weeks ago, one that Cat had participated in, the dark Witches' forces had been cut down. Only now was the temperature beginning to normalize. But even so, January in New Jersey was still cold.

Cat was grateful for the borrowed coat, and the fact that her boots had thick rubber soles. She silently applauded her footwear choice. It was a good thing she didn't go in for flimsy footwear. Stiletto heeled boots and the like. Being a cop made her shy away from the impractical. Besides, she was taller than most men she knew and didn't need heels.

They rounded a steep bend that was covered on either side with oaks and pines. Icicles hung from the lower branches and muddy snow covered the ground. She watched the path and kept her footing sure and steady. She raised her eyes when she saw it. Tate's cabin.

It was tucked away in the back of a ridge. Huge pines, oaks, and beeches surrounded it. Cat's eyes were big as saucers. This is not what she had expected at all.

It was a log cabin, but not the kind of run-down little shack she had anticipated. This structure was huge and had multiple levels.

The first floor had an arched walkway, and a slanted roof. Icicles and snow hung from the gutters and windows and reminded Cat of the frosting on a gingerbread house. But that was the only resemblance.

The cabin was not girly or childlike. It was powerful and solid and yet; it seemed to flow into the land and not take anything away from the natural beauty of the surrounding woods. Cat admired the thorough planning that went into building it and wondered who his architect was.

She followed Tate up the walkway. He purposely left large rocks and tree roots in the path. It made for a more natural setting and discouraged visitors. She smiled as she carefully stepped where he did. Tate always had an odd sense of humor.

He moved with the practiced ease of someone who knew their way well. Cat counted the times she would have slipped if she didn't have Werewolf reflexes. *Thirteen.* Her lucky number.

She marveled at the beauty of her home state. Leave it to Tate to find the most perfect section of the woods and claim it for himself. As if the area wasn't beautiful enough, Cat's breath left her when she got a glimpse of the enormous entryway door. It was absolutely stunning.

The wood matched the round logs that made up

the walls. The difference was in the scene that was carved into it. A huge Werewolf, head thrown back in an eternal howl at an invisible moon. The Wolf looked familiar, but surely her eyes were mistaken.

At the very least, she recognized his handiwork. Tate was a master wood carver and was in fact responsible for the aged wizard that sat in the middle of the Manor garden where an old oak had fallen three winters ago after being struck by lightning. She walked through the mini-botanical garden often just to catch a glimpse of it.

"Inside," the softly spoken word interrupted her thoughts. She was embarrassed to see he'd been standing with the door open for at least a minute.

Get your head on straight, girl, she thought to herself. The sight that greeted her next was almost better than the door. Inside, the log cabin was huge. There were multiple floors visible from the large octagonal living room area. Exposed ceiling beams made the room feel airy and bright, even though it was already night.

The upper floors had wide glass windows with shutters instead of blinds or curtains. *Bulletproof*, she guessed. There was both a fireplace and an old-fashioned wood stove. It was breathtaking in its complex yet utterly rustic design.

"How long have you had this place?" Cat didn't even bother trying to hide her astonishment.

"Huh, oh, I started building ten years ago."

"You built this? Like with your own two hands."

"Most of it, yes."

"Wow. Some hands you got there," she said in a low voice, but not low enough.

"You have no idea," his answer surprised her, but she played it off. Maybe she was cold, and her brain was indulging in some sort of hallucination because to her ears it sounded like Tate was flirting *with her*.

She dropped her backpack and pulled off her damp jacket. Well, *his jacket.* She hung it up on a hook near the door Fifteen minutes later she was convinced it was a hallucination after all. Tate was all business, starting the generator, lighting a fire, and securing all the windows and doors.

Cat was glad to remove some of her layers. Especially her shoes. She scrunched her toes in the deep carpet that sat in front of the fire and purred in her throat. Boy oh boy, did it feel good!

The round log walls were rustic and masculine, but the soft ivory furniture and the colorful throw rug made it warm and inviting. A Native American tapestry hung on one wall.

She listened to the sound of Tate's efficient movements as he moved about the kitchen, which was just off the living room. It was a really great room. Central to the floor plan. You could see and hear just about everything from there.

She heard a popping sound and was surprised to see him come back with two stemless wine glasses and an expensive-looking bottle of red wine. He handed her one of the half full glasses.

"Here, this will warm you up."

"Thanks," she accepted and was mortified at the pitch of her voice. Suddenly she was all throaty and sexy, like some late-night DJ? *Uh oh.* She cleared her throat and took a sip.

"So, um, did you contact Rafe yet?"

"The Manor is on lockdown, but I managed to get him a message before they shut off communications."

"Hm. Did he reply?"

"No," he watched her from under his long, dark eyelashes.

Cat was struck again by the sheer beauty of the man in front of her. *She had to stop this. She was not a kid stuck in puppy love anymore. Stupid teen crushes were beyond her nowadays.* Weren't they? But no matter how many times she repeated that in her head, she couldn't stop her heart from beating a faster, and her breath from getting caught in her chest, as he sat down on the edge of the couch just next to her.

She took another long sip from her glass and

tried her best to ignore the six-foot three-inch man next to her. The wine was a dark red, the bouquet bold and the flavor rich, just the way she liked it. She smiled with her eyes closed and tilted her head back on the couch. *Nothing like a little forced vacation*, she thought as she sipped again.

Tate went stone still as he watched that sexy little smile play on Cat's oh-so-tempting lips. She was just an arm's length away, her blonde head resting on his couch as she sat sipping his wine. The Wolf in him wanted to thump his chest and howl that he was a good provider, but the twenty-first century man remained immobile.

A trace of red liquid stained her lips, and Tate had to stop himself from leaning over and licking them clean. He felt his Wolf stir within. The full moon was close. He would know that regardless of whether Cat was near. It just made it all the more difficult to control his baser instincts.

He turned away just as she opened her ice-blue eyes. The color reminded him of who she was, a Maccon. Out of his reach. *Too good for the likes of you, boy,* his father's voice echoed in his brain. He ground his teeth together and she sat up.

"What's wrong?" Cat was confused. She thought for sure they would be safe now, but there he was anxious and riled up. He stood and stalked back to the kitchen with long, angry steps.

"Are you hungry?" His question was curt, but she took no offense. She understood all to well that Werewolves were cranky when they were hungry.

"Yeah. I could eat. Want some protein bars? I have a box in my backpack."

"Nah. We can do better than that. Look around if you want, I'll be back in a bit," he headed outside without his coat and shoes. Cat wanted to call after him, but she knew he needed neither. Tate was an excellent hunter.

True to his word, he returned less than half an hour later with a pair of plump rabbits. He cleaned and skinned them both within minutes. The meat was fresh and smelled marvelous as he basted them in small bits of dried garlic, thyme, parsley, and a can of petite diced tomatoes.

He added a glass of the dark red wine they were drinking and set the cast iron Dutch oven to simmer on the stove. Cat watched him as he cooked. He moved with the skill of a practiced chef. Grace and confidence in every nuance of movement.

She grew up with Werewolves. She was one herself, but no one had ever moved with the powerful beauty of the man in front of her. She wondered what he'd say if she called him beautiful. He'd probably scoff at her, but it was the truth. Her heart beat harder in her chest.

"Hungry? It'll be done soon," he set a small egg timer to twenty minutes and nodded at her glass before refilling it.

"I didn't know you cooked," Cat was mortified at her blasé statement, but she needed to try and calm the beating inside her chest.

"Well, there's a lot about me you don't know."

"Yeah, right? Like what?"

"Like this cabin, you didn't know I built it. I also like to cook. I read non-fiction and biographies. And I weave."

"Weave? Like what? *Hair?*" Cat nearly choked on her wine as she pictured him in a beauty salon. *LOL.*

"No, you dope, *tapestries.* I met a woman, a Werewolf, when I was about twenty. She was older than she looked. A hundred and five, she said. She was attending a Lenape Pow-wow at the Salem County Fairgrounds. Anyway she, uh, taught me some things. One of them was how to weave."

"I bet she did. So, what did she look like?" Cat hurt a little to hear the whimsy in his voice, but she couldn't begrudge him the past. She had no hold on him. She bit down her jealousy and asked her question with genuine curiosity.

"She was short, for a Werewolf. Long black hair

that she kept in braids and she had dark brown eyes like mine," Tate didn't see the pain his words inflicted on Cat.

The polar opposite of me, she thought to herself. Cat wiped her face and controlled the sob that was dying to come out. *After all these years.*

Oblivious to her feelings, Tate walked past the fireplace to a closed door. He opened it and motioned her inside. Cat followed.

"Wow," she was surprised to see he was not kidding. There was a large wooden loom in the center of the small, well lit room. On it was an almost finished rug.

"The colors. These are the colors of the Maccon crest. Gold, blue, white, and black."

"Yes. The colors of the Macconwood Pack. I thought it fitting."

"It's beautiful," Cat's voice was soft and reverent. She had never seen anything like it. And to think he made it with his bare hands.

She reached out tentatively to touch the unfinished cloth, but she pulled her hand back at the last minute. *Fool.* She had no business touching his things.

"I'm sorry," she began.

"No, it's okay, go ahead. I'm glad you like it," Tate reached for her hand and gently tugged till she was touching the soft dyed wool. She smiled up at him, her heart in her eyes.

She looked at their joined hands, and she couldn't help but stare. His skin was darker than hers, but smooth and beautiful. Cat liked how they looked against each other. Light complimenting dark and vice versa.

She moved to pull away, only to find herself caught in his long fingers. When she looked up it was straight into his black eyes. He held hers for a moment before turning to stare at their joined hands.

"Your skin is pale as milk and just as soft," his voice sounded rough, but it was hypnotizing all the same.

"Yours is darker, like bronze, and your skin is smooth," she moved closer to him without meaning too. Their bodies seemed to bend towards each other. *Another step, just one more inch…*

At the exact moment that they would have touched, the kitchen timer went off.

7

"That's the food," Tate let go of Cat's hand as if it were on fire.

He couldn't believe himself! What the heck was he doing, anyway? *Leave it alone, Tate. You're no damned good for her.* He wanted to put his fist through the wall.

Maybe he could if he was amped up enough. But he doubted it. These were solid pine logs. He'd probably just damage them and his hands in the process. He was a Werewolf, not a wrecking ball. *Best check on the food and get your hormones in check, pal!*

Cat almost shouted after him. She didn't care about food right then. Heck, she just wanted to touch him. All of him. But she kept her mouth shut. She let him leave the room.

She dropped her head forward and put her hands

on her knees. Her hair hung all the way over as she felt the blood rush to her face. She took a deep breath and shook her head. When she straightened again, she exhaled slowly and tried to get her head together. *You have goals, remember? Wolf Guard. Maybe even sheriff some day. Get your mind out of the gutter and just do your damn job.*

After her little pep talk, she listened to the sounds of Tate moving around in the kitchen. There sure was nothing sexier than a man who could cook. Cat sighed. She was hopeless.

Oh well, down the hatch. She chugged the rest of her wine. If she was going to make it through the night without throwing herself at him *again,* then she supposed she could do with a little liquid courage.

However, brief the sensations of intoxication were for Werewolves, the burning of the alcohol in her throat kept her mind off the man in the other room. She could almost see her blonde Wolf in her mind's eye rolling her blue eyes at that statement.

In truth, Cat was aware that the beast inside of her had claimed Tate years ago. Maybe even before that horrible night when he had rejected her. *That was then.* She swore her Wolf spoke to her again. But that wasn't possible. It wasn't the full moon yet.

The sound of a lid slamming onto the floor and a muffled curse turned Cat's attention to the kitchen.

"Do you need an extra set of hands in there?"

"Nah, I'm good," *Yeah, I could use your hands, I've got a couple of choice places for them too. Crap! Knock it off, Tate!* He repeated it over and over in his head. The only thing was, he didn't want to.

Cat looked so good, and she smelled even better. Like honey and lemon and fresh air. He wanted to bury his nose inside every inch of her and just inhale. He wondered if she tasted as good as she smelled.

"Shit!" he grabbed the dishrag and ran towards the sink. Did he really just set it on fire? He turned the faucet on and closed his eyes when he heard her voice. *Goddammit, Tate, just cook the food!*

"Is that fire?" Cat came into the kitchen sniffing the air and almost laughed when she saw the burnt rag.

"What the heck happened in here, *master chef?*"

"Quiet or you get no food!"

Cat inhaled. It smelled delicious. Her stomach growled; she was hungry. For more than just the rabbit.

"I apologize, please, feed me and I'll be good."

"Promise?"

Cat nodded at their friendly banter, though to be honest it felt more like flirting. She went to the cupboard and set the table. She approved of his plain stoneware plates and stainless-steel forks and knives.

They were no nonsense. Strong, dependable, and sturdy. She liked that in her flatware. *And her men.*

The rabbit was cooked to perfection. Cat sighed as she finished every last morsel on her plate. The meat was tender and flavorful. The perfect balance of herbs and spices tickled her tongue.

It made her savor every bite. The Wolf inside her purred at the knowledge that her chosen mate had caught her meal and prepared it for her.

"This is really good."

"Thank you. I'm glad you like it."

"I can't cook. I mean, I can order, and I can heat up, but I can't cook."

"Yeah, but I've seen you out-shoot even the best snipers we have in the Pack."

"I guess," Cat tried to force down the blush that heated up her cheeks. She couldn't help it though. She was pleased he had noticed her skill with a gun.

"You don't have to guess. You outshot me at the last Pack competition, and you tied with Seff. And he was a Ranger."

"I didn't think anyone noticed."

"Rafe did."

"Yeah, well, my brother isn't exactly one to give out compliments."

"That's not his fault, Zev was a little hard on him.

On both of you. I'm sorry I forget sometimes that you lived with him too."

"Yeah, well, I wish I could forget."

"What do you mean?"

"Nothing," she stood up with her dish and reached for his.

"You don't have to do that."

"Please, I don't mind. You cooked, I clean, fair is fair."

"Okay then, if you insist. You know, I can teach you some kitchen basics," immediately Tate realized the innuendo behind his innocent statement.

"Can you now?" Cat's grin widened, and she raised a blonde eyebrow.

"I just meant, you know, with the food-"

"Uh huh, what else could you have meant?" The innocence in her wide blue eyes made Tate doubt himself. Perhaps he imagined the saucy flirt he had just seen behind her grin? *Hmmm. Interesting.*

"Uh, I'm just going to check the perimeter. I'll be right back."

"Yup., I'll be here," Cat took her time washing the dishes. She carefully cleaned, dried, and put away everything they had used.

His cabin was amazing. She poked inside drawers and closets while he was out. He kept it well stocked with the essentials. Everything had its own hand carved nook or space. She loved being able to explore it without him.

It gave her access to pieces of his life she'd never be privy to. Cat rubbed her chest at the sudden pang she felt. Tate hadn't exactly invited her here because he wanted to. He had no choice in the matter. It was his duty. Kinda took the joy out of exploring. Cat walked back into the living room with her head bowed a little.

Okay, so you still got a thing for Mr. Tall, Dark, and Taciturn. Whatever, girl, grow out of it.

It didn't matter what she thought or how she ended up being there. Her heart did little flip flops when she recognized the sound of his footsteps as he walked back inside the cabin and locked the engraved front door behind him.

"Cat?"

"Yeah?"

"It's all clear, but I think we should sleep in the living room tonight. Just to be sure."

Cat's mouth went dry. She watched him walk into the living room in his jeans and t-shirt and wondered what she should do next. His eyes glowed a little in the firelight.

His hair, short now, was as dark as ever. She loved the look of it. Like a moonless midnight sky. Cat wanted to get up and run her fingers through it so badly that she sat on her hands.

"Uh, bathroom?"

"You mean the outhouse?"

"Oh God, no!"

"Well, there's a pump and a bucket outside. You could, *you know,* and I'll toss it outside. Then I could get you a pail of water to rinse in-"

"Are you freaking kidding me?" Cat could deal with no shower, but a girl had to pee before she went to sleep, and she was so not peeing in a bucket with him there!

"Yeah, actually, I am," Tate's devilish grin had her heart doing flips in her chest. Still, she could kill him for teasing her like that.

"Nah, seriously though, the first thing I did when I found this spot was I dug a well. The second thing I did was install a septic tank," Tate laughed as he spoke at the look on Cat's face. *Priceless.*

"I love the outdoors, but it's the twenty-first century and bathrooms are no longer considered a luxury. It's just down the hall."

"Hey, I think it's awesome. I happen to like indoor plumbing."

He laughed out loud as she made her way down the hall with only the light from the fire to guide her. She could see just fine, but still Cat mumbled a few not nice things just loud enough for him to hear. He laughed even harder.

She brought her cinnamon toothpaste with her into the bathroom. *It's okay, Cat, you can do this. It's just one night. With Tate. Alone in the woods.* She gulped a little too loudly.

Seriously, Cat, no worries. He's certainly not going to jump your bones. He doesn't even want you here. Not really. He probably doesn't even notice you're here. She closed the door to the bathroom and exhaled. It was more spacious than she would have guessed.

It was true that Tate's taste for interior design bordered on the simple, but Cat approved whole-heartedly. Everything was neat and had a certain rustic charm that she rather liked.

If only he had given them a chance. They would have been great together. But that was all in the past. She was a different person now. Career oriented. She had no time for girlhood crushes. She smiled sadly and turned to look at herself in the large oval mirror.

It was beautiful. Like something out of a fairy tale. It took up the entire wall. The edges were rough and unfinished, but that gave it a rustic charm. She could tell that it was very old and very heavy.

She saw her ice-blue eyes looking back at her from a frame of wavy blonde hair. The colors went from honey brown to platinum silver. People always envied her her hair, but she was used to it. She had good hair. She smiled politely when people asked her where she got it done and simply shook her head. It was all her.

She continued her perusal in the mirror. *Mirror, mirror, on the wall...hmm, yeah right,* she thought to herself. She touched her cheeks and pushed back her hair. Her cheekbones were high, making her face a little angular, maybe. But her skin was clear and creamy. Her lips soft and wide. *Not too bad,* she thought to herself. *But not enough.*

It had been years since she allowed herself to dwell on how she appealed to men. That man in the other room in particular. God knew he never wasted any time thinking about her. She looked down and her mouth dropped open. Maybe she was wrong about that? Or maybe he was just a considerate host.

On the navy-blue tile countertop was a new toothbrush still in its wrapper, a hairbrush, and a new bar of Ivory soap still in its box. A fresh powder blue towel sat next to them. *For her.*

Cat reached for the bar of soap before turning around. *Hmmm, shower or bath.* She couldn't resist the latter. The old-fashioned claw-foot bathtub sat across from a spacious shower stall tiled with the same small navy-blue squares.

She turned the faucet on, and for a minute

pictured herself sharing the large bathtub with Tate. There was certainly enough room for the two of them. *Whoa, down girl...*

Tate tried not to listen to what was going on in his bathroom, but it was more difficult than he would have thought. After a few minutes, the sound of running water drowned out the other sounds that he found so distracting. Like Cat's heartbeat, or the sound of her swallowing, her soft footsteps, her breath...

Think about something else. He sat down on the rug in front of the crackling wood fire. Cat was here. In his cabin. He could hardly wrap his head around the fact.

It was difficult for Tate to open up to others. That probably had a lot to do with his parents. His mother's suicide and then his father's abandoning him with the Macconwood Pack when he was just a kid did nothing for his self-esteem.

Rafe was probably his best friend, but nowadays, before that friendship, he was Tate's Alpha. He had sworn loyalty and obedience to Rafe under the light of the full moon when he first took his position in the Wolf Guard.

It was an honor to be chosen. Back in the day, the Wolf Guard was an extension of the Alpha's power. Not like traditional bodyguards, they did not protect the Alpha from physical harm, though each of them would die for him if necessary.

The Wolf Guard's job was to protect the Pack with the same ferocity as their Alpha. They were his right hand, his advisors, his eyes and ears on the ground. Tate couldn't believe that after all Rafe had done for him, he was even considering the possibility of betraying him.

How could he think of being with Cat? She was Rafe's baby sister, for God's sake! She was totally off limits to him. But why did he get so crazy with jealousy that he wanted to scream when she had thought he was Liam back in her bathroom at the Manor?

And why did the hair on the back of his neck stand up every time she walked into a room? *Dammit*, there was no denying it. He wanted her. Always. *Focus on something else, man.* The sound of the faucet turning off got his attention. She'd be finished soon, and he had been doing what exactly the entire time she was in there?

Great, dude. You're just standing here with your dick in your hand. Blankets! I should get some blankets. Finally, a good idea. At least, that way it would look like he was doing something with his time.

He moved to the wooden chest that sat in front of the sofa and pulled out two throw blankets. They were thin, but soft. He knew they would suffice for them both. Their kind were naturally warm.

He added a few logs to the fire and refilled their wineglasses. He didn't worry that they would get drunk. That was near impossible for Werewolves. He wondered for a moment if he should douse the fire, then shook it off.

When he built the cabin, he set the chimney very high so as to camouflage the smoke and not frighten the wildlife. He also set up several ancient Native American animal traps and alarms. If anything, or anyone got too close, Tate would know.

It seemed safe enough to leave the fire lit for now. The ones hunting Cat were not as skilled at tracking as he was. Even if he wasn't a Werewolf, he would be able to tell by the simple fact that they didn't follow the SUV back to where he had left it. If they had found it, an alarm would have sounded, and he would have been notified via email or text.

Still, he had to take this threat to Cat's safety seriously. He couldn't let anything happen to her. Not ever. She was Rafe's sister. She was Pack. It was his duty.

But that's not why he felt as nervous as a high school kid. Or why he was having trouble sitting still. *Was it too hot in there?*

Beads of perspiration formed on his brow. This

was ridiculous. He was acting like a damned pup! He shook his head in disgust and ran his hand over his face.

Forget this. Tate stripped off his t-shirt, yanking it over his head and sighing with relief when it was off. He looked at the crumbled-up pile of cotton in his hand dumbly. With another disgusted grunt, he tossed the damp garment across the floor.

Alright dude, chill out. He rubbed his hands through his short black hair, making it stand on end. There was a time when it reached all the way down his back. But he cut it off years ago. He still missed the length of it, though. Especially now.

His heart was thumping steadily inside of his chest. His ears perked up. His sense of smell seemed heightened. He was ready. On edge. His Wolf closer to him than ever before on a night before the full moon. *But why?*

He stood up and stretched his arms first, then his neck. He felt like a caged animal. Pacing the room was making it worse, but he simply could not sit still. *What was taking her so long?*

His question was answered when she emerged from the bathroom a few minutes later in a cloud of steam. The combination of soap, shampoo, and Cat's own fragrance made its way to his nostrils. And he breathed it in deep. Heat shot straight through his body. Tate stifled a growl. She smelled good.

She walked down the hall toweling her hair dry as she went. Her gait was slow and questioning. Uncharacteristic for Cat. She usually knew exactly where she wanted to go. Never mind who or what was there first.

When she entered a room, she took it over. She had this amazing power to make everyone go exactly where she wanted them. She wasn't forceful or nasty, just determined and maybe a little arrogant. But in a good way. *Just like a cat.* When she entered a place, she owned it.

Tate recalled times back at the Manor when the guys were all in the game room playing Xbox and hootin' and hollerin' over something or other and Cat would get home. She'd strut right in and regardless of who was sitting on her favorite side of the couch, she'd give them a look and *bam.* It was hers. Her whole attitude was like "thanks for keeping this warm for me." It drove Rafe nuts, but not Tate. He thought she was awesome.

So why was she taking her time in his tiny hallway? *Duh me.* Tate realized then that the way he was standing there was threatening. Not to a human, maybe, but Cat was a Werewolf. And he was acting territorial.

Crap! He sat down immediately. He was the more dominant out of the two of them, but still, he didn't want her to be uneasy. His Wolf seemed to growl at his thoughtlessness. Chiding him for his bad manners.

Cat nodded her thanks. And if that didn't make Tate feel even more like a heel! It wasn't her fault he was acting like a pup looking for a brawl.

He knew he couldn't find the right words to put her at ease, so he bit his tongue and waited for her to relax. Still and silent. Until she felt safe enough to sit down.

He tried not to stare at her, but it was difficult. He watched from lowered eyelids as she moved with the quiet grace that was all Cat.

Her golden hair was damp. Water droplets clung to the ends like diamonds in the firelight. Her eyes captivated him. They were a sharp, pale blue that reminded him of the ice-covered mountains he had seen once when Rafe sent him to Alaska on Pack business. They reflected the dancing flames coming from the fireplace and Tate felt his heartrate speed up.

She smelled fresh and clean. Ivory soap and *his* shampoo. Some organic rosemary and lavender concoction he had gotten from Seff's Witch. He liked the redheaded Sherry. When she gave him the soap, she told him in what he was sure was only a half-joking voice that it kept the fleas off.

At any rate, it smelled much, much better on Cat than it did on him. He took another whiff. *Grrr.* That time he couldn't quiet the growl. She seemed to smell better with every breath he took.

His gaze wandered lower. He stopped suddenly, and his jeans felt a little too tight. She was wearing one of his white t-shirts from the pile of clean clothing he kept in the bathroom cabinet. And from what he could gather, *nothing else*. Tate's mouth went dry.

"I hope you don't mind," her voice was husky and deep. The sound of it interrupted the internal war he was having with self-control, but he gave her his attention. Allowing himself to look his fill as she spoke.

"I, uh, borrowed your shirt," Cat touched the collar and smiled. It was a shy smile. Maybe a little unsure. He'd have to fix that.

"S'okay. It looks good on you, Cat," he nodded to her glass questioning. She smiled her assent. Her teeth straight and white. Her ice-blue eyes shining in the otherwise dimly lit room.

Dazzling. She was dazzling, just like that. No make up, no fancy clothes, just her in his old cotton t-shirt. Real and clean and fresh and beautiful. Tate had never wanted anything so damn much in his entire life.

"Thanks, Tate, you know, for *everything*, not just the wine," she moved to stand.

"Forget it, really. Sit," Tate wanted to smack himself on the forehead. She wasn't a dog! *Smooth, real smooth, dude.*

Still, she sat back down. He sincerely hoped it was not out of submission, but because she felt safe. He wondered if he should ask her if she'd be more comfortable in the other room, but just then she sat on the side of the rug opposite him and curled her long legs under her body.

The hem of his t-shirt fell high on her thighs. When she sat like that, it barely covered her at all. Any thoughts that she should go inside left his head. He grabbed the bottle and filled her wine.

Her scent drifted into his nostrils with each movement she made. It was like breathing in a hearth. Warm and comforting, fresh like spring grass, tempting like the summer sun, and mysterious like the moon. He wanted to roll around in it until it touched every single inch of him.

His Wolf seemed to stand at attention. Tate didn't question the new closeness he was experiencing with his Wolf half, if anything it made him feel quicker, stronger, and more at peace. He knew it had something to do with the battle the Pack had fought in just before Christmas. Rafe had made an alliance with the young Wolf who was destined to free them all. Tate was glad to be on her side.

He knew the fight wasn't over yet to break the ancient curse that kept Werewolves torn apart until each full moon, but he could feel the effects of that battle even now. His Wolf was near him. He heard his growl clearly inside his mind's eye. *Mine.*

The voice inside his mind was strong and absolutely certain. Tate found it more and more difficult to come up with excuses why he shouldn't do what his Wolf clearly wanted him to. *Take her. Claim her. Now.*

"Is the Manor still on lock down?" Cat managed to squeak out the question through tight lips. She seemed to have caught him off guard. His black eyes stared at her blankly. As if he needed a moment to remember the meaning of the words she had spoken aloud.

"Um, yes. The Manor will be completely shut down from all outside access for at least forty-eight hours."

"Oh, *soooo*, what do we do? Just wait it out here?"

"Yeah. About that, I am sorry, Cat, I know it's not something more, you know-"

"More what? You really don't know me at all, do

you, Tate? I guess Rafe's annoying kid sister didn't garner much attention from a brooding bad boy like you, huh?"

"Bad boy? Brooding? Me?"

"Yeah, you! You were always so quiet and mysterious. I was loud and obnoxious. And always tagging along after you guys."

"It was no big deal. I mean, you're Rafe's sister."

"Yeah, well, I'm *me*, you know. Not just Rafe's sister. Anyway, I *love* this. The cabin, the woods-" *You.*

"Really? You like log cabins?"

She didn't know whether to sigh or punch him in that annoying, yet devastatingly sexy grin that he wore. One perfect eyebrow arched over eyes black as wet asphalt. His teeth were white and sharp as he grinned and ducked just out of reach of her fist.

"Yes, you dope! Why is that so hard to believe? This place is great. In college, I spent every spring break out camping, well, as long as it wasn't a full moon," Cat shifted on the rug. It was difficult keeping her bare bottom covered, but she had washed and rinsed out her panties during her bath and they were too wet to put on. She ran a hand through her hair.

She knew she rambled when she felt anxious. She just couldn't believe her ears. Did he really think she was such a priss? She was a Werewolf! Of course, she loved the outdoors! And his cabin was absolutely beautiful!

Besides, she had grown up in pretty stark conditions. Maybe Tate wasn't as familiar with her home life as she had once thought. Her father's position as Pack Alpha led many to believe that she grew up a spoiled princess.

If only they knew the truth! Tate was around so much when she was a kid, that she took for granted that he knew all about Zev and his attitude towards his kids. *Less is more. Never buy new what you can fix. Excess is evil. Idle hands, Catriona, are the Devil's playthings!*

"Yeah, what did you do about that, anyway? You never came home for a full moon run with the rest of us," Tate's voice replaced the sound of her father's in her head. The last part wasn't a question exactly. Cat wondered for a moment if that meant he had noticed her absence a bit more than he let on.

It was true, Tate often wondered why Cat had shunned her home. Could it have been for a schoolgirl crush? That seemed excessive and a bit conceited even to his ears.

"Don't you know why?" her voice held a bittersweet sadness that was almost painful to hear. He had to stop himself from interrupting her. He needed to hear what she had to say.

He guessed that he was the initial cause for her hasty departure. She must have felt embarrassed. But after a month or two she had surely moved on. So why not come home?

God, how he waited for a chance to explain himself! He wanted her to understand why he had stopped that night on the beach. But before he could, she was gone. Off to that all-girl college in North Jersey.

He would have felt awkward visiting a place like that. Back then he was just a half-Lenape kid with no education, no money, no nothing. Her father would never have approved of him as a mate for his only daughter.

Zev Maccon had been very strict with her. Heck, Tate would be too if he was her father. Cat was stunning, even as a child. And back then he was a nobody. By the time she left for college, she was a damn knockout.

Of course, her father would want to protect her. Keep her innocent and coddled. He could see how that could get annoying. But why would she stay away from her home?

"I was never really invited to come back home after I left for school," she continued in that same melancholy tone of voice.

"But why would you need an invitation?"

"Zev made it pretty clear to me that I would not be welcome. You know how he was with women, Tate."

"How do you mean?" Confusion warred with anger as he listened to her. She sounded as if it was so obvious that her own father had not welcomed her into her own home. How could he have not seen that?

"Do you remember seeing any women around the old place? How about on a run? Please, my father *hated* women. Especially females within the Pack. He never allowed them to run with the males. He never allowed them to do much besides get married and have pups," her voice grew angry.

Tate vaguely recalled the way it had been. He supposed Zev had been a throwback, but a lot of the older Wolves were. Rafe was working to change all that, make the Pack more progressive. But Tate knew that a lot of the Pack was still decades behind in women's lib. Having the Alpha's own sister work as a cop in town hadn't gone over very well at first, but Rafe along with Tate and the other guard made sure that it was accepted and even applauded in some circles.

Tate had to bite down on the surge of protective anger that welled up inside of him. He wanted to hurt Zev and anyone else who had caused her to feel that way, but before he could respond she continued.

"Anyway, then Seff started dating Sherry in the middle of my first semester and she helped me find a small group of Wolves to run with. One was a sophomore and lived on campus with me. We set up a sort of college aged mini-Pack. We ran together, supported each other, I still keep in touch with some of them."

"Wow, I had no idea," he really didn't. Especially not about Zev. Heck, Tate had admired the old Wolf. He had after all taken him in and given him a home.

"Yeah, well, I sorta missed home, but you knew my father. He was never one for messy emotions or public *or private* displays of affection," in truth Cat had only missed Rafe and his friends. *Tate especially*.

"I mean, my father was never really that doting wonderful TV sitcom kind of father, you know, and I mean to either of his children. But I missed being near my family and the ocean and the pine barrens around the Manor. That's why I'm home now."

"I'll admit, Cat, I was shocked that you disappeared like that and then you stayed away so long. I hoped for a while that I would get a chance to explain."

"Really? I mean, come on, Tate, you of all people know why I left the way I did."

"I didn't mean to run you out of your home, Catriona. I am so sorry if that's how it seemed. I was only trying to protect you."

Cat's blue eyes narrowed. Protect her? From

what? She felt the sting of his rejection as sharply in her mind as if it had happened only moments ago.

She had always pictured him making fun of that night. Of the silly little girl she used to be. and how she threw herself at him. And yet right then he sounded almost remorseful.

His expression was sincere. Her wolf recognized the truth behind it. He seemed almost earnest. Cat found herself softening, but just at the last second, she turned her eyes and stared at the firelight. She didn't want to believe the tiny glimmer of hope that planted itself in her heart.

"Look, you don't have to do this, okay? We don't have to talk about this. It's ancient history. I'm over it," she brushed a whisper of blonde hair off her shoulders and continued her study of the fire. She watched as wood burned to cinder and ash.

Maybe love was like that. *Like fire*. It burned hot and bright for a while. Then it destroyed. It left nothing but dust. Pitiful evidence that something had once raged so strongly in that place that nothing else could survive there.

Was that what she was now? Had her young heart wasted itself on someone who didn't love her back? Would she ever love again?

Tate sat up a little straighter. His Wolf recognized the command in her voice, and he wanted to challenge it. The man couldn't help himself, he leaned in closer.

She was too busy talking to recognize the change in his posture. He wasn't really concerned with the subject matter, as long as she kept ignoring him. It was something about being over *it*? What she really meant was *over him*.

He knew how to read between the lines, and yet, he got the impression she wasn't telling the entire truth. She wasn't lying exactly, but her scent and the rapid beating of her heart were not indicative of someone over *anything*.

He felt his chest swell and his ears perk up. Whatever she may have said, Cat reacted to him. He inched closer. *A matter of pride*, he told himself.

He wasn't going to act on it. No, he had enough self-control to be able to stop himself. The black Wolf inside him growled and snapped his teeth. The hunt was on.

"So, you're over it, huh? You have no residual feelings or anything from that night?"

"I mean, sure, I'm embarrassed, but you were right about everything, I was just a kid with a crush," she didn't sound as sure as she wanted to.

Cat cleared her throat and took a sip from her glass, where the dark red liquid had soothed before, now it seemed to choke her. That wasn't her fault, though. Tate had somehow managed to move closer to her without her realizing it.

"Nothing but a little crush, right? And now I have absolutely no effect on you. Correct?"

Sinewy ropes of muscle corded around his tall frame. His bare chest moved with each breath and Cat was hard pressed not to stare. Acres of bronzed skin glowed in the light from the fire. She licked her lips, how she wanted to reach out and run her fingers across his smooth torso!

She quickly looked up and found herself caught in his line of vision. Flames danced in the black depths of his eyes and she saw his midnight black Wolf peering out at her. Cat wanted to move across the room. She got the distinct impression she was being hunted.

Her Wolf purred in her mind's eye, and Cat knew then that she had already recognized him. She had chosen him long ago and now she was ready to submit. Scared that his closeness would give her away, Cat turned her head and toyed with the hem of her shirt. *Great choice, Cat, maybe next time, walk around naked?*

He brushed a strand of hair that had somehow gotten stuck to her cheek back behind her ear. The small movement had Cat wanting to lean into his feather light touch. *God*, he smelled good.

She cleared her throat and looked around the room for something else to talk about. *You can do this; you can sit here and talk to Tate. You are an adult, for God's sake!*

"So, uh, when, uh, how, oh-" it was no good, she was simply tongue-tied.

He lowered his hand and stretched it out besides hers. Not touching, but close enough that she felt his energy. It vibrated off of him in rolling waves. *Strength, power, loyalty, bravery, light,* her Wolf seemed to name everything she was getting from him. And she approved.

Focus on something else, Cat. She swallowed, still tasting the wine on her tongue. Only now it was a bit sour.

She knew better than to back away. The Wolf inside of him would truly see her as prey if she made even the smallest of movements. She had her own Wolf though. And Cat knew how to remain under the radar. Hadn't she been doing that for years?

"So, uh, what kind of wood is this?"

"What?"

"What kind of wood did you use to build? Is it local?"

"Yes, actually, it is local. I used eastern white pine for the walls and roof. I brought in some cedar and mahogany logs for the interior. Closets and doors, stuff like that. I like the different colors and stria-tions in the different typed of wood. It took me four years to build this place and I'm still considering additions...," Tate's voice was deep and rough as he talked about trees and his cabin.

The timbre of his voice seemed to initiate a response that Cat had never expected. She managed not to hear a single word that came out of his mouth. All her focus was on keeping still.

Even the tiniest movement could trigger a response that Cat wasn't sure she wanted. The way he loomed over her, the way his eyes glowed as he looked her over, all these things told her his Wolf was very much present. And like hers, he had decided.

She inhaled slowly. Tate's scent filled her nostrils. He smelled like, like *coming home*. The home she always wanted and never had.

Her eyes darted up and met his. Maybe she didn't mind being the prey. Just this once. Maybe she wanted to get caught. By him. Only him.

Every bit of his six-foot three-inch frame seemed to fill the room. He was lean, but not skinny. Far from it. Thick muscles corded his entire body. Not from any gym either. Sure, Tate worked out. Like the rest of the Pack, he had a tremendous amount of energy and the need to physically expel it was natural for Werewolves. But he preferred the outdoors.

Cat knew he kept a large garden at the Manor. And now she knew he did woodwork, carpentry, weaving, and plenty of hiking. His time outdoors made him even more real. Not like the wannabes she knew at the sheriff's department who strutted around the female officers with their spin cycle bodies and store-bought abs. She preferred his natural physique to anything they had to offer.

Tate's shoulders were wide, and his skin was smooth with only a smattering of hair. Quite unusual for Werewolves. Despite his size, he managed to look as graceful as a dancer when he moved.

He told her once upon a time, back when she was a kid who asked too many questions, that yes, he was Native American. He was proud of his Lenni Lenape blood. He was also pretty sure that he had some Cherokee too from his mother's side.

Cat was so hung up on him back then that she went to the Maccon City Public Library and read whatever she could find on the "true people" of the New Jersey, New York, Pennsylvania, and Delaware region.

The Lenni Lenape were peaceful people and hard-working. She spent many nights picturing him back then. In the days of the European settlers, when the

Lenape would have been among the first to greet the strange pale men. His black hair would have hung down his back, the way it used to.

He would have been a warrior. *Like he is now, Wolf Guard, strong, loyal, and proud.* Yes, she could envision him clearly. Bare-chested and fierce. A protector. A just man and a mighty Wolf. The perfect reason for the settlers to fear the natives.

Tate was proud of his heritage, but close-mouthed about it for the most part. She had so many questions for him, but she didn't want to seem pushy or nosy. She had no rights to him. Something she knew all too well.

Her own ancestors had come from England and Scotland. She didn't know much about them. Her father hadn't been prone to family narratives. Someday she would ask Rafe more about where they came from.

It would be good to know. In case she had children one day. It was difficult for female Werewolves to conceive, but if she did manage to carry to term, her children would want to know who they were. Where they came from.

She looked at Tate's hand. The sides of his thumb brushed lightly against hers. Shivers ran down her spine and she wondered how their children would look. His coloring mixed with hers. Blue eyes and tan skin. Black eyes and blonde hair. Either way, their children would be beautiful.

She raised her eyes and found herself caught in his gaze. Hunger radiated from him. Desire pouring out into her. She gasped aloud. Their scents mingled together, and Cat found she couldn't hold still any longer. Heck, she didn't want to.

One sign, that's all she needed. One sign that he wanted this too and she would ask him to do what she wanted him to all those years ago.

"Tate?" The question hung in the air. Thick and tangible. She waited for him to respond.

His eyes grew darker and his lids were half closed. He licked his lips and leaned towards her; his hand wrapped around her neck as he pulled her gently forward.

"Cat?" There was a question in his voice. One that she had waited years to hear from him. Anticipation bubbled up inside of her.

"Yes, Tate, yes," she answered.

His lips closed over hers.

Cat couldn't believe this was happening. One minute she was drinking wine and talking about her college days, and the next minute Tate was kissing her!

The hard length of him pressed against her through his worn denim jeans. She could feel his heart pounding through the thin cotton shirt she wore. The barrier felt wrong and unnatural. She wanted to rip it off. Closer. She needed to be closer to him.

His tongue entered her mouth with long, slow strokes. Cat opened her mouth for him. She kissed him with everything she had. Lips, tongue, teeth. She moaned aloud when he did the same. He ground his hips into hers. She felt the rush of sweet anticipation pool between her thighs.

"Oh, God, Cat, you taste so good, better than I ever imagined," he licked the salty skin on the side of her throat.

She swallowed hard. He was so good at this! Cat felt a *purr* building inside of her. Her throat rumbled with the force of it. She was almost embarrassed, but he seemed to like it. Tate licked and sucked even harder.

"I can *feel* you purring, *mmmm*. Let's see how you like it when I do this," Tate licked her lips once, then again. First the lower one, then the top. He smiled as he ducked her mouth. Always moving just out of reach when all she wanted was to cling to his lips with hers and taste him!

He moved down, *lower*. Kneeling on the floor, he positioned himself just so, a devilish grin on his face. The one that used to make her heart pound when she was still in school. God, she loved that grin!

Before she could think or remark on it, he closed his mouth on her firm breast. Right over the white cotton of her borrowed shirt, Tate found the taut bud of her nipple. He circled it with his teeth first, gently scraping the sensitized flesh. Then he used his tongue. Finally, he closed his full lips over it. Then he sucked. *Hard.*

Cat moaned and bucked underneath him. Heat soared through her body, right to her core as he nibbled on her flesh. She wanted to take off the shirt! Remove the flimsy barrier between them. As if he read her mind, Tate stood up.

She nodded at his unasked question. Grabbing his head between her hands and pulling him down hard so that his face was level with hers. She kissed him. The way she wanted to all those years ago. The way she still dreamed about if she was truly being honest with herself.

She didn't know why this was happening right then, but Cat knew she couldn't stop herself if she tried. Not now. Especially when she heard Tate groan with pleasure as she nibbled his lower lip.

He pulled back, and it was all she could do not to follow him. He wore the most serious expression she had ever seen on his face. With slow, precise movements, his hands travelled from the top of her head to her neck. His thumbs grazed her chin as he exhaled.

He took the collar of her shirt, well, *his shirt actually*, in both hands. He looked into her eyes and, in one swift movement, he tore the thing in two pieces.

She was completely exposed. As naked as the day she was born. Her body awash in the orangey glow of the flames. Cat bit her lower lip and waited.

"*Beautiful.* God, Cat, if you want me to stop you better tell me now, otherwise I don't think I'll be able to," Tate's voice was a lower octave than she had ever heard before.

He was barely in control of himself. His Wolf eyes gleaming out at her from time to time. She liked knowing she had that effect on him. It made her feel powerful and sexy too. She slowly opened her thighs for his perusal and tugged him by the waistband of his jeans.

"Tate, I swear to God, if you stop now, I'll kill you," she gripped his hair as he leaned down and nipped at his neck playfully.

On a more serious note, her hands travelled down his bare back until she reached the delicious curve of his firm buttocks. Once there, she squeezed. His powerful frame trembled at her touch. He was vulnerable too. And that only made Cat want him more.

He pushed himself off her, and she felt cold immediately. Had she pushed him too far? Was he rejecting her? Did he think she was too wanton? Cat didn't know if she could go through that again and come out whole. Her eyes widened.

"Cat, look at me. I want you to watch what it is you do to me, what I've been trying to hide from you for years," he stood up slowly.

She watched as he easily unwound his body from the floor. His body was a finely honed instrument.

Lethal and beautiful at the same time. She loved looking at him. His hands went to the button of his fly and he proceeded to open his jeans with devastating patience.

Cat thought she'd burst from watching him. He moved so slowly and deliberately. He was perfect. All his perfection outlined in the light of the fire.

Every inch of his muscular body seemed amplified in the play of shadow and light. He looked like that ancient warrior she had so often imagined. Fierce, powerful, strong. And she wanted him so damn badly.

For too long she felt empty inside. Sure, she had her brother, but Cat's family life left a lot to be desired. She had focused on her career after Tate had turned her down on prom night. She wasn't sorry exactly; she did love her job. But something or *someone* was missing from her life. She wondered if she wasn't looking at him right then.

Nudity was not as difficult for Wolves as for normals. But when Cat looked at Tate fully aroused and unclothed for the first time, she gasped. Her eyes wavered from his coal-black eyes back down to where his thick erection sprung from his hard, muscled body.

He was so big, so hard, and so beautiful she wanted to lick him from tip to shaft. Used to taking what she wanted, Cat rose to her knees in front of him. She took his enormous length in her hands and instinctively she pumped him once, then twice.

Tate sucked in a breath of air as she circled him with her soft as milk hands. With her eyes never leaving his face, she put the tip of his swollen cock into her warm mouth and sucked.

Tate hissed out a sharp breath as she took him inside of her perfect mouth. The moist heat there was almost enough to make him explode right then. *Get control of yourself.*

Tate rested his hands on her shoulders as she did things to him with her mouth that he had never experienced. He was no virgin, but *dammit* if Cat didn't make him feel like one.

He growled and moved his hands to that golden head of hers that drove him wild. He had dreamt of getting his hands on her hair for so long, he just never thought it would be like this.

"Oh *God*, Cat!" He bit back a groan and dropped his head back as she continued her tantalizing exploration.

Perfection. The woman is perfection. Naturally beautiful and smart. And she was devouring every inch of him with her hands, lips, tongue, and teeth. Tate sucked in a breath through tight lips. *Hot damn.*

Cat's hands travelled further down his body. He tensed. He hadn't felt that way since he was a teenager. Heck, maybe he never felt that way. Not with anyone else. Ever.

Cat. His Cat. Finally....

With her long nails, she traced the muscles that corded his thighs and calves. She cupped his buttocks and gave them a strong squeeze before gripping his hips and taking him deeper in her throat.

Oh, damn...Hold it, Tate, not yet...

Finally, as if she anticipated just where he needed her, she traced the line of his scrotum and cupped him with one hand while she gripped the bottom of his shaft with the other. She moved her hot, wet mouth to the very tip and sucked. Hard.

Tate growled. He damn near lost it himself right then.

"No more, no more. Come here, Catriona, I need you," he lifted her up off the floor with both his hands easily.

She went willingly. Her blue eyes were hazy and glazed over with pleasure. And he hadn't even started yet.

He swung her body up by her firm ass and she immediately circled his hips with her long legs. Tate grunted and let the head of his cock rest just inside of her. She was tight and so very hot. He wanted to slam into her. But not yet. *Slowly*. He needed to go slowly.

She bucked impatiently. And he grinned. She

wanted him. Maybe even half as much as he wanted to be nestled deep inside of her.

He wanted to lose himself in the depths of her body, to ease the formidable ache that was growing inside of him. He had never experienced anything like it before. *But not yet*. No matter how loudly his Wolf roared. *Claim her. Mark her. Mine.*

"Not yet, Catriona, not just yet. First things first."

He smiled and lowered his head to her lips. Sucking and biting, then licking to soothe. What was it Anthony Keidis sang on one of his favorite *Red Hot Chili Pepper* albums of all time? "*Pleasure spiked with pain.*" That's what this was. *Grrr... Delicious.*

He covered her breast with one large hand, and he rolled her taut nipple between his fingers. His entire body seemed to pulsate with longing. All he wanted to do was take her. Long and hard. Still, he resisted pushing into her for all he was worth.

Instead, he backed her against the hard log cabin wall and rested her buttocks on one particularly fat curve that he had carved out as a shelf. With one flick of his wrist, he knocked down the few knick-knacks he had collected. A pond rock, a seashell, an empty frame he had carved from a piece of driftwood.

None of it as important as the woman in his arms.

He unlocked his mouth from hers and bent his

dark head to minister to her neck. She gripped the wall for support. Tate used that to his advantage. He took both her firm breasts in his hands and tugged on her nipples until she cried out in pleasure.

He watched with pride as she tossed her head from side to side and grabbed his wide shoulder with one hand. He sank to his knees and put one plump nipple in his mouth. He suckled her greedily. And damn him if she didn't taste like the sweetest thing he had ever experienced!

Like spicy heat and pure desire, blinding sunshine and spring rain. She was temptation itself. Personified lust. Her tight body as succulent as the ripest peach. Tate's eyes rolled back as he licked and sucked every inch of her perfect breasts.

Slowly, ever so slowly. He worked his way down her sculpted abs. He fit both hands around her small waist. She was fit and gorgeous. All woman. All his.

He took his time at her belly button, licking and kissing her, loving the way she gasped with her wide mouth open and her teeth biting her bottom lip. *Mmm...later.*

Tate made a meal out of her. Using both of his hands, he pushed her knees gently apart. When he finally made his way to the plump bud at the center of her long smooth thighs, Cat began to thrash about nervously. Like a caged animal.

"Shhh, baby, I got you. I got you now," Tate whispered as he leaned in closer. He let his hot breath touch her just where he wanted to put his tongue. To let her know just what he intended to do.

"Tate?" Her voice sounded breathless. Her question nervous.

She dug her strong nails into the muscles on his shoulders. But he didn't mind. His upper body was coated in a thin sheen of sweat, but she held on as his hands gripped her upper thighs.

He spread her legs apart even further and looked at her. She was gorgeous. Tate always thought of a woman's body as some sort of magical mystery. But here he was, looking at the very center of Cat. And loving every inch of her.

He reached out to part her, *there*. Her strangled cry was nearly his undoing. He looked at her reverently. He felt something stir inside of him, his Wolf, down to whatever magic or mysticism bound them together. Something profound. *Mine.*

"Oh, baby. You're beautiful. Fucking beautiful. And now, you are finally mine," he whispered the last as he moved his dark head closer to her. His long tongue snaked out of his mouth and he tasted her. His entire being was completely focused on her in that moment.

Cat moaned aloud. The feelings coursing through

her were unfamiliar and yet instinctually she circled his head with her legs and pumped her hips. God, he was making her burn in places she didn't even know she had.

Would he believe she had never allowed anyone such privilege with her body? Would he think she was wanton for throwing her head back even as she opened her legs and screamed his name?

Cat asked herself these questions only briefly. No. Tate was a Wolf like she was. He knew she didn't lie. And if he didn't know it yet, he would soon find out if they went any further that Cat was as untouched as she was the day she dropped her dress at the beach.

How could she allow anyone else to do this to her? Not when her heart, mind, soul and Wolf belonged to the man on his knees. And how she wanted him to stay there! *Yes, please, oh, oh yesssss.*

Her screams were delightful to his ears. His fingers held her thighs tightly. Maybe too tightly. He worried he might bruise her milky white skin, but the Wolf inside him howled his pleasure. *Mark her. She is mine.* Pure unadulterated instinct drove Tate. He lifted his head, his fangs a little longer than usual, and he bit down on her inner thigh.

Blood filled his mouth. *The blood of his mate.* And he swallowed. Both their scents grew stronger then. A new smell. Part him, part her. He moved frantically.

Sucking, licking, taking, consuming. His Wolf had claimed her. As for the man, well, he sure as hell wanted her. *Mine.*

Only when she cried out and shuddered beneath his tongue did he lift his head. Despite her frantic attempts to tug him up. His lips curled into a half-smile, half-snarl as he rose to his feet.

Tall, naked, and proud. He looked every inch the warrior. And she wanted him to claim her so badly. She purred and bucked. Her teeth snapping as she lifted a hand to his chest and his stomach.

His black eyes glowed. His Wolf as close as he had ever felt him before. The rush was exhilarating and frightening all at once. An incredible feeling.

Tate fit his swollen head to her center. His need to take her stronger than his need to breathe. *One last time, ask her one last time.*

"Cat? Yes or no?" He could hardly make out the words. His voice an almost unrecognizable grumble. Low and deep. More Wolf than human.

"Tate...now, I need you now," she answered him softly. Her Wolf as in control as his was, it would seem.

Her entire body felt as if it was on fire. She had just shattered beneath his mouth. But this, this would be something else entirely. She needed him. Wanted him. *Now. Oh God, now.*

He pushed inside of her. He raised his eyes to meet her wide ones. She was tight, so tight. Hot, too. And very, very wet. *Virgin?* His head begged the question, but his Wolf didn't need him to voice it. He knew she was meant for him and him alone.

Pride made him move faster than he intended too. She cried out his name. It was a breathtaking combination of pleasure and pain. *A beautiful sound*, he thought. Just before he lost the ability to think at all.

His first few thrusts were hard and slow. He plunged himself all the way inside of her agonizingly tight body only to come all the way out again. Slowly at first. *Sweet torture.* Then a steady pace. *Oh, God.* Finally, he moved with frantic urgency. *Grrrr...Mine.*

White hot light erupted behind his eyelids. It encircled her entire body as both he and Cat came together in chorus of growls and cries.

Tate couldn't think straight. He didn't even want to try. His whole body, both his beings, seemed to rejoice in the knowledge that he had just experienced true ecstasy.

Their sweat soaked bodies were prone in an exhausted heap on top of the thin blankets that he had put down for them earlier. Just on top of the rug by the softly glowing fireplace.

He added another log to the dying flames. Then

he came back to Cat's side and placed a soft kiss on her lips. She brushed his short hair away from his forehead. Her pink lips tilted into a smile that he reciprocated.

He felt that smile all the way to his toes. She was beautiful like that. Stunning. A soft glow seemed to emanate from her entire body. Unlike the usual Wolf magic that seemed to light up every Werewolf he knew.

It was as if their lovemaking had altered her chemical make-up. He didn't think he'd ever grow tired of looking at her like that. Gorgeously rumpled and nude. In his home.

He couldn't put a word to the emotion he felt welling up inside of him. *Happiness?* Was this true happiness? He damn well thought so.

"Cat?"

"Mm?"

"Are you okay?"

"Uh, huh."

"Are you, uh, *happy?*"

"Happy? Yes, Tate, I'm happy. Hmm, I've never been happier," her smile was groggy and contented. She snuggled closer to him.

Mmmm. He took a deep breath. He was so loving the erotic combination of his and her scents as they encircled them both.

"I think, -"

"Don't Tate, please don't overthink this, let's just savor the moment."

Tate's eyes narrowed. It sounded to him like maybe Cat thought this was a onetime thing between them. Doubts clawed their way into his mind. His Wolf bared his sharp fangs at them.

No. It is done. Tate tried to regain control of the turn his thoughts were taking. And of his Wolf too. If and when Cat did have second thoughts, he'd deal with that then. But not before. Besides, it may very well be too late. Now was probably a bad time to tell her he had marked her with that bite on her thigh.

He gripped her waist with a possessive hand and swept it up and down the length of her body. His Wolf seemed to chant her name over and over again. *Catriona, Catriona, Cat..my Cat...*

Cat listened to the wind as it whistled through the trees surrounding the cabin. Her supernatural hearing picked up on things like that all the time. It eased her overactive mind.

Was it her, or was Tate brooding? She hoped he wasn't regretting what they had just done together. It was better than anything she had ever imagined. She never imagined she would feel quite like this. Like she wasn't alone anymore. Like she had another half.

It was an intense feeling. A little scary too. But so very good. *Prrrrrr.*

She pictured the surrounding woods. How she loved living in New Jersey! It had everything. Mountains, lakes, cities, beaches, hiking trails, state parks, quaint suburbs, and awesome restaurants. Seriously, the food was amazing.

Cat loved being able to experience all the seasons too. There was just so much to see. She never grew tired of exploring the region. And if she did, New York City was a car ride away.

She loved her job and hoped to elevate herself in the Sheriff's department. Loads of opportunity for women there! She had no intention of leaving. She wondered what Tate would think of that. A lot of Wolves liked their women to stay at home.

Cat saw nothing wrong with that. It just wasn't for her. Besides, she felt it should be up to the woman. Either way she wouldn't want to leave Macconwood Manor. With New Jersey being a supernatural hub, she needed to stay close to Rafe.

Who knew, maybe he would see her new relationship with Tate as more reason to make her a Guard? Lately there was loads of paranormal activity and it all seemed to be centered in the Garden State. Never a dull moment. That was for sure.

She stretched out her long legs. *Possibilities.* Her

head was swimming with them. Just outside the large windows it was dark and cold outside, but inside, with Tate next to her and the low fire still glowing, she was warm and feeling better than she ever had before.

He ran a long lean hand up her thigh, around the slight curve of her buttocks to rest on her hip. *Just right.* His touch was perfect. As if he knew just how she liked it. She leaned into his caress, purring deep in her throat as she did. He really had great hands.

"You're still the only Wolf I know who purrs," she heard the smile in his voice without opening her eyes, "You know something? I don't think I ever heard you howl before. Do you yowl like a cat the way you purr like one?"

"*Prrrrrrr.* My name is Cat, but I am all Wolf. And I only purr when I am really happy," she closed her eyes as his hands found new, more interesting places to touch and rub.

"I wonder, if I do this, will you purr louder?"

Cat watched his fingers move down her flat belly to the soft blonde curls beneath. She sucked in a sharp breath. She was still a little tender from before. But it was so sweet. She couldn't resist parting for him.

She wondered if he would be gentle this time. Cat wasn't sure if she even wanted that. Not when the

Wolf inside of her was begging him to take her. Hard and heavy.

Slow, go slow. Tate dipped his finger into her moist center. He couldn't help his predatory smile when she sucked in another breath and parted her lips.

He added another and shifted her, ever so gently, so that she was flat on her back. He moved with slow accuracy. Pinning her to the floor while hovering slightly over her. Electricity seemed to fill the space between them, and Tate leaned into the delicious sizzle as he nudged her knees apart with his own.

He moved between her legs. Tate's chest pressed down into her belly as he licked a trail from her neck to her firm breasts. The pink buds tightened under his ministrations and pride filled him as she whimpered her delight.

He lifted her hands to his head, and she gripped his hair and pushed him down. Lower. He kissed and nibbled his way down her body. Taking great pains to lick and taste every inch of her until he reached her inner thighs.

Cat nearly jumped out of her skin when his tongue found the swollen nub at her center that was begging for his attention. She was taut and ready for him. Her legs spread wider of their own volition. She tightened her grip on his short hair in her hands and pulled.

He added another finger, and she whimpered again. Together with his tongue and fingers, Tate licked and sucked and delved into her. He savored the honey taste that seemed to get stronger with each lick.

She was the epitome of perfection. *Breathtaking.* He flashed his eyes up and saw her head thrown back, mouth open, and damn him if he didn't get harder.

He knew instinctively that he was the only person who ever gave her such intense pleasure. It made him want to howl with pride. He felt as if his whole purpose was to make her *feel.*

Cat had always seemed out of his reach. That shining pinnacle that he could never be worthy of. But here she was. With him. In his cabin. His space. That he made with his own hands. And though he knew she could protect herself, the Werewolf he was swore to keep her safe. To keep *her. Mine.*

Cat's moans grew louder. Tate felt himself grow harder and longer. As if that were even possible. But it was true. He needed to be inside of her! Now!

He quickly withdrew his hand and tongue. He wanted, no, he *needed* her. *God, how he needed.* He leaned down and kissed her lips. Letting her taste the honey sweetness that was all Cat. Then he entered her.

She was hot and sweet. *Honey.* And all his.

He tightened his arms around her as they moved together. In unison. As if they were made for each other.

He watched her eyes dilate with each shift of their hips. They moved together, faster and faster. She was perfectly in time with him. Soft moans and throaty growls came from both, and Tate felt as though his heart would pound right out of his chest.

Cat's ice-blue eyes met his. He saw the Wolf behind them, and he felt his rise to greet her. *Mine.*

Her beautiful face tilted backwards, and Tate wanted to howl with the gift that was her bare throat. He closed his mouth over it. Gently, ever so gently. Then he bit down hard enough to mark her, once again, but softly enough that she would take pleasure from it.

"You're mine now," he growled in a gruff voice. His eyes glowed as his Wolf peeked through and Tate licked the side of her neck and pumped harder.

10

"Tell me something about your childhood, something good," Cat smiled and ran her hand over Tate's smooth chest.

His skin was all bronzed and muscled. Hard and smooth at the same time. A feast for her hands and eyes. She waited patiently as he considered her question.

"I cannot remember much of my childhood. My father and mother were young when they had me. Still in their teens. They were poor and pretty much alone in the world. They were never happy. I can remember short bursts of time before my mother killed herself. Like flashbacks from a movie of my life with her. Back then she used to sing. Old native songs of magical wars and times when supernatural crea-tures walked the Earth without hiding. My father used to call her crazy. That time was forgotten before men learned to write stories. Those songs were lost to many. He called her too young to possibly know them. But I always felt like she was singing the truth."

"I'm sorry, Tate, for your loss. I didn't mean to bring up something sad. I understand, you know, my mom's gone too."

"It's okay. I'm not a child anymore. I like those memories. I almost forgot about them. Anyway, what about you? Tell me something good from your childhood," Tate's voice was deep and husky. Cat loved the way it made her vibrate all the way down to her toes.

Hmmm...her childhood? Yuck. Not her favorite thing to talk about. It wasn't that she had such an awful childhood. She was clothed, fed, and she *did* have a father. Technically. But she didn't want to talk about Zev. Or his warped idea about parenthood.

Tate already had an idea of what her life had been like. She wanted to just leave it at that for now. Besides, she didn't want to spoil the moment. Cat wasn't certain he meant this to be a permanent thing. Although her Wolf had already considered herself mated and marked. Cat wasn't so quick to rush in with her heart in her hands. *Not just yet, anyway.*

Let's see, a memory. Hmmm. She brightened as she recalled one particularly fond memory from when she was a little girl. She felt her smile deepen and knew she must look like a kid, but she didn't mind. This was a good one. Tate would enjoy it! She was certain of that.

After all, Cat had observed Tate for years. Chasing after her brother and his buddies, Tate had been an object of fascination for her since she was in pigtails. She knew him better than she knew herself. At least, that's how she felt.

Cat rolled onto her belly, giving him an unobstructed view of her toned legs and sculpted backside. What could she say, she had a great ass! That much she knew for sure. She appreciated the little caress he gave it as he snuggled closer to listen to her tale.

"Once, a few years before my Change, I had this great babysitter! It was the night of the full moon, and my father and Rafe were out on a run. My dad got me this babysitter because he said I was too young to stay alone. I was so mad! I mean, what ten-year-old girl wouldn't be?"

"Especially you," he smiled, and Cat nearly lost her place. He could knock the breath out of her with that smile. His dark eyes full of laughter and something else. Something she didn't dare put a name to. *Not yet*.

"Uh, anyway, the old woman who came over

turned out to be my grandmother. She was a normal, but her father was a Werewolf and so was her daughter, my mother. She had this accent, you know? Like some people from North Jersey do? She said 'watuh' for water, and 'mirruh' for mirror."

"Yes, I know what you mean. I conduct Pack business for Rafe in Hoboken and Jersey City quite often. There's something about that Hudson County accent that I find intriguing," she narrowed her eyes, not sure if he was making fun or not.

"No, seriously. There's this Wolf family that lives on Hudson Street. They have a bunch of kids," Cat raised her eyebrows at Tate's description, "What? I like kids. Anyway, you know Rafe started this program where he and his Guard spend time with some families with pups. So sometimes I visit. They all speak with that kind of accent. It's cute."

"I didn't realize you were so active in the Pack family outreach program."

"Yeah, well, it's cool. And I was the one who investigated when their oldest didn't make it after his first Change. I want to make sure the younger ones do; the program gives me the ability to contact them and form a relationship with the kids that will hopefully get them to open up to me in the future. I'm sorry I distracted you, please continue," the change in his tone was subtle, but loaded with feeling. Cat could feel the depth of his sincerity down to her toes.

It warmed her to know that this big bad Wolf Guard was deeply involved with the outreach program designed to help the Pack's young. She wondered if he knew she had helped Rafe with the initial idea for the program? That was another thing they had in common. After all, the children were the future of their Pack.

It only made sense. Zev had ignored them, but Rafe refused to make the same mistake. An idea began to take hold in her mind, but she pushed it away for now. Now all she wanted was to be near Tate. And to share this intimacy, she had never really had with anyone else before. She kissed him on his shoulder. His salty skin tasted good. Almost too good.

"I'm sorry. I know your job is difficult sometimes."

"Yours is too. Now, go on, finish your story, I really want to know what your grandmother told you. Was it a family secret or something, a fairytale maybe?"

She hesitated at first, not sure if he was really interested or not. Tate kissed her on her head and insisted again. So she continued. Confident he did want to hear.

"She told me the tale of the first of Wolves who founded the Macconwood Pack. They travelled over from the British Isles hundreds of years ago. Their names were Alice and Owen. She had this old cloth with her, like a tapestry I guess. It was thin and faded, and she kept it wrapped up in tissue paper that smelled like lavender. On it were two Wolves on one side and a man and woman on the other holding hands. It was beautiful. I didn't understand what it said, but she explained that it said their names. It said A-i-l-i-s and E-o-g-h-a-n, old Celtic spellings for their names."

"I have heard Rafe mention them, but I do not know their story. Will you tell it to me, Catriona?" Tate's voice was deep, and it rang with sincerity.

As a cop, that much would have been obvious to her. As a Werewolf, it was more than that. His desire to learn more and to hear her tell it inspired confidence in her. He wasn't feigning interest, he really wanted to know. Cat kissed him once on the lips and continued.

"Okay. Well, what I remember is that Eoghan was a young dominant Wolf. The son of the Alpha, strong and brave, destined to take over his Pack. He was betrothed to a very beautiful female Wolf. The daughter of a high standing Wolf from a neighboring Pack. Her name was Ailis."

"She was tall and willowy, with hair like golden thread. Unlike most She-Wolves who were thin and muscular, Ailis was all things feminine, which were to the tastes of the time. She was soft and curvy with a voluptuous figure. Pink lips, noble cheekbones, wide eyes the color of bluebells. But most of all she was honest, obedient, and loyal. The perfect bride," Cat was never one for long speeches. She ducked her eyes as she spoke, but Tate reached out and tucked a stray hair behind her ear, at the same time lifting her chin to look at him.

"You know, I rather like thin and muscular. And Cat, there is absolutely nothing un-feminine about you," she felt the blush heat her cheeks and ducked her face. But Tate was having none of that. He lifted her face by the chin with a gentle but firm grip.

"You are beautiful. Got it?"

"Uh huh," she licked her lips. If he kept looking at her like that, she'd never finish her story.

"What happened next?"

"Well, on their wedding night Eoghan's younger brother, Lyall, became jealous of all of his brother's good fortune. Like insanely jealous. So Lyall bargained with a dark Witch and had his brother cursed. While Eoghan struggled through a terrible fever dream, his younger brother stole his bride on their wedding day."

"Now this is where it gets tricky. You see, no one knows for sure how Eoghan fought through the dark Witch's trap, but he managed to break free of the fever dream and upon finding Ailis gone, he went after his brother and his bride."

"I'd kill him. Brother or not," Tate growled the words, and she watched as his Wolf shined from his eyes. *God,* he was amazing. Powerful and beautiful. She wondered if he meant that for her sake. Neither of them said anything about love or commitment, but Cat was Wolf and she knew what those bites had meant. She only wondered if the man felt the same way as his Wolf. *Marked. Mine.*

"The couple had not consummated their marriage. In fact, they spent precious little time alone, as was the custom back then. Lyall's plan was to mark Ailis and take her away from Eoghan. As far as he knew, the couple had no matebond. He figured he was safe under the dark Witch's protection and without the matebond Eoghan would never find his bride."

"I've heard of that. *Matebonding.* Does it even happen anymore?"

"I don't know. I think so. We should ask Rafe."

"Well, his might be different since his wife is a normal. But anyway, it sounds beautiful, right? Having a perfect communion with another? Like pieces of your soul and theirs have mixed into some-thing else, something new," Tate lifted her hair to his face and breathed it in. Cat wondered if that was longing in his voice. Whatever it was, it made her heart pound almost as much as his words did.

Matebonds were something of a myth to modern Werewolves. They seemed to happen less and less often. But, oh boy, you better watch out when they did! They were the stuff of legends. Cat knew that if Tate and she were to be together, they would mate-bond. Without a doubt.

"Well, to Lyall's surprise, Eoghan managed to catch their trail. Lyall had her locked in a dungeon in the Witch's dark fortress. Now this place was built to stop all manner of man from entering. A cop's worst nightmare, you know. High walls, few windows, one door heavily manned. And it was three weeks till the full moon."

"Lyall figured he was safe. As he made his way to Alilis' chamber, he pulled open the curtain from the window and shoved her beautiful face through the metal bars, so she could see her husband as he paced below them, helpless and impotent. He had his men hold her down as he yelled down to his brother what-ever the obscenities there were at the time. Lyall told Eoghan how he planned to rape her right there within hearing. And he promised to name their first-born after Eoghan."

"As Lyall neared her, the strangest thing happened. Ailis snarled and snapped her teeth. She threw her head back and again from side to side. As if she were possessed or having some kind of unholy fit. You know people were very superstitious back then. Even the supernaturals. So, the guards backed away, and she crouched down on the cold floor on all fours. Ailis threw her golden head back and in her human body, she howled. A cry so loud and so fierce that the other men in the room fell to their knees and covered their ears. She persisted on and on despite Lyall's shouts for his guards to restrain her. Within minutes Eoghan charged up the hall, but he wasn't just Eoghan. He was his Wolf. Fully formed. Huge with black fur and one white forepaw."

"His ice-blue eyes found his brother half naked, and on the floor, blood coming from his ears. Of course, that didn't stop him from ripping out Lyall's throat. Ailis stopped howling and stood with her hand on her Wolf-husband's back. Together they left the fortress, but not before setting it on fire. With Lyall's body inside, of course. His father, the Pack Alpha, forgave Eoghan his crime, but he was forced to make a home across the ocean. And so, he did. In the Pine Barrens of New Jersey."

"Wow," Tate's one-word response was truly appropriate.

"Yeah, isn't it great? It's one of my favorite childhood memories."

"And this is your ancestor?"

"Well, yeah, I guess. But even if they weren't, isn't the story awesome?"

"Heck yeah! Bloody and romantic! My favorite," but Tate wasn't thinking of forgotten tales or faded memories. He was looking at the woman beside him. *Mine*.

11

After eating some surprisingly awesome peanut butter and strawberry jelly crackers made by Cat herself, she stretched out on the soft carpet in front of the fire. Every dream she had ever had from the time she was in junior high culminated that night. Tate was, in a word, amazing.

He didn't mention love or commitment, but she felt something, some powerful emotion, radiating from him in waves like rays from the sun. She didn't care what it was, as long as it was something.

She didn't know if that made her stupid or weak. Cat just knew that she finally had what she had always wanted. *Tate.* And if she was really being honest with herself, she'd admit it. She loved him, and her Wolf had accepted him as mate. Heck, she demanded he be her one and only mate.

The only problem was Tate. He didn't say one word about it. Maybe it was just a matter of formalities, or maybe he didn't want commitment. She'd deal with that when the time came. *Enjoy this time however long it lasts*, she told herself.

For her, it could only ever be Tate. She felt energy coursing through her veins in a sort of frenzied contentment at being near him. She couldn't imagine herself feeling that way with anyone else.

A crash sounded outside, and Tate vaulted up from his place beside her, a growl deep in his throat. Cat was right behind him, fully awake and alert. He stretched his hand out in front of her. An act of protection. It should have antagonized her feminist nature.

But she didn't feel upset or angry. She rather liked the idea that he thought of her as his to protect. Besides, if she was honest, she thought of him the same way. It was a Werewolf thing.

"Wait here," his brisk command, however, did rub her the wrong way.

She yanked on his shirt and her still damp pair of leggings. As he buttoned up his jeans and went for his weapon. She walked over to the backpack she had hauled through the woods and pulled out her semi-automatic.

"Not on your life," was her response.

His black eyes glowed as he turned to her, then he tilted his head. His Wolf was speaking to him in a way he had never communicated before. Tate felt his connection to his Wolf rush through him as strongly as it did on any full moon. His heart pounded through his Wolf's words. *She is strong. She is a warrior. Protect her, but do not hinder.*

He nodded gruffly. Struggling slightly with the loss of that connection, but also reeling from the fact that it had happened at all. What did this mean? He didn't know, had no words for it, but he was feeling anxious now. He hardly noticed as Cat nodded back.

She moved behind him, and her scent filled his nostrils. Refocusing him. *Mine. Protect. Honor.* Together they quietly exited the cabin through the side door. They stepped barefooted onto the snow-laden floor. It must have started hours ago. A few inches had already accumulated on the frozen ground.

It had been too cold most of the winter for snow. But the last few weeks the temperature had evened out. Ever since Rafe had them fight alongside the teenage Werewolf against the Scarred Sisters, a coven of Dark Witches who had been dealing with demons and in doing so they had a severe effect on the weather. But the snow was finally here. And in full force. Heavy flakes fell from the air and the entire forest was whited out.

Cat imagined for a second that she was trapped inside a snow globe. The entire world seemed to be covered in white. The pale glow of the moonlight made it even brighter than usual for that time of night. But her Wolf eyes needed little light to see. She crouched beside Tate as he examined a broken branch.

"Someone was here. Watching us through the window. This branch has been cut," his voice was tense.

Cat knew what this meant. They were here, and they did this deliberately. *Bastards!* They thought they could frighten them with a stick. *They didn't know them.*

She turned around to guard his rear. Back to back, they squatted behind a large oak tree as Tate closed his eyes. He needed to focus so that his senses could tell him where danger lurked.

It took longer than usual. His focus was not as clear as it should be. That brief communion with his Wolf left him a little raw. And he was too concerned with Cat's well-being. That was not something he was used to, or that he necessarily liked. Doubts and old fears crept into his mind. *Not good enough. A nobody.*

He felt the pressure from her body as she leaned into him. It was as if she knew what he was thinking. Whatever the reason, the heaviness of her body felt good. His Wolf was reassured, and Tate let his senses take over.

Slowly he felt peace and a supernatural hum of power settle over him. He drew strength from his Pack bonds as he reached out with his mind.

Suddenly he opened his eyes.

"Cat, there are at least three of them. I can smell them. They are Wolves, males, but not Pack. You need to get back to the cabin. There is a room, a root cellar really, underneath the floorboards of the kitchen. Go and lock yourself in."

"No. I want to stay with you."

"Look, I can't do my job if I am worried about you. And I can't help but worry about you, Cat. Please."

It was the please that silenced her. She nodded her head and Tate left her with a gruff shake of his head. He thought she'd be safest in the cabin. But Cat had no intention of going back there. She needed to prove to him she could be an asset. She could be a Wolf Guard.

Lost in her own reverie, Cat didn't catch the scent

before it was too late. He came out of nowhere. His greasy hand cupped over her mouth and the putrid stink of his foul breath entered her nostrils as he hissed in her ear.

"I knew you'd be easy to catch, bitch. Skoll will be so happy when I bring you to him."

Tate roared in the distance and she heard the sounds of his fight from where she stood. She thought of every maneuver she knew, but it was useless. The grip he had her in was too tight. She'd never be able to get loose.

"I'm going to ask for some time with you before the boss slits that pretty throat! What do you say, sugar, a little thrill before you die? *Ha ha ha*," he squeezed her ass as he wrapped her legs and wrists in shackles and heavy chains.

Cat had to work hard not to puke all over him. She spat right in his face when he squeezed her left breast with his greasy hand. She didn't even flinch when he backhanded her.

"Don't touch me, you bastard!"

"Goddamn, bitch, you'll pay, but first, we see Skoll," he sat down and revved the engine of an ATV that was hidden nearby. Cat bit back a whimper. He was going to take her away!

She'd need to bide her time. She allowed herself to be pulled down behind him. She could never run away with the shackles and chains. They were just too heavy, and he had locked them to the ATV. But she had to do something! Without him seeing, she ripped the hem of her shirt and dropped it on the floor. The white blended in so her captor didn't notice it. But Tate would! She'd lead him right to them.

Tate circled the pair of Wolves who had invaded his property with barely contained rage. Werewolves were highly territorial, and his Wolf was growling for their deaths. They trespassed on what was his and he'd make them pay.

The sound of a motor made him pause. His heart pounded heavily in his chest. *Danger. Cat. She was in danger!* All his restraint left in that single moment.

There was no time for subtlety or to think about tactics. He called on all his inner strength and with a mighty roar from his lips, he attacked. The younger man was easy to take down. He was careless and cocky.

A roundhouse kick. A few punches to his stomach, then his face. The third punch broke his nose. Blood spurted everywhere and as the young Wolf looked at it on his hands, his eyes rolled into the top of his head and *boom*. He crashed to the ground.

The second Wolf was not so easy. He had watched Tate defeat his companion from the sidelines. He understood Tate's urgency, and he used it against him.

"So, you wanna play with me now, Injun Joe? Let's go! In my day, we killed fuckers like you for breakfast and pushed the rest of you into places none of us wanted! I was there, I fought alongside Custer! You won't get the best of me," Tate listened to the insults and let them slide right off him. He meant to make Tate careless. To waste his time. But Tate knew better.

"You're all talk, son, and I don't have time right now," Tate advanced and with an old boxing one, two punch the old Wolf with the bad attitude went down.

Tate didn't bother tying either of them up. *Cat.* He needed to find Cat. He searched near the house for a trace of her. Tate bit back a string of curses when he found none. He couldn't afford to lose focus. Of course, she wouldn't have done as he said! Not her. Not his Cat.

He circled back to the oak where they had last been together and he sniffed around. Literally. His Wolf bond was coming and going in waves. It would come in strong, then abruptly fade. Like bad satellite TV or a screwy Wi-Fi connection.

Tate stopped pacing. He was getting nowhere. He needed to refocus. Okay, he last saw her here. What happened next? That's what he needed to find out.

12

The second slap stung Cat's left cheek, and she tasted blood inside her mouth. Her head pounded, and she knew she wouldn't stay conscious much longer. That would be a relief in ways. Cold water forced her eyes open, and she gasped through her pain.

"Oh no, no sleep for you, bitch. The boss says you's all mine to play with just after you tell him the security codes to that cocksucker brother of yours' house! Now what's the codes? Hmm? Sweet pie! What are they?"

Spit flew from his lips as Cat's abductor screeched in her face. She could see his madness peeking out through his muddy brown eyes. This Wolf had been without a proper Pack for too long. He was not in his right mind. Probably would never be again.

"I want to speak to Skoll."

"You ain't fit to speak to him, bitch! I says when you can and can't. Tell me the codes and I'll tell him and then you and me gonna have us a party!"

"I'd rather die!"

"Oh, you will, sweet pie, that you will. But not till I stick you good! I'll have you squealing like a little piggy," he growled the last word and a long string of saliva spilled from his crooked teeth.

Cat had to force herself to not back up in her chair. No, not in front of him. She needed to maintain some control, if only for her self-preservation. Inside, she was beginning to lose her nerve.

It was a relief when he walked outside of the broken-down wooden shack where he was holding her in order to take a phone call. Stupid old Wolf. Didn't he know she could hear through the thin wood walls? She knew Skoll. She didn't quite get his endgame, but she knew he wouldn't want this cretin to rape her. Not if he planned on using her to get to Rafe.

She stilled herself to better hear the conversation. A well-timed yell might be her only chance to stop this guy. It didn't matter though. He was on the phone with another lackey. Not Skoll. She pictured the cruel Wolf with his slicked back black hair in a low ponytail, his black shirt paired with black pants. Like some pseudo *Miami Vice* villain. Sure, he gave Cat the creeps, but he played by rules. This guy, not so much.

Dammit! Cat knew from her police training that her captor had no control. Added to that, her Werewolf senses told her that he had lost his mind years ago. Some Wolves did. It was one of the side effects of the curse of St. Natalis. The one that kept them from Changing but once a month.

Without his boss to tell him what to do, Cat knew that he wouldn't be able to resist his baser instincts to rape and maim. He was an animal. Not Pack. He had no structure, limits, support, or laws. An anarchist. *Rogue.* Her Wolf snarled in her mind. And she called out to her mate with all her might.

Cat hoped to God that Tate was okay. She knew he would come for her. In time. It was in his nature. A Wolf Guard was loyal, brave, and determined, He would not leave her to her fate. She knew that as sure as she was still breathing. But right now, she needed a plan.

She ground her teeth and nearly gasped at the pain in her cheek. The bastard might have fractured her jaw with that last smack. No matter. She was Wolf, she would heal. Right now, she needed to focus.

Tate picked up the torn piece of white cotton and nearly whooped aloud. Cat had left him a trail to follow! Damn he loved that woman! And then he stopped stone still.

He loved that woman. Yes. He did. And he would get her back and rip the throat out of the son of a bitch that dared take her from him.

Suddenly Tate's chest seemed to implode with a burst of feeling and a rush of energy unlike any he had every felt. In his mind's eye, he saw a cord. A shimmery, thin thread that pulsated with golden, silvery light. Like magic. It felt like love. It was warm and kind. It came from the center of his soul and in his heart. He knew where it would lead. Home. To Cat. *Mine.*

He loosed a short howl and took off on his bare feet through the snow-covered ground in the direction his heart was telling him to go. Rocks and tree roots cut at his feet and seemed to stop him. Tate trampled them and forged ahead. Strength coursed through him. The kind of which he felt once a month at most. During the full moon.

After nearly fifteen minutes of strenuous running uphill, Tate found the trail had ended. An ATV was parked behind a tree, and Cat's scent was all over it. So was a splatter of something red.

He reached down and touched it. Blood. One sniff and he knew it was hers. He snarled and turned in every direction, trying to find her. But it was as if she had disappeared.

He wanted to run to her. To find her and crush her close to him. But she was nowhere. He closed his eyes. The magic rope that bound them together insisted this was the spot. Then why couldn't he see her? He paced. Full of rage at his impotence.

Cat squirmed in her seat as the shackles that bound her seemed to drain her strength. She pulled against them, but that only made her weaker. *Odd.* She was a Werewolf and was stronger than she looked. A simple metal chain would have broken under her strength, but this. This was no simple chain. The mad Wolf that was her captor came back into the dirty room where she was being held. Only this time he wasn't alone.

The woman was rank with rot. She smelled like decay and ash to Cat's sensitive nose. Immediately she knew what this was. She understood why the chains were making her weak. *Magic. A Dark Witch.*

"Here she is. Now Skoll promised me a boon and I want first dibs at this bitch so don't mess her up too much."

"Quiet, fool! This *bitch* is not your toy. Not yet. Do you hear that she-Wolf? I am happy to keep you safe from this one, but only if you tell me the security codes to the Manor."

"No. I don't care what you do. I won't tell you a damn thing."

"Really? Well, how about I tell you in excruciating detail just how it will feel when he pulls down those leggings and rapes you raw, dog! Now tell me what I need to know. I promise, we won't harm your brother. Just his mate. That normal isn't one of you, anyway. Rafe will be spared, but she must die. Now the codes," the Witch wore layer upon layer of black tattered skirts and matching gauzy top. She looked like something out of a nightmare with her missing left ear and large scars that ran down her cheeks.

Cat knew that kind of self-mutilation was done by Dark Witches who communed with Demons. *Shit.* This was not good. She wished she had a chance to tell Tate she loved him before dying. But she would die before she would tell this Witch anything!

"*Hm*, a stubborn one. I do not admire martyrs. It is easy to sacrifice yourself. Tell me, are you willing to sacrifice another? Maybe one other in particular?"

"What are you talking about?" Cat felt as if her stomach dropped into her feet. What did she mean? *God no. Please no.*

"Show her!"

"My pleasure, lookee here, bitch, this the guy you think will save you? Ha, he don't even know you're here! Ha ha ha," his evil chuckle made Cat shiver with fury.

She wanted out of that chair, so she could scratch his damn eyes out. *Not Tate. No not him.*

"Go ahead scream, he can't hear ya!"

Cat narrowed her gaze. Her heart thundered inside of her and she felt a pull she had never felt before. Her Wolf was strong inside of her. A feeling she couldn't mistake for anything else. Only this couldn't happen. Not yet. Could it?

"Oh shit! Her eyes! What the hell?"

Cat blocked out the surrounding noise. A hurricane of emotion welled up inside her. A storm like no other. Cat saw inside of herself and coming from her chest was a silvery gold thread. A rope, if you will, and it bound her to the bearer of the other end. Her mate. Her heart's desire. *Tate Nighthawk. Mine.*

Cat smiled, her white teeth sharp and glistening. She tossed her head back as the full force of her emotions ran through her and she howled. Cat howled and howled. She barely heard the roar of her mate as he burst through the magical barrier that kept him from being able to see or scent her.

His Wolf was visible through his eyes and she doubted much of the man was in control at that moment. He went right for the Dark Witch.

When Tate heard Cat's howl, he nearly screamed

for joy. She was alive. But instinct took over, and he found himself running full speed at a magic barrier. His Wolf was at the forefront of his mind and he wanted blood. So Tate let him out.

He broke through the front door and took in everything in a split second. Cat was in chains and bleeding from her lip. Her beautiful face bruised and battered. A Werewolf huddled in the corner. Scared and mad, that one. And a Witch stood shocked and still. Her scars making her more horrific a site than anything he had seen in a while.

He went straight for her throat. In two seconds, he ripped out her carotid artery and snapped both of her arms in two. When he turned for the other, pride made him halt his steps.

Cat was out of her chains. She lunged and suddenly had the man's head in her long-nailed hands. She snarled, her icy blue eyes glowing with her Wolf. With one sharp twist, she snapped his neck before he could raise another hand or say another vile word to her.

Seconds later, she found herself enveloped in Tate's arms. She was panting. Out of breath and high on adrenaline. Hot tears poured down her bruised face as she sobbed in his arms.

"Oh, Tate! God, I'm sorry, I'm crying, this isn't

like me, I don't want you to think I'm weak or spoiled or, -"

"Cat! Shhhh! It's okay, you are okay. My God, I could never think that of you! You are so brave! So unspoiled! Cat, you are the best person I know. I love you, Cat."

"What?"

"I love you! Don't you know that?"

Cat threw her arms and legs around Tate. He caught her easily and squeezed her, murmuring words of love. She had never heard anything so beautiful in her entire life. She hardly noticed when he sat down on the ATV with her still wrapped around him and sped towards the cabin.

Once they were there, Tate brought her inside. He took her straight to the bathroom and ministered to her wounds.

Tate took his time, intent on looking over every inch of her. He turned the faucet on the large claw-foot bathtub. Steaming water poured out of the spout, Cat sat on the cushioned stool, and watched as he added two scoops of bath salts.

"Sherry sent me these too. They should speed up healing."

"*Mmmm*. It smells like vanilla and orange and lemon zest. Ow, it hurts when I talk."

"Then don't talk, baby."

Tate undressed Cat carefully. He scooped her up and placed her inside of the tub before removing his own clothing. Once inside the warm water, Cat felt her aches and pains immediately leave. She was shocked as more tears fell silently down her face. Tate reached a handout towards her chin and lifted.

"Don't be ashamed, Catriona. Look, I am crying too. I am crying because my heart is so relieved to have you back. I went damn near out of my mind when you were gone. But do you know how I found you? Do you know why?"

Cat shook her head and stared at him in wonder as she traced the tears that fell from his softly glowing eyes.

"Because you are my mate, Cat, my true mate. And I am yours. We have a *matebond*. I saw it! It's gold and silver and beautiful, and it led me to you. But you weren't there. I wanted to run, to keep looking, but my Wolf demanded I stay there. Then do you know what happened?"

Cat still couldn't talk. She curled up on his lap in the water and shook her head.

"You *howled*. Cat, you howled! And it was like a wall came down and my Wolf jumped right through the rubble to get to you. My Cat, my mate, my love."

"Oh Tate, I love you too."

He hugged her fiercely then. It was the first time

she had said it out loud. And damn, it sounded good to his ears. It felt good too.

She sat up straight and Tate's entire body took notice. Her lips found his in a kiss unlike any other they had shared.

"Will it hurt you if we make love?" Cat loved him so much, especially after he asked her that question.

"Oh no, Tate, that's one thing that will never ever hurt me."

She turned her body so that she straddled him, sloshing water over the side as she did so.

"I need you, Tate, right now," she guided the head of his swollen shaft and she thrust down with all her might.

Tate groaned and suckled her breasts as she rode him. Hard and hot and fast. She was so tight, so torturously sweet as she pumped him for all he was worth. They groaned together in a chorus of ecstasy as his hot seed filled her.

They had just finished drying each other off when Tate's cell rang. He picked it up without hesitation.

"Yes," Tate's answers were clipped, his tone respectful. But Cat didn't need to listen to Tate's responses to know who was on the other end of the call. She heard her brother's voice quite clearly.

What puzzled her was the sound of Lt. Matt Larentia's voice. What on earth was he doing there?

And why was he furiously demanding to know where Cat was?

"We will be home in a few hours. Rafe? There is something you should know," Tate didn't get a chance to finish his sentence. Cat was glad. She wasn't exactly sure it was a good idea to advertise their new relationship status just yet.

Tate must have felt her hesitation. He turned the full force of his midnight stare on her and lifted her chin till she was forced to meet his eyes.

"Cat? Just so you know, the first thing I intend to do when we get back to the Manor is tell your brother that you and I are mated. That is, if you're okay with that."

"I am so okay with that," Cat smiled and grabbed the nape of Tate's neck. Pulling him down in a lip searing kiss.

Closing-up the cabin, making sure it was locked and secured, took half the time with both of them working together. The hike back was also short and direct once Tate no longer suspected they were being followed.

The threat was, for now, over. Relief and exhaustion warred inside of Cat for top position. She would have liked to give into both except she didn't want to be lackadaisical when she returned home.

During the few hours it took to drive back to

Macconwood Manor, Tate talked with Catriona about all the little things. Movies he liked, books he's read. Small talk. She shared details about her life that she had never told another living soul.

Like how she only used cinnamon toothpaste and never, ever dyed her hair. She watched the Hallmark Channel like a fiend and old MacGyver reruns were her favorite. Surprisingly enough, he was a fan too.

"I understand more about your job than you think, Tate, I mean normals are these precious mortal creatures and they hurt each other and commit crimes all the time for no good reason. I understand the despair you feel when you have to talk to the family of a new Wolf who just couldn't take the pain and didn't know how to ask for help," Cat's voice was soft, but her words meant a lot to him.

"I know you do, Cat. It's why I asked you to sit with me in the kitchen a few nights ago. I was feeling raw, and I needed peace. You gave it to me," Tate squeezed her hand and Cat pulled it up to her lips and kissed it.

"If only there was some place they could go to; you know? Kids, *normals*, *supernaturals*, doesn't matter which, could be both. They all need help and there should be somewhere they could go to get it. Without judgement, you know?"

"Hmm. That's a great idea, Cat. A really great idea."

The rest of the talk on their trip home was not nearly as serious. They laughed and joked, and Cat even nodded out for the length of a song or two. Then Tate pulled onto one of the private roads leading to the Manor. The snow had finally stopped, but a fresh blanket of white covered the long road and the surrounding grounds. It glistened in the moonlight like a million scattered diamonds. He looked at Cat through the corner of his eye as she slowly blinked her eyes and woke up. And for a moment Tate felt peaceful.

"Did I fall asleep?"

"Just a Cat-nap."

"Ha ha. You been saving that one for me?"

"You know it, baby. Hey look, we're home."

Randall met them at the first security gate and high-fived Tate before handing him a new cell and grabbing his old one.

"Number's the same, but this one has all the new codes and upgrades. I'll transfer your personal data tonight. Wassup Cat? All good?"

"Yeah, Randall, all good," she smiled and then blushed furiously when he stuck his head in the car and breathed. His head turned first to look at Tate, then back at her and vice versa.

"Oh, man! It's about time, bro! Um, you should know that there is a sort of surprise waiting for you inside though. Not sure if it's good or not," Randall's words were muffled as his voice dropped and Cat had a hard time understanding him over his beard. It was about twelve inches long now and dark as the rest of his shaggy head.

He was quieter than most of the Wolves. He didn't go in for parties and such. Cat had always thought of him as kind of a sad, geeky type.

All that software development and gaming had left some serious gaps in his social life. From what she knew he was a sick kid, before his Change. Stayed indoors a lot and was glued to the computer.

"Thanks for the heads up, man. Want a ride back to the big house?" Tate unlocked the doors to the SUV, but Randall was already shaking his head no.

"Nah, I'm going for a run. See you two later," with that he turned and started jogging towards the woods. Tate waved him off, and they continued to drive down the private road.

Two more unmanned security booths and they were in the private garage used by Rafe, the Wolf Guard, and Cat.

"You ready?"

Cat sighed and looked at the door that would lead them inside. She was a little nervous, there was no use denying it. But overall, she was glad to be home.

Tate held out his hand, and she took it. Together they entered one of the main living room areas. Their hearing told them which one to head to. The boys were sitting around playing cards while Rafe and Charley and another man sat around a small table in complete silence. They looked as if they hadn't heard them enter the room. But Cat knew better.

Rafe's eyes zeroed in on her immediately. The familiar icy blue gaze went over her from head to foot before he blinked. She recognized it as his way of checking her for injury. And when he lingered on her face, she knew she hadn't healed as much as she would have liked.

"Rafe? Would you like a full report now?" Tate's formal question almost knocked the confidence right out of Cat. But then she realized he had one eyebrow raised and no matter how she pulled, he would not let go of her hand.

Rafe stood up from the table. He was easily the largest man in the room. His face showed no emotion at all. And for a moment Cat thought they were in big trouble. Then she caught sight of Charley. Rafe's wife poked her head out from behind her husband, and her cheerful smile was contagious.

"Oh, stop it, you big oaf!" Charley nudged her

husband in the ribs with her elbow and he "oom-phed" before flashing an appreciative smile at her backside as she passed him by and grabbed Cat in a welcome back hug. She moved on to Tate and hugged him the same way. Like a mama welcoming back her children.

"Uh, Charley? Are you okay?"

"Oh, Cat! I am so happy for you both!"

"What, uh, oh, okay, so everyone knows?"

"Cat, before you and Tate tell us about what went down out there. Lt. Larentia here has something he'd like to tell you. In the other room, maybe? Lieutenant?"

"That won't be necessary. We are all Werewolves, well except for Mrs. Maccon of course, no offense," Cat stared at the older man with a million questions in her eyes.

"None taken, Lieutenant," Charley's answer barely registered with her.

The entire room seemed to fade away. The only thing she was sure of was that Tate was holding strong to her hand. And Lieutenant Matt Larentia was standing in front of her with worry, grief, sadness, and a bit of anxiety exuding from his pores. He ducked his head down. Cat thought he seemed ashamed, but just as quickly he looked back up at her.

"You know, your eyes are exactly like Claire's."

Cat nodded. She knew she took after her mother's side of the family. There was none of Zev Maccon in her at all. Rafe had inherited their father's black hair and large build. Cat had always assumed her height was from her father's side. Her mother was much shorter at five and a half feet tall, but their eyes were the same.

Rafe tensed, and Cat had the feeling he knew something she didn't. But she remained silent and waited for Lt. Larentia to continue.

"Claire was always a sweet kid. We, uh, we went to school together. High school. We were sweethearts. I took her to prom. I wanted to marry her. But uh, Zev, Zev had a contract, a betrothal contract and demanded she marry him or be killed as Pack law states. I wanted to fight him for her, but she begged me not to. She said she'd rather I lived, got married to someone else, then died at his hands. He was always a tough son of a bitch."

Cat's heart thudded in her chest. She moved closer to Tate without realizing it, and he put his arm around her. The heat and solidity of him standing next to her gave her strength. She had a feeling she'd need it.

"Twenty-seven years ago, when Rafe here was in grade school and I was just an officer, a bunch of kids, normals, stole his bike and kicked his butt. Your mom called the office, and they sent me. When I was taking the report I guess, well, I guess something happened between us or what had been there before had never really died. At least not for me it hadn't. My God, I loved that woman. You must know that. I would never have shamed her, never hurt her. But I loved her so much. One thing led to another. When she told me she was pregnant with you, I told her we'd run away. Leave this place and make a new life. But she wouldn't leave her son. I couldn't make her do that."

Cat gasped. Her hand was over her mouth and hot tears poured down her bruised face. It all made so much sense to her. Why her father, no not her father, why *Zev* had hated her. Why her mother had run away. It was because she belonged to another in her heart! *Poor mom just couldn't take it anymore.*

Cat could relate to that. But why, oh why didn't she take her and Rafe away too? Cat's emotions were moving so fast, she hardly noticed Tate's hand on her arm in slow, soothing strokes.

"Anyway, Zev, he, he visited me. Told me he knew what we had done. He promised to raise you as his own flesh and blood. He told me he wouldn't punish Claire. Zev said he would forgive her. That son of a bitch was the meanest damn thing alive. And I am ashamed that I did not have the power to stop him. I tried, I did, but he broke me. Both my legs, both my arms. Broke them and kept me tied up in his barn so that he could re-break them when they would heal. Months felt like years in there. Little water, kibble to eat, hardly any light. I was not freed until after you were born. Then he released me and told me that if I tried to come near either of you again, he would do that to you both. I had no choice. I couldn't let him do that to you. I am sorry, I am so sorry. I just thought you needed to know."

"But why? Why now? Why not a year ago or five years ago? Or when that son of a bitch died? How could you not tell me?!," Cat's voice grew louder as she went on.

"I am so sorry. For everything. I already told your brother this, a few years back, but please, don't, don't be angry at him for not telling you. I made him swear a blood oath to keep my secret as Pack Alpha. He had no choice."

"Rafe?"

"I'm sorry, Cat. I couldn't break my oath."

"That's okay, big brother. I understand. Gee, I guess I'm not a Maccon after all."

"Actually, your mother was the Maccon, Zev took her last name," Lt. Larentia interrupted with a sheepish grin on his face.

"Wow. I never knew that. I wouldn't have looked either, not after Mom left, -"

"You think your mom left? She didn't leave. He sent her away. To be a prisoner at some other Pack. I've been trying to find her for years."

"What?" Both Cat and Rafe looked at each other, then at Lt. Larentia.

"You mean our mother is alive? And she's being held somewhere?" Rafe roared the last. He looked to Seff who was already on his feet, cell phone in hand.

"We will look into this immediately. Thank you, Matt, you are prime Pack and you will always be welcome here," Rafe turned around, his chest heaving with emotion. Charley moved to his side. But Cat remained still.

"Dad? Can I call you that?"

"Dammit girl, of course you can. I waited my whole life to hear you say it," He opened his arms and Cat slowly went into them. Father and daughter reunited at last.

"Let me introduce you to Tate, he's my-"

"Yeah, what exactly is with you two? Spill!" Liam jumped over the couch and sat at the small table, hands on his knees, waiting rather impatiently for her to explain.

"Actually, why don't you start the story from the beginning."

Rafe's orders were usually followed to a t, but Cat and Tate managed to leave out the irrelevant parts.

All that mattered to Cat was that she had finally found her heart. And it was where she always knew it would be. With Tate.

EPILOGUE

"So, everything, uh, came together in the end?" Cat winced as Liam so crudely summed up the events of the last few days. Seff smacked his brother in the back of the head while the others looked around, trying not to laugh.

Rafe remained stone-faced until his wife squeezed his knee, then he leaned forward to speak.

"Everyone out of the room, except for you two."

Tate glanced at Cat. She looked worried. He narrowed his eyes. He loved Rafe. Loved his position in the Pack. Hell, he worked damn hard to make it that far. But there was no way in hell he was giving up Cat. Even if that meant defying his Alpha.

"Rafe, I-" Cat addressed her brother directly, but was silenced with a glare.

She heard the other Wolves in the hallway. She knew Liam had his ear pressed against the door. The damn nosy pup!

"So, the two of you have *matebonded?* Without asking my permission, my blessing? You, Tate, you just went and had your way with my baby sister?!," Rafe growled and put force into his words, causing both Cat and Tate to bow a little.

"Rafe, I'm a grown woman!"

"Silence! I'm the Alpha here and you do not have my permission to speak!"

"Rafe with all due respect, I am your Wolf Guard, I love and trust you, but she is my mate. We are bonded, and don't you ever talk to her like that," Tate struggled to stand upright. It was a fight, but he did, and though he kept his eyes averted, he stood tall. Ready to die for his mate.

"Ah, that is what I was looking for. My love, do you have any words?"

Charley stepped around her husband and took his large hand in hers.

"Yes, when's the wedding?"

With that, Rafe let go of his Alpha control and broke into a wide smile. He grabbed his sister in a bear hug and allowed her to swat him for making them sweat like that.

Tate allowed Charley to kiss his cheek, but when it came time to shake hands with Rafe, he paused.

"So, you've known? All this time?"

'What that you were in love with my sister? Dude, I'm the Alpha. Of course, I've known!"

"But I thought you didn't approve?"

"No, that's what you wanted to think. I just never made it known. After all, Cat deserves someone who knows his worth. Someone who would fight for her. You are that someone, Tate. Only now you know it too."

Later that night Tate and Cat snuggled together in their new bedroom in one of the guest houses on the manor. A gift from Rafe and Charley. They chose the one closest to the pool and gym. It had three bedrooms, a full kitchen, living room, office, and two bathrooms.

Charley offered to help Cat redecorate, and she accepted. Her brother's wife had a way with colors and textures that could make any house into a home. Cat was glad she offered.

She stretched in their king-sized bed and looked at her lover, *her mate*, and smiled. A very feline smile, for a Wolf anyway.

"What? Is something wrong?" His sleepy voice told her their last bout of lovemaking had left him spent. She was glad of it. Proud to know she had the ability to satisfy him as much as he did her.

"No, nothing is wrong," she traced her long fingernails across the muscles of his bronzed chest and smiled as he leaned into her touch, "I love you, Tate. I always have."

"I love you too, Catriona," his response was immediate. He took her hand and kissed the fingertips, all the while looking into her eyes. His eyes glowed with his Wolf, with his love, his loyalty to her, the true communion of their souls, and their unbreakable matebond as he looked at her.

Cat gasped at the intensity of it all. Her heart sped up. Whatever the future held, she knew they would face it together. Like they would in their new project. She was glad to have the approval of not only her boss at the Sheriff's Department, but of her Alpha as well.

"I can't wait to start working on the Macconwood-Nighthawk Teen Outreach Program. It's such a great idea, Tate, together we are going to do such great things."

"Hey, we came up with it together. And yes, we are going to do great things, Cat. Especially with you as my partner. So, tell me, how does it feel to be a Wolf Guard?"

"Amazing! But not as amazing as being your

mate," Cat grinned. She couldn't believe it herself. Rafe had finally asked her to be part of his Guard.

"Well, how about it Cat?" That's all Rafe had said after everything had been said and done. She remembered narrowing her eyes and tackling her brother to the ground in a hug so tight he was almost embarrassed.

He gave her a squeeze and rolled to his feet easily before sternly commanding her to never tackle her Alpha again. She smiled as she thought about it now. Tate's deep voice shook her from her reverie and Cat perked up.

"I can't tell you how glad I am that you feel that way, Cat, because I, uh, was wondering, if maybe you'd like to be my wife too?" Tate paused, wanting to gauge Cat's reaction to his proposal.

For a moment, he was worried that she might say no. After all, she was a modern woman. Maybe she didn't believe in marriage? Tate would abide by anything she said. She was his mate and traditional marriage or not, that wouldn't change.

He watched a wide array of emotions play across Cat's upturned face. Surprise, love, worry, angst, shock, fear, pleasure. And then she did something only Cat would do. She tackled him and brought her lips down hard on his, her entire body purring with affection.

"I love you, Tate Nighthawk, and I'd be damn proud to be your wife!"

"So, it's yes?"

"Of course, it's yes!"

That night Cat howled. Not because she was in danger, but because she was in love. Forever and always.

The end.

CHARLEY'S BABY SURPRISE: RAFE AND CHARLEY

THE MACCONWOOD PACK TALES 4

A MASCONWOOD PACK TALE
CHARLEY'S
baby surprise
The Masconwood Pack
INTERNATIONAL BESTSELLING AUTHOR
C.D. GORRI

BLURB

Can Alpha wolf, Rafe Maccon, survive his mate's pregnancy?

Charley is adapting to married life in her new home with her husband, Alpha Wolf, Rafe Maccon, and the eight Wolf Guards who live with them. Learning the rules to this new supernatural world isn't always easy, especially when she finds herself pregnant after just a few weeks of marriage.

Rafe Maccon never had anyone of his own before. He is determined to love, cherish, and most of all, protect his bride. His mated Wolf instincts go into overdrive once he discovers Charley is pregnant!

Will Charley cave to Rafe's demands or will this Alpha learn the meaning of compromise?

PROLOGUE

Six weeks after their wedding...

"Guess what, Rafe?"

"What is it, my sweet Carlotta?"

"We are having a baby!"

Rafe Maccon could not believe his ears. He sat on the edge of his enormous bed as his petite wife emerged from their private bathroom with her long curly hair hanging down her back. She held a small plastic stick in one hand and a box in the other that read *Home Pregnancy Kit*. She was positively glowing even in her simple cotton nightgown that he found sexy as hell.

Understanding slowly dawned on the Alpha Wolf, and he dropped the bottle of water he'd been drinking. He ignored the sound of liquid splashing on the wood floors as he ran to his mate and lifted her gently off the ground! *Pregnant! Must keep safe!*

He cradled her to his chest and kissed her temple. She flung her arms around his neck and pulled until his lips met hers. Lips that he kept closed as he tried to absorb the enormity of the situation. Werewolf pregnancies were not easy. True, his Carlotta was a normal, but chances were their child would not be. *What did this mean for his beloved mate? Would she be okay?*

"A baby?"

"Yes! Can you believe it? A baby of our own! Are you as happy as I am?" She bit her lip as she watched him. What could he do except smile and hold her tight to his chest?

"Carlotta, you are something else, my love," pride and joy mixed with terror and worry as he sat down on the bed with her cradled in his arms. *Precious cargo.*

"Isn't it great?" She laughed and squirmed to straddle him. Normally, this was one of his favorite positions, but he was feeling less enthusiastic as all sorts of fears and worries reared their ugly heads.

"Yes, it's great news," Rafe nodded, but his heart was pounding inside his chest.

Pregnancies sometimes things went wrong. Even normal ones. Werewolf pregnancies were unpredictable at best. Physical difficulties of her condition aside, Rafe had other worries.

One enormous issue was his less than stellar childhood. His father, Zev Maccon, was an absolute monster. He'd punished his children and their mother for years until claiming Rafe's mother had died. He'd only just learned his mother had not abandoned him as he'd thought and furthermore, she was still alive. He had yet to track her down, but they were working on it. That information came from Lt. Matt Larentia, his mother's first love and the father of his younger sister, Catriona.

The only good thing about his past was that his father was firmly buried there. The dead could not hurt him *or his*. That didn't stop Rafe from doubting his ability to overcome such a history. Maybe he wasn't ready for fatherhood. He'd only just found his mate. Maybe he needed more time alone with her. *Too bad*, his inner Wolf growled. *Ready or not, here comes parenthood.*

He smiled at his Carlotta's physical cues, but he had no idea what his wife was talking about. She was gushing on and on about baby names, clothes, toys, and furniture. She was happy. Deliriously happy judging from the euphoria on her beautiful face. *And he was being a dick.*

He slid her off his lap to rest beside him as she

continued to chatter away. Rafe snuggled her closer, enfolding her in his arms. *Mine. Protect.*

He breathed in her scent and tried to calm His Wolf who was right there at the forefront of his mind. He listened patiently and tried to remain attentive, but his brain was churning.

"I'll call one of our Pack physicians to come to the manor as soon as possible to give you a physical examination. You've met Dr. Rayne Davis before, right?"

"Sure, at the Christmas ball. And I think your sister mentioned her, but shouldn't we wait till I'm further along?" Charley sighed against him and nuzzled his arm basking in the joy of becoming a mother for the first time.

Normally, the Alpha would take that as a cue that his mate wanted him, but he needed to be gentle with her. Absolutely no sex, well, not until the doctor gave the okay. *And maybe not even then.*

He would do everything he could to protect his mate and their young. *His young. A baby!* Even if that meant abstaining from her sweet touch. *God, help him.*

"Oh Rafe, I'm so happy! We are going to be such great parents," she sighed and snuggled closer.

He wished he could share in her confidence. Not that he doubted his feisty wife would be an amazing mother. Hadn't she charmed every single one of his

Wolf Guard with her beautiful singing voice, her gentle but firm handling of some of their antics, her teasing wit, and her outrageously delicious cooking?

She was perfect. Warm, loving, and braver than any normal he'd ever met. She was not the problem, it was Rafe. Growing up with little to no affection meant he lacked certain skills a father should have.

He didn't want to disappoint Carlotta, but he also didn't know if he had it in him to be a dad. One thing was certain, he'd take care of her and the baby. That much, he could do.

"I love you, Carlotta. I'll protect both of you, I swear it."

ate next Fall...

L   "Seven months!" Charley huffed as she climbed the stairs to the master bedroom she shared with her husband, Alpha Wolf of the Macconwood Pack, Rafe Maccon and, not her favorite person right now. In fact, she found her darling hubby to be nothing if not irritating these last few months!

Her sister-in-law, Cat Maccon Nighthawk smirked as she followed slowly behind Charley. They'd become the best of friends since Charley's spur of the moment marriage to Rafe. That is, after a few of his adorable, yet felony-inclined Wolf Guard kidnapped her for him! *The loveable jerks!*

"Oh Charley, I'm sure it hasn't been that long," said Tulla Graves with her teasing southern accent.

She'd recently married Wolf Guard and resident tech expert, Randall Graves.

Tulla was a welcome addition to the household where Charley had been the only resident *normal* until her arrival. Her adorable son, Daniel, was at school at the moment, but Charley doted on the gifted little boy as much as anyone else in the household. A good friend and full of tips for the first-time mother, Charley sought her advice time and again. Especially since her husband's disappearing act. The two women meant a lot to her.

She teared up just thinking of how Cat and Tulla had rallied to support her during the last few months. Especially when one overbearing Wolf refused to allow her to leave the premises alone, deeming it unnecessary exposure to danger. Not that he would take time off his schedule to accompany her anywhere.

In fact, he couldn't bear to be in the same room with her lately. Today's shopping trip, unscheduled as it was, was almost called to a halt before Cat and Tulla came to her rescue. As a Wolf Guard herself, Cat insisted Charley would be safe and, if that wasn't good enough, Tulla had a special cell phone outfitted with a custom tracking app and emergency signal designed by her husband should they need help. *My highhanded tyrant of a husband thinks he can ignore me and run my life! Ha!*

Not that she would trade her life for anything. Charley might be angry with Rafe, but she loved being a part of the secret world of the supernatural that he had introduced her to. As Alpha of the Macconwood Pack, he had an enormous responsibility to his Wolves, but he'd always made sure she knew she came first with him. And now so would their child.

"I swear I'm going to brain your overbearing brother one of these days, Cat! I am so not joking!"

The women stifled their giggles and Charley glared behind her, careful not to lose balance. She held on to the banister and shrugged as Cat stilled her face. Tulla mimicked the pose, showing no hint of mirth. They had insisted on carrying Charley's purchases upstairs for her, and with all the extra weight she'd been hulking around the past seven months, Charley was not inclined to argue. And boy did she have a lot of purchases!

The three women spent the entire afternoon at the mall and Charley admittedly went a little overboard with her gold card. She couldn't help it. Retail therapy was a well-known cure for the blues. *Just not today.* The large meat-lovers pizza and fudge brownie explosion they'd shared for lunch didn't even make a dent in her feelings of despondency.

Being with Cat, and looking into her clear, ice-blue eyes, had only reminded Charley of Rafe. The two siblings shared the Maccon eye color, but that was it. Where Cat was tall and willowy with blonde hair and a toned build, Rafe was big as a house with rippling muscles and impossibly dark, jet-black hair, with equally dark lashes surrounding his eyes. He was so freaking hot. And she was so freaking hormonal lately that she wanted to laugh, cry, and throw something all at once whenever she thought of him. Which was pretty much every second of the day. *Darn him!*

Of course, watching Tulla blush every time her husband sent her a text was just as painful to watch. The two of them were as inseparable as she and Rafe had been when they were first married. As newlyweds, it was to be expected, but she couldn't help but feel jealous. Especially, when Tulla sighed and giggled like a high school student with her first beau. Rafe had sent her one text while she was out: *Text me when you are home safe.* Not exactly full of love and romance. *Sigh.*

"What has my darling big brother done now, Charley?"

"It's more about what he isn't doing," she mumbled as she opened the door to their bedroom.

"Uh oh, trouble in paradise, sugar?" Tulla asked.

Charley just grunted. She was beyond frustrated with her big, gorgeous husband. Her hormones must be really out of whack if she wanted to throttle him one minute and lick him from head to toe the next. Not that she could do that even if she wanted. The jerk refused to touch her!

Her OB/GYN and Pack doctor, Dr. Rayne Davis gave them "the okay" to resume normal sexual activity months ago. Still, Rafe insisted they exercise caution. *To keep you both safe, Carlotta.* Charley was patient with him those first few weeks. *New father jitters*, she'd said. *They'd get through them together*, only they hadn't.

Not that she regretted her pregnancy, she was more than thrilled to be having his baby. And even without the intimacy of sex, those first few months were a dream. He'd pampered her with special little gifts and delectable treats to satisfy her cravings. He'd kiss her and hold her. He even stayed up with her when, as luck would have it, she got night sickness instead of morning sickness. But even after all that passed, he refused her. No matter how she tried to seduce him. She had thought he was just being over-protective, but now she was scared it was something else.

Think of the baby. She did. Often. Happy as she was to be a first-time mother, Charley was seriously struggling lately to keep that happiness afloat. Especially with Rafe's increasingly chilly attitude towards her. As if that wasn't enough, she had other things on her mind, concerns, and fears that she found herself facing alone. *Should she breastfeed? Cloth diapers or disposable? Natural childbirth or epidural? And what was the deal with pacifiers?*

She sighed disgustedly and kicked off her flats. *Could things get any worse?* Her ankles were swollen, her stomach was huge, and her back was killing her after being on her feet all day.

"Charley, maybe he's just scared," Tulla began as they entered the master bedroom.

"No way! He's the Alpha, Tulla. He eats bad guys for breakfast!"

"True, but you can't possibly doubt his love," she replied.

"No, he loves me, I know. But it's like a fondness or something. It's, it's different now," she choked back her tears, determined to retain some pride, "I think he's just not attracted to me anymore."

"Oh, Charley! No-" Cat said.

"It's true, he finds me repulsive," she couldn't

stem the tears after she spoke the last few words in a defeated voice she hardly recognized as her own. She barely registered Cat's panicked gaze at Tulla who wrapped her arms around Charley and murmured soothing words that did nothing to heal her bruised heart.

He finds me revolting. It was the only reason Charley could think of that made sense. Maybe Rafe couldn't stand how big she'd become? Not that she could blame him, she was a freaking blimp. *But it's not my fault,* she wanted to shout!

She did everything the doctor told her too. She watched what she ate. Plenty of clean protein and fresh veggies. Okay, she indulged in the occasional pizza and brownie ice cream sundae but come on! Sometimes, it was necessary.

She exercised regularly, walking for thirty minutes every day outdoors when the weather allowed or on the state-of-the-art treadmill in the Macconwood Manor gym. Sometimes she even swam in their heated indoor pool. Charley looked down at her enormous belly as she moved out of Tulla's embrace to the bed she shared with her husband.

Well, *used to share with him*, she thought sadly. It had been months since he'd slept with her. Of course, he blamed it on work. Being the Alpha was not an easy job, and he'd been busy tracking their elusive enemy, the rogue Wolf, Skoll.

Skoll was a thorn in Rafe's side, but Charley was sort of beholden to him. After all, he was the catalyst that sent Rafe's Wolves looking for a mate for their Alpha. Skoll had thought to challenge Rafe's ascension to Alpha by bringing up an old Pack law that stated he needed to be married to retain the position. Too much of a coward to challenge Rafe outright, he'd used devious methods to threaten the security of the Macconwood Pack.

Okay, so maybe Charley wasn't beholden to him. He was a serious jerk! Especially after he tried to have Cat kidnapped just weeks after Charley and Rafe married. Yeah, she could understand why Rafe wanted him found and dealt with. Then there was the ongoing search for Rafe's and Cat's mother, who he'd recently discovered was still alive. Yeah, her husband had a lot on his plate. *But what about me, his wife?* Surely, he would feel better if he leaned on her, confided in her, even just a little bit. Like he used to.

"He doesn't even sleep in here anymore. Sometimes, I feel like we're not married at all."

"What? That's not like him to leave you alone," Tulla looked concerned as she started emptying the shopping bags. Cat moved to sit next to Charley.

"Oh, I'm not alone. Every single night, one of the

other Guards is outside my door. *Keeping watch.* I feel like the whole damn house knows every time I get up to pee. Which, unfortunately, is very, *very* often."

Charley sighed. Her tall, beautiful sister-in-law put a toned arm around her back and gave her a squeeze. Charley couldn't help it; the unspoken sympathy made her start crying again. There was nothing she could do to stop the sobs, and with both women on either side of her, she found she didn't want to. They'd understand.

Finding Rafe had been like a dream come true for her. Well, once you got past the whole kidnapping thing at the beginning of their relationship. She smiled through tears as she recalled that night.

She'd been waiting at a bus stop, on her way to a blind date that she was actually dreading when a van pulled up next to her. Before she knew what was happening, she was grabbed from behind and basically kidnapped to the Jersey Shore.

It seemed her husband's idiotic though well-meaning Wolf Guard had taken it upon themselves to find him a mate. And, lucky for her, Charley had been picked. She'd been instantly attracted to the big, gorgeous Werewolf who would later be her husband.

He seemed to like her too. As in he couldn't get enough of her those first few days. After a whirlwind romance, they were married and forged a *matebond,* the stuff of legends apparently. *Only, maybe they hadn't?* Charley was told that *matebonding* was a true rarity among Werewolves. True mates had a special connection, a mind link some said, an unbreakable tie said others, either way, she was no longer sure.

All she knew was she'd given herself, heart, body, and soul, to Rafe. In return, he'd given her himself and a home. Not a house, a real home with family, love, and hope for the future. It was like some modern-day fairy tale. She never thought she would see the day where she'd doubt his love for even a second. Especially not after she told him she was pregnant with his child.

She thought he'd be just as ecstatic as she was. Sure, he'd been worried about intimacy in the beginning, and she had calmly accepted that. But after the doctor had given them the okay, well, she'd expected them to resume the physical side of their relationship. Only, they hadn't. Rafe hadn't touched her with serious sexual intent in months.

The separation was starting to take a visible toll on Charley and their relationship as a whole. She hardly saw him anymore except at meals and during doctor visits. The truth was, he'd been avoiding her.

"Charley, honey, I am sure he's just got a lot on his mind. We didn't have a great dad, you know, maybe he's nervous about becoming a father," Cat spoke up.

Charley blew her nose and sat up straight. *Could it be that simple?* Cat's words suddenly sounded very wise to Charley.

"Men aren't notorious for their good thinking skills, you know, I bet Cat is right! He could just be feeling a bit nervous," agreed Tulla.

"You think? I mean, I know that I never knew Zev Maccon, but from what I hear, Rafe is nothing like his father," Charley wiped her eyes with a new tissue and looked at both women.

"Well, that's true, but still, his fear could be real. Why don't you talk to him about it?" Cat said encouragingly.

"I would, but when? I hardly see him anymore."

"He's in his office right now, Tate just texted me that he'd left him in there with a pile of paperwork to see to."

"Did he?"

"Uh huh," she said, and Charley almost missed the wink she gave Tulla, "He, uh, mentioned that Rafe looked utterly exhausted too. Poor guy, not getting enough rest and all."

Cat looked at Charley with amusement in her big blue eyes. She was a true beauty, her sister-in-law, and as far as Charley knew, she just might be right about her husband.

"Well, your stuff is all put away, except this, I'll

talk to you later," Tulla slid out the door after handing Charley a certain pink striped bag that held a silky confection inside.

Cat said her goodbyes to Charley immediately after with some excuse about having to meet her husband, Tate, for a game of billiards. Charley hardly noticed. She undressed slowly and stepped into the warm shower.

It took her all of ten minutes under the strong spray of water to make up her mind. She was going to confront the big man she married, but first things first. She wanted to be fresh and clean before she went to see him.

It was almost ten o'clock at night by the time she was finished dressing and gathered enough courage to leave the bedroom. This wing of the Manor would be quiet about now. She inhaled a deep breath taking in the long, silky maternity nightgown that she wore in the full-length bathroom mirror.

It was a dream of a nightgown, she bought it just that day. It had two side slits and dipped low in the front showing off her even larger than normal breasts. *Designed to make a pregnant woman feel as sexy as she looked*, that was what the cashier had said. She put on the matching robe, making sure she was decently covered. Werewolves had serious tendencies towards jealousy and interested or not, she would never want to insult her husband by exposing herself to anyone other than him.

Oh, but it really was a pretty set. Even the robe with its embroidered roses and sheer sleeves. Charley sighed and brushed her long hair out with a wide comb until it curled softly over her shoulders and back. She'd been letting it grow for months now. Rafe loved her hair. At least, he always said so. *I really hope this works,* she thought and rested her hands on the top of her swollen abdomen.

Seff McAllister was sitting in a chair just outside their door. He was reading an old, leather-bound book when she opened the bedroom door. His ready smile told her he'd heard her coming as he quickly rose to his feet.

"Hey there," the Pack Beta nodded at her, and she smiled back.

He was unassuming in his appearance, with light brown hair conventionally cut and a thinner build than the other Wolves, he looked almost non-threatening. *Almost.* Except for the lightning quick reflexes that she'd witnessed and the wicked gleam that shone in his eyes from time to time. He had a ferocity she'd only heard about and right then she was glad of that.

"Going to find our fearless leader?" he asked.

"Yes. You can go on now, Seff. Thank you."

"Alright then, but you tell him you sent me away or else I'll never hear the end of it."

"You got it," she said and smiled.

She couldn't believe how nervous she felt. She used to share everything with Rafe, but the distance between them was growing every single day they were apart.

She had to stop it. She needed to bridge the gap. To save her marriage

❦ 2 ❦

Charley walked barefoot down the long corridor to Rafe's office. She smiled to herself. The room held fond memories for her. They'd been married inside those four walls. *And afterwards*, they'd made love on the desk with a frenzied, all-consuming need. Since then, they'd had several similar interludes just as passionate in that room and others. *Just not lately*.

She'd been a virgin when she met Rafe. Untouched and ripe for the picking. *And how!* He taught her everything he knew about making love and some things, well, she'd like to think *she taught him*. He brought her to delirious heights of physical pleasure, each interlude unique, but breathlessly tender and passionate. His love a beacon that she could find anywhere, only it didn't seem to be there anymore. He wasn't there anymore.

Maybe Cat was right. Maybe Rafe had fears of his own. It was just so difficult for her to imagine. He'd always seemed unbreakable. One thing she was sure of was, she was not giving up on her marriage without a fight.

She opened the door quietly. The near pitch black took a second for her to get used to, but she noticed her husband's form almost immediately after that. His broad back was to her, and he was sitting in the big recliner near the fireplace. It was early fall, too warm to really need one, but Rafe always liked a good fire. It was pretty to look at, she admitted. *Poor baby. He must be exhausted.*

"Rafe?" she called his name softly. She walked across the plush carpet and faced him.

His eyes were closed, and he breathed easily in his sleep. He looked so tired. Heavy shadows sat under his eyes, and he'd lost some weight since the last time she really looked at him. She bit her lip nervously.

Werewolves, especially her Alpha, had enormous appetites. She felt guilty for all her earlier complaints. Whatever her husband was, he worked hard to ensure the health and safety of his entire Pack. He had so much responsibility. He shouldered it alone too.

Charley flushed with embarrassment. She'd been thinking only of herself.

She rubbed her belly and sighed. Well, maybe she could join him for a nap? She'd learned early in their relationship that Rafe was very strong, remarkably so even for a Werewolf. Charley knew she wouldn't hurt him by climbing onto his lap, so she did.

His familiar scent filled her nostrils. *Pine trees and fresh cut grass.* He always smelled earthy and clean to her. Since her pregnancy, her sense of smell was even stronger, and she picked up on the musk of his Wolf underneath the woodsy fragrance that was all him. *Mmm.* She loved it. Fact was she missed the way his scent would remain all over her after they made love. She missed *him.*

She curled closer to him, just content to be near him. She smoothed her hands over the soft flannel of his shirt that did nothing to hide the hard muscles of his chest. She loved his chest and the soft, spongy black hair that covered it.

She sighed and nuzzled closer. Suddenly, his arms came up around her as she turned her body to get comfortable. As if he instinctively felt her presence. She dropped her head back and sighed, loving the feel of him.

She gasped when she felt his nose dip closer and nuzzle her neck. Then his hands came up over her sides and lifted to cover her breasts completely. Sensitized from her pregnancy, Charley moaned at the sensations he was causing.

Rafe groaned his reply and flexed his hips in the wide chair. Charley felt the long, hard length of him against her backside. *It had been so long.* She knew they should talk, but right then all she wanted to do *was feel.* She leaned back into him and delighted in the way he sucked and kissed her neck while fondling her heavy breasts in his hands, paying close attention to the hard, tight buds.

"Carlotta," he whispered, a familiar, husky tone to his voice that she'd longed to hear for months now.

"Oh, Rafe," Charley trembled as his hands slid up and down the silky fabric, finally finding her thighs and parting them with a tender sort of roughness.

She felt his tongue trace her earlobe and down to the hollow in her neck as he adjusted them so that she sat on top of him, fully facing him. He lifted her nightgown and squeezed her hips and bare bottom until it was flush against him. *I am so glad I didn't wear underwear.*

She ran her hands along his muscular thighs delighting in the shiver that seemed to run through his large body. He kissed, licked, and nibbled while he freed himself from the confines of his pants. One hand squeezed a pebbled nipple while he sprung free from his pants. The heat from his hard, aroused body found her and Charley felt moisture pool between her thighs.

"Mine," he growled into her neck.

They both grunted as he entered her from behind with one, single, perfectly aimed thrust. He held her by her hip with one hand and her throat with the other, moving them both, up and down, in and out, until it was almost too much for her. Sensation after sensation built up until she was a quivering mass of desire and need.

All those long months of abstinence and frustration made her acutely aware of each place he touched, kissed, and claimed. With every ardent stroke of his hard body, Charley forgot the distance between them, forgot her past misery. *Oh, Rafe!*

"*Mine!*" He roared the word as he plunged one final time, his seed bursting inside of her. Not too soon either, Charley groaned his name as she became caught up in the shimmering magic of her own completion. His rough exhale tickled the back of her neck as she melted, boneless and completely sated against her husband. *Finally. My love.*

She knew the second the sated haze of their lovemaking faded and, reality finally caught up with her husband. *No Rafe, please don't.* His hands came around to her swollen belly and froze.

Charley hardly had time to catch her breath as he cursed roughly. He pushed her carefully off of him and then he stood up. Charley felt the loss of him as keenly as she would have a bucket of ice water. She could only stare with tears in her eyes as he jumped out of the chair behind her and fumbled with his pants.

"Look what we've done! Damn it, how?"

"I came looking for you," Charley began tentatively and moved to go to him, but he held her at arm's length.

"I thought it was a dream! *Goddammit*, I tried so hard to stay away!"

"Rafe, what are you saying?"

"Damn it, you should have woken me! This was a mistake-"

Charley felt as if the bottom just dropped out from underneath her. Without another word to her husband, she bolted from the room. She was sick with grief. *He doesn't want me anymore. I have to get out of here.*

Rafe stalked around his study. In a moment of pure panic, he tossed everything on his desk across the room with a resounding thud, but even that didn't satisfy his desire to crunch something. *What the fuck happened?*

He'd been so careful not to touch his mate these past few months, to make sure she and their young were safe! The need to be with her, to touch her and taste her, was so strong he found himself unable to resist. That was why he'd spent the last few weeks sleeping in his office.

He had to keep his dirty paws off her, for her sake and the baby's! He wasn't going to risk his family because he couldn't control his baser urges. *Must keep her safe. Mine.*

Only it seemed that he misjudged his feisty mate. A mistake he should never have made. Carlotta was the bravest person he knew; it was one of the reasons he loved her so.

She'd come to seek him out, and once she found him sleeping, she curled up on his lap. Looking for safety and reassurance and he, in his relaxed state, mistook her appearance for yet another erotic dream since he forced himself to sleep away from her. Then he did exactly what he swore he wouldn't do until after the baby came. He made love to his wife.

Rafe closed his eyes and exhaled. He could still smell her on his skin, *honey, and cherries*, sweet and sexy as hell. The sounds she made, the way she gave everything of herself freely, how he felt when he was inside her, dear God, there was nothing like making love to Carlotta. She was his life.

You could have put her and the baby in danger! He was furious with himself. How could he have lapsed like that? And why was she so angry? Didn't she know he'd do anything to keep her safe? *Fuck! Fuck! Fuck!*

He'd wait awhile, then he'd go make sure she was okay. *Not to touch her again.* She needed time to come down from the emotional and physical excitement. *Good, we have a plan. Yes. Okay.* Except, just as he formed said plan his Beta, Seff, came running into his office with a furious expression on his face.

"What the hell did you do to her?" Seff barked at him.

The Pack Beta should have known better than to speak like that to Rafe, but their relationship spanned many years. They were friends before Rafe's ascent to Alpha. Still, he couldn't help but growl and face the smaller man.

"What did you just say to me?" Rafe growled. Seff didn't back down though, he averted his eyes for a second before looking back to face his Alpha.

"I saw Charley running up the stairs to your room-"

"Oh God, did she fall?"

'Fall? No way! But she's packing her bags and when I knocked, she *ordered* me to get a car and bring it out front."

It was only then that Rafe noticed the keys in Seff's hand. Fear tightened his throat as the words sunk in. *She's leaving me? No!*

"What, did she say why?"

"No, she didn't tell me why, that's why I came to find you! To find out what the hell you did to make the Pack's Alpha female cry and want to leave her home?" Seff's voice darkened, and he took a stance that Rafe never thought he'd see from his Beta.

"Are you challenging me?" Rafe hated the time he had to waste on asking this, but he couldn't ignore a direct challenge. Especially not one from his closest friend.

"No, but I'm going to get the car because I swore to protect and obey Charley when you took her as your mate."

"Fine, get the car, but your ass will be sitting in it alone."

"About time you stopped talking to me and went after your wife."

Rafe glowered at Seff, but noted the satisfied smile on his Beta's face, as he ran around the corner and took the stairs two at a time. The sound of clothing being shoved into bags was loud in his ears as he paused outside his bedroom. *Their bedroom.*

What have I done? In his desperation to save his mate from the fate that so many in his Pack suffered during pregnancy, he'd pushed her away. He had somehow hurt her, and now she was leaving him. *God no!*

Rafe hesitated. Panicked that the idea of her going had never occurred to him. He treated this pregnancy as something they simply had to live through and overcome. *Like a disease. No wonder she wants to leave, you fucking idiot!*

He couldn't wait a second longer. He had to confront the situation. He knocked before he walked into the bedroom they'd shared. He couldn't hide his shock at seeing his beautiful mate bent over a duffle bag wearing yoga pants and a loose top as she struggled with the zipper.

"Carlotta?"

At the sound of his voice, she froze. Rafe swallowed. Fear gripped him in her sadistic claws. *Fucking bitch that she was, those claws tightened around his throat.* He swallowed again.

"Baby, what's going on?"

"What does it look like?"

"I don't understand."

"You don't understand? Try being me. One minute you're caught up in a whirlwind romance, the next your husband can't stand the sight of you!"

"What?! That's not true-"

"Not true? Yeah, I wouldn't have believed it either, especially after what we just did downstairs-"

"That was an accident, I'm sorry-"

"Oh my God! An accident?! Having sex with me was an accident?"

"I meant I was sleeping-"

"So, you had no idea you were actually having sex with me, oh that's perfect," she started zipping the bag and moved to lug it to the door, but he blocked her path. He had to make her listen.

"Carlotta, please, let's talk."

"The time for talking is over-"

"What? What are you saying?"

❈ 4 ❈

Charley stood there looking at her husband, her resolve weakening with every second that passed. *No. I can't do this again. Just tell him and get it over with.*

"Look, Rafe, I, I know you're repulsed by me, I don't know if it's because I'm so big or you hate the idea of touching a pregnant woman, but-" tears pricked her eyes and she turned from him in anger, "*Oh God!* Just forget it, I think we made a mistake and, I just can't stay here anymore-"

"No!" the word seemed torn from his lips, "That's not true, you know that's not true," he looked as horrified as she felt, but she refused to consider his feelings. *How could he do this to her?*

"Carlotta, please listen to me-"

"Listen to you? Who the heck *are* you? I don't

know you! You, you, you seduce me, marry me, promise to give me the world! I believed you, and I fell in love with you! I thought it was all perfect, then we find out we're gonna have a baby, and you show your true colors!"

"What do you mean?"

"I mean you are a liar! A big, hairy liar!" She punctuated that by throwing a shoe at him. He didn't even duck. He seemed frozen in place, but Charley could sense his tension. Well, that was just too bad. She had her own tension to deal with lately. He could handle his own.

"I have never lied to you, Carlotta- "

"Yes, you have! You promised to love me-"

"I do love you!" he roared.

"Bullshit," she yelled then attempted to calm herself before adding, "Rafe, you may have started out thinking you loved me, but it is clear you don't. You're right not to. I mean, what do I know about how to fit in your world anyway? All you big, gorgeous Werewolves have your own rules, don't you? Maybe you just messed up the one about finding a true mate? Maybe you can find someone else? Someone you find more attractive-"

"What the hell are you talking about?! You are my *only mate,* and you are so beautiful-"

"Oh please, you think you have to say that to me because you feel guilty about knocking me up?"

"*Knocking you up?* You are having our child, Carlotta! You are precious and amazing–"

"No, stop, just let me finish. I know the truth, Rafe," tears streamed down her face, but she forged on. She was afraid that if she stopped, he'd talk her into believing him. *She so wanted to believe him.*

"Rafe, it's too late. We both know that. You haven't willingly touched me in months. You won't have sex with me–"

"What the hell do you call what we just did?"

"Rafe," her voice grew deep, but she managed to keep it void of emotion, "we both know if you weren't asleep that would not have happened. I, I know you aren't in love with me, *like that*, not anymore. So, uh, let's just admit we made a mistake, and I'll finish packing and just go, and when the baby comes, I will let you know. Please, just get out of my way," she was crying again, but she couldn't help it. *Stupid, Charley, just get out of there already.*

She tried to move around him dragging one of her suitcases behind her, but he blocked her escape. He reached out to touch her. His fingers felt like fire when they touched her, she pulled back wrapping her arms around her swollen stomach. Months of getting the cold shoulder from him had taken its toll. This latest devastating blow was almost too much. If he touched her again, she would surely break into a thousand pieces. *Be strong, Charley.*

The way he reacted to what they had just shared was so harsh, and unlike him, she couldn't bare it. Charley simply couldn't stand the thought that he was revolted by making love with her. Especially because she'd felt wonderful finally having him inside of her.

All she could think about while it was happening was how perfect it was to have Rafe touching and kissing her. It was all she ever wanted. She thought it was beautiful, a way for them to re-connect, but he'd been horrified!

She had to leave. She had to escape. She couldn't bear to be in that room a moment longer. She tried to skirt around him again, but she was hardly agile in her condition. Never mind the fact that he dropped to his knees and held out his arms to stop her progress.

"God no! Baby, please, please wait," his voice was hoarse, and his hands shook when he reached up to lay them on top of hers as she guarded her rounded belly. She tried to pull away, but he held her firmly. *And gently.* She could never fault him with being careless with her person. *Her heart maybe.*

"Listen to me, please, Carlotta," he cleared his

throat, his eyes wide and wet with emotion. Charley gasped when she saw his tears, but she was too afraid to trust in them, "*Fuck, what have I done?*"

His anguished voice was revealing, but she didn't stop him from continuing, "Carlotta, I am so, so sorry. I never meant to hurt you. I swear! I promise you, I never expected that you thought that I-"

"Well, what am I supposed to think? You used to seek out my company, we were together all the time, a kiss here, a touch there, a kind word, a conversation, Rafe, *we made love every night*! Now, now you won't even sleep next to me. I know a lot of men don't like their wives' bodies during pregnancy, but I never thought you would be one of them, that's why I think you made a mistake with me-" she hated the way her voice dropped. She couldn't look at him now, couldn't bear to witness the pity she was sure she'd find in his icy blue gaze. *Eyes that had once worshipped her.*

"Carlotta, look at me," she didn't want to, but she was no coward, no matter how badly she wanted to run away just then. She sucked in a fortifying breath and met his stare, shocked to find not pity, but terror on his beloved face.

"I've handled this so fucking badly. Listen to me, *you are my mate*. My one true mate. The only mistake I've made, was letting you think that I felt anything other than love for you. *What a fucking idiot I've been!* I am so sorry. I've just been so worried about you and the baby. Werewolf pregnancies are difficult, very difficult the mortality rate is high, and I wanted to try and spare you any difficulty. I spoke to the Pack elders, they told me abstinence was best, I know I should have discussed it with you, but I didn't want to worry you," his explanation poured out of him while relief and anger at his revelations coursed through Charley's veins.

"You've been worried? I'm the one who's pregnant, you jerk! My body has been taken over, and I have no one! No one to talk to, to tell my secrets and fears to, to turn to in the middle of the night! You, you made me sleep alone for months!"

"But I placed a Guard outside your door. You were safe. I made sure of that! You were not alone."

"Oh yeah, so when I need my feet rubbed, or need someone to scratch my back, or I just want to be held and kissed, I should ask Seff to get in bed with me? How about Kurt or Dib or Liam?"

"If they dare touch you, I'll rip their throats out!" he growled through tight lips, and Charley's heart thumped in her chest. *He's jealous! Good.*

"Oh, now you're going to play the jealous husband! That's just great! Just, *ugh*, move out of my way Rafe!"

"No! You are not leaving me!"

"As if you would notice!"

"I'd die without you, Carlotta."

The room was silent after that declaration. Charley's heart pounded in her chest. He looked so earnest, and she was so torn, so upset, she didn't know what to think. She loved him so much!

"I'm sorry, baby, I swear I'll spend the rest of my life making it up to you. Please, don't leave me. Without you, nothing else matters."

"But–"

"No buts, baby. Stay. Please. I will do anything you say."

"You'll stop running away and making decisions for me without consulting me first?" She noticed the way his body tensed but gave him the chance to respond.

"I am an Alpha Wolf, baby, it is difficult for me to adjust to having a partner, I am used to getting my own way, but for you, I will try anything."

"Then I want things to go back to the way they were before we got pregnant."

"But you, the baby? What about–"

"That's the deal, Rafe. Either you start acting like my husband again, or we end this."

"I am your husband. We are mates. Nothing will ever change that."

"Rafe?"

"I mean it, anything you want."

"Sleep with me."

"You still want to sleep with me?"

"Yes," she said, beyond pride. She just wanted him back.

"Okay, I'll come to bed with you."

"I, I want that," she whispered as he rose to his feet.

"*Thank God.* I love you so much, baby, please don't ever doubt that" his huge arms swallowed her in a tight embrace, but not too tight of course.

"I never thought I would ever doubt that, but Rafe, I've been so lonely."

"Me too. I've been stupid. I am sorry," he bent down and lifted her in his arms.

"*Oof*! Put me down, I'm too heavy."

"Baby, you weigh nothing at all. And you are the most beautiful thing in the world to me."

"Still? Even with this soccer player, I'm carrying around?"

"You kidding me? I've never seen you more beautiful."

"Oh Rafe, I love you, but what about, *you know*?"

"We'll work it out together, from now on all decisions will be made together," he walked to their bed with her in his arms, an expression of such love and tenderness on his face that Charley almost didn't hear what he said.

Momentarily sated by his tender handling of her, Charley yawned against his hard body. He cocooned her in the warmth of his arms and covered them with the comforter, tossing the clothes she was packing on the floor. They could always clean up tomorrow.

Oh, Rafe, she thought as she drifted into sleep. She knew then that he genuinely loved her, but only time would tell what the future would hold.

Dr. Rayne Davis was a smallish brunette with large eyes and a wonderful bedside manner. She was not only a Werewolf, she was also one of the Pack's top physicians, and Charley's OB/GYN. She replaced the ultrasound wand and wiped the jelly off Charley's exposed stomach with a tissue.

"Well?" Rafe's face was grim with worry.

He'd been turning himself inside out with thoughts that something he'd done could have harmed his son or daughter. They'd decided early on to keep the sex a surprise.

Charley had thought it was because he was old-fashioned. He didn't have the heart to tell her it was because, unfortunately, so many supernatural young didn't survive birth. He wanted to ease any suffering she would surely feel if they lost the young by keeping it as clinical as possible. *Nothing would stop the pain, but our mate is strong*, his Wolf said in that corner of his mind's eye reserved for his other half.

"Listen, is that his heart?" Charley smiled.

"Yes, he *or she* sounds perfect," the doctor nodded.

His mate was so beautiful and fragile. His Carlotta sat against the examination table, swollen with his child, and he'd never wanted her more. He could kick himself for making her think he didn't desire her. *Hell*, he couldn't stop himself from touching her if he tried.

True, he'd sought the advice of the Pack elders without asking her, and he'd been told that sex wasn't a good idea when your wife was pregnant. It could hurt the baby. However, the temptation of his luscious wife was almost too great for him to handle. Especially now that she carried his young. The truth was, he wanted her all the time! That was why he started sleeping in his office. *And she thought he wanted to get away from her! As if!*

He'd have to make it up to her. After the baby was born, and both mother and child were safe, he'd show her just how much he wanted her. *Always.*

He just needed them protected. His Wolf growled at the thought that they could be harmed. He had to work to reign in his beast.

Now that the Curse of St. Natalis, the one that had kept Werewolves from their beasts on all nights save the full moon for thousands of years, was close to being broken, Werewolves had to learn all over again how to control their Wolves full time. The moon still held sway, but not so much for Rafe. He figured it was because, as Alpha, he was the strongest in his Pack. Still, it was new, exciting, and terrifying to feel his other half so keenly when the full moon was still weeks away.

His Wolf's instincts to protect, honor, obey and love his mate was awesome, but the man needed to remain in control. Yes, Charley craved that explosive physical contact that was so strong between them, but Rafe spent the last few months fighting hard against it.

Sleeping next to her sweet, soft form last night had damn near done him in. And when she'd rolled over and covered his legs with hers, he almost exploded from the contact. *Like a horny teenager still wet behind the ears.*

Her sweet honey scent had filled his nostrils, and it was all he could do not to follow his instincts and lick her from head to foot. She was delectable, funny, smart, and beautiful. Rafe was ashamed of himself for making her feel as if she wasn't. *I'll make it up to you, baby, after*, he vowed as he helped her to a sitting position.

"Well, you two must be excited. It is getting close to your due date. How are you feeling, Mrs. Maccon?"

"I feel fine, well, I'm huge, but I feel good."

"Well, your baby is firmly planted in there even though I can only get a side view. I can tell he or she is doing perfectly! Have you been taking your vitamins?"

"Yes, except I switched to the low iron brand, the other ones were giving me gas," Charley answered.

"What? Why didn't you tell me? Does she need more iron? Can she get it through diet?" Rafe crossed his arms over his chest as he demanded answers to his questions. *Why hadn't she told him she had gas pains? Cause you weren't there for her, moron!*

"Mr. Maccon," the doctor began in a calming tone, though she was careful to avert her eyes to her Alpha's dominance.

"I gave your wife two kinds of prenatal vitamins specifically for this purpose. Don't worry. She is getting everything she needs. The child too."

He felt his wife glaring at him and knew he'd stepped in it again. What was he supposed to do though? How could he take care of her if she kept things like that from him?

"Now, Mrs. Maccon, your blood pressure is

slightly elevated from the last time you were here though you are still within normal range. I'd like you to take it easy these last few weeks, supernatural pregnancies can be difficult, though we've made some serious strides in decreasing the risks the last few years."

"I thought not all Werewolf, and normal couples have supernatural young?" Charley asked with a hand on her belly.

"Well, that is true. There is no guarantee your child will be a Werewolf, but it is more than likely given your husband's genetics."

"Okay, um, is it true I'll be carrying for longer than nine months?"

"Um, well, truthfully, I've seen Werewolves and wives of Werewolves give birth anywhere from six to ten months after fertilization. Of course, the longer the baby is in there, the better chance he or she has of being viable."

Rafe's jaw clenched. He hated that terminology. As if she'd understood that the doctor turned to him, with her eyes still carefully averted. *Don't you cause harm to my mate! Grrr.*

"Don't worry, Mr. and Mrs. Maccon, I am going to do everything I can to make sure you are both healthy."

"Thank you, Dr. Davis, may I use the restroom

now?" Rafe helped Charley off the examination table as the doctor waved her towards the restroom. He watched his mate carefully until she closed the door, then he turned his attention to the doctor.

"Can I ask you a question?"

"Yes, sir, of course."

"My wife is concerned about, well, about sex, Dr. Davis."

"Ah, yes, well most pregnant women are uncomfortable with their size, and it is really just a matter of finding the right, ah, position-"

"No, you see, she wants to have sex. She thinks I don't find her attractive anymore, but I'm just trying to keep them safe. Can you tell her it isn't a good idea?"

"Mr. Maccon, with all due respect, your wife is experiencing a huge surge of hormones, and her body is constantly making demands of her. Many pregnant women crave sexual attention. If she feels good enough to have intercourse, then I suggest you oblige her."

"But what about the baby?"

"What about the baby? Has Mrs. Maccon experienced any pain or bleeding after intercourse?"

"No. Not that I know of."

"Then she's fine. Trust your wife, Mr. Maccon. She will tell you when it is no longer comfortable for her."

Rafe left the doctor's office slightly more assured. Carlotta, on the other hand, was radiant. She wore a long sage green colored tunic over velvety brown pants with the same-colored flats on her dainty little feet. Her hair was loose around her slightly flushed face, just the way he liked it. He kissed her lightly on the mouth and drove her to get a chocolate egg cream at the *Maccon City Dairy*.

"Good?"

"Yes, thanks."

"Anything for you, my love," he kissed her again, warming at her smile, then he drove them back home to Macconwood Manor.

He was still nervous, and it showed. He couldn't help it. His Wolf was working overtime, watching, and listening for anything and everything while they were out. His lack of sleep was catching up with him.

Charley yawned in the car. She was tired too. Rafe picked her up out of the car and carried her to their room despite her many protests. He ignored the amused glances from those members of his Wolf Guard who witnessed the entire thing.

"But I want to go to the game room and watch TV?"

"You can watch television in bed. You need rest."

"But Rafe!"

He kissed her gently on the mouth, shushing her protests. He needed her safe. He couldn't explain it. Not in words, but maybe if he showed her, without going too far. He nuzzled her cheek and lay her down on the comforter.

"If you lay with me for a bit, then I'll take a nap, deal?" She yawned, and he gave in. *How could he say no to her?*

"I love you, Carlotta," he gathered her close to his side and turned on the brand new flat screen he'd had installed for her in their bedroom.

He turned on one of those cooking shows she liked and muted the volume. Then he rubbed her back in slow, wide circles. She sighed and rolled onto her back, her luminous brown eyes smiling at him as she ran her hands up his shoulders.

"I heard, what the doctor said, Rafe," she began shyly, biting her lower lip. He followed the movement like the predator he was, waiting for the opportunity to pounce.

"What's that, baby?"

"She said we could *make love*, as long as I wanted to."

"Yeah?" he said following the movement of her hands as she flicked open the buttons of her shirt revealing the lacy bra she wore over her ripe breasts.

"Well, I want to Rafe," she'd no sooner said the

words than he was hovering over her. All good intentions aside, his mate was luscious and aroused. Their bond made it impossible for him to deny his response. *Be gentle*, he admonished himself.

He kissed her deeply, with long, slow strokes of his tongue that made her tremble against him. He peeled off her clothing until she was nude on their comforter.

"You have on too many clothes, take them off," she sighed as his tongue savored every sweet inch of her skin.

"Yes, ma'am," he growled and took off his shirt, reveling in her touch.

He cherished her body until he almost went mad with wanting her. Carlotta's breathing was heavy in her passion. She moaned as he brought her to the ultimate pleasure. Her unmistakable sobs and tremors increased his own drive to reach satisfaction. *So perfect. Mine. Grrr.*

Rafe knelt on their mattress and spread her gorgeous legs until she was completely open to him. He took his cock in his hand and rubbed the tip along her glistening lips. Her thighs trembled at the sensual onslaught. She sighed his name as he, careful of her abdomen and its precious cargo, pushed inside of her welcoming heat.

He thrust slowly, the long length of him buried to

the hilt. He ground himself against her, her muscles gripped him as he pushed her near the edge, and, this time, he fell off with her. Never, in all the times he made love to his wife, had he ever felt so complete. Like they reached a new level of togetherness with this one shared intimacy.

Within minutes, Carlotta's breathing evened out, and she drifted to sleep, safely tucked against him. *Always.* Rafe smoothed and kissed her hair away from her face. He tried to stem the worry from overflowing. He placed one giant hand carefully on her belly and jumped, almost waking her up, when he felt the baby kick.

His heart swelled with love and pride.

We will keep her safe. We will keep them safe! Ours! Grrr... Mine!

6

Late November…

"That's it! I will kill him!" Charley raged as Seff stood and blocked the door.

"I am sorry, Charley, but Rafe had to go to a meeting, and he said you weren't to leave the room."

"Too freaking bad! I thought we were past this!"

"I'm sure this has nothing to do with you guys personally, this is about safety. He said he'd explain when he came home-"

"I don't give a crap what he said! Seff, my back is killing me, and I want to go for a drive."

"Look, he didn't even get a chance to explain it to me, Charley."

"Then it must not be that important. I want to go, *now*, Seff."

"Charley be reasonable. It's raining, and it's dark."

"I don't care! Look, you can come with me."

"Charley-"

"Seff, either you take me for a drive right now, or I'm going to sic Buttercup on you!"

Right on cue, Charley's pet from when she'd lived alone came down the hall. The fluffy cat had his back up and his fangs bared. It was a well-known fact in the household that Buttercup was Charley's personal attack cat. If she was unhappy, her cat made sure the culprit was too.

Lately, the furball had taken to napping inside the hall closet. He'd taken a special liking to Rafe's favorite coat. Not a good look for the guy. It was rather difficult to exude the proper image of an Alpha werewolf when you were covered in orange cat hair. *Have a fight with Garfield and lose?* Poor Liam had made that joke once. Only once. Seff's little bro had a hard time talking for a few days after that one. At any rate, Seff had no desire to fight the fearsome creature.

"Okay, okay. I will take you for a ride in town, deal? But I'm telling Rafe you made me!"

An hour later...

Rafe pulled into the garage back at Macconwood Manor. *Fuck!* He could not believe this latest news. Skoll again! The fucker was one oily Wolf. They'd almost had him, but he'd slipped away. He spent the last hour with Randall and a few others devising new plans to track the bastard. He hadn't gotten around to informing his Beta yet, choosing to keep the Wolf watching over his beloved mate.

Carlotta was so happy lately. He was too. They'd been much closer ever since the near miss when he'd almost lost his mate because of his stupid fears and insecurities. But he would never let that happen. She was his life. He vowed to never let her go. *Mine.*

He was on full alert as he pulled up to the Manor's multi-car garage. Rafe sucked in a breath. The cherry-red Range Rover, the one he'd bought his wife as a belated Christmas gift, was missing. She loved that vehicle, and she would never let anyone take it without her. *That meant- oh shit!*

Rafe ran up the stairs three at a time. He first noticed that Seff was not stationed at the bedroom door. He went inside and noted the empty bed and the fact that his wife's purse was gone. Panic flared inside of him. His Carlotta was not there. He grabbed his cell and dialed.

He'd just left one of his top security teams, trained by his Wolf Guard, with strict instructions to contact him in case of any changes in their search. Now he advised them that they may be too late. *Fuck!* He needed to find his wife. *Now!*

Skoll was cruel and dangerous. A friend and follower of Rafe's maniacal father, he wanted to be

Alpha and bring things back to the way they were under his rule. Mainly dark and scary. *Hell no!*

Rafe would not be cowered, and Skoll had tried again and again to rob him of his rightful place. He'd been involved in a kidnapping attempt on Rafe's sister Cat and several other attacks on the Pack. Luckily for Cat, Tate Nighthawk, one of his best Guards, had been with her. The two were happily married now, and Cat was now one of his Wolf Guard, as she'd always wanted to be.

Despite his making up with his mate, that didn't mean he worried any less about her and their young. In fact, they'd argued that afternoon when he'd been called away, and he ordered Seff to guard her. He promised he'd explain when he got back, but it had taken much longer than he thought. The report he'd received was very disturbing. Skoll had been seen in the vicinity and with a known practitioner of Dark Magic.

Rafe himself had gone to the motel where his enemy had been seen, but there was no sign of Skoll. Only some rare ingredients and a couple of empty vials remained in the room. They'd bagged the stuff and sent it to a White Witch that the Pack was friendly with for identification.

Rafe already sent Kurt and Dib, two more of his Guard, to track the Dark Witch who'd been working for Skoll. *They'd pick him up for questioning.* After they left, he headed back home to put everyone on high alert. He'd been so preoccupied with his duties to his Pack, he hadn't thought to call Carlotta first.

What kind of fucking husband and father did that? Idiot! He failed them. His wife and young should have been his first concern. And they were, but he hadn't been quick enough. He heard her cell phone go off in their bedroom and his heart dropped to his stomach. She didn't have it with her. *Fuck.*

7

Charley waited impatiently inside the passenger side of the vehicle since Seff had been driving her high-end SUV. It had been a while since she could fit behind the wheel of her beloved Range Rover. The fact that Rafe finally got her, her very own vehicle, proof that he was opening up to the fact that she was a capable person, and that she could not drive it at the moment galled her to no end. She sighed and patted her ever-growing belly. *Don't worry, I won't take it out on you in future allowances or anything like that, my little buddy.*

She loved her baby and didn't really mind the no-driving thing. Nope, not the stretch marks, the fact that she could no longer see her feet, or the frequent trips to the bathroom either! It was all worth it in the end. She'd soon have a happy, healthy baby and all the little bothers would just fade away. For Rafe, she could do nothing else. Her man needed a win in his family life, and she was going to provide it by delivering a perfect baby!

The rain was coming down harder now, and though she'd been all gung-ho to go for a ride in the car, as it was the only thing that soothed her back pains this far along in her pregnancy, she'd been anxious to head back. Something was niggling the back of her mind. *It's okay, any minute now we will be headed back to the manor*, she thought to herself.

The drive had been a nice one. It settled those pesky gas pains that for some reason or other, she felt in her back. They usually came and went, but today, they had been plaguing her non-stop. *Just my luck.*

She'd been careful not to mention them to Rafe. He tended to worry, and when he did, he could be slightly suffocating. He'd have had her at the doctor's office immediately.

My lovable, overbearing teddy-Wolf, she thought. No need for that, a long drive in the Range Rover and some cold ginger ale and she was normally golden. She blamed her nerves on the fact that it didn't seem to be working.

Charley huffed out a breath as she began to feel the strain in her lower back. She lovingly patted her wide belly and smiled. This baby was going to be huge! The doctor had assured her, everything was just fine. Supernatural babies simply required a lot of fuel, and she didn't mind providing it! *Can you say pizza?*

The pine barrens that surrounded their home compound was as dense as it was dark. Rafe preferred to keep it *au natural*, meaning no unnatural lighting in this part of Macconwood Manor. The section reserved for full moon runs once a month and Manor residents only the rest of the time.

There was, of course, the public road that was very well-lit and paved, but she really had to pee and asked Seff to take them the back way. It was faster by about six minutes. That could have meant the difference between having to shampoo the inside of the car or not if her bad luck hadn't followed her around!

Seff had, of course, obliged her. He readily headed for the back road when no sooner had they entered the private property, they'd both heard a familiar pop. The car jiggled a bit, then pulled to the right. They had a flat and Charley's bladder was about to burst.

"No worries, I'll have the tire changed in a few minutes," he said.

Good thing, Seff could see in the dark though, not very well through all the rain. They were still a few miles to the house, and there was no way she was walking in all that weather. If only she hadn't left her cell at home! *Ugh.*

"You okay?" Seff asked with an apologetic smile on his face.

"Yeah, I've got a vice grip on my bladder though," she replied.

"I'll hurry," he said.

It was odd that the brand-new car would have blown a tire like that, but she didn't give it a second thought. She did feel bad however that she couldn't help him. Not that she had to worry, as a Werewolf, Seff was strong. *Not like Rafe, but close.* He'd have the job done and them back home soon enough. *Ow*, if only her back would stop bothering her!

"I am really sorry about this, Charley, can you hold it a little longer?"

"Yeah, don't worry about me, I'm sorry you have to change the flat in this weather."

"No worries. Stay put."

He smiled and zipped up his raincoat before heading around to the back, driver's side tire. There was a flat tire kit in the trunk somewhere, she was certain. Charley rested her head against the cushioned chair and closed her eyes. Maybe Rafe would give her a back rub when she got home? *Mmm. Oh yeah. That would be nice.*

She was concentrating on her breathing when she heard a thud. She tried to turn around in her seat, but she couldn't really move. There simply wasn't enough room. *What the heck?*

"Seff?" She called out and pressed the button to open her window.

Cold rain splashed her face, but Charley didn't even feel it as a man with furious black eyes and a slicked-back, ponytail grabbed her door handle before she could push the lock down. Fear coursed through her body as she looked at those familiar, coal-black eyes. It was *him*. Skoll.

"Come out, come out, *Mrs. Maccon*," he snarled and released her seatbelt. The man who wanted to unseat her husband as Alpha grabbed her wrist and pulled her forward. Charley groaned as she stumbled on the slippery pavement. She couldn't stop her forward propulsion, and she landed hard, hitting her knees on the rough asphalt.

"Ow!" Pain shot through her back as she tried to crawl away from him. *Dammit!* She was too slow, too awkward physically. This man was her husband's biggest enemy and threat! That meant he would use her and her child to hurt Rafe! He laughed at her, slowly stalking like a sick predator as she tried desperately to get away from him.

"No, no, no!" She cried as she tried to scramble to her feet, but the pain came again this time hitting her even lower in her back.

Skoll caught up to her easily. He chuckled deep in his throat as he lifted her to her feet without any thought to her condition. His hands bit into the sensitive skin of her wrists, drawing blood when she tried to pull away. The rain seemed to slow down, but Charley was already soaked and shivering as the temperature dropped. She fought his grip, but it was like fighting against handcuffs. He was simply too strong for her.

Charley tried to stem her fear, but it was no good. He'd already scented it. She could tell by the evil gleam in his black eyes that he liked it. The sicko was getting off on her fear and pain. She forced herself to stand still and firm. She wasn't going to give this creep one ounce of pleasure.

"What have you done with Seff?"

"Oh, that brown-haired pup? He's sleeping right now. A touch of Dark magic and, *bam*, knocked that Werewolf right on his ass! But looksee what I got here," he dropped his eyes to her large belly and placed his hand on it. Charley tried to pull away from him, but he was too strong.

"Let go of me, you piece of shit," she said between clenched teeth.

"Ah, the bitch reveals herself! You know, when I set up camp right in Rafe's backyard I thought maybe

I'd get a stray or two, but I never dreamed I'd catch his whore!"

"I mated to the Alpha of the Macconwood Pack, that makes me the female Alpha, I order you to release me!"

"Ha! You bitch, no *normal* will ever give me orders, but I might have some use for you and your bastard! Now move," he snarled and pulled her further into the trees.

She didn't want to leave the road, but Charley had no choice, but to follow. She gritted her teeth against the sharp pains that were coming more and more frequently and tried not to think the impossible. She was going into labor in the middle of the night, in the woods, during a thunderstorm, with her husband's worst enemy.

Skoll was tall and muscular, though there was something slimy and underhanded about his whole appearance. As if he were bathed in evil. He shoved her onto the ground in a little clearing where he'd assembled a lean-to of sorts.

"Make yourself comfortable," he mocked as he turned his back to her.

Charley sat up and tried to keep the pain from showing on her face. She'd been keeping track of her pains and a real and sudden fear gripped her. She was trapped outside, in the woods, with a maniac, and she was having contractions. *Oh crap!* Charley was in labor.

"Don't bother praying, it's two weeks till the moon is full. I've hidden this spot well. Your precious *mate* will never find you in time!"

Rafe, I am so sorry, she said in her mind as she watched Skoll light a lamp. The thought of being stuck here with him made her gag, but she kept silent. She didn't know what shape Seff was in, but she hoped he was healed by now and able to get help.

She didn't have much time left. Maybe she could try to reach him through their *matebond?* Charley closed her eyes and tried to concentrate. She never tried to reach Rafe through the magical Pack bond that connected them before, but she had to try.

ack at the manor...

Rafe had no time. Carlotta could be in danger. He ran for the front door and nearly plowed down Liam and Conall in the process. Conall's blonde spiked hair was even taller than usual as he took in his Alpha and, Liam dropped the video game he was holding as they became aware of Rafe's agitation.

"Have you seen Seff or my wife?" Rafe growled the words. He could hardly keep his Wolf from showing through his bright blue eyes.

"No, why? What's happening?" Conall asked.

"Seff said Charley wanted to go for a ride earlier, but that was while ago," Liam replied.

"He's not answering his phone. I need to find her now. There's been news about Skoll, it's not safe."

"Shit, um wait, let's track their phones," Conall opened an app and began a trace, but Rafe held up Charley's cell phone in his hand.

He was barely able to form words in his frenzied state. Rage and helplessness overwhelmed him. He didn't notice the grip he had on Charley's phone and before he knew it, he crushed it in his palm. Liam and Conall swallowed audibly.

"I have to find her now!"

"Wait one sec, Rafe-"

"I don't have time. She needs me, I can feel it."

"But it makes no sense to leave without having an idea of where to go, give the app a second to work-" Liam protested, but Rafe didn't hear him.

He went out into the rain and closed his eyes. He needed his mate. She was out there, somewhere. He had to find her. *Carlotta. Mine.* He felt a pull and knew instinctively it was her. She was in pain. *No!*

"Rafe, wait! Seff has his cell. He always does. Just give me one second, I almost have the coordinates," Conall was tracking Seff's cell with one hand and calling Randall with Liam's phone in the other.

"You trace Seff and the car, see if you can find them. Liam, get Dr. Davis over here, I'm going after my mate, something is wrong," his words were more growl than human.

Rafe tore off his shirt while he ran towards the woods. One second, he was on two legs as he tore out of his jeans, the next, he was on four. His huge black Wolf took off in the direction he'd felt his *matebond* pulling him towards.

Liam whined at Conall and nodded his head towards their Alpha. He was amazed that the man could change with the moon so far away. It was true the curse was almost broken, a young Wolf they knew named Grazi was trying to end it, but it still held power over them. Werewolves were still subject to the phases of the moon. And once they were free, well, they'd need to learn how to live with their beasts all over again. Rafe's perfect communion with his was an amazing accomplishment and awe inspiring. But the Wolves had no time to think on that. They had to track down Seff and Charley!

"I think he was headed the right way. Randall? Yeah, we'll meet you there," Conall hung up the phone, and he and Liam ran after their Alpha. He was way ahead of them, but they'd still make better time on their own feet than if they stopped to get a car. They only hoped he'd find her quickly.

All the members of the Wolf Guard loved and respected Charley. She was the best thing that ever happened to Rafe. They would do anything for her and the little one. The two men sprinted down the road refusing to let their fears and anxieties slow them down. Seff and Charley were safe, they had to be! They ran on swift feet as their Alpha made his way on four paws through the pitch-black woods.

Rafe jumped over the knotted roots and branches that littered the pine barrens that spread out wildly behind the manor. His property went on for miles and miles, preserved for the Pack as a safe area for moonlit runs and hunting. He'd never thought the breach they'd discovered earlier that night would end at his property. Someone was going to pay for this!

Rage burned inside of him as he ran harder than ever before through the cold rain. The drops felt like a thousand needles piercing his hide. His breath puffed out in clouds, and he silenced the urge to howl. *No need to alert his enemies.* His mate was close. Their bond was getting stronger, but she was in distress. He could feel her pain and the bitter taste of her fear. *Grrr.*

He'd tear out the throat of anyone who dared put his mate and his young in danger. If that bastard Skoll touched a single hair on her head, Rafe would have no qualms about ending his pathetic life. *Coward. Enemy.* Pack justice was swift and at times merciless, but no one threatened his family. *No one.*

Charley closed her eyes on a wave of pain that

brought her to her knees. She didn't know how long they'd been there, Skoll spent the time on his phone. He'd been arguing with someone though it was in a language she couldn't identify. He clicked off the cell and turned to face her as she gritted her teeth in pain.

"Ah, are you about to whelp then? I can smell your time is near. Pity, your time is near as is the end of your life, since I've no use for you. Now that young you carry may be valuable. I have the acquaintance of a Dark Witch who will use your baby's organs to fuel a magic that will end the Macconwood Pack!"

"You will never get your slimy hands on my baby!"

"Ha ha ha, want to bet?" He came towards her and Charley backed up as far as she could against the rotted wood wall.

Fear and pain warred with each other inside of her until she thought she'd pass out. He reached his thin arms towards her, and she screamed and swatted his hand away. That only made him angry. He raised his hand as if to backslap her. Charley huddled into herself, trying to protect her stomach from his blow. But it never came.

Before he could reach her, a black torpedo flew at him out of the dense stand of trees. Charley screamed. Could it be? She smiled through her pain as the familiar shape of her husband's Wolf went on the attack.

Skoll did not stand a chance. He had no time to retaliate against Rafe's violence. Her husband and mate had the villain by the neck, glowing eyes met hers as if to ask a question, at her nod, her Werewolf husband closed his jaws. *Hard.*

"Rafe! You found me! Oh, thank God, ahhhh!" She groaned in pain, and the Wolf leapt over the bloody corpse of his enemy to stand by her.

He nuzzled her face with his wet muzzle and licked her cheek. A whining sound came from him as she clung to him and cried into his dark fur. A second later she was against hard, muscular skin. Her husband ran his hands over her gently, though frantically, checking for injuries.

"Carlotta! Are you okay? What did he do? Did he hurt you?"

"No, he didn't get the chance! But- *ahhh!* Rafe! I, uh, I think the baby is coming!"

"What? Here? Now?!" Rafe's face blanched.

Charley screamed and held her stomach as a powerful contraction hit her. Her mate held her hand and helped her to stand once it had passed. She wanted to get as far away from Skoll and everything that bore his touch and his vile scent. The Wolf inside her husband thoroughly approved of the sentiment, at least she felt his approval. *The matebond.* She almost smiled, but the next contraction hit.

"Oh God, Rafe!"

"Come here, baby," he picked her up in his arms and walked her carefully through the trees to where her car was stranded. He was naked and barefoot, but he didn't even notice.

Conall and Liam just arrived as he put Charley down in the trunk of the car and nodded towards Seff's prone form. His Beta looked like a pile of clothing on the road, limp and unmoving.

Liam tossed Rafe a pair of sweats that he pulled out from under his shirt and moved towards their unmoving Packmate. Rafe pulled them on as Conall stooped down to check on Seff. He trusted them to check on the man, but he could not leave his mate's side. She squeezed his hand and gritted her teeth as another contraction hit her.

"What's wrong with him?" Rafe asked concerned for his Beta but preoccupied with his wife.

"I don't see an injury," Liam frowned. The younger Wolf Guard was obviously worried about his brother.

"It's *Dark Magic*, Skoll said a Witch helped him. Rafe!!" Charley screamed and tried to sit up.

"Call the doctor again! Get the ambulance here!"

"It's too late, the baby is coming now, Rafe!"

Rafe slid the long skirt his wife was wearing up her legs. He looked at her and waited for her to nod before he ripped her soaked cotton panties off her body. He didn't know much about delivering babies, but he knew the situation wasn't ideal. He grabbed the blanket that was in the backseat and covered her the best he could.

"*Oh shit!* The baby is coming. Carlotta, I can see the head. Okay, you can do this. You're braver than anyone I know, it's going to be okay," he murmured softly.

Funny thing was, all his previous panic and anxiety was all forgotten. In the face of danger and the threat of losing her twice, he knew that his mate was strong and courageous. She could handle this, and he would be there to help her. They could do this! He believed it with every fiber of his being. She was amazing.

"Rafe, I can't, I can't!"

"You can, my love, look at me. I was wrong, okay? I should have never tried to stay away from you. I thought I was protecting you, but I stifled you. I am so sorry about all that. Even afterwards, I was high-handed, but baby, you are amazing. I love you, you're my heart, you and this baby. We can do this together, I swear I will do everything I can to protect you, both of you, and I will love you till the last breath leaves my body," he cradled her head and kissed her softly.

She cried and kissed him back, and he felt his heart swell. Then she screamed as another contraction hit her. Rafe whined in sympathy and held her hand. He felt helpless.

The sounds of an ambulance reached his ears, and he almost cried with gratitude. He felt wild, *nervous*. His eyes went to Liam who flagged down the vehicle.

Charley gripped his hand, and he was amazed at the strength he felt there. Not that he should be. His mate was strong and brave and wonderful. She was going to make it, or, by God, neither was he.

Rafe switched positions, he stood by her head and supported her back while Dr. Davis came over with a gurney. By then his entire Wolf Guard and security detail were scanning the area. The rain had stopped, but it was still cold, and they were out in the open. His Wolf was bristling inside of him.

"Let's get her on the gurney, please, Mr. Maccon?"

Rafe lifted his wife and transferred her to the narrow ambulance bed. Dr. Davis made no move towards Carlotta which was wise. He couldn't allow anyone to touch her just yet. Not with his Wolf so tense. *Mine.*

"Mr. Maccon, I am going to look at your wife to see where we are, okay?" The doctor explained before she touched Charley and that was good. His Wolf allowed it even though he still felt raw and volatile.

"Okay, I see the head is almost out. Stop the gurney here, please. Looks like we're doing this right now."

"Here! She can't give birth here!"

"Tell your child that, Mr. Maccon," the doctor said with just enough respect in her voice to make up for the snark.

"Okay, Mrs. Maccon?"

"Call me Charley!"

"Okay, easy there, Charley, with the next contraction I want you to push. Okay, tuck your chin down and push now," Dr. Davis ordered, doing her best to remain calm under her Alpha's fierce scrutiny. *She wondered if he even realized how much he loved his wife.*

"Someone get Mr. Maccon some antiseptic wipes. Get the blood off him. He's about to become a father."

He hadn't noticed the blood splattered across his chest and hands. He'd killed tonight to save his mate, and he had no regrets, but he wouldn't hold his child with that traitor's blood on his hands.

A second later, he'd dumped a bottle of hand sanitizer all over himself and wiped it off with a bottle of water and a clean towel from the ambulance.

"Rafe! RAFE!" Charley screamed his name.

Rafe could hardly breathe. That piercing cry from his wife's lips sounded like agony. Everything afterwards was silent. In fact, no one made a sound for what seemed like forever. Then, he heard it, the most beautiful noise in the world. A soft mewling cry coming from a tiny bundle that Dr. Davis wrapped up and handed to his wife.

Tears poured down Charley's face as she held their baby. Rafe stepped towards her and put his arms around her, things went blurry for a second, and he realized that he was crying at the sight of their perfect child.

"Oh, my! Mr. Maccon?"

"Yes?"

"Please take your son from your wife."

"A son? It's a boy!"

"Yes, take him now. Charley get ready," the doctor ordered.

"Ow, Rafe! Oh, God! Ow! Ow!" Charley yelled as another contraction squeezed her still swollen belly. Rafe moved just in time to take his newborn son as Charley screamed into the night one more time. She bore down, and minutes later the unthinkable happened.

"It's another boy!"

"What? Twins!" Conall was grinning as the doctor

handed the second baby to Rafe, who now held two sons in his hands.

"But how?" His question was muffled by the groan coming from his wife. She looked as if she were still in a lot of pain and panic gripped his heart again.

"Honey? Carlotta?!"

"Wow! I don't believe this, I guess three is the magic number!"

"Wh-" Rafe was unable to form words at that point.

"Okay, ready, now push, Charley come on!" Dr. Davis was amazed. She'd heard of twins that were difficult to detect, but triplets?

"I can't, I can't! Ahhhh!" Charley was exhausted. Her body felt broken in two, but she felt another contraction and just had to push.

"Great job! Here comes baby number three, and, it's a girl!"

The doctor gave the newest addition over to Charley who looked radiant in her exhaustion. Rafe gathered around his wife and daughter with his sons in his hands. Babies, mother, and father were loaded into the ambulance, as a second vehicle came for Seff.

Rafe had protected his family. They were healthy and safe. His Wolf howled in his mind's eye. Their matebond glowed with the power of their love.

"Carlotta, you are full of surprises, my love," he said.

"Yeah, but I didn't know just how full!" She giggled and then yawned. She was exhausted. His brave, beautiful mate. Pride and love beamed from Rafe's face as he watched his mate nuzzle their children while the ambulance drove them to the hospital.

EPILOGUE

"Who's on duty tonight?"

"Me!"

"No, it's Uncle Conall's turn!"

"Back off, Conall! It's Uncle Dib's turn to stay up with the wee ones!"

Charley laughed from where she sat nursing her oldest son, Owen. His younger brother, Val, short for Valen, had just finished his meal and was napping in one of three bassinets that sat in the main living room. Rafe stood near her, rocking their daughter, Rafaella. Charley had insisted they name their daughter after him.

The babies had been home for a month now after spending a week in the hospital. They had stayed a few days for observation with an ever-watchful mama and papa to protect them.

"But how come we didn't suspect multiples?" Charley asked on the day they got ready to go home.

"Ah! Because," Dr. Davis said with a triumphant smile on her face, "These little ones are masters of disguise! You see, I never detected Charley was pregnant with more than one baby because their hearts when they are near each other, beat perfectly in time. Watch this," she proceeded to show the proud parents the unusual trait.

Such a thing, doctor and parents had never heard of before, but they all agreed to keep it under wraps as it was surely a part of their supernatural heritage. Rafe held his wife in bed that night after all three babies had been tucked in their cribs in the adjoining nursery.

Charley hated to be separated from them, but Rafe insisted even perfect mothers needed their sleep. Besides, they had eight live-in nannies! The one thing they'd never lack for was babysitters!

It was a good thing too. Triplets were bound to need a lot of care. Especially his children!

"Rafe?"

"Yes, my love," he asked as he lay with his head on her soft, belly.

"You are incredible," she smiled.

"I don't have anything on you, baby."

"I love you."

"Me too. You and the babies are everything I've ever wanted. I hope I am worthy of you all."

"Oh Rafe, you're a natural born father. The babies already recognize you and love you. And I do too."

"That's good mate of mine, because I am never letting you go."

The doctor had given the okay for them to be intimate and he'd relished the idea of getting his wife in bed all day. He waited a long time to show her how much he loved her, almost too long. That night he finally showed her, with every single fiber of his being.

Mine.

Liked this story? Want more? Check out the whole series The Macconwood Pack Tales on my website www.cdgorri.com.

If you are looking for more about the Macconwood Wolves, then try my Maccon City Shifters books. Or catch up on how the Alpha and his Wolf Guard found their mates in the Macconwood Pack Novel Series, from book1, Charley's Christmas Wolf, to book 8, Werewolf Fever.

Thank you so much for reading!
Del mare alla stella,
C.D. Gorri

HAVE YOU MET THE BARVALE CLAN BEARS?

Looking for a Paranormal Romance series that is loads of growly fun?

Meet the Barvale Clan first in the Bear Claw Tales! A complete shifter romance series about 4 brothers who discover and need to win their fated mates!
Titles are:
Bearly Breathing
Bearly There
Bearly Tamed
Bearly Mated

Followed by two more spin off series, the Barvale Clan Tales, featuring:
Polar Opposites
Polar Outbreak

Polar Compound
Polar Curve

and, of course, the Barvale Holiday Tales, beginning
with A Bear For Christmas
Hers to Bear
Thank You Beary Much
&
Bearing Gifts!
Look for more of these sexy, heartwarming holiday
inspired tales soon!

No cliffhangers. Steamy PNR fun.
Go and read your next happily ever after today!

The Falk Clan Tales are my stories surrounding four Dragon Shifter brothers and how they find their one true mates!

Each brother's chest is marked with his rose, the magical link to his heart and his magic. They each have a matching gemstone to go with it.

In *The Dragon's Valentine* we meet the eldest Falk brother, Callius. He is on a mission to find a Castle and his one true mate, one he can trust with his diamond rose....

She's given up on love, but he's just begun...

In *The Dragon's Christmas Gift* our attention shifts to Alexsander, the youngest brother of the four. He has resigned himself to a life alone, until he meets *her*...

His heart is frozen. Can she change his mind about love?

The Dragon's Heart is the story of Edric Falk who has vowed never to love again, but that changes when he meets his feisty mate, Joselyn Curacao.

Some wounds run deep. Can a Dragon's heart be unbroken?

Meet Nikolai Falk in the last Falk Clan Tale, *The Dragon's Secret.*

She just wants a little fun, he's looking for a lifetime.

*These first four books are now available in one convenient set. Look for Dragon Mates today.

Meet another long lost Falk brother in *The Dragon's Treasure.* Castor Falk breaks free from his prison in search of his kin, he finds his mate instead.

She doesn't believe in fairytales, until a Dragon comes knocking on her door.

The Dragon's Surprise features a new Dragon, Devine Graystone, and a female Werewolf who makes him think twice about his lonely state of being...

Nothing can surprise this six hundred-year-old Dragon, except maybe her.

Lastly, in *The Dragon's Dream* we meet a spunky she-Wolf who gives Nicholas Graystone a run for his money when it comes to romance. Can a Dragon really have it all?

He's a hardcore realist until she dares him to dream.

YA & STEAMY PARANORMAL ROMANCE AUTHOR URBAN FANTASY C.D. Gorri

OTHER TITLES BY C.D. GORRI

Other Titles by C.D. Gorri

Paranormal Romance Books:

Macconwood Pack Novel Series:

Charley's Christmas Wolf: A Macconwood Pack Novel 1

Cat's Howl: A Macconwood Pack Novel 2

Code Wolf: A Macconwood Pack Novel 3

The Witch and The Werewolf: A Macconwood Pack Novel 4

To Claim a Wolf: A Macconwood Pack Novel 5

Conall's Mate: A Macconwood Pack Novel 6

Her Solstice Wolf: A Macconwood Pack Novel 7

Werewolf Fever: A Macconwood Pack Novel 8

Also available in 2 boxed sets:

The Macconwood Pack Volume 1

The Macconwood Pack Volume 2

Macconwood Pack Tales Series:

Wolf Bride: The Story of Ailis and Eoghan A Macconwood

Pack Tale 1

Summer Bite: A Macconwood Pack Tale 2

His Winter Mate: A Macconwood Pack Tale 3

Snow Angel: A Macconwood Pack Tale 4

Charley's Baby Surprise: A Macconwood Pack Tale 5

Home for the Howlidays: A Macconwood Pack Tale 6

A Silver Wedding: A Macconwood Pack Tale 7

Mine Furever: A Macconwood Pack Tale 8

A Furry Little Christmas: A Macconwood Pack Tale 9

Also available in two boxed sets:

The Macconwood Pack Tales Volume 1

Shifters Furever: The Macconwood Pack Tales Volume 2

The Falk Clan Tales:

The Dragon's Valentine: A Falk Clan Novel 1

The Dragon's Christmas Gift: A Falk Clan Novel 2

The Dragon's Heart: A Falk Clan Novel 3

The Dragon's Secret: A Falk Clan Novel 4

The Dragon's Treasure: A Falk Clan Novel 5

The Dragon's Surprise: A Falk Clan Novel 6

The Dragon's Dream: A Falk Clan Novel 7

Dragon Mates: The Falk Clan Series Boxed Set Books 1-4

The Bear Claw Tales:

Bearly Breathing: A Bear Claw Tale 1

Bearly There: A Bear Claw Tale 2

Bearly Tamed: A Bear Claw Tale 3

Bearly Mated: A Bear Claw Tale 4

Also available in a boxed set:

The Complete Bear Claw Tales (Books 1-4)

The Barvale Clan Tales:

Polar Opposites: The Barvale Clan Tales 1

Polar Outbreak: The Barvale Clan Tales 2

Polar Compound: A Barvale Clan Tale 3

Polar Curve: A Barvale Clan Tale 4

Also available in a boxed set:

The Barvale Clan Tales (Books 1-4)

Barvale Holiday Tales:

A Bear For Christmas

Hers To Bear

Thank You Beary Much

Bearing Gifts

Also available in a boxed set:

The Barvale Holiday Tales (Books 1-3)

Purely Paranormal Romance Books:

Marked by the Devil: Purely Paranormal Romance Books

Mated to the Dragon King: Purely Paranormal Romance Books

Claimed by the Demon: Purely Paranormal Romance Books

Christmas with a Devil, a Dragon King, & a Demon: Purely Paranormal Romance Books

Vampire Lover: Purely Paranormal Romance Books

Grizzly Lover: Purely Paranormal Romance Books

Christmas With Her Chupacabra: Purely Paranormal Romance Books

Purely Paranormal Romance Books Anthology

The Wardens of Terra:

Bound by Air: The Wardens of Terra Book 1

Star Kissed: A Wardens of Terra Short

Waterlocked: The Wardens of Terra Book 2

Moon Kissed: A Wardens of Terra Short

*Now in a boxed set and in audio!

The Maverick Pride Tales:

Purrfectly Mated

Purrfectly Kissed

Purrfectly Trapped

Purrfectly Caught

Purrfectly Naughty

Purrfectly Bound

<u>Dire Wolf Mates:</u>

Shake That Sass

Breaking Sass

Pinch of Sass

Kickin' Sass

<u>Wyvern Protection Unit:</u>

Gift Wrapped Protector: WPU 1

<u>Standalones:</u>

The Enforcer

Blood Song: A Sanguinem Council Book

Spring Fling (co-written with P. Mattern)

<u>EveL Worlds:</u>

Chinchilla and the Devil: A FUCN'A Book

Sammi and the Jersey Bull: A FUCN'A Book

Mouse and the Ball: A FUCN'A Book

<u>The Guardians of Chaos:</u>

Wolf Shield: Guardians of Chaos Book1

Dragon Shield: Guardians of Chaos Book 2

Stallion Shield: Guardians of Chaos Book 3

Panther Shield: Guardians of Chaos 4

Witch Shield: Guardians of Chaos 5

<u>Hungry Fur Love</u>

Hungry Like Her Wolf: Magic and Mayhem Universe

Hungry For Her Bear: Magic and Mayhem Universe

<u>Shifters Unleashed Boxed Sets</u>

Check out these amazing anthologies where you can find some of my books and the works of other awesome authors!

Midnight Magic Anthology (Water Witch)

Rituals & Runes Anthology (Air Witch)

<u>Island Stripe Pride</u>

Tiger Claimed

Tiger Denied

<u>NYC Shifter Tales</u>

Cuff Linked

Sealed Fate

<u>A Howlin' Good Fairytale Retelling</u>

Sweet As Candy (as seen in Once Upon An Ever After)

<u>Coming Soon:</u>

Asterion

Vampire Shield: Guardians of Chaos 6

Tiger Rejected

For Fangs Sake

Hungry As Her Python: Magic and Mayhem Universe

If The Shoe Fits: A Howlin' Good Fairytale Retelling

Chickee and the Paparazzi: FUCN'A

The Wolf's Winter Wish: A Macconwood Pack Tale

The Hybrid Assassin

Tempted By Her Protector: WPU 2

Alien Protector: WPU 3

Elvish Protector: WPU 4

Thrilled By Her Protector: WPU 5

<u>Young Adult Urban Fantasy Books:</u>

Wolf Moon: A Grazi Kelly Novel Book 1

Hunter Moon: A Grazi Kelly Novel Book 2

Rebel Moon: A Grazi Kelly Novel Book 3

Winter Moon: A Grazi Kelly Novel Book 4

Chasing The Moon: A Grazi Kelly Short 5

Blood Moon: A Grazi Kelly Novel 6

*Get all 6 books NOW AVAILABLE IN A BOXED SET:

The Complete Grazi Kelly Novel Series

Casting Magic: The Angela Tanner Files 1

Keeping Magic: The Angela Tanner Files 2

<u>G'Witches Magical Mysteries Series</u>

Co-written with P. Mattern

G'Witches

G'Witches 2: The Harpy Harbinger

G'Witches 3: Summoning Secrets

EXCERPT FROM PURRFECTLY MATED

How the fuck did I wind up here?

It was all Elissa could do not to slam her face down on the table as she pondered that question for the umpteenth time since leaving her cozy Hoboken apartment to go on this so called date.

"So, babe," the over-stuffed, heavily-cologned, and downright fugly man said.

Her date of the evening looked like something out of a bad sitcom as he tried to lean over the stained tablecloth of the rundown hotel buffet room, he'd driven two hours to get to. Waggling his caterpillar-like eyebrows, he gave her the once over and Elissa's skin crawled.

Oh, hell no.

"I got a room upstairs, you know, for *after*," he

told her, nodding his head, and biting his lower lip in a manner she assumed he thought was provocative.

At best, it was nauseating.

FML.

How was this guy Elissa's date for the evening? What had she done to deserve this?

Little Gianni. Yup, that was how he'd introduced himself. And here she was. On a blind date with a guy who had the word 'little' in front of his name.

Well, what did she expect? Roses and champagne? In this economy? She didn't know where Cinder-fuck-ing-ella got her prince, but it sure as fuck wasn't in Jersey.

Elissa could only blame herself for agreeing to go on this blind date. Initially, the whole Little Gianni fiasco had been intended for her roommate.

Wait a second. Scratch that thought.

It *was* all Gretchen's fault. That ungrateful cow!

She tried to play it off like she was some sweet little homegrown maiden. Oh, just wait till Elissa got home. Gretchen was never going to hear the end of it.

She owed Elissa. Big time. Like a whole month of washing the dishes big time. The rat trap they shared in her hometown of Hoboken was all the two women could afford, and for the most part, they got along just fine.

In fact, they'd grown to be close friends over the three years they'd lived together. It was the only reason she'd ever agreed to this date from Hell.

Elissa sighed and looked over at Little Gianni. Maybe he wasn't all that bad?

"*BEEEELLLLLLLLCHHH!* 'Scuse me, doll. Better out, am I right?"

Gianni winked and Elissa wished for a black hole to open up and swallow her up right through the floor.

OMFG.

The man just burped out loud like he was in a frat boy belting contest, only those days passed him up about thirty years ago.

For fuck's sake. Gretchen, you so owe me.

Elissa cursed her roommate and tried not to groan. But Little Gianni wasn't quite done. The grown ass man lifted his leg and let one rip.

Right. Fucking. There.

Elissa was going to die before the end of the night.

Literally.

This is what you get when you do a friend a favor without asking for details! Idiota!

The voice of her Italian grandmother sounded in her brain. She tried to ignore it, willing herself not to wince at the man while he sucked air, and who knows what else, noisily through his coffee-stained teeth.

Ew. So gross.

That was the perfect word to describe it. The only word, in fact. The entire date was just so fucking gross. She still couldn't believe her sweet little roommate from Iowa, *Gretchen Kaepernick*, she of the wispy hair and baby blues, had set her up with this guy!

What the actual fuck was up with that?

Little Gianni was a slob. Actually, he looked just like her Uncle Nico, and that was not a good thing. Seriously, not good at all.

He wore his hair slicked back in a too tight ponytail that emphasized his rapidly receding hairline. As if that wasn't enough to put her off, he was sporting an enormous paunch. Now, being a curvy girl, Elissa appreciated food and was in no way against men showing the same appreciation.

She liked bigger men. Always had. But bigger did not mean you had to be sloppy. Little Gianni's stomach was literally hanging out from under a tight tan golf shirt that had definitely seen better days.

The man didn't even look like he had ever played a sport of any kind. With it, he wore brown polyester pants that were three inches above his ankles and unbuttoned at the waist.

He didn't look like he tried at all for this date.

What kind of guy did that? His shirt collar was bent and wrinkled, and all three buttons were open to his chest, revealing a mat of oily, dark hair and pimples.

Somehow, he'd managed to tuck the back of the shirt in, but the front simply would not hold in that stomach. What worried her more were the tight brown pants.

As he sat back and stretched, she wondered if she should take cover. They looked like they were one bite from exploding off his body. Elissa shuddered at the image.

Please God, if You have an ounce of mercy, don't let that happen, she prayed.

"Hang on, doll, I gotta take this," he said, and turned to answer his cell phone.

It was ringing to the tune of '70s disco music she hadn't heard since the last family reunion. Her eyes kept going to the huge stain on the front of his shirt. It was a little game she liked to call *what the hell is that*.

Coffee, she guessed.

"Up your ass, Bruno. I gotta have it by Monday," he cursed into the receiver.

Elissa winced at the spectacle he was making of them both. There were only a handful of people there, but still.

Deep breaths.

Ew. Maybe not.

She coughed as the strong body spray, that he'd obviously used a ton of in lieu of a shower, bad move in her opinion, invaded her lungs.

Oh, this was so bad.

Elissa was, by no means, a snob. But this guy looked like he'd stepped out of a bad 1980s mafia spoof film. What's worse, he kept smacking his lips together as he hung up the phone and looked her over from head to chest.

Thank fuck for the table, she thought, wishing she could hide her bosoms from his view.

"Ssssss," he hissed, like it was sexy or something.

She just grimaced. Elissa might be able to forgive a lot of quirks, but she hated mouth noises. Really hated them. It was a super pet peeve of hers. Never mind his totally inappropriate and unwelcomed leer.

She started counting the minutes, willing the date to be over already. Plenty of people would tell her she shouldn't be so choosy, but really? She was not this desperate.

Not yet anyway.

So, she was curvy and a little mouthy too. But was it wrong to want a man with good table manners? Even if men were thin on the ground for someone like her.

As a chef, she'd worked in a lot of restaurants

and even as a personal cook for professional couples. She'd seen her fair share of unhappy couples and downright uncomfortable marriages. But as far as she was concerned, all relationships went downhill when good table manners were dismissed.

Good manners were merely a sign that a person was thoughtful and respectful. At least, that was what Nonna had told her. Gianni here had clearly missed that lesson as a child. Elissa had to work not to groan in disgust as he slurped a raw clam down his gullet.

Shudder.

Was there no end to his feeding? That's what it reminded her of. Feeding time at the zoo.

OMG. That was rude, she scolded herself. But it wasn't like she said it out loud.

All she wanted to do was go home. At least she was comfortable. *She'd* worn her softest pair of black leggings for this disaster date, paired with one of her favorite tunics on top.

It was dark green with tiny black buttons down the front and showed just the right amount of cleavage. She'd gone for neat and tidy as opposed to downright sexy.

Good call, in her opinion. Elissa looked perfectly fine for a nice *getting to know you* dinner, which is what she thought she was getting when her roommate asked her to step in for her on a blind date that one of her best client's had set up for her.

Elissa shuddered now, thinking how good old Gianni here would've reacted to the red dress and heels she'd contemplated before checking the weather report.

Gulp.

The lewd man was already salivating, and she was so not having it. Fending off his unwanted advances was not how she wanted to finish the night.

Ew again.

Elissa shivered, slightly chilled despite the fact they were indoors. It was a cold, gloomy evening, and the forecast called for even more rain later that night. Not at all unusual for this time of year in the Garden State.

November was always chilly in the evenings, rainy too. Elissa tended to run warm, but she was glad she'd brought a jacket with her. Especially since her date refused to turn the heat on in the car.

When she'd asked, he'd looked offended and told her it wasted gas.

Um. Okay.

She checked her phone. It was only seven o'clock, but the two hour drive was still ahead of them. Maybe they could make it home before ten if they left soon.

Ugh. Did he just blow his nose?

"Allergies, doll. Say, you gonna eat that?" he asked before scooping a fry from her dish and swallowing it down.

Elissa was gonna kill her roomie. Gretchen was a hair and nail stylist. A lot of her clients were elderly, and they just loved her. They were always offering to set her up on blind dates with their nephews and grandsons.

Mostly, the sweet old ladies were kind. They swore they could find her curvy roommate the right man, assuming she was single because she was new to town. Well, when Elissa got home tonight, she was going to tell Gretchen she needed to fire the old lady who set this date up from being her client.

Like *ASAP*.

No one who liked Gretchen would've sent her out with this guy. Gianni reached over and touched her hand and Elissa pulled back, reaching for the napkin.

Gross.

"I sure hope you ain't a cold one, doll," he said, shaking his head.

"What?"

"Ain't gonna matter. I know just what you need, doll."

She was still wiping the greasy residue he'd transferred to her skin from the food he ate sans utensils.

This was too much. Elissa was beyond uncomfortable with all the leering and bad attempts at innuendo.

Plus, she was starving. One look at the dump he'd taken her to, and she knew she could never eat there. The chef in her wouldn't allow it.

To think they drove two hours for this! She'd practically frozen to death in his maroon Cadillac, listening to a CD of the Rat Pack, while Gianni crooned loudly, and off key, to the music.

Normally, she was a fan of the famous group of legendary singers. Having grown up in Hoboken, she couldn't not be a Sinatra fan. Though, to be honest, Dean Martin had always been her favorite.

Still, Elissa was a firm believer that there were just some people you did not try to imitate. Especially not if you were Little Gianni. While he was belting his heart out, he'd been trying to get his right hand on her thigh. She'd asked him politely to stop.

Twice.

Then she'd been forced to try something a little more drastic. Like spilling her hot tea on the offending hand the third time he'd tried it. Finally, he'd removed his hand from her leg. Not making a fourth attempt, which she was grateful for.

Elissa should've taken that behavior as a sign and gotten out of the car. But no. She'd wanted to do

Gretchen a solid. So, against her better judgement, she gave the creep another chance.

Idiota, her grandmother's voice echoed in her brain again.

The old woman had loved her. Elissa knew that without a doubt. She'd raised her after her own parents had passed on in a tragic automobile accident when Elissa was just twelve.

Her grandmother was a no-nonsense kind of lady who dished out priceless wisdom with brutally honest insights. It was the same way she dished out huge bowls of pasta with her amazing meatballs and home-made sauce. Not to mention a side order of back-breaking hugs that Elissa still missed.

Nonna cooked like that all the time. She made a huge pot of sauce every weekend, and she was happy to serve it to Elissa and her teammates and friends, especially after games and tournaments.

Soccer had been her sport of choice, and cooking had soon become her favorite hobby. Her grand-mother had encouraged her in both pursuits. Guiding her in one and cheering her on in the other. Elissa still missed her terribly.

"Hey babe, ain't you gonna eat nothin'? You know they charge twenty dollars just to sit down," Little Gianni interrupted her train of thought.

Elissa was forced to turn her mind back to the

present, which unfortunately included watching, *and hearing*, him as he sucked on his teeth and stuffed another breaded shrimp down his throat.

"I'm fine," she answered with a polite smile plastered on her face.

Just get home, Lissa. Just get him to take you home.

Elissa closed her eyes when he looked back down at his dish. Thank God for small favors, she mused. At least he was more interested in eating at the moment.

He'd taken her to the rattiest looking hotel and casino she'd ever seen in her life. And the buffet room?

Ew.

Seriously, the place had to be violating at least a dozen health codes. When Gianni had said Atlantic City, she'd thought at least the atmosphere would be exciting. But they were so far from the real glitz and entertainment, they might as well be anywhere else.

She sighed, looking at the plate she'd made for herself. Elissa couldn't even fake an interest in the food. As a chef, it was hard enough to dine out.

She was always judging the food, the service, the ingredients. How could she not? It was her business. And that was when the food was good!

This was not good. Not at all.

She'd been to hospitals that served better food.

Old yellow lights buzzed and blinked around the buffet, giving it an abandoned kind of feel. The menu was made up of mostly frozen then fried or baked cuisine.

Reheated actually. It was like a giant TV dinner buffet where every item was previously frozen when already cooked and warmed up in an oven.

It was the kind of food sold cheap at restaurant supply stores in bulk. Yeah, this was much worse than hospital food, in her opinion.

There was a worn carpet on the floor, a handful of scattered tables in the dining room, elevator music on in the background, and the entire place smelled like canned soup.

Not to mention not one of the five people there besides them was under sixty years old.

"Gianni," she said, leaning forward so as not to hurt his feelings.

"I thought you mentioned something about seeing a show tonight. Is it here?"

Please don't be here.

If he was taking her somewhere else, she could beg off and hire a cab to take her home. There was no way she was sitting through anything else with this man. Not now. Not ever.

"Ah, I see, babe, you want some entertainment first, I get it," he snickered loudly, and she blanched.

Whatever he thought was going to happen wasn't. She needed to disabuse him of the notion, and fast.

"Alright, alright. Lemme finish this, babe. Then we'll go up to the room I got for us," he said.

Before she could make sense of the ludicrous statement, he slurped another fried shrimp, don't ask how. Then he grabbed her arm and yanked her from the seat before she could even react.

Elissa tugged on his hold, but the man was immovable. Tossing a five-dollar bill on the table, Little Gianni snatched a toothpick from the hostess stand before dragging her outside.

Great, he was a cheap tipper, too.

All she wanted was to go home. Figuring the best way to do that would probably be to get him to the car, she let him lead the way.

Once inside, she would ask him to drive back to Hoboken so she could wring Gretchen's neck. Fuming, she pulled her arm out of his hand and walked behind him.

The rain was really pouring, and the cheap bastard had refused valet. Elissa ducked her head so she wouldn't get so wet. Of course, the jacket she'd brought was light and had no hood.

Gianni had an umbrella, but he didn't offer to hold it for her, and honestly, she did not relish the idea of getting any closer to him than necessary.

Seriously, not happening.

Now all she had to do was break the news. She had no intention of watching a show or returning to the hotel with him.

What could go wrong?

GRAB PURRFECTLY MATED TODAY.

EXCERPT FROM GRIZZLY LOVER

"Resa," Oliver fisted the note he'd found tucked under the secondhand keyboard he'd just finished paying off.

The instrument sat against one wall of the cramped room, right beside the only window in the small Brooklyn Heights apartment he'd been renting the past six months since he came to the city.

For a Grizzly Bear Shifter used to the wilds of the woods as his backyard, it was quite the change, but he just had to try to see if he could make a go of his music. Oliver had always been gifted with a good ear, but even as a cub, his mother had encouraged him to go and seek his destiny.

Brooklyn Heights was as close to Manhattan as he could afford with his meager savings, but what did money matter anyway? Especially when there was music to be written. The window faced the south brick wall of another small apartment complex identical to his.

It didn't matter what it looked like outside, as long as he was able to breathe some fresh air. At least on the fifth floor, it was somewhat fresher than the heavily congested streets below.

She was gone. His mind registered that fact as he took in the empty room. She'd left.

"No," he growled, and aimed his fist at the tiled counter top, cracking a few of the old ceramic squares in the process. Mrs. Goldstein, the landlady, would be pissed when she saw that.

Oliver's Bear roared inside of him and his heart contracted painfully in his chest. It was worse than being sucker punched by Thor his idiot cousin, who was as big and strong as his namesake. Why would Teresa say such cruel things? He couldn't believe it, couldn't fathom his sweet Resa saying such foul callous words about their relationship. He read the hated missive one more time.

Oliver,

It was fun while it lasted, but even you can't be so naïve as to think I could find true love with a nobody. I just wanted to get back at my father. Don't bother looking for me or calling, I will have already changed my number.

Teresa

Yes, it was her handwriting. He closed his eyes on the wave of anguish that washed over him. Gasping, he sunk to his knees while the beast inside of him roared and sTimped his massive claws in fury.

Mate, his Bear cried out, but Oliver refused to answer his other half.

How could she just leave him like this? He'd been so sure of her, of them. He was positive that she loved him too. Being with her was everything to him. She was his fated mate. It was the first time he had ever tasted happiness. A taste that was bitter now that he knew it was all one-sided.

The first time he'd seen the golden-haired beauty, Oliver's Grizzly Bear had stood up and taken notice. The second he'd breathed in her peaches and cream scent, his animal had roared one single word in his mind's eye that would change Oliver's life forever.

Mate.

Following his heart, he'd approached the soft spoken, elegantly dressed Teresa Witherspoon after spying her at the park day after day. She'd sit on one of the cleaner benches and read from a book of seventeenth century cavalier poets.

"You like Lovelace? Looking at you I pictured a Donne fan," Oliver said when he'd finally found the nerve to approach her.

"Spiritualist poetry doesn't appeal as much to me I guess. I like Lovelace and Suckling. They're fun and witty."

"But they're just trying to get in a girl's pants with their poetry. You approve?" he grinned.

"It's not so much the seduction that appeals to me, it's the living in the moment. Carpe diem and all that," she shrugged.

There was something so tragically sad about her that his heart had squeezed in his chest with longing. He'd wanted to make her smile. Heck, he even pretended to stumble in the grass, laid himself flat just to get her to walk over and touch him. And she had, put her soft, long hands right on him to see if he was alright. He'd stolen a kiss and had never looked back. Until now. The dream was over. She'd left him.

Oliver's Bear roared in his grief. That last night they were together, he'd told her the truth about what he was. The fact that there were more things in the world than she had ever imagined.

Oliver Pax had committed a most grievous sin against his Clan. He'd confessed to a normal, a human woman, that he was a Grizzly Bear Shifter.

It was allowed under certain circumstances, like when the woman in question was your fated mate. He'd thought she'd taken it well, after all, they'd made wild, passionate love immediately after. Hell, he'd been so caught up in the moment, he'd marked her with his bite, tying himself to her irrevocably, but now she was gone.

What would become of him? Would he go mad like so many other Shifters who'd lost their mates? He had heard the stories. The tales of broken matings and rogue Shifters who needed to be put down.

Oliver tipped the bottle of whiskey back emptying its fiery contents down his throat. Then he threw the hated thing across the room. Something about the muted violence of the act satisfied his animal's need for savagery. The Bear inside of him wanted to tear the whole world down, but maybe work would be a better outlet, he thought.

Oliver sat down at his banged-up keyboard and began to play. He poured out his bruised heart. Wrote lyrics and tied them together with a fairy tale as old as they come. The Beast of Brooklyn Heights was born that day. And the rest, as they say, was history.

GRAB GRIZZLY LOVER NOW.

EXCERPT FROM BEARING GIFTS

"Thanks for coming tonight, Charity," Abigail Jensen, a nurse who worked at the Barvale Senior Center spoke softly as Charity hung her coat and hat on the rack near the desk.

It was already snowing, and she only had a few minutes, but Abigail never called her if it wasn't an emergency. Charity just had a way with people, and she enjoyed spending her time helping put others at ease if she could. True, she had about fifteen minutes before she needed to leave on time, otherwise she would be late for her shift, and tonight was important.

"No worries. You know I enjoy spending time with the residents, Abigail."

"I know, but normally you come on the weekends.

Mr. K is a special case, and we have tried everything to make him feel at ease. His wife had to have emergency hip replacement surgery, and he is only here while she recovers, but he's been despondent without her."

"Wow, he must really love her," Charity whispered. She shuffled the box that held a single bear claw inside and followed Abby down the hall. Seated in a wheelchair in the middle of his room was an elderly man with white hair and a beard. He had a hand-knitted red scarf draped around his neck, and his hands were clasped together.

"Good evening, Mr. K. I brought you a visitor," Abigail announced, and Charity walked in.

"Hello, I'm Charity—"

"I don't need any charity, I need my Elaine," he muttered grumpily.

"I understand. If I had a wife or husband, I would miss her too, but the center isn't all bad, you know. I usually come by on weekends and bring treats like this and crafts or movies. Sometimes, we play card games and once we had a talent show."

"A talent show? And what can you do, my dear?" he asked, engaging already, and Charity smiled at the win.

"Well, Mr. K, not to brag, but I am a terrible dancer, and I can't carry a tune," she confided.

"I will leave you two to it," Abigail said and turned to leave.

For the next fifteen minutes, Charity chatted with the exceedingly kind Mr. K, answering questions, and getting the older gentleman to open up about his wife. Her recovery was slow going, but he talked to her every single day. That kind of devotion was really touching, and Charity's heart swelled hoping someday, she would have that kind of love for herself.

"So, do you still believe in Santa?" he asked.

"Oh, I don't know. When I was little, I used to stay up and wait to hear him, but I never did. I think that would be amazing—"

"Even now that you are a grownup? I am surprised."

"Why? Adults need magic too," she told him.

"That is true, my dear. This was so lovely, Charity. Thank you for visiting me," Mr. K said, taking her hand as she stood to leave.

"It was my pleasure."

"You know, Christmas is in just a few days. I hope you sent your letter to Santa already," he whispered conspiratorially, and she laughed.

"I sure did," she replied, and kissed his weathered cheek.

"Oh, how nice! I am going to tell my Elaine she

must get well faster, a younger woman has her sights on me," he teased.

"You do that, and I bet she will be better in no time. You are quite the catch, Mr. K!" Charity chuckled.

"Seriously, my child, I want to thank you, very much so. I do not know many young women who would stop by to chat with a grumpy old stranger."

"You're not grumpy, Mr. K, just sad, and it is understandable. I bet you're worried something awful about your wife, and I want you to know I will be praying for her speedy recovery. I am sorry to cut our talk short, though, but I have to go."

"I see. Hot date?" he asked.

"Ha! No, I have to go to work."

"And after, is that when you will meet your boyfriend?"

"Actually, I am single—"

"I can see from the look in your eyes that is not exactly a choice, is it, Charity?"

"Well, I have a crush on someone, and tonight I am going to tell him. I'm kinda nervous," she confessed.

"My dear, if he has even one brain cell still functioning in his head, he will scoop you up and run away with you. I know quality when I see it, and you have it, child. Yes, indeed," he said and patted her hand. "You be a good girl now."

"Yes, sir. Thank you, Mr. K. I hope I will get to see you before your stay is over. Merry Christmas," she said, and waved goodbye as she raced to her car.

She did not hear the elderly man whisper his reply softly as he watched her go with sparkling blue eyes, "I'll be watching you, Charity Smith."

He knows if you've been bad or good...

GRAB YOUR COPY OF BEARING GIFTS TODAY.

ABOUT THE AUTHOR

C.D. Gorri is a USA Today Bestselling author of steamy paranormal romance and urban fantasy. She is the creator of the Grazi Kelly Universe.

Join her mailing list here: https://www.cdgorri.com/newsletter

An avid reader with a profound love for books and literature, when she is not writing or taking care of her family, she can usually be found with a book or tablet in hand. C.D. lives in her home state of New Jersey where many of her characters or stories are based. Her tales are fast paced yet detailed with satisfying conclusions.

If you enjoy powerful heroines and loyal heroes who face relatable problems in supernatural settings, journey into the Grazi Kelly Universe today. You will find sassy, curvy heroines and sexy, love-driven heroes who find their HEAs between the pages. Were-wolves, Bears, Dragons, Tigers, Witches, Romani, Lynxes, Foxes, Thunderbirds, Vampires, and many more Shifters and supernatural creatures dwell within her worlds. The most important thing is every mate in this universe is fated, loyal, and true lovers always get their happily ever afters.

Want to know how it all began? Enter the Grazi Kelly Universe with Wolf Moon: A Grazi Kelly Novel or pick up Charley's Christmas Wolf and dive into the Macconwood Pack Novel Series today.

For a complete list of C.D. Gorri's books visit her website here:

https://www.cdgorri.com/complete-book-list/

Thank you and happy reading!

del mare alla stella,
    C.D. Gorri

Follow C.D. Gorri here:
    http://www.cdgorri.com
    https://www.facebook.com/Cdgorribooks
    https://www.bookbub.com/authors/c-d-gorri

https://twitter.com/cgor22

https://instagram.com/cdgorri/

https://www.goodreads.com/cdgorri

https://www.tiktok.com/@cdgorriauthor